"Why did you kiss me?" Lance asked.

His voice had deepened, no longer flippant and teasing, but somewhat solemn.

He asked as though he really wanted to know.

Because I couldn't stop myself. Because he'd been so kind and careful and comforting to her that morning. Because his lips were so warm and somehow soft, even though the rest of him was so rugged. She cleared her throat. "I already told you. I was extra emotional that day."

His eyes narrowed. "You sure that's all it was?"

"Of course," she lied, straight to his face, locking her jaw for good measure.

"That's a shame. Because I happen to think you're pretty damn fine, too." There was a light in his eyes—a heat that made them downright dangerous.

She looked away. "That's the whiskey talking, cowboy," she said through a forced laugh.

His huge hand reached up and cupped her cheek, steering her gaze back to his. "No. It's not."

Air lodged into her lungs, giving her chest that wonderful, tight sensation, like any moment it would burst open and the flood of desire would carry her away.

No. No more getting carried away.

"It's not the whiskey," he murmured, his face lowering to hers...

Hometown Cowboy

A ROCKY MOUNTAIN RIDERS NOVEL

SARA RICHARDSON

FOREVER

NEW YORK   BOSTON

Copyright © 2017 by Sara Richardson
Excerpt of *Comeback Cowboy* copyright © 2017 by Sara Richardson
Cover design by Elizabeth Turner
Cover copyright © 2017 by Hachette Book Group, Inc.

Forever
Hachette Book Group
1290 Avenue of the Americas
New York, NY 10104
forever-romance.com
twitter.com/foreverromance

First Edition: February 2017

Forever is an imprint of Grand Central Publishing.
The Forever name and logo are trademarks of Hachette Book Group, Inc.

The publisher is not responsible for websites (or their content) that are not owned by the publisher.

The Hachette Speakers Bureau provides a wide range of authors for speaking events. To find out more, go to www.hachettespeakersbureau.com or call (866) 376-6591.

ISBN 978-1-4555-4075-4 (mass market edition)
ISBN 978-1-4555-4073-0 (ebook edition)

Printed in the United States of America

OPM

10 9 8 7 6 5 4 3 2 1

To Debbie McIntire,
a wonderful reader who is now a friend.

Hometown
Cowboy

Prologue

Funny how you can remember every detail about the most significant day of your life. Not the best day of your life necessarily, but the day that shaped you, the day that you were forced to find your strength.

Lance Cortez wandered to the bay window in his living room and stared out at the land that had been in his family since the Spaniards had crossed the mountains into Colorado and founded the town of Topaz Falls.

From his house situated on the valley floor, it seemed he could see every acre, from the razor-edges of Topaz Mountain to the pointed tips of the evergreens that studded the steep slopes. Even in the dimness of that eerie space preceding the dawn, he could make out the stables up the hill, the bullpens across from the pasture, and the house farther on down the hill where his father still lived. The house where he'd grown up. It was a ranch style, built from the logs of those trees on the mountain. Anchored by a wraparound porch.

Sixteen years ago, before dawn, he'd stood on that porch right there and watched his mother walk out of his life. He didn't know what had woken him that day. Maybe the sound of the dog barking or the door creaking. But when he'd stumbled down the hallway, he'd caught her dragging her suitcase across that old porch.

"Where are you going?" he'd asked, not liking the weakness that had started to spread over his body like a dark shadow. Something in him already knew. She'd been distant for months, there but not.

His mother had paused on the sidewalk at the bottom of those porch steps, but she hadn't looked at him. "I have to go away for a while," she'd said. "I can't do this anymore."

He'd wanted to ask why, but couldn't. He couldn't open his mouth, couldn't unfist his hands. She was leaving them. And he wondered if it had anything to do with the underage drinking ticket he'd gotten two days before. At fourteen, he knew he was a holy terror.

Or maybe it was the fact that his father was away so much, traveling to the rodeos, giving all of his time to a sport his mother hated.

"I'm sorry, Lance," his mother had said. There were no tears in her eyes, but her voice caught. "I'm so sorry."

That word gathered up the sadness that had weighted his bones and spun it into a whorl of anger. If she was sorry then why was she going?

"I hope you'll understand someday."

He didn't. Sixteen years later, he had yet to understand how a mother could walk out on her husband and three boys who needed her. He'd been fourteen. He could take care of himself. But what about Lucas? At ten, he'd only just started the sixth grade. And Levi. Hell, he was still wetting the bed at seven.

Without another word, she'd walked away and hauled her suitcase into the old pickup. Energy had burned through him, tempting him to run down those steps and somehow force her to stay. He couldn't, though. He knew it. He saw it in her eyes.

She'd already left them behind.

The engine had started and the tires ground against gravel. Lance had watched until the darkness swallowed the taillights and she was gone.

When he'd stepped back into the house, he was a different kid. Refusing to shed even one tear, he'd made himself a cup of coffee and omelets for his brothers. When his father came back that afternoon, he'd told him she was gone.

They'd never said another word about it.

In the months and years that followed, he'd tried to make up for her abandonment. He'd quit being such a delinquent. Watched over his brothers when their father was out searching for something to remedy his own pain. Became a bull-riding champion in his own right. But he couldn't undo the damage she'd left in her wake. It took seven years after she left for things to fall apart.

He wished he would've been watching Levi that night he'd set the fire. Wished he'd been able to stop it before it killed the livestock. Wished he could've stopped it before it ruined them all. Lucas had wanted to take the blame, to protect their younger brother just like he always did, and Lance let him. They'd made a plan. Kept quiet about it. He'd been so sure Lucas would get off easy.

But he'd been wrong. Even though his brother had been

only seventeen, they'd charged him as an adult and sent him to prison.

Nothing had ever been the same after that. Levi threw himself into bull riding and hadn't been home in years. After Lucas got out of prison, he refused to come home. He'd gone on to work for a stock contractor down south and hadn't been home since.

All because of one day. One rejection. One person who was supposed to care for them turning her back instead.

Funny how you remember the details of days like that. The words, the sounds, the feelings that'd turned your body cold. Funny how you spend every day for the rest of your life trying to forget them.

Turning his back on the view of that porch, Lance headed for the kitchen.

It was time to put the coffee on.

Chapter One

Sorry, sir." Jessa Mae Love threw out her arms to block the heavyset man who tried to sit on the stool next to her. "This seat is taken."

He eyed her, the coarseness of his five o'clock shadow giving his face a particularly menacing quality. Still, she held her ground.

"You been sittin' there by yourself for an hour, lady," he pointed out, scratching at his beer belly. "And this is the best spot to watch the game."

"It's true. I have been sitting here for a while." She smiled politely and shimmied her shoulders straighter, lest he think she was intimidated by his bulk. "But my *boyfriend* is meeting me. We have an important date tonight and I know he'll be here any minute." She checked the screen of her cell phone again, the glowing numbers blaring an insult in her face. Seven o'clock. *Seven o'clock?*

Cam was never late. He'd been planning this date for

more than a week. Since she was coming straight from the animal rescue shelter she owned, they'd agreed to meet at the Tumble Inn Bar for a drink before he took her to the new Italian restaurant on Main Street. "He'll be here," she said to the man. "Cam is *very* reliable."

"Whatever," the man grumbled, hunching himself on a stool three down from her.

Signaling to the bartender, she ordered another glass of pinot. "And why don't you go ahead and bring a Bud Light for my boyfriend?" she asked with a squeak of insecurity. But that was silly because Cam would be there. He'd show up and give her a kiss and apologize for being so late because...his car broke down. Or maybe his mother called and he couldn't get off the phone with her.

"He won't let me down," she muttered to cool the heat that rose to her face. He would *never* stand her up in this crowded bar—in front of the whole town.

Everyone considered the Tumble Inn the classiest watering hole in Topaz Falls, Colorado. And that was simply because you weren't allowed to throw peanut shells on the floor. It was nice enough—an old brick auto shop garage that had been converted years ago. They'd restored the original garage doors and in the summer, they opened them to the patio, which was strung with colorful hanging globe lights. Gil Wilson, the owner, had kept up with the times, bringing in modern furniture and decor. He also offered the best happy hour in town, which would explain why it was so crowded on a Wednesday night.

She stole a quick glance over her shoulder. Were people starting to stare?

Plastering on a smile, she called Cam. *Again.*

His voice mail picked up. *Again.*

"Hey, it's me." She lowered her voice. "I'm kind of worried. Maybe I got the time wrong? Did we say we'd meet at six? Or seven? I guess it doesn't matter. I'm here at the bar. Waiting for you..." A deafening silence echoed back in her ear. "Okay. Well I'm sure you're on your way. I'll see you soon."

She set down the phone and took a long sip of wine. Everything was fine. It was true she hadn't had very good luck with men, but Cam was different.

She drummed her fingers against the bar to keep her hand from trembling. Over the past ten years, she'd been *almost* engaged approximately three times. Approximately, because she wasn't all that sure that a twist tie from the high school cafeteria counted as a betrothal, although her seventeen-year-old heart had thought it to be wildly romantic at the time. Little did she know, one year later, her high school sweetheart—the one who'd gotten down on one knee in the middle of the cafeteria to recite one of Shakespeare's sonnets in front of nearly the whole school (did she mention he was in the drama club?)—would go off to college and meet the Phi Beta Kappa sisters who'd splurged on breast implants instead of fashionable new glasses like Jessa's. Breast implants seemed to get you more bang for your buck in college. Who knew?

She pushed her glasses up on her nose and snuck a glance at the big man who'd tried to steal Cam's seat earlier.

"Still no boyfriend, huh?" he asked as though he suspected she'd made up the whole thing.

"He's on his way." Her voice climbed the ladder of desperation. "He'll be here soon."

"Sure he will." The man went back to nursing his beer and tilted his head to see some football game on the television screen across the room.

She was about to flip him off when an incoming text chimed on her phone. From Cam! "It's him," she called, holding up the phone to prove she wasn't delusional.

"Lucky guy," Big Man muttered, rolling his eyes.

"You got that right." She focused on the screen to read the text.

Jessa, I left this morning to move back to Denver.

Wait. *What?* The words blurred. A typo. It must be a typo. Damn that autocorrect.

"What's the word?" Big Man asked. "He comin' or can I take that seat?"

"Um. Uh..." Fear wedged itself into her throat as she scrolled through the rest of the words.

I didn't see a future for me there. In Topaz Falls or with you. Sorry. I know this would've been better in person, but I couldn't do it. You're too nice. I know you'll find the right person. It's just not me.

Yours,

Cam

"Yours? *Yours?*" Ha. That was laughable. Cam had never been hers. Just like the others. Hadn't mattered how *nice* she'd been. She'd been jilted. *Again.* This time by her animal rescue's largest donor. And, yes, the man she'd been sleeping with... because he'd seemed like a good idea at the time. Women had slim pickings around Topaz Falls, population 2,345.

"Is he coming or not?" Big Man asked, still eyeing the empty stool.

"No. He's not coming." A laugh bubbled out, bordering on hysteria. "He broke up with me! By text!"

A hush came over the bar, but who cared? Let them all stare. Poor Jessa. Dumped again.

"It's not like he's a prize," she said, turning to address them all. "He's a technology consultant, for God's sake. Not Chris Hemsworth." Not that she knew what being a technology consultant meant. But it'd sounded good when she'd met him after she found his stray puggle wandering downtown six months ago. Peabody had pranced right up to her on the street and peed on her leg, the little shit. Now, Jessa was a dog person—an *animal* person—but that puggle had it out for her from day one.

When Cam had come in to retrieve his little beast from the shelter, stars had circled in her eyes. He was the first attractive man she'd seen since all those bull riders had passed through town three months ago. So unfair for those smokin' hot cowboys to gather in town and get the women all revved up only to leave them the next day.

In all honesty, Cam was no cowboy. Though his slight bulk suggested he spent a good portion of every day sitting in front of a computer screen, his soft brown eyes had a kind shimmer that instantly drew you in. He'd been good to her— taking her out to fancy restaurants and buying her flowers just because. Also, because she'd saved his beloved varmint from the potential fate of being mauled by a mountain lion, he'd made monthly donations to the shelter, which had kept them going.

Now he was gone.

"I can't believe this. How could he break up with me?"

Everyone around her had gone back to their own conversations, either unwilling to answer or pretending they didn't hear. So she turned to Big Man. "I guess you're happy about this, huh? Now the seat's all yours."

He didn't even look at her. "Nope. I'm good right where I am, thanks."

Oh, sure. After all that, now he didn't want to sit by her? "Fine. That's fine. It's all fine." Raising the glass to her lips, she drained the rest of her wine in one gulp.

"You know what?" she asked Big Man, not caring one iota that he seemed hell-bent on ignoring her. "I'm done." This had to stop. The falling in love thing. It always started innocently enough. A man would ask her out and they'd go on a few dates. She'd swear that this time she wouldn't get too attached too soon, but before she knew it, she was looking up wedding venues and bridal gowns and honeymoon destinations online. She couldn't help it. Her heart had always been a sucker for romance. Her father had said it was her best quality—that she could love someone so quickly, that she could give her heart to others so easily. He got it because he was the same way. Her mother, of course, labeled it her worst quality. *You're simply in love with the idea of being in love*, her wise mother would say. And it was true. Was that so *wrong*?

"Hey, Jessa."

The gruffness of the quiet voice, aged by years of good cigars, snapped up her head. She turned.

Luis Cortez stood behind her, hunched in his bowlegged stance. Clad in worn jeans and sporting his pro rodeo belt buckle, he looked like he'd just stepped off the set of an old western, face tanned and leathery, white hair tufted after a long ride on his trusty steed.

"Hi there, Luis," she mumbled, trying to hold her head high. Luis was her lone volunteer at the shelter, and he just might be the only one in town who loved animals as much as she did. He'd also been her dad's best friend and since she'd come back to town last year to settle her father's estate, she'd spent a lot of time with the man.

Maybe that was part of her problem with finding the love of her life. She spent most of her free time with a sixty-seven-year-old man...

"You all right?" Luis asked, gimping to the stool next to her. Seeing as how he was a retired bull-riding legend, it was a wonder he could walk at all.

"Uh." That was a complicated question. "Yes." She cleared the tremble out of her voice. "I'm fine. Great." She would be, anyway. As soon as the sting wore off.

"Thought you and Cam had a date tonight." Luis shifted with a wince, as though his arthritis was flaring again. "Where is he anyway? I was hopin' I could talk him into puttin' in his donation early this month. We gotta replace half the roof before the snow comes."

Cam. That name was her newest curse word. *Cam him! Cam it!* Feeling the burn of humiliation pulse across her cheeks, she turned on her phone and pushed it over to him so he could read the text. "Cam broke up with me." Luis had obviously missed the little announcement she'd made earlier.

He held up the phone and squinted, mouthing the words as he read. The older man looked as outraged as she was, bless him. "Man wasn't good enough for you, anyways, Jess. He's a damn fool."

"I have a knack for picking the fools." Just ask her mother. Every time she went through one of these breakups, Carla Roth, DO, would remind her of how bad the odds were for finding true love. Her mother had never married her father. She didn't believe in monogamy. *One person out of six billion?* she'd ask. *That is highly unlikely, Jessa.*

It might be unlikely, but the odds weren't enough to kill the dream. Not for her. Neither was the lack of any significant relationship in her mother's life. Jessa had grown up being shuffled back and forth—summers and Christmas in Topaz Falls with her father and the rest of the year with her college professor mother who didn't believe in love, secretly watching old romantic classics and movies like *Sleepless in Seattle* and *You've Got Mail* with wistful tears stinging in her eyes.

"Don't worry, Jess," Luis said in his kind way. "You'll find someone."

Big Man snorted.

Before she could backhand him, Luis gave her shoulder a pat. "My boys ain't married yet," he reminded her, as if she would *ever* be able to forget the Cortez brothers. Every woman's fantasy.

Lance, the oldest, had followed in his father's footsteps, though rumor had it this would be his last season on the circuit. He trained nonstop and had little time for anything else in his life, considering he left the ranch only about once a month. The thought of him married almost made her laugh. Over the years, he'd built quite the reputation with women, though she had no personal experience. Even with her father being one of his father's best friends, Lance had said maybe five words to her in all the years she'd known him. He seemed to prefer a woman who'd let him off the hook easily, and God knew there were plenty of them following those cowboys around.

Then there was Levi. Oh, hallelujah, Levi. One of God's greatest gifts to women. She'd had a fling with him the summer of their sophomore year, but after that he'd left home to train with some big-shot rodeo mentor and rarely came home.

There was a third Cortez brother, but Luis didn't talk

about him. Lucas, the middle child, had been sent to prison for arson when he was seventeen.

"Sure wish I'd see more of Levi," Luis said wistfully. "He ain't been home in a long time."

Her eyebrows lifted with interest. "So, um..." She pretended to examine a broken nail to prove she didn't care too much. "How is Levi, anyway?"

"That boy needs to get his head out of his ass. He's reckless. He's gonna get himself killed out there."

Jessa doubted that. Levi Cortez was making a name for himself in the rodeo world.

"Lance, now, he's the only one of my boys who's got his head on straight," Luis went on. "He always was a smart kid."

From what she'd seen, the oldest Cortez brother had never been a kid, but she didn't say so. After their mom ditched the family, Lance took over a more parental role. Not that she had any right to analyze him. "He's handsome, too," she offered, because every time she did happen to run into him, his luscious eyes had completely tied up her tongue. Yes, indeedy, Lance happened to be a looker. Though it was in a much different way than his cocky brother. "He looks the most like you," she said with a wink.

Luis's lips puckered in that crotchety, don't-want-to-smile-but-can't-help-it grin she loved to see. Her dad used to have one like that, too.

"Anyway...," the man said, obviously trying to change the subject. "What're we gonna do with Cam gone? I assume he didn't leave any money behind for the shelter."

"Not that I know of." Apparently, he hadn't left anything. Not even the toothbrush she'd kept at his house, Cam it.

"You got any other donors yet?"

"Not yet." She'd been so preoccupied with the most recent love—infatuation—of her life that she hadn't exactly made time to go trolling for other interested parties. Her dad had a big heart, but he'd always hated to ask for money, so when she'd come to take over, the list of benefactors had been...well...nonexistent. In one year, she'd already used most of what little money he'd left her to purchase supplies and complete the critical repairs. She could live off her savings for a couple more months, and at least keep up with the payroll, but after that things didn't look too promising. She'd probably have to lay off her night shift guy.

With Cam's generosity, she hadn't been too worried. Until now, of course.

"Don't you worry, Jess. Somethin'll work out." Luis's confidence almost made her believe it. "You're doin' okay. You know that? Buzz would be proud."

She smiled a little. Yes, her father definitely would've been proud to see his old place cleaned up. When she'd finished veterinary school and started on her MBA, he'd been so excited. He'd owned the rescue for thirty years but had never taken one business class. Which meant the place never made any money. He'd barely had enough to live on.

She had planned to change all of that. They'd planned it together. While she worked her way through business school, they'd talked on the phone twice a week, discussing how they could expand the place. Then, a month before she finished school, her father had a heart attack. He'd been out on a hike with Luis. Maybe that was why the man felt the need to take care of her, check in on her, help her fix things up around the house.

Familiar tears burned. She'd never blame Luis, though. That was exactly the way her dad would've chosen to go. Out on the side of a mountain, doing something he loved.

"We'll find a way, Jess." Pure determination turned the man's face statuelike, making him look as pensive as his eldest son. "All we need is some inspiration." Which he always insisted you couldn't find while stuck indoors. "I'm headin' up the mountain tomorrow. You wanna come?"

She brushed a grateful pat across the man's gnarled hand. "I can't, Luis. Thank you."

As much as she'd like to spend the day on the mountain, drowning her sorrows about Cam and the rescue's current financial situation in the fresh mountain air, she had things to do. This breakup had to be the dawn of a new era for her. She was tired of being passed over like yesterday's pastries. To hell with relationships. With romance. She didn't have time for it anyway. She had walls to paint and supplies to purchase and animals to rescue. Which meant she also had generous donors to find.

She shot a quick glance down at her attire. Might be a good idea to invest in herself first. Typically, she used her Visa only for emergencies, but this could be considered disaster prevention, right? She needed a new wardrobe. Something more professional. How could she schmooze potential stakeholders looking like she'd just come from a half-price sale at the New Life Secondhand Store?

"You sure you don't want to come?" Luis prompted.

"I'd love to but I have to go shopping." Right after their book club meeting, she'd enlist her friends to help her reinvent herself so she could reinvent her nonprofit.

By the time she was done, the Helping Paws Animal Rescue and Shelter would be everything her father dreamed it would be.

It would keep the memory of his love alive.

Chapter Two

Easy, now, Wild Willy." Raising his hands in stick-'em-up surrender, Lance eased closer to the barn stall, where his favorite training bull was backed against the wall, snorting and pawing at the ground like he was seeing red. *Fuck.* Sweat soaked the bull's brown coat and for some reason those horns looked even more lethal in the dim light.

On a normal day, he didn't enjoy standing eye-to-eye with one of his bovine athletes—especially before he'd finished his coffee—but this mean bastard had given him no choice.

Just as the coffeepot had started to hiss, Tucker, the stable manager and training wrangler, had come barreling into Lance's kitchen hollerin' about how Wild Willy had gone ape shit in the field. Seemed his favorite cow was flirting with another bull. In the process of proving his manhood by charging Ball Buster, Wild Willy had stepped in a hole and come out of the debacle with a limp. Which meant Lance had the pleasure of assessing the injury to see if they had to call out the vet.

"All over a woman," he muttered. Last he'd checked, he was a bull rider, but some days he felt more like he was stuck on an episode of *The Bachelor*.

"Trust me, fella," he said, easing closer to Wild Willy, who'd calmed some and was now chawing on a bundle of hay. "She's not worth it." Relationships in general weren't worth it. "You're better off alone." Why put in all of that effort when almost every relationship ended with two people walking in opposite directions? Or two cows, in this case. "All right, Wild Willy. Let's get a look at that hind leg." Keeping a safe distance on the outside of the pen, he tested the bull with a sweep of his hand down its flank, which only riled it up again. The dumbass jolted away, slamming its rear end into the wall.

Shiiiiit. Whipping a bandanna out of his back pocket, Lance mopped sweat from his forehead. "You're not gonna make this easy on me, are you?" he asked, backing off to give Wild Willy some space.

The bull tossed its head and snorted a confirmation.

"Don't forget who feeds you. I *own* you." And he needed this big guy right now. Only a few weeks until World Finals, and he had a hell of a lot of work to do to get ready. This season had pretty much sucked. Only one title and a whole lot of back talkin' from fans about how he should've retired two years ago.

"Well, maybe I'm not ready to retire," he said to the bull. Hell, he was only thirty. He could still go out on top. Even with his joints creaking the way they did. He'd ignored pain before, especially when he had somethin' to prove. This wouldn't be the first time.

But it might be the last.

No. Couldn't think about that. Couldn't think about how everything he'd worked for his whole life would likely end after this competition. What would he have after it was over?

Instead of dwelling on that fun question, he faced the bull. He'd rather face a lethal bull than uncertainty any day. "Steady now." He ripped the bull's halter off a nearby nail in the wall. "Don't make me get the tranquilizer—"

"Lance?" A woman's voice echoed from outside the stall. Not just any woman, Naomi Sullivan, the ranch's book-keeper and all around caretaker of the whole lot of them. "Are you in there?" she called again. And she didn't sound calm.

Raising a finger to Wild Willy's snout, Lance tried to match the crazy in the bull's eyes. "This is not over." He tossed down the halter and stepped outside into the early morning sunlight. The sky was still pink. It cast a bluish haze over the hand-hewn log buildings that made up the Cortez Family Ranch. Smoke still puttered out of the main house's chimney from the fire he'd started in the woodstove last night. That's how early it was. Too damn early for another crisis, but from the looks of Naomi's bedraggled reddish hair and wide green eyes, something had her panties all bunched up.

Naomi had been a family friend forever. The sister they'd never had. So he could tell when she was stressed. And now would be one of those times. "What's up?" he asked, thinking of nothing but the steaming hot coffee waiting in his kitchen.

"Sorry to bother you." She was heaving like she'd run all the way up the hill from her house. She lived with them on the ranch. After her husband had taken off and left her with a baby girl ten years ago, Lance had offered her a job and invited her to move into the guesthouse on the property. Not that she was a charity case. She was damn good with numbers. Always had been. However, she did tend to run high in the drama department.

He gave her a smile to simmer her down. "You're not bothering me. Everything all right?"

She looked around as though torn. "I'm worried about your dad. I haven't seen him since yesterday." In addition to doing the books for the ranch, she kept an eye on his father, which had become a heroic task as of late. As if she hadn't already proven herself a saint, the woman had offered to cook and clean for Luis. She was the one who made sure he took his blood pressure meds.

"He said he was going for a hike and wouldn't need dinner," Naomi went on. "But when I brought over his breakfast this morning, he wasn't around."

Of course he wasn't. Because lately his dear old dad had taken to wandering off without bothering to tell anyone where he was going. If he wasn't volunteering at that animal shelter in town, he was somewhere out on the mountain, head in the clouds as he relived better days.

Naomi wrung her hands in front of her small waist. "I noticed his backpack was gone. Along with his sleeping bag." She reached into her pocket and held up a prescription bottle. "But he left his medication behind."

Which meant a thousand things could've happened to him out there. He could've gotten disoriented. Could've passed out. Could've lost his balance and fallen off a cliff. He was sixty-seven years old, for shit's sake. A fact Lance had to keep reminding him of over and over. He didn't belong out on that mountain alone.

"I'm worried about him." Naomi was on the verge of tears now, and if there was one thing he hated more than having to act like his father's babysitter, it was a woman crying. "Should we call out search and rescue?"

Hell no. He didn't say it, but he wasn't about to call out search and rescue. They'd called those guys six times in the past year, all because Luis Cortez had taken to wandering off alone somewhere on the three thousand acres they owned. God only knew how much of the taxpayers' money they'd already wasted. Not to mention he didn't want to put any lives at risk for a man who was probably just out for an extended stroll.

Lance laid a hand on Naomi's shoulder and steered her back toward her house. Looked like his training would have to wait. Again. "I'm sure Dad's fine. Probably just wanted a night under the stars." That's what he usually said when Lance dragged him back home from one of his impromptu camping trips. A new layer of sweat burned his forehead. If the man kept wandering away he swore he would implant a GPS chip into his father's arm so he could start tracking the old coot.

"What if he's hurt?" Naomi asked, grabbing his arm like she needed support. "Oh God, Lance. I should've checked on him last night. After everything he's done for me, I hate to think of him out there alone."

"Hey." He stopped and turned her to face him. She seemed to worry about everything. Everyone. And he knew the weight of that burden. She didn't need it. She had a daughter to raise. Much as she mothered him, he took it upon himself to protect her, to make sure she didn't have to worry.

"He's *fine*. Don't forget, he does this all the time." His father was worse than an untrained Labrador the way he got distracted and roamed away. "I don't want you to worry, got that? I'll take care of it." The same way he always did.

"How do you even know where to look?"

"I don't. But Jessa might." She spent more time with Luis than pretty much anyone. If it was any other woman, he'd worry she was on a gold-digging expedition, but Jessa didn't exactly scream temptress.

Naomi's face brightened. "Great idea. Jessa will know how to find him."

"Sure she will." He prodded her up the porch steps. "Now you go on in and take care of Gracie. Tell her we can do a riding lesson this afternoon, if she's up for it." Naomi's ten-year-old was currently the only female he chose to spend time with and that was just fine with him.

Naomi shook her head with a wide smile. "*If* she wants to? Are you kidding? You should hear her bragging to all of her friends about how she has the most handsome riding instructor in the whole wide world. She actually told them all you look like Ryder from *Tangled*. You should've heard the squealing." She trotted up the steps to her modest guesthouse and turned back to him with a smirk on her face. "Me? I'd take Gerard Butler. No offense."

"None taken." They'd determined long ago that they'd be a bad fit. Course, he'd be a bad fit with pretty much anyone.

"See you later." Naomi waved him off. "Tell Jessa I said hey. And be nice to her, Lance. I saw her at book club..."

He happened to know that book club was a fancy way of saying wine and chocolate club, but whatever.

"She got dumped again."

Shiiiiit. Wasn't this his lucky day? "As long as she's not crying," he muttered, heading down the road. Boots pounding the packed dirt, he passed the main house, passed that steaming hot cup of coffee waiting in his kitchen, and kept right on movin' until he'd reached his truck, cursing the whole way.

* * *

This couldn't be right. Jessa turned to get a profile view of her body. *Hello!* When she saw that the label on the bra said Bold Lift, she'd had no idea what it meant. In a matter of two minutes, she'd somehow gained at least two cup sizes. She gawked at herself in the mirror. *Wow.* Those babies were really out there. When she looked down at her toes, her chin practically hit her cleavage. Not to mention the straps were already digging into her skin. Why did satin and lace feel so itchy compared to cotton?

Turning her back on the spectacle in the mirror, she gazed longingly at an old cotton bra hanging on the knob of her closet door. But no. *No.* It was time for her to kick it up a notch. She had a lot to offer and she was about to show it to the world.

When she'd called her mother last night to inform her that she'd lost her main donor (carefully omitting the fact that he'd also happened to be her boyfriend), the woman had gotten right down to business. "You'll only appear as professional as you feel," she'd said. Then she'd advised her on how to build a wardrobe that would help her "dress for success."

Jessa had written everything down.

Expensive undergarments. Check! Even though the bra squeezed her tighter than a corset, she'd wear it. Along with the new thong she'd bought to match. Because smart, stylish women apparently wore uncomfortable undergarments.

Carefully avoiding a glance at the backside of her body, she backed out of her bedroom and into the small bathroom. When it came to how she looked in a thong, she subscribed to the ignorance-is-bliss mentality.

After doing her makeup the way she'd learned on Pinterest last night, she dashed to the closet to select one of the new outfits she'd bought. Today was a big day. She'd set up meetings at the local real estate office, the bank, and the town chamber to see about developing some partnerships with businesses in town. Not that any of them had seemed particularly excited to talk to her, but she'd change their minds. Which meant she had to look her best.

To her credit, her mom had never nagged her about the way she dressed, though it was obvious that style had never been important to Jessa. It'd never mattered what she wore, seeing as how she spent her time with animals. She'd been bled on, vomited on, pooped on, peed on...so she'd never actually had a reason to wear nice clothes. Most of her life, scrubs, yoga pants, and T-shirts had suited her just fine.

But Dr. Carla Roth was refined, elegant, brilliant, and incredibly sophisticated. Even as a professor, her mother wore beautiful silk blouses and wrap dresses with heels. At a cocktail party, the woman glittered like royalty. She'd won three of the university's largest grants by simply charming old men at various university functions.

Unlike Jessa, her mother had never had her heart broken. Not once. And that was exactly the kind of woman Jessa needed to become.

Her book club friends—Naomi Sullivan, Cassidy Greer, and Darla Michelson—had been all too eager to help her craft a new look.

The whole group had led her down Main Street, parading

through the clothing boutiques, arms full of adventurous new garments for her to try on.

But now, hanging in her closet, the skirts and brightly colored tunics didn't appeal to her the way they had last night when everyone was oohhhing and aahing at her in the dressing rooms.

She snatched a flowery blouse off a hanger. What did that go with again? Was it the blue skirt? The red capri pants that her friends swore made her look exactly like Katharine Hepburn? All the new colors and patterns in her closet started to blur together in a whorl of confusion. *Whoa.* This could take a while. She needed coffee. Stat.

Leaving the clothes behind, she dashed through the living room to the kitchen and scooped heaping tablespoons of coffee into the French press. The familiar scent of her morning routine soothed the mounting tension from her hands. She could do this. She could match a shirt and shorts, for the love of God. It wasn't rocket science. She had an MBA, Cam it!

After filling the kettle, she set it on the stove and cranked the burner. It was the flowery shirt that went with the capris, right?

Shit. She had no idea. It was time to call for backup. Snatching her cell phone off the counter, she summoned her mother.

"Hello?" Her mother sounded a bit out of breath, which meant Jessa had probably interrupted her morning yoga practice.

"Hi, Mom," she said, glancing down at her body. Come to think of it, she might benefit from a morning yoga practice, too. The only morning practice she embraced regularly involved pastries.

"Jessa?" her mother wheezed. "Is everything all right, honey?"

"Everything's good!" she said, trying to sound chipper. "I bought all those clothes you told me to get."

"That's wonderful! I'm so happy for you." Her mother sounded more relieved than happy. "You're *finally* investing in yourself. It's going to make such a difference. You won't believe what new clothes can do for your self-confidence."

"Yeah. Um. It's pretty exciting." But it'd be even better if she could actually *dress* herself in the new clothes. "So listen. I have some important meetings today and I'm not sure what top to wear with my red capri pants."

"Hmmm..." Her mother mused as though this decision ranked right up there with purchasing a house. "Were you able to find a white asymmetric blouse?"

"Uh—" What was an asymmetric blouse again?

A knock sounded. At the front door. Yes, that would be the door, which was neatly centered between the two large bay windows a mere twenty feet from where she stood. In the kitchen. Wearing only a bra and thong.

Okay. She edged her back against the refrigerator. Sheer curtains had seemed like a good idea when she'd picked them out last year, but she was starting to regret that decision. Clearly, she hadn't thought through the implications of what would happen when she wanted to make herself a cup of coffee dressed only in a thong and Bold Lift bra.

"Jessa?" her mother said loudly. "Did I lose you?"

"No. I'm still here," she whispered.

Another round of hearty pounding pried a squeal from her lips. What the hell was happening? Who'd knock on her door before seven? Was her house on fire or something?

"Honey? Is everything all right?" her mother asked.

"Yes," she hissed. "But I'll have to call you back." Before her mother could answer, she clicked off her phone and set it down. Holding her breath, she stood perfectly still and quiet—minus the loud drumbeat of her heart.

The knocking didn't stop.

"Hello?" A man's deep rumbling voice sent her heart off to the races again. There was something vaguely familiar about it...

"It's Lance Cortez. I need to talk to you."

Lance! Oh. Holy. No. This was *not* happening. She gazed longingly at the other side of the living room to the safe darkness of the tiny hallway that led to her bedroom. There was no way she'd get through there without him seeing *some*thing. Like her ass, maybe. Cam it!

Get the front door with the windows, the ignorant Home Depot salesman had advised. *It'll let in the most light.* Yes, and now it would also give Lance a clear view of a very full moon.

She flattened her body against the cabinets, craning her neck, and sure enough, he stood right there on her front porch, now peering through that lovely window on the door.

Oh, God. Her lungs heaved so hard it felt like the Bold Lift Bra was about to bust at the seams. *Calm down*, she instructed herself. *He'll go away.* He had to go away.

"Jessa! I know you're in there. Your car's here," he called again, rapping the door with that big manly fist of his. "I need to talk to you. It's an emergency."

Tell me about it! Maybe she could call 9-1-1 and have him escorted off her porch...

Footsteps thudded on the front porch, moving closer.

Sweet lord! Lance Cortez was peeking through the bay window!

"Hang on a sec!" she yelled, then hit the deck, pressing her body against the wood floor. Lifting her head, she assessed the distance to the hallway. It might as well have been twenty miles.

Okay. Think. What would Naomi do? That was an easy one. She never would've gotten herself into this situation in the first place because Naomi had the ability to get dressed without the assistance of coffee.

"Jessa, I really need a word," Lance called again.

"Be there in a minute!" Despite the fact that she was basically naked, sweat itched on her back. Her room. She had to get to her room. And there was only one way. She'd have to army crawl. As long as she stayed on this side of the couch, Lance probably wouldn't be able to see her from the window. It was risky, but what other option did she have? He obviously wasn't going away.

Here goes. Trying to remain one with the floor, she squirmed forward, shimmying past the bookshelf. *Squirm, pull, squirm, pull.* She edged against the couch, bare skin grazing the cold wood planks.

Yes. Yes! It was working. Almost halfway now...

A scratch stung her hip as something sharp caught the delicate strap of her thong.

Uh oh. Contorting her body, she tried to get a better look. A loose staple from the re-upholstery job she'd done on the couch had hooked her adorable brand-new panties. *Cam it!* She should've known a staple gun wasn't enough to hold a couch cover together. *Thanks a lot, Pinterest.*

"Jessa!" More pounding.

"Hold on! Give me a minute!" she called, trying to wring the panic from her tone. What the hell was his problem, anyway? Couldn't he take a hint? She pushed onto her side to free herself from the staple, but her legs smacked into the end table. The whole thing toppled over with a deafening crash. *Ow! Shit!* She rolled over, gripping the backs of her calves. At the same time, the thong stretched, ripped, and snapped, falling to the floor underneath her.

"Jessa?" Lance yelled through the door. "What was that?" The doorknob clanged like he was trying to get in. "Is everything okay?"

Hot tears filled her eyes. "Fine!" Minus the throbbing in her legs and the fact that she'd just shredded a fifty-dollar thong.

"Are you sure?" he persisted, the sonofabitch. "That sounded bad. Is the key still out here?"

The key? Oh, dear God, the key! Her dad had always left a house key underneath the flowerpot...

A new wave of terror surged, blinding her with white-hot fear.

The sound of metal clanged in the lock.

"No!" She squealed, scrambling to hide herself behind a small square throw pillow from the couch. "Please! Don't come—"

The door sprang open.

Right as Lance stepped around the couch, she shifted the pillow to cover her lower hemisphere.

"What're you—?" He halted like he'd been shot, his gaze bouncing from her eyes to her bra and then, sure enough, down to the pillow.

"Turn around! Cover your eyes," she wailed. For the love of God! Humiliation curdled into anger. "Why'd you have to come in? Who just barges into someone's house, huh?" Why couldn't he have waited on the porch like she'd asked?

"Uh..." He seemed to be frozen in place. "Sorry. I heard the crash. Thought you were hurt..."

Was he gawking? His lips had parted with surprise. And then there were his eyes. Wide and unblinking. Men didn't usually look at her like that...

"What the hell happened?" he asked, finally finding the decency to turn around and stare out the bay window.

Securing the pillow against her lower abdomen with one hand, she covered her Boldly Lifted chest with her arm in case he decided to peek again. "I had a bit of an accident." She should make something up. Something really exciting. Something like she and a mystery man were playing this kinky game...

"Are you hurt?" Lance asked, his head swiveling toward her again.

She kept herself covered. Oh, yes. She was hurt. On more than one level. "I'm fine," she choked out. "Can you get my robe? It's hanging up in the bathroom at the end of the hall."

"Right. Your robe." He sort of side-shuffled his way down the hall and back, before tossing the robe at her without turning around.

Clutching her salvation, she scurried up to a standing position, the backs of her calves still aching, and wrapped the fabric around her, tying the belt securely at her waist.

Lance peeked over his shoulder as if to check on her, then turned all the way around.

She wasn't sure if she was out of breath due to the terrible thong ordeal or to the fact that the elusive Lance Cortez looked so different up close. She's seen him around town since she'd been back, but she'd never *looked* at him that closely. He'd never looked at her the way he was now, either.

Eyes open slightly wider than a normal person's, lips parted like he couldn't remember what it was he'd wanted to say.

Yes, well, neither could she. Not with the sight of his dark hair, which curled slightly at the edges. It was mussed like he'd been nervously running his hand through it all morning. And those eyes. An arctic blue-gray. Cutting. He wore a dark red flannel shirt with the sleeves pushed up over his bulky forearms. His jeans were faded and worn like he worked hard, which she'd heard he did.

"So…" His voice had this deep soothing reverberation that made her want to curl up against him. "Did you fall or something?"

Or something. "I was in the kitchen making coffee," she informed him, trying to smooth her hair into soft waves like it had been before she'd gone to battle with the couch. "Wasn't expecting anyone to show up at my door…" Especially the enigma that was Lance Cortez. "So I panicked and was trying to get back to my room without giving you a show." Which was clearly too much to ask from the universe.

"Oh." His gaze seemed to fixate on the leopard-print thong that lay a mere two feet from his boots.

As swiftly as possible, she swiped it off the floor and shoved it into the pocket of her robe. "Um. Did you need something, Lance?" Because her humiliation meter was about tapped out for the day and it wasn't even seven o'clock.

"Right. Yes." That intense gaze pierced her eyes. "Dad spent the night out on the mountain and I need you to tell me how to find him."

The news shocked her into stillness. "He spent the night out there?" Luis hadn't said a word about camping when she'd talked to him Wednesday night. Though he did camp occasionally, he usually told her his plans.

"I'm sure he's fine," he went on. "His sleeping bag is gone, which means he planned on being out all night. But he didn't bring his meds."

Though she tried not to panic, her mind hopped on a runaway train car of worst-case scenarios. So many things could've happened to him...he could've taken a fall. He could've gotten turned around. He could've had a heart attack like her father...

Lance's weight shifted. He cleared his throat. "So, have you seen him?"

"Not since Wednesday." It was hard to swallow past the emerging rock formation in her throat. Because Luis had asked her to go up the mountain with him. And she'd said no.

"Are you okay?"

"I'm..." What if something had happened to him and he was all alone because she didn't go with him?

A shrill whistle sliced into her thoughts.

Lance looked around. "You got water on the stove?"

Blinking fast enough to sop up threatening tears, she nodded quickly. "I was making coffee..."

"Coffee sounds great," Lance said. And if that wasn't shocking enough, he sat himself down on her couch.

Heat blanketed her, making the robe feel like a fur coat. He wanted to sit and have coffee with her? While she wore her robe? "But...um...maybe...well...okay..." The words stumbled over one another, mimicking the erratic beat of her heart. *No. Don't you dare*, she told that stubborn thing.

No matter how beautiful Lance Cortez was, she was done with romance.

Chapter Three

He'd only stayed for the coffee, so he'd best stop looking at Jessa like she was on the menu.

Lance did his best to reel in his tongue and crank his jaw closed. But... *damn*.

It had to be the thong. And the bra. And the robe. Who knew Jessa Mae Love owned sexy lingerie? Not him. It would've been better if he'd known, if he'd been prepared to see her like that—all half naked and done up like a no-strings-attached fantasy. Her legs were much longer than he'd ever realized. Long, tanned, and defined. Lethal combination. Must be all of that hiking she did.

Though he knew better, his gaze followed her to the kitchen. Yes, Jessa had spent every summer in Topaz Falls for as long as he could remember. He'd known of her, even a little bit about her, considering their fathers were more like brothers than friends. He'd seen her around the ranch, but he'd never looked at her too closely. How could he have ever missed that bust, which he'd gotten a nice view of before he remembered his manners and turned away. He may not get out much, but he was still a man. And he had perfect eyesight. He noticed things like that. Somehow on Jessa, he'd missed it until the moment he'd seen her lying on the floor. All of a sudden, there they were, two perfect breasts staring him in the face, and he was awake on a whole new level. Even without coffee.

The unrecognizable woman in front of him—could he even call her Jessa anymore?—worked quickly in the kitchen, clutching the top of the robe like she wanted to bolt it together. He almost wished she could.

After she'd removed the screaming teakettle from the stove and poured water into a French press, she sort of scuttled past him. "I should go change," she said in a huskily sexy voice that didn't seem to fit her. Or at least it hadn't. Before the lingerie...

"I'll throw on some clothes," she went on, nervously shifting her eyes. "Then we can talk about Luis."

Yes. Clothes. That would be best. Because if she put on more clothes, maybe he could focus on something besides these details he'd never noticed about her. Like the soft way her blondish hair cascaded past her shoulders. Or the way her earnest, unsure, brown-eyed gaze had stirred something inside him. Instead of answering her, he simply averted his eyes and nodded, giving her permission to go, giving himself space to get his shit together. Because he'd just spent a good five minutes checking out Jessa Mae Love. Town animal activist. Best friend to his sixty-seven-year-old father. Which was weird.

God, this was so weird...

"Um. Be right back." Her skin blotched bright pink before

she whirled and scampered down the hall, that short robe riding up enough to make his eyes pop open wider so he could get a better look before he checked himself again. Jessa Mae Love. He tried to picture her the way he'd always seen her—wearing tan hiking pants, a T-shirt, hair pulled back tightly into a ponytail, and those eyes obscured by thick-rimmed glasses. But the image kept morphing back into sexy robe babe. No way would he get her out of his head now.

He pushed off the couch and did a lap around her living room to get the blood flowing somewhere besides his crotch.

Trying to distract himself from the action happening in her bedroom down the hall, he looked around. The house was the typical 1940s bungalow. Jessa's father, Buzz, had lived there for more than thirty years. A few years ago, his father had dragged Lance to a poker game here. Back then, dark wood paneling covered the walls. A hazy smell of cigar smoke contaminated the furniture. It'd been the typical elderly bachelor pad—everything old, moldy, and most likely purchased from garage sales. But Jessa had really lightened things up.

She'd painted the wood paneling bright white and knocked down the wall that used to separate the kitchen from the small living room. There were pops of orange and turquoise in pillows and curtains. Instead of trinkets, a wall of white bookshelves was filled with academic-looking hardbacks. He paused in front of the white sofa and studied the picture that hung on the wall behind it. Jessa and Buzz standing on Topaz Mountain. He leaned in closer. She had on the typical Jessa uniform—pants and a loose-fitting T-shirt—but on closer inspection, it did appear that the woman had always been more well-endowed than he'd given her credit for...

"Sorry that took so long."

He spun, knocking his knee on the edge of an old trunk that acted as a coffee table, and held back the wince.

"I'll get the coffee. Should be done now," she murmured, nervously fisting her delicate hands.

"Sounds good." His head *was* pounding for a hit of caffeine, but the rest of his body pounded for different reasons. Apparently, Jessa had suddenly decided to start wearing shorts. Short shorts and a faded V-neck T-shirt that pointed his gaze to the very spot he'd been trying to avoid.

"Have a seat." She gestured to the couch and sashayed across the room and into the small kitchen.

For the second time that morning, he had to remind himself to close his mouth. He sank to the couch, glancing at the picture book on her coffee table instead of her ass. Which was shaped and firm, he couldn't help but notice. And if he sat here much longer, he might be tempted to do more than notice, which meant he should fast track this little meeting.

With that in mind, he shifted forward, widened his stance, and rested his elbows on his knees. "So, got any idea where my dad might be?"

"I'm not *exactly* sure," Jessa answered, working quickly to fill two mugs in the kitchen. "But if I had to guess, I'd say he's somewhere up near the north ridge."

"And the north ridge is...?" His face heated. Yes, he owned the land, but he never had time to get out and explore it. Not the way Jessa and his father did.

"It's about eight miles up the mountain." Carrying two steaming mugs, Jessa walked—no *swayed* those curvy hips—back across the living room and handed one to him. She sat on the very edge of a leather chair opposite the couch. "I saw him Wednesday," she said, her brown eyes reddening. "He asked me if I wanted to go up with him. And I said no." The last word teetered on the edge of a whimper.

Oh, shit. Don't do it. Don't cry. "He'll be fine," he said before a tear could fall.

Jessa bit into her lower lip. Something he might like to try sometime...

"I thought he'd ask Tucker to go with him since I couldn't. No one should be out there alone. Ever." A tear did slip out then, and he shocked himself by reaching over to cover her hand with his. Not because he wanted to touch her. Hell no. That had nothing to do with this. Her dad had passed away last year and it obviously still got to her, that's all. He could imagine how that would feel. Didn't know what he'd do if he lost his own father. "Dad's out there all the time," he reminded her. "He likes to be alone. And it's not your responsibility to babysit him." That burden rested solely on his shoulders. And with his training schedule, he hadn't done much of a good job of it lately.

Jessa stared at his hand covering hers like she didn't quite know what to make of it. Yeah, neither did he. So he withdrew it, lifted the coffee mug to his lips, and took a good long sip. Heaven. It was liquid heaven. Bitter but creamy. Exactly the way he made it for himself. The realization shook him up again. He set down the mug before he spilled it. "You put a tablespoon of cream in it." Real cream. None of that fake flavored shit.

Jessa startled, her eyes worried. "You don't like it?"

"No. I mean...yes." He paused to unscramble his thoughts. "That's exactly how I make it." But she hadn't asked him if he wanted cream.

A soft smile plumped her lips and made them look as delicious as the coffee. "That's how Luis drinks it every day at the shelter. I figured maybe that was how you liked it, too."

"Good guess." He sipped again, hoping the caffeine would clarify his thoughts, because they kept wandering and now was not the time to get distracted by a woman. He had to find his dad so he could get back to the ranch and take care of Wild Willy. Otherwise he wouldn't be able to resume his training and then he'd be five hundred miles up shit creek.

"So he didn't tell you where he planned to camp?" Jessa asked, crossing those long legs. Her voice had a formal ring to it, like she was about as uncomfortable with the current situation as he was.

He focused on his coffee. "No. But he does this all the time." Definitely more than Jessa knew about.

"He can't sit still," she said through a fond smile. "He hates to be confined."

"Yeah, well, if he doesn't start sitting still more often, I'll *have* to confine him." He couldn't watch the man 24/7. Not with Worlds coming up.

Not that he needed to have that discussion with Jessa. He'd already said too much.

Lance finished off his coffee and plunked the mug onto the trunk. "So can you tell me how to get up there? To the north ridge?"

"There's really no easy way." She stood and collected their mugs, rushing them to the kitchen. "You'll have to take the ATV up most of the way," she called as she rinsed them in the sink. "Until the talus field. Then you go on foot about another mile or so until you see the outcropping."

The what huh?

She traipsed back to her chair and sat. "Then you run

into the boulder field." Her eyes glittered with excitement. "That's where it gets fun."

"Sounds simple." Yeah, about as simple as getting his body to behave when he took his gaze to the point of her V-neck shirt. Holy hell. This was gonna take him all day.

"It's actually pretty complicated. I'll have to come with you," she murmured, the rounded apples of her cheeks flushing with an intensity he'd never seen on her face. Of course, he'd never really looked before.

"You want to come?" His mouth went dry. He'd have to spend the whole day trying not to notice how sexy she suddenly was?

"I *have* to come. There's no way you'll find him on your own."

Damn it all. She was right.

* * *

Jessa did her darnedest to stuff down the worry that threatened to make her seem overdramatic. Lance was so calm about the whole thing. So sure his father would be fine. Luis went out on the mountain all the time. Sometimes alone. He knew the terrain. Knew every survival skill he'd ever need...

She gazed out at the peaks from Naomi's front porch, where she and her friend had gathered to wait for Lance to bring down the ATV. The mountains looked beautiful, powdered with snow at the very tops, the late fall sun casting a spotlight on every chiseled detail. *He'll be fine*, she told herself again, trying to mentally separate today from the trauma of last year. And yet her stomach refused to settle.

In an attempt to distract herself, she filled Naomi in on her eventful morning.

"Let me get this straight." Her friend's luminous green eyes doubled in size. "Lance came *in*to your house. Sat on your couch. And had coffee with you?" she repeated for what had to be the fifth time.

Jessa's skin warmed as though the high-altitude sun was beating down right on her face, but nope, they were nice and shaded. It was simply a hearty Lance Cortez–induced blush. Not even the brisk mountain breeze could douse it, though goose bumps prickled her legs. God, she shouldn't be wearing shorts on a search-and-rescue operation. But they'd left her house in such a hurry she hadn't even had time to change into more appropriate attire.

A few feet away, Naomi's sweet daughter, Gracie, sang to herself on the porch swing.

Jessa leaned in close so the girl wouldn't hear. "*Yes.* He came into my house. And I was naked," she moaned, reliving that humiliating moment when Lance had stepped around the couch and the bottom fell out of his jaw.

Naomi's eyes narrowed in a way that quirked her lips. "Better naked than wearing your old hiking pants," she offered.

"Thanks." She'd hoped a quick chat with her friend would bolster her confidence, seeing as how she had to spend an entire day with Lance and somehow not succumb to her typical awkward ways, but so far the woman wasn't helping. "This isn't funny! You should've seen the way he looked at me." At first he'd looked shocked, then it seemed more like lust, but then, as he'd finished his coffee, his expression had looked almost disgusted. "I don't think he likes me very much."

"Lance doesn't like anyone," Naomi reminded her. "But that's why this is so perfect."

"I'm not following." This didn't sound perfect to her. She had to spend a whole day with someone who didn't like people. And he was so beautiful to look at. Which meant she was guaranteed to make a fool out of herself again.

"He's tough to read," Naomi admitted. "But it's the perfect opportunity for you to try out your new look. See if you can win him over. It'll be great practice for finding donors for the shelter."

Now it was her turn to laugh. "Win him over? Lance Cortez?" That was like a duck trying to win over a lion. "Do you know me at all? I have no clue how to charm a man."

"Well you coulda fooled me," her friend said, looking her up and down. "Seriously. You look hot. The contacts, the makeup, the hair..." She reached over and fluffed the soft waves Jessa had blown dry earlier. "You've always been beautiful, and now everyone's going to know it."

Jessa smoothed her hair nervously. "I'm not sure it'll make much of a difference."

"Trust me," Naomi insisted. "It *will* make a difference. You look great," she emphasized. "Pretty soon you'll have donors lined up down the block."

"If you say so." But after Lance came over, she canceled all of her meetings. Donors weren't her biggest concern today. Not right now. She squeezed her friend's hands, feeling her own tremble. "Do you really think Luis is okay out there?" she asked, almost breathless. Memories of getting the phone call that her father had collapsed out on the mountain bore down on her.

"I was worried, too, honey," Naomi said, not letting go of her hands. "But Lance is right. His dad is a true mountain man. He's not lost. He's not missing. He just needs to be more responsible and remember to bring along his medication next time."

"Right." She nodded as though the words had alleviated her fears.

"You and Lance will find him," Naomi went on, turning back to the driveway.

Somewhere in the distance, an engine sounded. Nerves gripped Jessa's stomach. She hoped so. She hoped they'd find Luis right away. She also hoped she could spend the day with Lance and somehow resist that dark, hot cowboy thing he had going on...

But when he came speeding around the corner on the ATV, dirt flying from the wheels, that hard body tensed and strong, her heart floated away from her again.

He skidded to a stop in front of the green lawn and pulled off his helmet.

"Uncle Lance!" Gracie squealed, launching herself off the porch and into his arms just as he stood.

Laughing, he swung her around, and that smile on Lance's face—the unguarded expression of happiness—bolted Jessa's feet right to the wooden planks beneath her. Then and there her heart dissolved into warm mush and something inside her sang. She knew she could never see him the same way again.

Lance glanced over at her, some of that messy dark hair spilling over his forehead, and their eyes locked. The singing turned into a warm hum. It was like that scene in *West Side Story*, when Tony and Maria first see each other across the dance floor. Everything else blurs into a meaningless background and it's just the two of them, staring longingly into each other's eyes. Well, she was longing. It was hard to tell what he thought.

Lance was the first to blink. "Hey, Jessa," he said casually, like the universe hadn't just exploded into a million glittering diamonds that made everything sparkle. Was she imagining it or did his voice gentle the syllables of her name?

"Hi." Jessa nearly sighed.

"All right, buckaroo." Lance set a still-giggling Gracie gently on the ground. "I've got to go. But we'll get to that riding lesson later."

The girl's eyes were sparkling the same way Jessa imagined hers still were. "Promise?" Gracie asked, hands clasped underneath her chin, the little charmer.

"Pinkie swear." He held up his little finger to finalize the deal and Jessa could've sworn her ovaries ached.

Naomi pushed her from behind, and it was a good thing because otherwise she might've stood in that spot all day long staring at Lance.

"So you two have a good time," her friend said, giving her another good nudge in his direction. "Let me know as soon as you find Luis. Tell him I'll have his lunch waiting."

"Will do." Lance looked at her. "Ready?"

No. She was clearly not ready, seeing as how she could feel her heart starting to wander away from her again. Somehow, with one look, Lance had obliterated her ambition to put romance on the backburner.

Oh God. If that had happened with one look, how would she spend the whole day with him? She shot a desperate look at Naomi, but her friend only nudged her toward the steps, her whole face beaming a calculated smile.

As if she knew Jessa was already in over her head.

Chapter Four

White-hot rays of sun cut across his vision and blinded Lance the second he turned back to the ATV. It was a damn good thing the sun blinded him, too, because *something* had to direct his attention away from Jessa so he'd quit noticing how the brightness lit her long, sleek hair. And how her hips swayed in that womanly way. Not to mention how her tanned legs tensed with her steps, shaped and strong but delicate, too.

Damn those shorts. Who the hell wore shorts on a rescue operation, anyway?

Someone with sexy legs, jackass. Not like it was a crime. The woman was allowed to wear whatever she wanted. He never used to care what she wore before. Until sexy robe babe, that is. He kept his head down and navigated the path across Naomi's lawn. *Man.* His father owed him for this mess. If the man would've stayed put, he never would've had to call on Jessa. Never would've noticed her sex appeal. *This is Jessa Mae*, he reminded himself for the hundredth time.

Blinking against the morning sun, he casually sauntered to the driveway. Jessa had already made it to the ATV, booking it down the walkway as if she could feel the snort of a pissed-off bull on her tail. Seemed she wasn't thrilled about spending the day with him, either. When she'd seen him swinging Gracie around, the woman's face had been stony and expressionless. She'd stared at him for a full minute at first, and her eyes had avoided him ever since. Kind of the way he attempted to carefully avoid looking at her. But that was about to get a lot harder because dear old Dad had taken the other ATV out for his little escape, which meant there was only one left. For him and Jessa. To ride together...

Without glancing back at him, she plunked one of the helmets onto her head and tugged the chinstrap into place. Then she swung a leg over the machine and took the handlebars in her hands, staring straight ahead.

"What are you doing?" Lance asked quickening his pace.

Jessa cranked on the handle, starting the thing up. "I'm driving," she yelled over the engine noise.

He skidded to a stop. "*You're* driving?" He hadn't counted on...spooning her from behind.

"You don't know where to go," she yelled again, handing over his helmet like she wanted to get this over with. "I bet I know exactly where he went."

He reached over her and shut off the engine. "You can tell me where to go. *I* should drive."

Jessa didn't budge, but she threw up the face shield on her helmet. "I've been up there a lot more than you have. *I* know the terrain."

"And *I* can handle the ATV," he said, before he thought

better of it. Not that he wanted to insult her, but she was pretty petite to maneuver a machine like this. Especially with the weight of two riders.

Fire filled her narrowed eyes. "I'm driving," she said, turning the key to start the engine back up. "So you can either get on the back or I'll go by myself."

"Fine," he ground out, pulling the helmet down so she wouldn't see the scowl that tightened his face.

Careful not to touch her, he eased his leg over the seat and slid on, bracing his hands against his thighs, unsure where else to put them.

Jessa glanced over her shoulder. "You need to hold on," she advised him, flicking the helmet's shield up so he could gaze into her exotic brown eyes. They flashed with determination but wouldn't quite meet his.

"I am holding on." To himself. That was much safer. He didn't want to feel her soft skin beneath his fingertips. Didn't want to feel anything for her at all.

With a slight shrug, Jessa flicked down the helmet's face shield and turned back to the handlebars.

He clamped his legs tight and secured his feet on the ATV's sturdy base. That'd be enough to hold him in place. How fast could Jessa possibly drive any—

The engine squealed then clinked, there was the grind of metal gears, and they shot off like a missile on target.

"Shit!" His arms flew up and before the momentum threw him right off the back, he wrapped them around her waist, pulling his chest against her back to steady himself.

Her shoulders tensed against him, but she kept her head straight, focused on driving, and it was a damn good thing because they must've been going twenty miles per hour straight up the side of the mountain. "You always drive like this?" he growled over the wind. He'd have to think twice about letting her and his father go up the mountain together again.

"I just want to get there," she yelled back, turning enough that he could see the worry tensing her jaw.

Right. She'd lost her father only a year ago. On the same mountain they were currently blitzing up. And he couldn't imagine that...losing his dad. He'd already lost Lucas, then Levi. One by one the people he'd cared about had walked out of his life. If he lost his dad, he'd lose everyone who mattered. Everyone he had left. Friends weren't the same. Parents anchored you to your heritage, reminded you who you were when it got hard to remember. Far as he knew, Jessa didn't see her mom much. She'd been close with her dad. An ache snuck into his chest as he peered at her profile. Beneath her helmet, her face had hardened into a mask of desperation.

He didn't like seeing her that way. Worried. A little scared. It did something to him, made sympathy prickle through him, which made his arms soften around her...more like he was holding her instead of holding on for dear life. "Hey." He leaned in close so he wouldn't have to shout so loud. "He's all right." This was Luis Cortez they were talking about. The man who'd wrestled a mountain lion off one of his horses, according to local legends. "He's probably gonna be all pissed off that we came up here after him." In fact, he knew his dad would be pissed.

The ATV slowed, then stuttered to a stop, reducing the engine noise to a low hum. Jessa glanced back at him. "Do you really think so?" she asked in a small wobbling tone. Even with the face shield in place he could see the paleness that had taken over her complexion.

"Yeah." He flicked up his face shield, then went for hers so their eyes could lock. So he could reach through her fears. "And I'll tell you one thing," he said with a smirk. "I'm riding down the mountain with *him*."

A shadow of a smile flickered across her lips. "You don't like my driving." The revelation seemed to amuse her. "That's surprising considering you ride maniacal bulls for a living."

"That's a hell of a lot safer than sitting behind you on this thing." He meant that in more ways than one. Because the sun haloed her in a mystifying glow and for the first time ever he realized she wasn't only pretty. Jessa was stunning— beautiful and real and deep.

"Hey," she scolded, her eyes narrowing. "I'm being safe. I'd never endanger—"

"I'm teasing you," he interrupted before she got her leopard-print thong all bunched. "Trying to lighten things up."

"Oh." She looked down.

"I'm not worried about him, Jessa," he said more softly. "Really. The only reason I rushed over to your place was because he doesn't have his blood pressure medication." He grinned at her. "That and I've gotta get back to my training. The sooner we find him the sooner I can get back on my bull."

"Right. Thanks, Lance." Jessa's eyes shied away from his, unsure and guarded and humble. She cleared her throat and lowered the shield to cover up her delicate face, which definitely wasn't pale anymore. Color had shaded her cheeks with the same heat he felt flickering somewhere deep.

Her scent reached him, floating into the cloud of exhaust that had started to dissipate. Some type of vanilla, but light and subtle. It'd been a while since he'd inhaled a woman's scent and a sigh expanded through him, ending in a sharp pain that descended behind his ribs. He'd lusted after plenty of women. The buckle bunnies who'd followed him around the circuit in the early days, who'd always made good on their promise of offering him a fun, uncomplicated night. That had been a different kind of ache, though. It'd never traveled any farther north than his brass belt buckle.

"Ready then?" she murmured, the words muffled. Scooting herself into position, she clamped her hands onto the handlebars again, then cranked the engine.

"Ready." Heart pulsing in small bursts of a long-forgotten desire, Lance threaded his arms around her waist again, letting her back rest against his chest, this time with no hesitation.

* * *

Heaven help her, Jessa had to start focusing on something besides the way Lance's hardened muscled chest shielded her back. The way his sinewed arms guarded her in a strong embrace. *Something else...something else...*

The cool, crisp air. The rays of sun poking through white puffy clouds overhead. Pine trees, tall and gangly. *Shit!* She dodged one that seemed to jump out of nowhere, jerking the handlebars in a way that brought Lance even closer.

"We almost there?" he asked through her helmet. And yes, she'd be the first to admit that the last twenty minutes of her driving hadn't been the best in her life. But he was the one to blame for that. Being all sweet to her. Draping his body all over hers from behind. That had made it a bit hard to concentrate on not hitting broad tree trunks or massive boulders. "Getting close," she yelled so he wouldn't hear the tremble in her voice.

She'd sworn off men, damn it. Sworn off love. All well and good in her head, but God, she wished she could cut out her heart and leave it behind. Already it had ballooned in her chest, rising higher, soaring with the same sappy emotions that had gotten her into so much trouble in the past. And who was she kidding? Lance. Lance Cortez! Bull-riding god who'd been known to shack up with the groupies who made it their life's mission to sleep with a bull rider. Or all of the bull riders. She swore those women kept a checklist in their back pockets.

That thought was all it took to deflate her heart. It couldn't take more disappointment. More pain. Lance Cortez had a certain reputation. Rumor had it that he'd never spent a full night with a woman. He'd slept with plenty of them, but he never stayed in their bed until morning. Remembering that made it easier to focus. They were out here to find Luis. That was all.

Standing up a bit, she peered over the next small rise. This was one of the trickier spots. She slowed the ATV, easing it up the side of a steep incline so Lance wouldn't be thrust into her again. They were getting close to the boulder field, the place she and Luis always parked when they hiked together.

Easing herself forward, she made a futile attempt to put space between her back and Lance's chest, leaning over the handlebars as she navigated the rocky slope. Just as they crested the rise, a smear of blue caught her eye. Luis's ATV. She plowed straight for it, then cranked the brake, skidding to stop right next to it. Hands shaky and tingling, she ripped off her helmet and let it fall to the ground. "He's not here." She glanced around. They were high enough that the trees had thinned; only an occasional gnarled pine tree twisted from the snow and wind during the harsh winters. But there was no sign of Luis. No backpack. No evidence of a camp.

"He must've gone off on foot," Lance said from behind her.

An ominous feeling swept over her, thinning her breath. She stared at the boulder field, the scattered granite that stretched all the way to the mountain's pointed summit. "I thought we'd find him here." She'd been so sure. They'd gone off on foot many times, but always in different directions. And there weren't many places to camp past this point. The terrain got rocky, steeper. Less than a mile up from this place was the spot where her own father had collapsed. Where his heart had given out. Panic fluttered her nerves.

"He couldn't have gone very far," Lance said, coming up beside her, seeming to assess the land. "Looks pretty unforgiving." For the first time gravity weighted his tone.

"It is," she whispered. She and Luis had hiked around here. Once, she'd even gotten him to take her to the spot where her father had died. Tears bit at the rims of her eyes.

From here, it took about another twenty minutes to hike up to the place Luis had taken her father that day. Was that where'd he'd gone? Did he visit the place often? Was it still as hard for him as it was for her? Before she could stop them, the tears spilled over in warm streaks, sadness flowing out of her once again.

"Hey." Lance rested a hand on her shoulder. "You okay?"

"Yes." But the tears kept streaming out and she was powerless to stop them. "Sorry," she muttered, annoyed with herself. She hadn't counted on this being so hard. "I'm worried." And God, she missed her father. Missed being someone's little girl.

Taking her shoulders in those large manly hands, Lance helped her climb off the ATV and turned her to face him, crouching so their eyes were level. "Dad's fine. Trust me. I know."

"How?" she whimpered.

He shrugged, shook his head a little. "This'll sound crazy, but he and I have this connection. If something was wrong, I'd know. I'd feel it."

The words almost prompted a sob. Why hadn't she known? The day her father had died, she'd gone about her life, seeing her furry patients, meeting her roommate for a drink during happy hour. That's where she'd been when she'd gotten the call. She should've felt something...should've felt the loss even before she knew. He was her father.

She gazed at the boulder field, everything blurred and gray despite the bright sunshine, and once again she wondered if he'd suffered. If he'd been in pain. If he'd been scared. Luis hadn't told her much, couldn't seem to talk about it. But he'd said her father had gone ahead and was already on the ground by the time he got there.

"Don't cry, Jessa." Lance held her face in his hands and swiped away the tears with his thumbs. "Like I said, he's okay. I know it. We'll find him."

She nodded, attempting to sniffle back a year of sadness. "I believe you." And yet she couldn't get a grip, not up here so close to her dad's final moments. "It's just...my father." She swallowed so hard her throat ached. "Sometimes it's hard to be up here." God those tears burned her eyes. "I wish I would've been with him. I wish I could've been holding his hand when he..." She couldn't bring herself to say it. It was so horrible. So, so horrible to think of him out here in pain and terrified as the world dimmed and life faded from his body. Instinctively, her hand reached up to finger the necklace he'd given her. It had been his last gift. A rose gold heart with a small diamond embedded inside.

"It's real pretty," Lance said, looking down at the charm. "He give it to you?"

She nodded, tensing her throat so her voice wouldn't wobble. "I miss him. I should've been around more."

She half expected Lance to lecture her on living in the past, on not letting the regrets take over, like so many other people had done. Instead, he pulled her against him, wrapping her up in the comfort and peace of a long, sturdy hug. And despite the potential dangers, she let her head rest against him. She breathed in the calming scent of leather and coffee.

"I wish I knew what those minutes were like." The minutes before he closed his eyes and gave in. Maybe that would bring her peace. Maybe it would give her the permission to let her regrets go.

Lance moved back slightly and took her chin in his hand. She felt the roughness of his skin, the calluses, the coarseness of scabs from healing scrapes. Gently, he tilted her head up until she was staring straight at the sky. So blue, the color itself seemed alive, bottomless in its perfection. Fluffy clouds billowed and moved and floated, a fluid dance. And the sun, so bright and clear it seemed to make everything sparkle.

"That's what he would've been looking at," he murmured, the deep vibration of his voice close to her temple. "The sky, the mountains."

Jessa let her eyes soak it all in until she felt so full with the beauty and wonder of the world, she had to close them. "It's beautiful." Didn't matter how many times she saw it. This view, these mountains, that endless royal sky always struck her. And her dad had loved it, too. He would've wanted this to be the last thing he ever saw.

"It's peaceful up here," Lance said, looking up, too. "Maybe a little what Heaven's like."

The words held a gift, a surprise ray of hope that penetrated her doubts. "You believe in Heaven?"

Those lips quirked in a small smile, and even though he was so dark, with that mussed hair and tanned sun-drenched skin, his eyes were lit with energy. "I like to believe there's something more."

More. The word spread over her like a healing salve, alleviating the lingering throb from the wounds of loss. All these years, she'd been wrong about Lance. She'd thought him to be closed off and grouchy, a man of few words who got annoyed easily, but now she realized she'd misjudged him. He might not do small talk, but a seven-word sentence from Lance meant more than paragraphs from most people.

Her eyes opened and color flooded in. The first thing she saw were his lips, right there, inches from hers. The tendons that threaded her joints together loosened and sparks crackled in her heart. She inhaled his musky scent, let her gaze rest in his. Such beautiful clear eyes. Deep and wise. And yes, she seemed to be moving in closer now but she couldn't fight that pull, couldn't stop the hard cry of need and desire that pushed her into him. Her palms came to rest on his chest as her lips grazed his. But that one light touch wasn't enough. Wasn't nearly enough . . . so she went for it— a full-on kiss, lips fused to his, sighing, searching . . .

Except his chest tensed and he seemed to step back. An

icy realization splashed her face, dousing the passion that had ignited. Lance didn't want to be kissing her. He'd offered her a kind word because she was upset. That was all.

That was all.

Throat thick and pulsing, she slowly eased back, the warmth that had bathed her lips turning cold.

Lance stood stock-still, his own lips parted, arms out as though he'd lost his balance, chest suspended like he wasn't sure if he should breathe in or out.

"Oh my God." Invisible flames of humiliation licked at her cheeks. "I'm so sorry." She'd freaking kissed him! Less than a day after swearing off men, she'd let that swirl of emotion and desire and hope sweep her up into its kingdom of seduction. Her skin tingled. The sunlight seemed too bright. "I didn't mean to...I shouldn't have..." *Kissed* him. On the lips. Like they'd been transported into some sappy chick flick. They were supposed to be searching for Luis! Holy baldheaded cats, what the hell was the matter with her? She couldn't even go one day without swooning. She needed help. Romantics Anonymous. *Hello, my name is Jessa and I'm addicted to love...*

Might as well face it.

Lance simply stood there, saying nothing, an unreadable expression frozen on his face.

Not surprising. He was clearly in a state of shock. Or disbelief? Repulsion? It was impossible to tell. That fight or flight survival instinct kicked her hard under the ribs. "We should find your dad," she said quickly, turning so he wouldn't see the fierce blush that had brought her about two inches from passing out. "Let's go this way."

With desperation in her steps, she tromped toward the boulder field before she could screw up anything else.

Chapter Five

Two seconds ago, he could've sworn Jessa's lips were pressed to his, warm and wet and the slightest bit naughty. If it hadn't been for the smear of some honey-flavored lip gloss on his bottom lip, he would've thought he'd imagined the whole thing because she was gone. As in out of sight. And he was still standing in the same position he'd assumed when she knocked his world off its axis and kissed him.

Shit. He'd screwed that up. Royally. Who could blame him, though? He'd never expected *Jessa* to press herself against him and kiss him. Never expected the rush it brought in him, either. She'd caught him off guard, knocked him off balance. And yes, he could see how stiffening and stepping back may have sent her a certain message, but it was a reflex. Either regain balance or land on his ass. His body had reacted and made the choice for him.

He squinted in the direction that Jessa had stormed off.

The boulder field was sloped and she'd already disappeared on the other side of the rise. "Jessa!" he yelled, not exactly sure how to find her. But he had to. Had to find her, somehow undo the awkwardness he must've made her feel. And they still had to find his dad, too. So he stepped off the way she'd gone, trying to follow her path. He skirted around a hunk of granite as tall as him. Went over a smaller boulder, then hoisted himself up and gazed around. *There.* She was weaving her way through the rocks about thirty yards up.

"Hey!" he called again. "Wait up." He climbed down, trying to formulate an explanation in his head. Except he didn't have one. Usually when women started crying in front of him, his forehead would crank itself tight and he'd slowly back away, scanning for a fast escape. But he kind of hadn't minded comforting Jessa. He certainly hadn't minded the feel of her soft breasts against his chest and her silky lips locked on his...

In fact, he didn't mind this whole excursion as much as he'd thought he would.

Though Jessa slowed her pace, she didn't stop to wait for him. Her chin had lifted with determination, her eyes focused ahead and her arms swooshing at her sides.

The sight drew out a smile. Sure, he felt bad that she seemed embarrassed, but God she was captivating with that fortitude. Continuing on like the whole thing hadn't bothered her at all. He'd met women before who would've whined about his reaction, who would've gone for the guilt trip. Not Jessa. She'd simply hauled off and left him standing there like she didn't need him anyway.

By the time he'd closed in on her, he was out of breath. "Are you okay?" He tried to hide the wheeze in his lungs through a hearty throat clearing.

"Spectacular," she muttered, stomping on.

His hand snagged her shoulder and forced her to stop. "Come on. It's not a big deal." At least it shouldn't have been. Hell, he'd been kissed by his fair share of women. A couple had even caught him off guard before. None had rendered him unable to walk, however. Or to think straight. His eyes searched hers.

They were dark, but the sunlight made the flecks of bronze in them glisten. There was a force in her gaze. She didn't shy away or narrow her eyes angrily at him. She simply stared back, open and unfazed.

"I was surprised," he admitted, leaving out the whole truth. Surprised and thrown off balance by his body's fast response to her. "And I—"

"Can we forget it?" she interrupted. "Please? I'm just emotional. Maybe even a little hormonal this week. You know how it goes."

"Uh." No. He didn't. He *really* didn't.

"And let's face it," she went on. "You're PDF, so it's not my fault, exactly."

"PDF?" he repeated. He sucked at acronyms. Had to use Google to decode most of Levi's Facebook posts. He'd never been good with words. *PDF... PDF...* "Poor dumb fool?"

Those glistening baby browns rolled. "Pretty. Damn. Fine. Don't you get out?"

"Not as much as you would think," he admitted. Lately he hadn't gotten out at all. He was supposed to be training his ass off.

"So you can see how something like that would've happened," she said, lifting her chin again. "The emotions. The whole smoldering cowboy thing you've got going on. But I'd really appreciate it if we could forget it. Like, completely erase it from our memories. Because, Lance, I've sworn off men. Romance. All of it, really. Gotta shift my focus, you know? Don't need it messing up my life anymore. So please. This never happened."

He'd never enjoyed a woman babbling. Ever. Until today. "Okay. I guess. But—"

"Nope. See, 'but' is a segue back into the same topic we just agreed to forget. As in never mention it; never even *remember* it. We entered into a verbal agreement, which can be legally binding in the state of Colorado," she finished, looking quite proud of herself.

"Can it now?" He didn't even try to hide his amusement. He'd known Jessa for years. Or at least he'd known about her. To him, she'd always been Buzz Love's daughter, the gangly girl with the glasses. He thought her to be nice though somewhat shy, maybe even awkward. But they'd never had a real conversation before this morning. She was actually fun to talk to.

"Yes," she uttered with a definitive nod. "As a matter of fact it can."

"What if I said go ahead and sue me?" He pressed his gaze into hers again. "Because I'm not sure I'll be able to forget. I didn't *mind* you kissing me."

She laughed. "Right. You didn't mind." The words mocked him. "Your shoulders felt like concrete. And the way you stepped back…I actually thought you were gonna bolt." But she waved a hand through the air as if it didn't matter. "Listen, I get it. You're Lance Cortez. Sort of famous. Rugged. Hot. I'm just Jessa. Normal girl who smells like animals half the time."

Not right now she didn't. Right now she smelled like the vanilla beans Naomi sometimes set around his father's kitchen. And what was wrong with normal? Kind of refreshing to have a woman say things like they were instead of what she thought he wanted to hear for once.

"Besides all of that, I've sworn off kissing." She turned away and started to hike again, giving him no choice but to follow.

"That seems a little extreme." He kept his eyes focused on the ground so he wouldn't trip over a rock and look like a dumb ass. "Isn't there something else you could swear off? Sugar? Chocolate? Alcohol? Seems to me kissing is one of those things that's actually good for you." Especially when it led to sex. Weren't there a bunch of health benefits associated with sex? Sure seemed like it. Not that kissing Jessa would lead to sex. Because how weird would that be? Having sex with this woman who hung out with his father? Who wanted marriage and kids and the whole bit so badly she'd been engaged multiple times? His body didn't seem to think it would be weird, though. The quick flash of a conjured image was enough to activate the launch sequence. Steam seemed to radiate off his face and cloud the brisk mountain air.

"Actually, I happen to think alcohol and chocolate are much healthier than kissing. At least in my experience," Jessa insisted, scrambling to climb over a tall boulder that blocked their path. She moved effortlessly. Her feet and hands knew exactly where to go. While she finessed it, he awkwardly scaled the thing with sheer strength.

When they'd gotten past the obstacle he slipped in front of her. Wouldn't be as easy for her to get around *him*.

"So that's it then," he challenged.

"That's it." Her gaze didn't waver and he didn't doubt that she meant it.

"Oh, wait. Actually, one more thing. I'd really appreciate it if you didn't say anything to anyone else. The girls would *kill* me if they knew I'd already slipped up and—"

A shrill whistle cut her off. For a second he thought he'd imagined it, but then it rang out again.

"Luis," she whispered, gripping Lance's coat. "That's your dad."

* * *

"How do you know it's him?" Lance jogged alongside her, seeming to be hardly out of breath while she hiccupped and gagged on the thin mountain air.

"He told me if I ever needed help out here, I should whistle exactly like that," she sputtered, clutching at the pains needling her chest. And then Luis had said he'd find her. He'd told her if he ever heard that whistle, he'd rescue her. A second wind lifted her head and churned her legs faster. "We have to find him." Her eyes drank in the endless blue-gray peaks spread all around them. He could be anywhere. Who knew where that whistle had echoed from…

The shrill sound pierced the air again. They were getting closer. Jessa skidded down a steep section of loose talus, losing her balance and flailing to catch herself.

Lance held on to her arm. "Take it easy. Don't need to do two rescues."

She ignored him, ripping out of his grip. "He's in trouble," she wheezed, her heartbeat throbbing in her temples. Luis was in trouble and he was alone.

Another whistle veered her to the left. She slowed to pick her way down a boulder-strewn slope. So close. It sounded so close…

"There!" Lance darted in front of her and pointed toward a huge rounded boulder.

She strained to see.

Luis stood near it, still and alert.

"Are you okay?" blared from her mouth with surprising force, given how she could hardly breathe.

The man spun and relief whooshed in, filling her lungs, calming that surge of adrenaline. He looked like the same Luis, nothing broken, nothing bleeding. His white hair was bedraggled, but other than that, he seemed fine.

Lance made it to his father before her. "What the hell, Dad?" Now he did seem to run out of breath. And he looked pale, too. Rattled. Like maybe he'd been as worried as her on their little sprint down here.

Jessa doubled over to catch her breath.

"What's the problem, son?" the man asked, clearly clueless as to how worried they'd been.

"What's the *problem*?" Lance's tone inched toward a yell.

"We thought something terrible happened to you," Jessa broke in, before Lance could jump all over him. "You were gone all night. And no one knew where you went." She wasn't yelling, but a bit of a whimper snuck through. If anything had happened to him—

"Course I was gone all night," he said, as ornery and gruff as ever. "I have every right to go out and camp on my land whenever the hell I want."

Jessa cut a glance at Lance. His face had gone red. Molten.

"The hell you do," he ground out. "It's not safe for you to come out here alone."

Now that she agreed with. What if her father had been out here alone when he'd had the heart attack? They never would've known what had happened to him. They may have never found his body. She pressed the back of her hand against her lips before a sob snuck out.

Luis seemed to assess her with those watery gray eyes. "I didn't mean to worry anyone," he said more gently. "I'm fine. Everything's fine."

"Then why were you whistling?" she whispered, still battling how the memories of her dad and her relief at seeing Luis swirled her in a fog of emotion.

"Can't find the damn ATV," Luis said, gazing around. "Woke up at sunrise and been lookin' for it ever since. Left it parked right here. I know I did. Someone must've taken it."

"No," Lance snapped, his body rigid. "Actually you didn't leave it right here."

The worry that had just started to dissipate clouded Jessa's heart again. "You parked it where we always park," she said, studying him, searching his eyes for a sign that he remembered. "Over on the east side of the mountain."

Luis simply blinked at her. He looked...confused. Disoriented. And she'd never seen him that way out here. He always knew where things were, which direction was which, how to get from one point to another. On all of their hikes, he'd been the one to lead her.

"This *is* the east side," he insisted, with a stubborn lift to his stubbled jaw. "I ought to know. This is my land."

She glanced at Lance, but he simply shrugged it off. His head tilted to the right. "Topaz Mountain is right there, which means that way is east. You must've gotten turned around." Whirling, he pointed toward the ridge. "The ATVs are this way. Let's go."

Luis stepped off, too, hiking up the backpack that held all of his gear and passing his son as though he had something to prove. Jessa followed behind, watching him, and something was definitely off. His feet seemed to be stumbling more than usual. Was his balance unsteady?

When Luis had gotten far enough ahead of them that he couldn't hear, she jogged to Lance. "Something's not right," she said.

"Tell me about it." He shook his head. "He can never admit when he's wrong about anything."

She tugged on his arm until he stopped and faced her. "That's not what I mean."

"So what do you mean?" he asked, inching into her space. He was so broad she couldn't see around him. His thick callused hands came to rest on his hips.

Her heart fluttered like a caged butterfly searching for a way out. "I just... I've never seen him get turned around out here."

Once again, Lance's shoulders lifted in that laid-back-cowboy shrug. "It could happen to anyone. Especially if he didn't sleep all that great. He's probably tired."

No. It'd happened to her multiple times but it didn't happen to Luis. She glanced at the older man, still stalking toward the east side of the mountain in a huff. "What if something's wrong? Health-wise or something?"

Sympathy softened Lance's eyes. "It's not like what happened to your dad. Nothing's wrong. I see the man every day. Trust me. He's healthy as a horse."

A sigh sank in her chest. Maybe Lance saw only what he wanted to see. "What if we hadn't come looking for him? How long would it have taken him to find his way?" Or would he have wandered off and gotten lost? If he couldn't even find the ATV, what else would he forget?

"He would've found his way eventually," Lance insisted, as though he was unwilling to consider the alternative.

Well, it was easy to see where he'd gotten his stubbornness. Jessa raised her head and stared him down. "I don't think he should go out alone anymore."

"I couldn't agree more," he said, checking behind his shoulder as though he wanted to make sure his father was out of earshot. "Which is why I'd like you to stay with him for a while."

Her mouth fell open. "Excuse me?" She must not have heard him right.

"I can't babysit him every second. Not for the next few weeks. I'm training for Worlds."

Right. The biggest competition on the bull-riding stage. A laugh tumbled out. "So you want *me* to babysit him." Did he even realize how ridiculous that sounded?

Lance took a step closer, and it wasn't fair how those large silvery eyes of his could look so pleading. "He already spends most of his free time at your rescue thing anyway."

Rescue thing? Heat swathed her forehead. "I'm pretty sure you meant to say my father's animal rescue organization, which happens to be his legacy." *You hot jackass.*

"Right." His lips twitched as though he was trying to hold back a smile. "That's what I meant. You already spend a lot of time with him. We can tell him your house is being fumigated or something and you can move in with him for a few weeks. The upper story of his house is furnished and everything."

"Oh, well in that case." She let the sarcasm in her tone speak for her. "Are you crazy? The man is sixty-seven years old. He's not going to let me babysit him." If he realized what was really going on, Luis would have a conniption.

"He likes you," Lance countered, his eyes melting into some kind of irresistible plea. The same one she often saw on wounded animals. Good God. Sometimes life just wasn't fair.

"In fact, I think he might like you better than he likes me," he said, going for the kill shot with a delicious little smirk. "I can't keep my eye on him when I'm out training. And I don't trust him to be alone. Can't have him wandering off anymore."

Under the power of his gaze, her will had started to cave, but she shook her head, desperately holding on to the shard of pride she had left. "No. I'm sorry. I *do* have a life, you know. I can't drop everything and babysit your—"

"I'll give you half of my winnings," he interrupted.

Jessa staggered back a step. This was absurd. "I won't take your money."

"Fine, then. I'll donate it to your shelter. Half of everything I win at Worlds."

Half of everything? She didn't know much about bull riding, but she knew those purses were worth a lot of money. "That's...wow...a chunk of change..."

He stepped in closer, lowered his head to hers. "I'm gonna win this year. I just need the time to train."

Determination had steeled his face, his voice, and she didn't doubt he'd win. He'd won a World title before, though it had been years back. But he was the real thing—the rider who persevered through every injury, through every disappointment. And given how disappointing she'd heard the past year had been for him in the arena, he'd do whatever it took to get one more title. "I don't want to take your winnings." But she kind of did, too. Not for herself, but for the shelter. That'd give her plenty to make the repairs and improvements they needed, to buy supplies and upgrade their facility until she could establish a good donor base.

"I'm not doing it for the money," Lance uttered, his voice full of conviction.

No. It clearly went much deeper for him. She could read it in his eyes. He had something to prove to the world. She'd seen the articles in the town newspaper. She'd heard what everyone was saying. While Luis had somehow managed to continue competing as a living legend until the age of thirty-eight, they thought Lance had lost his spark. Some people in town said he should've quit a long time ago. How would that feel? To always be stuck in the shadow of your great father? To have the world thinking you're done before you're ready to be?

"Please, Jessa," he said laying a hand on her forearm and effectively wiping out her last scrap of dignified resolve. "I need your help." Judging from the twitch in his jaw, those might've been the most difficult words he'd ever managed to say.

Yeah, who was she kidding? She couldn't say no to the man. Couldn't turn down a large donation to the shelter.

"Fine. I'll do it," she said, starting to walk past him.

On one condition, she should have added. That he'd steer clear of her so she wouldn't lose her heart again.

Chapter Six

Topaz Falls didn't exactly offer much in the way of nightlife. Not that Jessa had ever minded. Since she'd moved here full time last year, her idea of nightlife had been snuggling up with whatever animals she was caring for at the time and enjoying a rom com movie marathon from the comfort of her couch. But one Friday evening last winter, as she was getting settled in for one of her favorites, she realized she was out of chocolate truffles and she simply couldn't watch the fabulous *Chocolat* without any chocolate. So she'd thrown on a hat and a coat and braved a blizzard to walk eight blocks to The Chocolate Therapist, the town's only confectionery and wine bar.

Normally the town was dead at nine o'clock on a snowy Friday night in December, and sure enough The Chocolate Therapist had been closed. Her heart had sunk until she'd noticed a light on somewhere near the back of the store. In a move of desperation, she'd knocked on the door.

The owner, Darla Michelson, had answered. She had one of those friendly inviting faces, with dancing blue eyes and smile lines instead of crow's-feet, all framed by an unruly but adorable nest of curly black hair with hip red streaks. In a halo of light, Darla had hurried to unlock the door and when Jessa explained the situation, the woman had invited her in and had not only filled up a takeout box with the creamiest, loveliest truffles she'd ever seen, Darla also invited her to stay for the book club meeting she was hosting in the back room.

She might not have if she hadn't been freezing, if her pinky toes hadn't been numb. The prospect of staying somewhere warm and cheerful, with that rich chocolate scent billowing all around her, far outweighed the cold, lonely walk home. Darla had taken her coat and poured her a glass of mulled wine that tasted like Heaven. Then she'd taken her into a small back room, which happened to be set up like the coziest living room Jessa had ever seen. There were an overstuffed couch and two lopsided recliners clustered around an antique coffee table. Happy pink and green pillows freshened up the worn sofa while polka-dotted lampshades brightened the whole space.

Cassidy Greer, who was a local EMT, and Naomi had popped off the couch enthusiastically to greet her. They were so warm and friendly, bright rays of sunshine in the winter of her lingering grief. That night, for the first time since her father had passed away, the feeling of loneliness that had shrouded Jessa fell away and the first signs of spring started to bud in her heart.

After that, every week, she headed to The Chocolate Therapist, and it really had become her healing. The chocolate and wine, yes of course, but even more so these women who'd become like her sisters. Maybe it was their shared grief. Darla had lost her husband to cancer two years before, which made her a young widow at thirty-four. Sweet young Cassidy had lost her brother Cash in a bull-riding accident five years previously. And Naomi had been left behind by a husband who wanted nothing to do with her or their amazing daughter. That first night, they'd bonded. Pain has a funny way of bringing people together, and they'd spent the whole night sharing their life stories over countless mugs of mulled wine and God only knew how many boxes of truffles. They were all so different—on the book side of things Darla preferred straight-up smut, Naomi was addicted to self-help books, Cassidy read only suspense and thrillers, and Jessa, of course, was all about sweet character-driven romance novels that told idyllic stories with happy endings. Their vast differences didn't matter, though. They hardly ever discussed the books they were reading, anyway. Every discussion somehow diverged into talking about life, their problems, and the joys or hurts or triumphs they were facing.

Jessa had never had a group of friends like that before, with whom she could say anything she wanted without guarding herself or considering how silly or ignorant or pathetic she might sound. With them she could just be.

So when Darla called an extra meeting, Jessa had hurried right over, expecting to discuss their latest selection. But instead of their normal discussion, it had started to feel like an interrogation. Like always, they were gathered around the coffee table. Red sangria had replaced the mulled wine once the snow had started to melt. Tonight, Darla had made the most addictive chocolate-covered strawberries—white, dark, and cinnamon flavored. Everything had been going wonderfully, until Jessa mentioned Lance's proposition. That's when the gasps and questions had started.

"Lance asked you to move in with him?" Naomi demanded, dabbing a smear of chocolate from the corner of her lips.

"Isn't that a little fast?" Darla chimed in, leaning over to refill her sangria for the fourth time in an hour. Owning a wine bar means you build up quite the tolerance.

"Yeah, you've been on only one date," Cassidy added. Though she had the most somber blue eyes Jessa had ever seen, Cassidy's grin revealed her dimples. She was the quietest in the group, but also could win the award for the wittiest. Not to mention the most reliable. She covered weekends at the shelter so Jessa could have some time off.

They were teasing, she knew that, but she wished she could fan the blush away from her face. The truth was, she knew it was a bad idea, moving to the ranch, babysitting Lance's father for the next couple of weeks. Especially with the way Lance affected her. She'd kissed the man after being in his presence for all of an hour. Not that she could let these women ever find out. She'd never hear the end of it. They were already teasing her enough. And that had to stop before she crumbled and told them everything.

Trying to maintain an air of indifference, she leaned back into the couch cushion as if their chatter didn't faze her. "First of all, he didn't ask me to move in with *him*," she said for at least the fifth time. "He asked me to move in with his *father*."

"That's not weird or anything," Cassidy quipped, sharing a look with Darla.

Jessa gave the women a look of her own. "Second, we have *not* been on any dates. This is strictly a business arrangement." And she intended to keep it that way. All she'd have to do is recall the repulsed stiffening of his upper body when she'd gone to kiss him. That should make it easier.

"He's already seen you naked," Naomi pointed out before popping another strawberry into her mouth.

"Bet he wouldn't mind seeing that again," Cassidy teased. "Like tonight. In his bedroom."

Jessa squirmed. Could not let herself go there. Lance was off-limits. So was romance. And sex. Definitely sex because, in her opinion, those two things went together.

She picked up her glass and took a sip to cool herself down. When was the last time she'd broken out in a sweat simply sitting still?

"I've always wondered how Lance would be in bed," Darla said, licking the chocolate covering off a strawberry. She tended to wonder that about everyone. Did a lot of experimenting, too, though she claimed she'd never fall in love again. "I bet he's rowdy." She bit into the strawberry with a gleam in her eyes.

"That's something I hope I never have to hear about," Naomi answered sternly. Though she was close to Lance, Naomi had been Lucas Cortez's high school sweetheart until he'd gone and gotten himself sent off to prison for arson. She still talked about him sometimes, though. Seemed to wonder what could've been, like everyone does once in a while. Or more than once in a while if you were Jessa. Which is exactly why she'd sworn off men for now. "You can tease me all you want, but nothing is going to happen between Lance and me." He'd made it perfectly clear. "He promised to donate money to the rescue. That's the only reason I agreed." That and Lance's ridiculously convincing wounded puppy eyes.

"Maybe he wanted you around more," Naomi suggested.

Jessa only laughed.

"I'm serious," her friend insisted. "I never dreamed he'd ask someone to move to the ranch. He usually avoids people at all costs." She tilted her head and studied Jessa in a way that made her want to hide. Naomi had one of those intense gazes that made you wonder if she could read your mind. "But he obviously doesn't mind having you around. Which is a little suspicious. He could've asked *me* to keep a better eye on Luis. I already live there."

"You've got enough to do," Jessa shot back, refusing to let hope root itself in her heart. "He knows Luis and I are friends. That's all it is." He knew the man wouldn't put up a fight if Jessa moved in. Luis would do anything for her and his son knew it. "Couldn't be better timing, actually," she said in her best businesslike tone. "Because I'm not interested anyway." Or at least she shouldn't be. Therefore, she'd simply avoid Lance, keep an eye on Luis, and start making plans to upgrade the shelter. That would keep her busy, and before she knew it, the time would be up.

"If your face gets this red when you're not interested, I'd hate to see what happens when you *are* interested," Darla said sweetly.

"It's warm in here," she lied. Actually, there was a wonderful cool breeze floating through the open window.

"I have a feeling it's about to get hotter," Naomi said, elbowing Darla. The three of them laughed in that happy tipsy way.

Jessa fought off another blush with a sip of sangria. She held an ice cube in her mouth and simply rolled her eyes at them, denying that thoughts of Lance generated any heat within her. Which only made her skin burn hotter.

She had only one more night to fix that problem.

* * *

His father had gotten older, no doubt about that. Lance eyed him from across the kitchen table. Wisdom pooled in the grayness of the man's eyes, but they sagged, too. Jagged lines that had started as crow's-feet at the corners now fissured down into his cheeks, which were wrinkled and spotted with age. Most times he didn't look at his father's face for too long, but now he forced his gaze to be still, to note the details, the changes.

If it were up to him, he'd still see Luis Cortez the same way he had when he was a boy. He used to stand on the corral fence whooping while his dad rode, his spirit and strength a force Lance had dreamed of one day harnessing himself. Didn't matter how many times he was thrown, his father always got up, shook off the dust, and shoved his foot right back in that stirrup. Nothing could break the man, nothing inside the corral and nothing outside the corral, either. Even after his mother had left and Lance had worried it might break them both, Luis had simply soldiered on. But no one was indestructible. Not even the toughest cowboy. Life wears on you, little by little, not shattering you all at once, but chipping away from the inside where the damage isn't always visible. Lance had lived enough to know that.

"What're you still doin' here?" Luis asked, scraping the last of the eggs and crumbled bits of bacon off his plate and shoveling them into his mouth. "I thought you'd be training on Ball Buster this mornin'."

"I'm waiting until Jessa gets here." And trying to figure out how time had gone so fast, how his father had gone from an unbreakable wrangler to an old man who lost ATVs. He shook the thought away. It was age, that's all. Old people forgot stuff. It was bound to happen to Luis sometime. Lance reached for the coffeepot and poured himself a refill. "You're okay if she stays here for a while?" he asked, cupping his hands around the mug. The robust scent sparked the memory of drinking coffee with Jessa yesterday, which conjured up the images of her lying almost naked on the floor again.

"Why's Jessa coming?" his father asked from behind a blank stare.

Worry dulled his body's sudden arousal. "We talked about this last night." Maybe the man's hearing was going out...

"Right," Luis said gruffly, eyes cast down at the table as though he was trying to remember.

"Her place is being fumigated," Lance reminded him. "She's got an insect problem."

Luis grunted his disapproval. "She shouldn't have to pay for something like that. What's she got? I could take care of it for free."

A grin broke through Lance's concern. His dad might be aging, but he'd never quit striving to be the hero. Age couldn't take away something like that. "She wanted to leave it to the professionals this time," he said before Luis could ask more questions. "So can she stay here or not?"

"Course she can. Got that whole upstairs that don't get used anyway."

"Great. She should be here by eight." At least he hoped she'd be there. She'd sure left in a hurry after they'd gotten Luis back down the mountain. He'd hoped they'd have time to go over the plan, but next thing he knew, Jessa was gone.

"Well, I'd best get moving." His father stood and carted his dishes to the sink. "I was gonna head up for a hike before I mend the corral fences later on."

Shit. Lance had meant to have a little talk with him about the whole hiking alone thing last night, but hadn't gotten around to it. Okay. He'd completely avoided it. But it looked as though it might be time to force the issue. He stood, too. "I don't think it's a good idea for you to go up the mountain on your own anymore."

Right on cue, his father's shoulders straightened. "Pardon?"

"You forgot where you parked the ATV," Lance said, trying to be careful.

"I didn't forget," Luis shot back. "I was this close to finding it." He held an inch of space between his thumb and pointer finger. "Another ten minutes and I would've been on my way down. You didn't need to come find me."

Of course not. Luis Cortez didn't need anything from anyone. Lance tried to quiet the fight rising in his father's eyes. "All I'm saying is, I'd like you to take somebody with you. What if something *did* happen? I don't want you out there alone."

"Nothin's gonna happen," his father insisted. "I don't need a babysitter out in my own backyard." He went to walk away but Lance stepped in front of him.

"I'll get you a satellite phone then." With a GPS tracker. That way he'd always be able to find him.

"I'm not bringing a phone into the wilderness. I go to get away from that shit."

"Come on, Dad. I'm just—"

A knock sounded at the front door.

"Good morning," Jessa called through the screen.

Sighing out the disgruntled annoyance, Lance gave his father a look before winding through the living room, then down the hallway to the front door.

Jessa stood on the other side. She was dressed differently—more like the old Jessa, in a faded yellow T-shirt and long hiking shorts. Her feathery blond hair had been loosely pulled back and that easy smile was intact. Lance had an urge to hug her. Somehow the sight of her made his body lighter. She was so...easygoing. And that was a rarity in his life at the moment.

"Hey." He stepped out onto the porch and closed the door so his father wouldn't hear anything.

"Everything all set?" she whispered. Her hand curled over the handle of a small wheeled suitcase.

"Yeah. I told Dad your place has an infestation. He's fine with you staying a few weeks." As long as he never found out the real reason...

"Great." She went to pick up her suitcase, but Lance reached out and snatched the handle before she could grasp it. It was light, as unburdened as she seemed to be. "One other thing you should know. I was trying to talk to him about not going up the mountain alone anymore," he half-whispered.

Jessa laughed and somehow the heartiness of it tempted him to join her.

"Bet that went over well," she said.

"Yeah. Not so much." But just being near her for two minutes had purged the tension from his head. "I told him I'd get him a satellite phone, but he wasn't interested."

"I'll work on it," she promised.

He set down the suitcase. "Thank you."

"I can't make any promises. He might not listen to me, either."

"No." He stepped closer. "Thank you for being here. For doing this."

"Oh." She stumbled back a step as if she'd been caught off guard. "Sure. It's nothing."

That was the biggest understatement he'd ever heard. "Actually, it's a lot. And I really appreciate it." She had no guarantees going into this. She didn't know if he'd win, if she'd get anything out of it. Somehow that made it more generous. "There's no way I could handle all of this on my own with the finals coming up," he admitted. Hell, he'd have to put in twice the training hours as those twenty-something guys he was going up against or he'd be humiliated on the biggest stage in bull riding. And there it was...his greatest fear worming its way to the surface of his life. That he really was washed up and too old like everyone said.

"I'm happy to help," Jessa said, smiling again but still keeping her distance. "I love your dad."

She might love his father, but after the awkward exchange yesterday, she didn't seem to want to be anywhere near *him*. Unfortunately for her, Lance wasn't in a real big hurry to get inside.

"Besides that," she went on, "you promised me enough money to make a difference at the shelter. And I happen to think you'll win."

"Really?" She'd be about the only one in the world.

"Sure." She seemed to look him over, size him up. "You've got more experience than those young guys, which means you probably have more composure. You know what to expect. And it looks to me like you're still in pretty good shape." Her eyes shied away from his. "So yes. I think you'll win this year."

The words left his tongue fumbling for something to say. It's a gift when someone believes in you at a time no one else does. When you've lost some of the belief in yourself. Before he could say anything, the front door opened.

"Jessa." Luis already had on his hiking backpack, the stubborn bastard.

"Morning, Luis," she greeted warmly as she leaned in to hug him.

His dad's face seemed to soften whenever Jessa was around, as if she were the daughter he'd never had. "I was headed up the mountain," Luis said, nowhere near as ornery as he'd been with Lance.

Her eyes lit with genuine excitement. "I'd love to come with you. Maybe we should bring the fishing poles."

"Good idea," Luis agreed, already clomping down the porch steps. "Lance can get your things to your room."

"Oh, perfect. Thank you." She winked at Lance and it said so much, that they were co-conspirators, allies, and maybe even friends.

Clutching her light, carefree suitcase in his hand, he turned and watched the two of them hike up the driveway.

Jessa had come for his father, to watch over him, to take care of him. So why did he want her to be here for him, too?

Chapter Seven

So far so good. Jessa tossed another fence post into the ATV's trailer and clapped her gloves together. Clouds of dust puffed into the air, disappearing against the sky's blue radiance. So far she'd managed to avoid Lance all morning. The hike with Luis had eaten up a good three hours, and it had been nothing short of spectacular—the sky clear and blue, just the right breeze sighing through the pine trees. Luis had been in top form, his pace quick and his footsteps sure. Without even a slight hesitation, he'd led her right to the pond nestled into the swell of land at tree line, and between the two of them they'd caught five rainbow trout. Hers had been the largest, she'd pointed out. Luis had simply smiled in his long-suffering way.

Her concerns about being in such close quarters with Lance had started to dissipate with the morning's chill. This wouldn't be so hard. Luis liked to keep busy and the two of them would spend a good portion of time at the shelter during the week. That would leave little time for running into Lance. This morning when she saw him on that porch, a whole flock of butterflies had migrated into her chest, nesting all around her heart and humming with that tantalizing purr. That's why she couldn't allow herself to be close to him. Not alone, anyway. She didn't trust herself one iota. Something else took over when Lance gazed at her. Some*one* else. Her inner slut.

"You got all those posts loaded up already?" Luis careened around the corner hauling a sledgehammer over his shoulder, and for the life of her she couldn't figure out what she'd been so worried about. Apparently the whole getting lost in the mountains thing was an isolated incident because today, Luis looked strong and determined and completely capable. There was nothing feeble about him.

Jessa glanced into the shed where she'd been searching for the fence posts he'd asked for. "I think that's all of them." When Luis said he had to mend some fences on the property, she'd jumped at the chance to help him, just in case he had any more balance issues. But he seemed fine. Plus, it had given her an excuse to hide in the shed and stay busy so she wouldn't risk a Lance sighting.

"All right, let's head on up to the corral then." Luis slid onto the ATV, but Jessa froze next to it.

The butterflies still hibernating in her chest stirred. "The corral?" As in the place where Lance would be training?

"Yeah. Got a bunch of fences all but fallin' down up there." Luis cranked the handlebar and the ATV roared to life. "Gotta get 'em fixed up 'fore one of the horses gets out," he shouted above the noise.

He released the brake and nodded her over. Jessa moved slowly toward the ATV, like her shoes were made of lead.

She'd promised to help Luis with the fences, so she couldn't back out now. Hopefully Lance would be so busy he wouldn't even notice her.

She climbed onto the ATV and buckled her arms around Luis's waist.

Instead of peeling out and tearing up the driveway like he so often did, Luis eased the ATV along. He peered back at her. "Is there somethin' goin' on I don't know about?"

Her shoulders locked. Had he figured out this whole thing was a sham? "What do you mean?" she managed to reply without an echo of fear. Lance would kill her if Luis found out what they were doing.

The ATV stopped. Luis turned his upper body, those wise eyes studying her. "I mean you and my boy seem to have gotten close," he said behind a hint of a smile. "I was surprised when he asked if you could stay with me."

She gulped back a relieved breath. "We're just friends. He's trying to help me out."

The man gave her a nod, then turned around and they puttered along again. "I wouldn't be put out. If it was more than that."

She forced a laugh but it felt like the beef jerky they'd snacked on earlier had gotten stuck in her throat. There *shouldn't* be anything more. He'd backed away when she kissed him, and given the man's reputation, anything more would only lead to heartbreak for her. "Nope. Nothing more." The bat-shit crazy butterflies in her chest called her bluff.

Thankfully, Luis let it go. She'd never been a good liar and had never been good at hiding her emotions, either. They always made their way to her face, out there for the world to see. Which was why she couldn't face Luis. As soon as he parked the ATV, just down the hill from the corral, she slid off and started to unload the fence posts, working with a repetitive precision. She would not look at the corral. She would pretend it wasn't there. She would—

"Come on, Uncle Lance! Hold on!"

Jessa's head snapped up and her eyes honed in on the very scene she'd been trying to avoid. Oh, hell-to-the-no. Across the corral, Gracie stood on the second fence rail, teetering precariously on her sparkly pink cowgirl boots while she gripped the top rail with her hands. Naomi stood next to her, body set as though ready to catch her daughter. Tucker, the Cortez's stable manager, stood next to Naomi, eyes glued to a stopwatch.

Before she could stop herself, Jessa darted her gaze to the right and yes, ladies and gentlemen, there was Lance Cortez in all of his bull-riding glory. Chap-clad legs cinched down over the steer's wide girth, back arched, free arm whipping over his head in a graceful rhythm. Sweat drenched his blue T-shirt, making it cling to every chiseled muscle, and that black cowboy hat on his head made him look downright dangerous.

The maniacal bull snorted and jackknifed his body, but Lance held on, those powerful arms fully engaged, and God they had to be as big around as the fence posts she was loading. Then there were his hands. There was something so seductive about large, rugged hands skilled in the art of holding on. She'd like to bet they were skilled in other arts, too.

A slow heated breath eased out as she thought about all of the places those hands could hold her body.

Lance continued the dance—that's how he made it look, graceful and choreographed—riding that steer like he owned it. In complete control.

Wooooowwww. She couldn't move. Couldn't take her eyes off him.

His body was actually built for this, muscle stacked on muscle, tendons as thick as ropes. The more the bull bucked, the more Lance seemed to come alive.

Awe surged through her, nearly buckling her knees, turning her arms weak.

The fence post dropped from her hands and slammed onto her toes. Pain shredded through her feet.

"Ow!" she screamed as she fell to her knees to push the thing off.

The post rolled down to the ATV.

"Oh no!" she heard Gracie screech. "Hold on, Uncle Lance!"

Jessa looked up. Lance had turned his head in her direction, which threw off his form. The beast below him bucked and kicked its legs in the air.

Jessa scrambled to her knees.

Lance was trying to recover, hands both grasping, but his body was being tossed violently. With a final snorting fury, the bull threw his head back, a horn connecting with Lance, then leaped and sent him flying toward the fence.

"Oh God!" Jessa shot to her feet and hobble-ran the perimeter. It was horrible seeing him sprawled there. He could be dead!

Tucker was already out in the corral, luring the bull away from Lance. Somehow Jessa managed to squeeze herself between the fence posts and sprint to him, but her foot caught a rock. Momentum pitched her forward and launched her right on top of Lance.

His wide eyes stared into hers. They were open. And he was breathing.

"Are you okay?" she choked out. The lingering pain in her toes throbbed with the fast pulse of her heart.

"Of course I'm okay," he said with an amused smile. "That's not the first time I've been tossed, Jessa."

His eyes were so pretty. Grayish blue with heavy thick lashes.

"Are *you* okay?" he asked, lifting his head.

Oh. Right. She was still lying on him. "I'm fine," she said quickly, rolling off to the side, then standing before he could get a glimpse of the humiliation that radiated across her face.

Lance stood, too. His shirt was torn and blood stained the right side beneath his chest plate.

"You're bleeding." She reached out to touch the wound, but he stepped back quickly.

"It's fine. Ball Buster caught me with his horn. Again, not the first time."

So back off, his movements seemed to scream. The same humiliation that heated her face traveled down her throat. She glanced around. Naomi and Gracie were staring. Luis was on the other side of the fence watching the whole spectacle. Tucker had corralled the bull and was now gazing at her and Lance, too. The same question seemed to have stumped all of them: Why had she panicked and run to him when no one else watching—even the ten-year-old—seemed the least bit concerned?

Why indeed.

"I'm sorry," she half-whispered. "I mean, I thought you were hurt…"

"I'm fine," he said again, this time with a gruff undertone. "It's part of the job. I'm used to it."

"Right. Good. I'm glad you're fine," she muttered, turning to slink away. "I should get back to the fence, then."

Truth was, she never should've left the damn fence. Never should've glanced at him. Never should've agreed to this in the first place. Her toes scuffed the dirt as she walked away from him. From everyone.

"That was a good one, Uncle Lance," she heard Gracie prattle behind her. "And it was so funny when Jessa fell right on top of you!"

Yeah. Funny. Jessa kept walking. Fast. Head down, arms pumping at her sides, propelling her away from the girl's giggles.

She knew Naomi was behind her, and it didn't matter how fast she walked, somehow her friend matched her stride.

"So wow, you're really not interested in him, huh?" the woman teased.

Jessa stopped. Luis had started digging out a fence post nearby and he didn't need to hear this. "Why would I be interested in him? Every time I get near him his body goes rigid like he's terrified I'll actually touch him. Like he might get cooties if he lets himself get too close." She *shouldn't* be interested. He'd sent plenty of vibes to ward her off. Instead she seemed to want him more. Go figure.

"Come on." Naomi swatted at her. "It's no big deal. I bet no one else could tell. They don't know you like I do." She elbowed her as though trying to make her smile. "They probably just think you're a drama queen."

"Only when Lance is around." She peeked over her shoulder. Tucker was playing chase with Gracie and Lance had disappeared. "I shouldn't be doing this. Staying here."

"Lance would be lucky to have you." Naomi hooked her arm through Jessa's and started towing her toward Luis. "In fact, you're too good for him. The man hasn't had a real relationship with anyone. Ever. And you want it all. Dating. Romance. Marriage. He's completely ignorant. Trust me."

"I know." She sighed. "So what should I do?"

Her friend pulled her in for a half hug. "Stay and help Luis," she whispered. "And see Lance for who he really is. Not for who you want him to become."

* * *

Son of a— That hurt like hell. Lance gritted his teeth and pressed a bandage into the gaping wound Ball Buster had slashed across his ribs. Somehow the bull had managed to get under his chest plate and give him a nasty cut. Not to mention that weight of a serious bruise crushing the air from his lungs.

He latched the first aid kit and hung it back on the nail behind the stable door. When he'd heard Jessa cry out in pain, he'd turned, which gave Ball Buster the perfect opportunity to kick, toss his head back, and catch Lance with his horn. Damn it, he should've stayed focused. Should've tuned out everything else. Usually he could. Except when Jessa was around, evidently.

"You okay?" Tucker stuck his head into the stables. "Didn't realize you took off."

"I'm good." He braced his shoulders so his voice wouldn't wheeze. His whole chest ached like a mother, but no one else needed to know that. He couldn't slow down on his training. Couldn't lose a day. His longest time all morning had been six seconds and that wasn't gonna cut it for Worlds.

"That last one was only four," Tucker informed him. "Not your fault. You got distracted." The man raised his brows and looked him over. "Not like you to get distracted out there."

"Yeah, well, I'm not used to hearing women scream," he grumbled.

"That's surprising, given your revolving bedroom door," Tucker said through a hearty laugh.

Lance shook his head. He'd set himself up for that one. Wasn't worth reminding Tucker that he'd grown up since his early days on the circuit. "I'm not used to hearing *Jessa* scream." That was the plain truth of it. It'd scared him, the pain in her voice. Pulled him right out of the zone.

His friend stepped into the shadows, a funny grin on his face. "I like Jessa. She's good people."

"Yeah." Clumsy, but a good person. She'd pretty much be a saint in his book if she could stick it out with his father for the next couple of weeks.

"So..." Tucker leaned against the wall. "Somethin' goin' on between you two?"

"No." Lance dodged past him and headed out the door and into the sunlight. "Nothing's going on." At least nothing he needed to discuss with Tucker. "She's doing me a favor. Staying with Dad so I can train and not worry about him." Tucker would never give up his secret.

"That all she's doin'?" Tucker called from behind him.

Lance stopped. "Yes." He turned. "Why?"

His friend smirked. "She sure seemed worried about you."

"She's probably not used to seeing stuff like that." Most people were shocked the first time they saw a rider get thrown. Usually it looked worse than it was. Not today, but usually. Thankfully she'd walked away before she could see how much pain he was in. Knowing Jessa, she'd force him to go to the hospital to have his ribs looked at. And he sure as hell couldn't fit that into his schedule today.

"Maybe I'll ask her out," his friend said, poking him in the ribs.

Pain splintered through his bones. *Motherfucker*. Lance sucked in a breath and held it until the stabbing sensation subsided.

"You wouldn't mind, would ya?"

He didn't know if his blood ran hot because of the pain he was in or because of the smug look on his friend's face. He shouldn't mind. Tucker wasn't a bad guy. He was funny, as loyal as they came. The man would do anything for anyone who needed help. But he couldn't stomach the thought of his hands on Jessa. "She's taking a break from dating," Lance informed him. "Said she's sworn off the whole thing so she can focus on the shelter."

"Don't seem right. A woman as good-looking as Jessa not dating anyone."

"Yeah, well, what're you gonna do?" He was fine with it. Her not dating anyone. Didn't bother him none. The thought of her dating someone else? Now that was a different story. One he didn't care to analyze. He straightened his shoulders, battling a wince. "Make sure Ball Buster is ready. I'm going again."

"You sure?" Tucker stared at him like he'd lost it. "Maybe you ought to call it a day. That was a nasty fall. You're movin' kinda slow."

"I'm going again," he repeated. And this time, it didn't matter who screamed. He would hold on for eight seconds.

Chapter Eight

Jessa stood at the kitchen window halfheartedly scrubbing dinner dishes in the sink while she watched the sun slide behind Topaz Mountain. She'd lived in the mountains for almost a year, but the sunsets still stunned her. Darkness had started to spread down the mountain, inviting the sky to come alive with surreal bursts of orange and pink.

She sighed, arms and back weighted with a day of work.

"You don't gotta do the dishes." Luis lumbered over to her. "You're the guest. I can handle it." He eased the lasagna pan off the counter.

"Don't be silly." She turned to smile at him. "I actually like doing the dishes." Strange. At home, she let them pile up in the sink until she *had* to do them. But here, after sharing dinner with someone, it made her happy to stand at the sink, the feel of her hands drenched in the warm, sudsy water. It was nice, not being alone for a meal. It felt more purposeful, somehow.

"Fine, then. But I'm on dish duty tomorrow." Luis set the pan back on the counter. His hands trembled like they had all throughout dinner. Small little tremors she'd pretended not to notice, even when he'd dropped his fork, when he'd knocked over his glass.

Damn arthritis, he'd said, but she'd never noticed tremors before. Stiffness, sure. But not the shaking. She'd casually asked him what his doctor thought about the arthritis, if he was taking anything for it, but he'd quickly changed the subject.

Without turning her head, she stole a quick look at him over her shoulder. While they were eating the lasagna Naomi had brought over, Jessa had noticed the signs of fatigue tugging at his eyes. They'd had polite conversation, but he hadn't said much. The spark he'd had while hiking and working on the fences earlier seemed to have dimmed.

She turned her attention back to the window, to the sunset. "You can go to bed if you want." It was almost seven and they'd had a full day. Back when her father was alive and she'd visit, he'd always fall asleep in his chair after dinner. Until she woke him and sent him off to bed. "I can finish up here."

"You sure you don't mind?" Luis shocked her by saying. She'd expected an argument. "After all that work, I'm done in for the day." Weariness softened his typical gruff tenor.

Jessa shook the water off her hands and turned. "I'm sure. I'll finish up in the kitchen, have a cup of tea, and probably head to bed myself." Well, maybe not bed, but a little book therapy. After the whole debacle with Lance, she'd downloaded a new book on her Kindle. *You Don't Need Him: How to Make Yourself Believe It.* It had gotten three and a half stars...

"All right, then. See you in the morning." Luis plodded out of the kitchen and disappeared down the hallway.

Jessa did her best to sigh out the concern that knotted her stomach. Luis had every right to be tired. He was almost seventy, after all. The man had earned the right to go to bed before eight o'clock at night. She snatched another plate off the pile, plunging it deep into the sink and scouring until the last bits of tomato sauce had been cleaned off.

Outside, the shadows had deepened. Instead of brilliant colors, the sky had muted into a rose-tinted softness, the mountains forming a jagged, dark silhouette. Inhaling the crisp, wood-scented air through the open window, she finished up the last of the dishes and swiped a towel from the stove to start drying.

A click sounded at the back door, interrupting her soft humming. Lance walked into the kitchen, still dusty from his day out in the corral, although it appeared he'd changed into a clean T-shirt.

"Hey." She tried to say it casually, but the quick ascent of her heart made her voice effervescent.

"Hey." He looked around the empty room. "Where's Dad?"

"He seemed tired," she said, focusing hard on drying the dish in her hands so she could avoid the insta-blush that plagued her when she looked directly into his eyes. "Are you hungry? I can reheat some of Naomi's lasagna..."

"Nah. I'm fine, thanks." He walked over and leaned against the counter next to her. "How'd today go?"

His nearness sent her heart spiraling. Damn infatuation. "Things were good," she murmured. "Great actually." Minus the memorable scene of her tackling that man right there. But it was best to make this conversation strictly business.

"We were out on the mountain for a good three hours and there were no problems at all," she reported.

"Good. That's great." Lance stuffed his hands into his pockets and simply stood there gazing at her.

Which made her work extra hard on drying those plates. When she'd finished and stashed them in the cupboard, Lance still stood there. She couldn't take the silence anymore. "So I'm sorry about the whole falling on you thing," she babbled. "I didn't mean to, it just looked like you were hurt—maybe even dead—and I kind of panicked, which I now realize was ridiculous, but at the time I didn't think it through..." *Stop talking. Please stop talking.* But her mouth rarely obeyed her brain. "I didn't *mean* to land on you. I tripped," she said, as though he'd demanded an explanation. "There was a rock and I didn't see it and—"

"It's fine," Lance said through the beginning of a smile. "It didn't bother me."

Mmm-hmmm. Right. She turned to him, not caring that her face was on fire. "The thing is...it kind of seemed like it *did* bother you. Like you got all rigid and glared at me. So I wanted you to know, I didn't mean to make a scene." Though it seemed to be one of her specialties in life.

"You're right." He wore a full-on smile now, the one that quirked his lips and tugged at the corners of his eyes. "I did get all rigid and glare at you."

Well, at least he admitted it. "Don't worry. It won't happen again." Because she would keep her distance. No more humiliating herself in front of Lance. Tomorrow was a new day.

Lance said nothing, but his eyes stayed with hers as he started to roll the edge of his T-shirt, up over the button fly of his jeans, up over a carved, tanned six-pack...

Heat sparked in her chest. She shouldn't be looking. Shouldn't be *ogling*. What was he doing? This was highly unfair...

Finally, he rolled the shirt up his chest...

"Holy mother of God." She gawked at the blood-soaked bandage and the purple and blue splotches that mottled his skin.

"That's why I was so rigid," he said, rolling the shirt back down. "And that's why I glared. It hurt."

Air hissed out of her mouth. "Lance. Geez." How in the world was the man even standing? Breathing?

"It's not as bad as it looks. I've had worse."

Worse? Her ribs ached just thinking about it. She shook her head and tossed the towel aside. "Why do you do that to yourself?" She couldn't imagine it. Couldn't imagine subjecting herself to pain like that day in and day out.

"Why do you rescue wounded and lost animals?" he asked her pointedly.

"Because I love it." She did, but that wasn't the whole reason, and it seemed Lance knew that, because he waited for her to expand.

"And...?" he prompted when she didn't speak.

Damn, he was more perceptive than she'd given him credit for. "Aaannd," she sassed. "Because it's something I can do to carry on my father's legacy." It gave her a connection to him, a way to honor him.

"We have a lot in common," he said as though resting his case.

Maybe so. But dwelling on the things they had in common would not help her put out the flames of infatuation. "You need to redo that bandage," she said, changing the subject. "Did you even clean the wound?"

"No," he admitted, standing straighter. "I was training all afternoon."

Now it was her turn to glare at him. "*Training?* Your ribs might be broken. And not to mention, that cut should probably be stitched. It's definitely going to scar."

"It's not a big deal," he insisted stubbornly.

Not a big deal. Ha! He might be perceptive but he was not as smart as she'd thought. "Have you ever heard of infection? You would not believe the infections I've treated. Wounds fester, Lance. They get full of bacteria and then they get worse and worse until—"

"Fine," he interrupted before she could offer him the gory details. "I'll wash it out."

"Wash it out." She shook her head, already heading for the first aid kit she'd seen in the bathroom earlier. "We can't just wash it out. We're using the strong stuff." She marched back into the kitchen and laid out the kit, seeing what she had to work with.

"Take off your shirt," she ordered.

"Gladly." That naughty smile of his flashed, but she shamed him with a look. This was not a joke. She's seen animals go septic as the result of an infected wound.

He peeled off the shirt gingerly, as if every movement caused him pain, and she forced herself not to examine the muscles, the hard flesh. She had to go into full doctor mode.

Leaning in, she carefully removed the bandage and examined the wound. It had started on one side as a puncture wound, then tore across his flesh with jagged margins. "This is going to hurt," she informed him.

He squeezed his eyes shut. "It already does."

Jessa glanced around. He wouldn't make it through this without something...

There. On top of the fridge sat a small collection of Jack Daniel's bottles. She hurried over and reached for one, then unscrewed the cap. "Here." She held it out to Lance.

He accepted with a grin. "You trying to get me drunk?"

"Yes," she confirmed, digging through drawers until she found a clean rag. "Trust me. You're going to want to be good and drunk for this." Especially if one of his ribs happened to be cracked underneath that gash. The thought brought on a shiver. How had he trained all afternoon with an injury like this?

"All right, then. Bottoms up." Lance raised the bottle to his lips and took a hearty gulp.

Jessa ran the washrag underneath scalding hot water and squirted on some of the antibacterial soap. "Take another shot," she said, inspecting the wound again. A bandage wasn't gonna cut it. They needed something to hold the edges together.

Lance obeyed, albeit wincing. He set down the bottle and swiped his arm across his mouth. "God, that stuff is awful."

The words surprised her. "You don't drink?"

"Sure, a beer once in a while. When I'm not training. But I've never liked the hard stuff."

"Well, you'll like it now. Trust me." She nodded toward the bottle.

Making a disgusted face, Lance downed another shot. "Gah." He pushed it far away. "That's enough. I'll be fine."

"Suit yourself." Jessa approached him with the cloth. "I'll start by cleaning the edges of the wound. We have to clear away the dried blood so we can flush it out." It was best to start prepping him now. This would be the easy part.

Lance straightened his upper body, tensing those carved muscles. "Right. Okay. Go for it."

Doctor mode, she reminded herself, deliberately over-looking the way his upper body flexed. It was just flesh and muscle. *Lots* of muscle...

Ahem. She steadied her hands and carefully pressed the cloth against his skin, lightly running it along the cut's borders.

His chest expanded with a breath, and he let it out slowly.

"Am I hurting you?" she asked, already knowing the answer.

"No worse than I've been hurting," he answered with gritted teeth.

She pulled back a little. "I'm trying to be careful." But that would be difficult as soon as she got into the wound. Hence the use of whiskey. "I have to flush it out a bit." She hurried to the sink and filled a glass with hot water. "This'll sting," she warned. Holding a towel beneath the cut, she poured water over the damaged flesh.

Sure enough, Lance flinched, but she kept her hand and the towel strong against his lower chest.

When the cup had emptied, she blotted the wound with the towel. "You really should have this stitched up," she said again.

"I'm not going to the hospital." His voice had gotten a bit lazy. It appeared the whiskey had done its job.

"Well, I can try to pull it all together with butterfly strips." She riffled through the first aid kit until she found the antibacterial ointment, gauze, and tape.

With the cleaning part over, Lance seemed to relax. "So why did you think I was glaring at *you* earlier?" he asked, searching out her eyes.

Shrugging, she carefully swabbed the ointment thoroughly over the wound. "I guess I thought you were annoyed."

His shoulders flinched, but he seemed focused on her instead of the pain. "Why?"

"Because I made a scene." With a towel, she carefully cleaned off the excess ointment, then cut the gauze. "Because I was worried about you." Using some butterfly strips, she secured the bandage and pulled the edges of his skin together.

"Why would I mind if you were worried about me?" he asked, gazing down at her, his eyes soft and open.

"I don't know." She gently pressed her fingers against the wound, making sure the dressing would hold. "You seemed put off. Just like you were when I accidentally kissed you."

Lance's breathing had gone shallow, but he didn't wince. "I already told you. I didn't mind the kiss. You're the one who said you shouldn't be kissing anyone."

"I shouldn't," she insisted defiantly, peeling the paper off a large bandage, and thanking God she had something to focus on besides his eyes. She plastered the sticky waterproof covering over the dressing and stepped back to admire her work. Yes, her work. Not his pecs...

"Then why did you kiss me?" Lance asked. His voice had deepened, no longer flippant and teasing, but somewhat solemn.

He asked as though he really wanted to know.

Because I couldn't stop myself. Because he'd been so kind and careful and comforting to her that morning. Because his lips were warm and somehow soft, even though the rest of him was so rugged. She cleared her throat. "I already told you. I was extra emotional that day."

His eyes narrowed. "You sure that's all it was?"

"Of course," she lied, straight to his face, locking her jaw for good measure.

"That's a shame. Because I happen to think you're PDF, too." There was a light in his eyes—a heat that made them downright dangerous.

She looked away. "That's the whiskey talking, cowboy," she said through a forced laugh.

His huge hand reached up and cupped her cheek, steering her gaze back to his. "No. It's not."

Air lodged in her lungs, giving her chest that wonderful, tight sensation, like any moment it would burst open and the flood of desire would carry her away.

No. No more getting carried away.

"It's not the whiskey," he murmured, his face lowering to hers. "You're stunning. And funny. And good."

See him as he is… Naomi's words echoed back to her. She did. She saw everything in his eyes. They were so close. So clear. Holding her gaze with a shameless tenderness.

"Kiss me again, Jessa," he tempted. "And I'll prove how much I don't mind."

This time she did laugh. She couldn't hold it back. Pressure had built inside of her, and it had to come out somehow. "You're not attracted to me." Lance Cortez didn't *want* her…

He took her hand and pressed her palm to the crotch of his jeans.

Beneath her fingers a hard bulge made her gasp. *Wow.* Okay, so that was quite impressive…

"That's how much I want you," he uttered. "I haven't kissed you. Haven't even touched you. I'm hard just looking at you. Just being near you." He let go of her hand.

She quickly pulled it to her side. She was not supposed to be doing this. Not now. And yet she couldn't run away. Couldn't even move. Lance still had his shirt off. Oh, why did he have to have his shirt off? He had a body made for touching. So tight and hard, sturdy and strong.

He watched her, saying nothing. Doing nothing. Just watching her.

Naomi had a point. He wasn't marriage material. But should that matter? It wasn't like she was ready to get married tomorrow or anything.

And Lance was still standing there. Shirtless. Watching her with those sexy heavy-lidded eyes.

This was her problem. She overanalyzed things. Thought too much. Tried to plan. A very good-looking man was standing right in front of her. Muscles gleaming in the soft light. Wanting her so badly his groin had to be aching. Asking her to kiss him.

Screw it. No more planning. She might have sworn off relationships, but technically she hadn't sworn off kissing. A surge of adrenaline empowered her. "You're sure?" she asked, desire flooding her throat. Her feet shuffled closer to him, until she stood against his solid body. "You want me to kiss you? Because your life might never be the same after this."

"That's quite the promise." His gaze lowered to her lips.

Jessa swallowed hard. Had she ever kissed a man? Well, besides that awkward moment with Lance on the mountain. She'd never instigated it. Men usually kissed her. Should she just go for it and press her lips into his? Maul him? Ease into it?

"You sure know how to build anticipation," Lance teased.

Her face flamed. "Sorry. I'm...I guess I've never been the one to start it..." And awkward Jessa was back.

"I can start it," he offered. "If it makes you feel better."

"Um, yes please."

His smile grew and his gaze captured hers. They were magnetic, those eyes. The power of his gaze held her still, everything except for her shoulders, which rose and fell with expectant breaths. Nerves seemed to flow through her blood and lodge in her chest, filling it until it pulled tight at the seams again.

Taking his sweet time, Lance slid his fingers underneath her chin and drew her face to his, eyes watching hers—no, conquering hers—overriding the subtle knowledge that this was not the best idea she'd ever had.

"I thought you weren't supposed to be doing this," he murmured, his lips nearly fused to hers.

Talk about building anticipation. That deep, rich coffee scent. The way the stubble on his face grazed her skin. Jessa's head got light. "I talked myself into it," she whispered, bracing her hand securely against the countertop next to him so she didn't collapse.

"I'm glad." His fingers stroked the skin at her jaw as his lips lowered over hers.

Her eyes fell shut and blocked out everything except for the feel of his mouth, the curve of it, the wet warmth, the way his lips melted into hers. They were firm, but tender, too, so skilled and wonderful it broke open her chest.

Heat flowed in until she was dizzy with it, drowning in it, but just as she lost the power to stand on her own, Lance's hands moved to her hips and hitched her closer to his body. She let herself lean into him, sliding her hands up his ripped chest, lightly sweeping her fingers over the bandage. God, he was perfection.

His lips moved to her ear, while his fingers carefully brushed her hair out of the way. "I think you're right," he breathed. "My life might never be the same." His tongue traced the ridge of her ear while his heavy breaths grazed her neck and made her legs falter.

He must've felt her wobble, because he wrapped his arms around her and crushed her body against his. "Damn, Jessa…" He kissed his way down her neck. "You smell good."

"Vanilla sugar shower gel," she gasped, letting her head tilt to the side.

"Mmmm. I like it." He slid his tongue back up her neck and his lips found hers again. This time he kissed her harder, like he wanted more.

Yes. More. There could be so much more…

Lance shifted, guiding her until her back was against the refrigerator. Things were falling, magnets and papers, but none of that mattered because Lance was pressed against her, his tongue stroking hers, his hips grinding against her body. The feel of him hard and desperate against her sent her heart spiraling. A frantic moan escaped, and Lance smiled against her lips. She let her head fall back so she could draw in a breath, but she hit the refrigerator.

A loud crash froze her. Lance pulled away. Those bottles of Jack Daniel's that had been on top of the fridge now lay next to their feet.

"At least they didn't break." Lance started to laugh but she pressed her hand against his mouth. "It's not funny! What if your dad—"

"What in God's name is that racket?" came from down the hall.

"Oh no," she hissed. "Oh God…"

Lance still had a big silly grin on his face. "It's nothing, Dad," he called, but the man came charging around the corner anyway.

Jessa pushed back and pretended to inspect the bandage. "Well, there we go. Everything looks good." She glanced up and forced a smile, but she'd like to bet he could see the vein in her forehead pulsing. "Hey, Luis. Sorry about the noise. I was bandaging Lance up and we accidentally knocked over the bottles." Her bright red face had to be a dead giveaway that the whole sentence was a lie. Not to mention her dilated eyes.

"Uh. Thanks, Jessa," Lance said, reaching past her for his shirt.

"No problem," she intoned, as if answering a complete stranger. "Next time, don't wait so long to get it cleaned up."

A spark smiled in his eyes. "I definitely won't."

Whew. She fought the compulsion to fan her face with a towel.

"Guess I should get going then." Lance clapped his dad's shoulder on his way out the door. "Night, Pops."

Luis didn't respond. He simply watched his son leave, then he turned to Jessa. "So nothing's going on between you two."

She invoked her laser focus to put away the first aid supplies. "Uh-huh. Nope. Nothing."

"From what I could tell that was a whole lot of nothing," Luis muttered as he plodded back down the hall.

That was one way to put it. A whole lot of nothing.

Chapter Nine

The world came back into focus slowly, the way it did when he woke from a dead sleep. Cold air blasted his face. The door slammed shut behind him. Lance stuttered to a stop on the front porch. He should go back in there. Shouldn't end the night with Jessa like that. Should he? Hell. He didn't know. It was still hard to think, but it had nothing to do with the shots of whiskey he'd downed.

He faced the door. What had just happened in there? He'd never planned on kissing her. He'd only wanted to check in, make sure his dad hadn't given her a hard time today. But then she'd ordered his shirt off. And the way she got so close, her delicate fingers pressing against his skin. It should've hurt like hell while she worked on him, but instead it only charged him up, making his body ache with the need for more until it was all he could think about.

She'd taken her time cleaning the cut, applying the bandages so carefully. She'd taken care of him. No one had ever taken care of him...

On the other side of the door, lights glowed. Which meant she hadn't gone to bed yet. Knowing his father, he'd gone back to bed right away. Probably pretended he didn't suspect anything, just like he always had when Lance was growing up. If he pretended he didn't see, they didn't have to talk about it. For once, he was glad Luis didn't like to meddle.

He took a step toward the door, the porch's bright light casting his shadow across the wooden planks.

The ache for a woman's soft touch gripped him. He could still feel her body under his hands, petite but toned. Could still feel her lips burning against his. But he really shouldn't go back in there, because this time he might not be able to stop himself, no matter who walked into the room.

A dog's low bark drifted somewhere behind him. He didn't even have to turn around to figure out who it belonged to. Bogart, Naomi's German shepherd, came trotting regally up the porch steps. Which meant Naomi wouldn't be far behind. He should've anticipated that, seeing as how her house was right across the driveway. She'd probably been spying.

"Well, well, well." Naomi walked into view beneath the porch light, staring up at him like a pissed-off librarian, mouth in a thin line, arms crossed in a stance of unyielding disappointment.

Yeah, there was no way out of this. Lance sauntered down the steps to meet her.

"What're you doing here?" she asked before he could say hello.

He reached down to pat Bogart's perked ears. "Came by to check in with Jessa." The wind picked up, carrying the strong pine scent. He should've been cold without his coat on, but the fire Jessa had lit inside him was still going strong.

"Mmm-hmm. Mmmm-hmmm," Naomi mocked. "You came to check in." Her narrowed eyes invited him to a silent interrogation, which he avoided by glancing down at the dog.

He sucked at lying. "Hey there, Bogart. Out for your nightly stroll?"

"Don't try to change the subject." Naomi's growl was almost as low as the dog's. "Seriously. Your hair is sticking up like someone just ran her fingers through it. What happened in there?"

Actually, he still wasn't exactly sure, but Naomi wouldn't let him off that easy. He leaned a shoulder against the front porch column. "I really did come to check in."

She raised her brows, admonishing him to continue.

"But then she saw the damage Ball Buster inflicted earlier, so she wanted to fix me up." He lifted his shirt to show her the bandage.

The woman rolled her eyes with a hearty shake of her head. "Fix you up?" she snorted. "So let me guess. You took your shirt off to show her the goods and she threw herself at you."

"It was definitely my fault," he admitted. Things had started out innocently enough. She'd seemed genuinely horrified when she saw the wound. Then he had to go and dare her to kiss him again. He shook his head. "She didn't throw herself at me." He'd gone after her. He didn't know what it was about Jessa, but he seemed to lose what little self-control he had when she was around.

"Damn it, Lance." Naomi took a shot at his shoulder.

At least she didn't nail him in the ribs. He backed away before she got any ideas. "We just kissed." Even as the words tumbled out, the argument fell apart. It'd turned into more than a kiss in about two seconds. Two more minutes and he would've had her clothes off. He would've been buried so deep inside her he might never have found his way out.

"Jessa doesn't know how to just kiss," Naomi informed him, one hand placed on her hip in a sassy way that reminded him of Gracie.

He might be losing his touch, too. Used to be a kiss was simply a necessary stepping stone to get a woman where he wanted her, but he couldn't get Jessa out of his head. Hell, he could go for another round of kissing right now. Maybe at his place, so his father wouldn't interrupt this time...

"Oh no you don't." Naomi shook a finger in his face. "You and Jessa is not happening. So stop thinking about it."

He shoved away her finger. "How do you know what I'm thinking?"

"Oh please. Your eyes are all glazed over and you're practically drooling." Her glare could've incinerated him. "Don't do this to her, Lance. She's not like those women who follow you around everywhere."

Actually, that had stopped a long time ago. "They're not there to see me. Not anymore." There were younger guys. Guys who were happy to take them home for a night.

Naomi glared up at him, jutting out her right hip slightly, a signal that she was about to change her approach. "Do you want to get married? Have kids? Has that changed for you?"

"No." Didn't have to think about the answer. He'd never wanted that. Any idealistic views he'd had about love had been obliterated the day his mother looked him in the face, then turned her back on him. He didn't intend to build a life with someone only to watch it fall apart the way it had for his father. The way it had for their family.

"Jessa does," Naomi said. "She wants all of that. A commitment. A family. A man to spend the rest of her life with. She believes in that. We might not, but she does."

"I know." People talked about how many times she'd been engaged. He doubted she'd ever gone on "just a date." She seemed to want something that'd last a lifetime. Everyone in town knew Jessa had that dreamy-eyed view of love. Sometimes he envied that. It wasn't like her parents had some fairy-tale romance, but she still held on to the hope it could happen. What would that be like? He had no clue what it felt like to believe in something.

Naomi stepped closer. She was short, but she sure could look intimidating when she wanted to. "She's been jerked around enough. I can't be responsible for it happening again."

"You? Why would you be responsible?"

"I'm the one who helped her change her look so she could start winning over donors for the shelter. And I told her to use you as a guinea pig. I told her to try to win you over."

That was worth a laugh. "You told her to use me?" Not that he minded...

But Naomi wasn't seeing any humor in the situation. "Come on, Lance." She sighed. "You never even noticed her until she started to dress sexier. Until she wore her contacts. Put on makeup."

Maybe not, but he hadn't had a reason to notice Jessa, either. He didn't exactly get out much. Besides, it wasn't the makeup. He couldn't give a damn about the makeup. That's not what tempted him to kiss her tonight. That's not what drove him to keep kissing her until his mind and body were lost in fantasyland. "She wasn't wearing makeup tonight. And why would you tell her to change her look?" Why did women do that to each other?

"She *wanted* to," Naomi shot back. "And I never thought you'd take advantage of it. I never thought she'd fall for *you*, of all people."

Fall for him. He thought about the way she'd touched him. The way she'd smiled up at him. It all seemed genuine, but… "Maybe she's not falling for me. Maybe it's all part of your little plan."

"No." Naomi's head shook the possibility away. "When she ran over to you today… I knew. She cares about you. And you can't take advantage of that. It's not right."

He blew out a breath. Wow, women sure knew how to use guilt to trip people up. "I didn't mean to take advantage of her." He hadn't meant for anything to happen between them. Maybe if he hadn't seen her naked…

"You and Jessa want two different things. She has a big heart, Lance. And I don't want her to get hurt again." That was the final blow. It didn't matter how much he wanted to kiss her again. Didn't matter how much she turned him on.

"I don't want her to get hurt, either." She deserved to find what she wanted. He couldn't stand in the way of that. "I'll talk to her. Tomorrow. I'll get things straightened out."

But first he had to straighten himself out.

* * *

Morning looked different after sharing a hot kiss with Lance Cortez. Jessa opened her eyes. After last night, everything was different. Sunlight flooded the room, streaming lazily in through the large picture window that framed Topaz Mountain. The cliffs appeared to be so close it seemed she could reach out and brush her fingers along their rugged peaks. She stretched out in the creaky bed and let the rays of light warm her face. She'd never dreamed she'd be so comfortable staying in Luis's house. The room was so simple—a brass queen bed, an old scratched antique dresser, and a wooden rocking chair in the corner. There were no frills, no pops of color, but somehow the simplicity of it put her at ease. You didn't need much when you had that view staring you in the face first thing every morning.

She closed her eyes, letting herself fall back through the hours to last night. A deep vibrato still fluttered her heart. Had Lance really kissed her? Had he really said he wanted her? The images were so soft and hazy, overcast by a thick cloud of desire.

And yet the memories sizzled through her, an assurance that it was real. It had all happened. The kiss, his strong hands on her body, his tongue against her skin. Her body woke with a start, feeling the sensations again.

Noise sounded from downstairs—the creaking of the kitchen's wood floors, running water. Luis must be up.

A shot of embarrassment jolted her out of bed. She rarely slept past seven and it was almost eight. Quickly, she shed her flannel pajamas and pulled on yoga pants and a long-sleeved T-shirt. Stopping in the bathroom, she smoothed her hair and pulled it back into a ponytail. Her eyes looked tired, but happy, too, as though she was still luxuriating in the exhilarating pleasure of being touched and held.

She'd *never* been touched and held exactly the way Lance had done it.

A bounce snuck into her step as she made her way down the narrow wooden staircase. She found Luis in the kitchen.

"Good morning." She greeted the older man with a happy wave. She couldn't help it. Everything felt lighter. It was so freeing not worrying about things with Lance. Not devising a strategy for how to avoid him or overanalyze what last night meant. It had felt so natural and easy. They'd had fun. He'd been good to her. And that was all that mattered. Instead of lying awake agonizing over what might come from it all, she'd slept deeply and restfully. Such a contrast to pretty much every other man she'd ever kissed.

"Morning." Luis nodded with a small smile. He had to have known there was more going on than they cared to admit last night, but she knew him well enough to know he'd never bring it up. He was a *live and let live* type of person.

Jessa sashayed past him and filled a glass of water. She liked to down eight ounces first thing every morning. "Can I make breakfast?" she asked, after she'd finished the glass. Nothing said Sunday morning like her father's sweet potato and egg hash.

"Nah, you don't have to cook for me, Jessa." Luis slipped on a heavy flannel coat. "Besides, Sundays we all go up to Lance's place for breakfast. Me and Naomi and Gracie."

"Oh." Her heart thumped a bit harder. One kiss and she'd been conditioned. She heard the man's name and instantly her lady parts warmed right up.

"Better get your coat," Luis added. "Cold out this morning. The dew's as thick as icing out there."

"Um." She sneaked a quick glance at herself in the microwave's spotted glass. So yeah. She definitely wasn't looking her best. She hadn't showered, hadn't even officially gotten dressed.

She reached up and patted the straggler hairs into place. "You know, I can stay here. I'm sure he doesn't need one more person to feed."

"Unless I miss my guess, he'll want you there." Luis looked her over, those kind eyes crinkled and wise.

And...omniscient. That was the word. Though they were watered down with age, Luis's eyes were so focused and intent they seemed to see everything. "He'll be glad to see you. Trust me. I know my son."

Would he? The thought baited a smile. Would he be as happy to see her as she would be to see him? Already her heart was twirling like she had when her mother would dress her in a frilly skirt.

"Let's get a move on. Luis waved her over to the front door. "We don't want the grub to get cold."

Her hesitation melted away. Luis knew his son. And things didn't have to be awkward. They'd kissed, that's all. Okay, made out. But only for about three minutes. He'd probably made out with a lot of women for much longer than that.

She pulled her coat off the rack and slipped it on, then bent to jam her feet into her shoes. "Should we bring anything?" She'd seen some fruit lying around. She could cut it up and make a salad...

"Nah. Lance cooks for everyone on Sundays." He held open the door for her. "Not sure where he learned. I never could do much in the kitchen."

She paused on her way out to the porch, nerves boiling with the anticipation of seeing him. "You're sure he won't mind if I come?"

Luis looked at her, his face serious and sincere. "You're practically part of the family. I always promised your dad we'd watch out for you if anything ever happened to him. He'd want you to be part of our family."

Unexpected tears pricked at her eyes. Luis had said things like that before, but she'd never felt it hit so close to her heart. In a way, she did feel like she fit. She'd agreed to stay only to do Lance a favor, but truthfully she loved it at the ranch—the surrounding peaks, the old creaking floors, the acres of open space surrounding them. The people. "Thank you." She squeezed his shoulder and followed him down the steps to the driveway.

It *was* chilly, but beautiful, too. The early morning sunlight gleamed so bright it almost hurt to look. Thick morning dew made the ground sparkle. They crunched over the dirt in a sort of awed silence, taking in the pure air, the warm sun, the shimmering blue sky. The closer they got to Lance's house, the more her insides warmed, the more her heart beat with eagerness. Even though she couldn't wait to see him again, it wasn't because she wanted something out of him. For once in her life, she had no expectations. She simply wanted to be around him. To know him better. To see him smile like he had last night.

The thought made her smile as she followed Luis up the porch steps.

She'd heard Lance had built his own house a few years ago, and it was gorgeous, all log and stone. A wraparound porch wound around the entire thing, making it cozy and welcoming. She passed a wicker swing, which looked like the perfect spot to sit out with a glass of wine on a cool autumn night...

"Here we go." Luis opened the front door, not bothering to knock.

The inside of Lance's house was as impressive as the outside. Jessa crept across the slate-tiled entryway, trying to take in everything at once. The comforting smell of black coffee, the warm tones on the walls, the framed scenes she recognized from around the ranch. The main floor was a completely open concept, a living room with leather furniture clustered near a large stone fireplace on one wall. Beyond that, the space opened into the masculine gourmet kitchen with dark wood cabinets and grayish concrete countertops.

A large dining table sat in front of a beautiful bay window, and it was already laden with dishes and food—some sort of decadent-looking coffee cake, a pan of eggs, a plate of crisp bacon.

God, it smelled heavenly.

A set of French doors near the kitchen busted open. Gracie came skipping through, followed by Naomi and Lance.

Oh, Lance. A faint humming purred inside her. If it was possible he looked even better than he had last night. Fitted faded Levi's and an unbuttoned flannel with a tattered henley underneath.

Heat flashed the way it had when he'd first pressed his lips into hers.

"We saw some deers!" Gracie cried, skipping over. "A mama and two little ones."

"Wow." Jessa knelt down to her level and folded her into a hug. "I'd love to see them," she said, as though she didn't see deer walking down the street every day in Topaz Falls.

Naomi ruffled her daughter's red curls. "You could've seen them if this little princess hadn't scared them away."

"I was trying to be quiet but they were so cute." Gracie grinned up at her, those jewel-like eyes shining. "One of the babies got this close!" She held her hands about six inches apart while her mother laughed.

Jessa laughed, too. The little girl had some mad skills in the art of exaggeration.

As soon as the laughter faded, an awkward silence settled. Awkward because Lance still stood by the doors, his arms crossed, staring at her.

"Come on, sweet girl," Naomi said, steering her daughter away. "Let's get those grubby hands washed up before breakfast."

As she passed, Naomi gave Jessa a small smile. A tad sympathetic?

Unease spread through her, taming the elation she'd felt since she'd woken up. Why was Naomi looking at her as if she felt sorry for her?

"Grub ready yet?" Luis asked his son, heading for the table without waiting for an answer. "I'm starvin'."

"Uh. Yeah." Lance seemed to shake himself out of whatever held him in a trance. "Just about. You can have a seat if you want."

Luis didn't have to be told twice. He crossed to the far end of the room and sat himself at the head of the dining table.

Lance approached Jessa, but he didn't look at her. Not really. His eyes shifted. "You came." The words weren't happy. They weren't even welcoming. And for someone who'd been so adamant about kissing her last night, he sure was keeping a chilly distance intact.

"Um, yeah." She tried to make eye contact with him, but he looked away. "Luis insisted. I hope that's okay."

"Sure." He seemed to shrug it off like he didn't care either way before he left her standing there and went to the coffeepot in the kitchen.

Gracie skipped back into the great room. "Papa!" Since Naomi's parents had moved to Florida a few years ago, Luis was the closest thing Gracie had to a local grandpa.

He rose from his chair and lifted her into the air while she squealed. Then he set her down in the chair next to his, and their heads bent together as she chattered about the deer.

Jessa watched Lance move stonily in the kitchen, her feet rooted to the floor. Suddenly she felt like she shouldn't be there. Like she didn't belong after all.

Naomi came to stand by her. A little too close. "So how was your night?" she whispered.

"Oh. Fine. Good." She squirmed out of her coat and walked over to hang it on the rack near the front door so they were out of earshot.

"Anything unusual happen?" Naomi asked too innocently. She obviously knew something had happened, and why should that surprise her? The woman lived right across the driveway from Luis.

"How did you know?" Jessa sighed.

"I saw Lance leaving." Naomi glanced toward the other side of the room, where everyone was still otherwise occupied.

"It was nothing," she insisted feebly. Obviously. Lance was completely ignoring her.

"Nothing? Really? Because your face is beet red."

"It's warm in here." She tugged her shirt out a few times to let in some air.

Her friend yanked on her elbow and pulled her closer to the front door. "Have you changed your mind? About banning relationships from your life for a while?"

"No." But she had to admit she could. She could change her mind pretty easily with the right motivation. "We kissed. It's not like I'm hearing wedding bells or anything."

"Good." Naomi let her go. "Because we've already talked about this. He's not commitment material."

"Maybe that's because he hasn't met the right woman." She was just thinking out loud here, but that would make sense. Lance didn't have much time to date. The women she'd heard he'd been with weren't exactly commitment material, either. Besides... "I'm not in a hurry for anything to happen. I liked kissing him." She wouldn't even try to deny it. "But I don't need some big commitment right now anyway."

Naomi rolled her eyes. "Sure, you say that now. But what about in a month when you're more invested? What happens then?"

For once, she didn't know. And she didn't have to. "I'll work that out then."

"And get hurt again," her friend said gently. "Trust me. Lance has baggage. You don't want to be the one to have to deal with his mommy issues. That's exactly why I—"

"Hey, Jessa."

Her head snapped so fast she felt a pull in her neck. Lance was looking at her now. He was even talking to her.

"Can you help me get the drinks ready?" he asked, still hanging out by the coffeepot.

Naomi rolled her eyes, but Jessa simply bumped past her. "Sure. I'd be happy to."

Chapter Ten

Jessa drifted to the other side of the counter and glanced at him as though waiting for instructions. Which was good. Distance would be key for this conversation. When he'd walked in and seen her standing there it hit like a shock-wave. He noticed her lips first. The lips that were so smooth and giving against his last night. Then her eyes. Friendly and open, smiling in a way that made him want to smile, too. She had on yoga pants that showcased her tight ass. The tight ass his hands had held just last night. It pretty much looked like she'd rolled right out of bed and come on over. Seeing her disheveled in that sexy carefree way made his brain give out and the little speech he'd rehearsed last night faded into the desire to touch her again.

But he couldn't. So she'd stay over there and he'd stay over here and then maybe he could remember what it was he was supposed to say to her. He checked on the others, who were seated at the table, already piling food onto their plates while Gracie informed them of every fact she knew about deer.

"Sooo...should I pour coffee for everyone?" Jessa asked, stepping into his line of vision.

Their eyes connected and he forced himself not to look away again. "In a second." He shuffled a few steps closer. "Actually, we need to talk first."

Something changed on her face. Her smile fell away, and the bright, wide eyes that kept demanding his attention narrowed. "Okay. So talk." She folded her arms and leaned against the counter, glaring as though she already knew what he was going to say.

Damn it. How had he planned to start this again? "Well..." He cleared his throat. The noise level over at the table rose as Gracie giggled about something his dad had said. Jessa didn't seem to notice. Her glare was relentless.

He blew out a breath. If anyone wondered why he didn't do relationships, this would be a good example. He sucked at having honest, hard conversations. Since there was no easy way to put it, he'd best just get it out there. "I shouldn't have kissed you," he said, quietly enough that the others wouldn't hear.

Jessa's unreadable expression didn't change but her jaw twitched. "And why is that?"

Why was that again? Staring at her made it hard to remember. He glanced down at his plain, uncomplicated boots. "I'm pretty sure we want different things."

When silence thrummed into his ears, he looked up at her.

Her facial expression hadn't budged an inch. "What is it you want, Lance?" The words came out solid and hard. She didn't seem to care much if anyone else heard.

He shoved his hands into his pockets so he wouldn't flip

off Naomi from across the room. What the hell did she know? Talking had been a bad idea. "I want simplicity."

Jessa shocked him with a smirk. Where had all this attitude and sass come from? He'd always heard she was a softie. He must've heard wrong.

"And what is it you think I want?" Her tone came within an inch of mocking him.

"Uh." Was this a trap? He'd learned early in his dating career never to answer a question that could have potentially catastrophic consequences. Truth was, he didn't know what she wanted. Not exactly. He knew what Naomi thought Jessa wanted. But Jessa was waiting.

He blew out the frustration in a hefty sigh. "Look. This isn't about you. I don't do relationships. I'm not interested in that." Life was so much easier without those ties. "I shouldn't have taken those shots last night." Not that he could blame his body's reaction to her on the whiskey. "You're great, but—"

"Did I do something that led you to believe I wanted a relationship with you?" she interrupted in that same bold, *screw you* tone.

"No." *Wow.* This was the last time he'd follow Naomi's advice on anything. Talk about a crash and burn. "But Naomi seemed to think—"

"Did it ever occur to you that maybe *I* wanted a fling?" Jessa marched closer. "That maybe I'm sick of relationships and just want to have fun with no strings attached for once in my life?"

"No." Somehow he managed to get the word out even with his jaw hanging open. That had definitely never occurred to him.

"Would it be so hard to believe that I'm not out searching

for a husband?" she demanded, hands positioned on the rounded curve of her sexy hips.

"Well..." What could he say to that without risking her foot in his balls? She'd built quite the reputation for herself. Wasn't his fault word got around. "Isn't that what you want?"

She laughed. The woman laughed at him. "*You* kissed *me*." Her pointer finger slashed the air between them. "*You* said you were attracted to *me*."

"I am." Damn was he attracted to her. Her shoulders were straight and tight, her perky breasts begging for some attention. And her face had flushed with the same passion he'd seen last night.

"Then what the hell is your problem, Lance, huh?" she demanded.

When she put it that way...he glanced over at the table again.

Gracie and his father were still chatting while they ate, but Naomi was glaring at him. *Oh, right.* That kicked his memory into gear. He was supposed to be putting boundaries between them to save Jessa some heartache. "I don't want you to get hurt." He felt like he was reading a damn script. What he really wanted to tell her was that he'd never been more turned on than he was right now and would she like a tour of his bedroom?

"Maybe I'm the one who'll hurt you." Her head tilted in a flippant gesture. "Did you ever think about that?"

"Noooo," he admitted. But he could be down with some pain...

"Screw you, Lance. I don't need your pity *or* your protection." She marched over to him, and he felt his heart lift at the prospect of her body being against his again.

"You know what I *do* want?" she asked, her voice lowered into an alluring growl.

He could only shake his head. Shock and intrigue surged through him in a way he'd never felt.

"I want some fucking coffee." She bumped past him to the coffeepot. Without a glance back, she filled herself a mug and sashayed over to the table, leaving him staring after her, his body as primed and ready as it'd been last night.

* * *

She was so done. And not just with breakfast, either. Jessa blotted her mouth with a napkin and tossed it onto her empty plate. Lance might be a complete jerk-wad, but he knew how to make breakfast. Normally, she would be a polite guest and offer to help clean up the dishes, but she had to get out of there. Now.

All through breakfast she'd felt Lance's eyes searching her out. But she had studiously avoided him, gushing over Gracie instead. Thank God there was an adorable ten-year-old at the table to distract everyone from the fat-ass purple polka-dotted elephant in the room. Because Naomi had obviously discussed last night's kiss with Lance in great detail, and Luis might be nearing seventy, but he wasn't blind. He had to have witnessed something of what had transpired between her and Lance in the kitchen—an encounter that still had her knees quaking, by the way.

So during the meal the adults in the room had hardly looked at one another, instead enthusiastically indulging Gracie's spirited ideas about how adding pigs to the ranch could be super fun. Because look how much Wilbur livened things up in *Charlotte's Web*. Gracie was always on a mission to bring more animals into the fold. She was a girl after her own heart.

A lull in the conversation presented Jessa with the opportunity she'd been waiting for for at least a half hour. "Well, this has been great," she said, her gaze skimming right over all of them. "But I should check in at the shelter. Make sure Cassidy's holding up okay." It wasn't like Cassidy couldn't handle it, but Jessa couldn't handle *this*. The poor broken-hearted Jessa routine. When she'd realized what Lance was trying to get at in the kitchen, something inside of her had erupted. She was *not* emotionally fragile. And she sure as hell didn't need a man—even Lance Cortez—to be her key to a happy life.

She was done being poor nice Jessa.

The eruption had left behind a force that built inside her, fortifying her. With this newfound courage, she popped right out of her chair. "Thanks for a lovely breakfast," she said to no one in particular. But she did beam a real smile at Gracie. "See you soon, sweet girl."

The girl blew her a kiss, which Jessa returned before she spun and made a break for the door.

"Wait." A chair scraped the plank floors and before she could get too far, Lance slipped in front of her. She forced herself to stare back at him, working her mouth into a line of indifference. "Yes?"

"Don't you need help at the shelter today?" he asked, widening his eyes and glancing in his father's direction.

Right. She was supposed to be on babysitting duty. After everything that had transpired between them, that's what it came down to. That's why she was here. Lance hadn't forgotten and she shouldn't, either. Irritation simmered, but she didn't want to take it out on Luis. It wasn't his fault his son was clueless.

"Actually I could really use some help." Blocking out Lance, she turned to his father. "Do you have time to come today? I might have to do inventory on supplies."

The older man's mustache twitched. "Sure," he said. If he was trying to hide his amusement, he was doing a terrible job. "Gets me outta doin' the dishes." He planted a kiss on the top of Gracie's head and dragged himself out of the chair.

"Great. Thanks." With a prim smile, she sidestepped Lance and led a hearty charge out the front door to the tune of the "Hallelujah" chorus playing in her head. Not surprisingly, Lance didn't try to stop her.

Outside, the day had brightened and the scents of fall permeated the air—dried grass, crisp leaves. Not that she enjoyed it. Her volcanic heart still fumed. As far as she could remember, she hadn't said anything pathetic to Lance. Sure, she'd tried to kiss him, and yes, she'd admired him, but she wasn't Scarlett freaking O'Hara. She hadn't been *pining* after him. She hadn't begged him to kiss her. And maybe she would enjoy a fling. She didn't know for sure, but it was possible. Now she'd never know, since Lance had gone and made it a huge deal.

We want different things. God. How did he know anything about what she wanted? Her feet pounded the dirt harder. He didn't. Mostly because he hadn't bothered to ask her.

Luis tromped along by her side. "You want to talk about it?" he asked in his pleasant way.

"Not especially." There was nothing to talk about. Nothing to think about, except the work she had to do today. Swearing off men had been the right decision all along, but then Lance had come along and screwed it up by kissing her, before doing a complete one-eighty and telling her he wasn't looking for a commitment.

And people thought *she* had issues.

After running into Luis's house to change into some jeans and her *Stay Calm and Help Animals* T-shirt, she led Luis to her truck, which was parked off to the side of his garage. Driving away from the ranch felt freeing. She flicked on the radio and let the country music coax out the tension.

Luis stared ahead, his fingers drumming on his knees to the beat. "Lance took it the hardest when his mom left," he said, his jaw tight. "I never knew what to do. How to talk to him about it. We just tried to survive."

The words caught her off guard. Even though they'd spent a lot of time together, Luis had never mentioned his ex-wife before. She turned down the radio. "Sometimes that's all you can do," she said, her shoulders softening.

"Point is, he didn't learn anything good about relationships. Not from me," the man went on, though he didn't look at her. Luis didn't have to expand. She'd heard the rumors about him after his wife left. He'd had affairs with married women, taking full advantage of his status as a renowned bull rider. For a while, he'd been quite the Casanova. But she didn't hold that against him. She knew how it felt to have a broken heart, to search for something that would soothe away the loneliness, even if it was only temporary.

Luis stared blankly out the windshield. "It's one of the things I regret the most."

Letting silence settle, Jessa turned onto Main Street. The sidewalks were full of people strolling, pausing to window shop at the eclectic mix of boutiques and shops. It was a beautiful day, bright and vivid, yet she couldn't help but feel that a cloud hung over them. Sure, Lance hadn't had it easy after his mom left, but a lot of people hadn't. And Luis had already paid a steep price for his actions. He'd lost a son. After Lucas was sent to prison, the man had cleaned up his act. From what she'd heard, he stayed home with Lance and Levi more, tried to fix things with his boys. People *could* change. But they had to want it.

Stopping at the lone traffic light, she waved at Mrs. Eckles, who owned the bakery across the street. "I didn't exactly learn about healthy relationships from my parents, either," she reminded Luis. But that didn't have to stop her from having a healthy relationship with someone else. "And you know what, Luis? Lance's issues aren't your fault." He had a choice. He could decide what he wanted for his life. It seemed he already had, so there was no point in dwelling on the situation. "Anyway, we don't have to talk about Lance. Like I've said before, there's nothing to talk about." They had a business arrangement and things had gotten too personal. She wouldn't make that mistake again.

On the south end of Main Street, she veered to the right and pulled up in front of the shelter. The building itself wasn't attractive. Before her father had bought it, it had been an old diner, a plain square brick building with a shingled roof. Some people around town called it an eyesore, but it served its purpose. Before Buzz had passed, she'd planned to give it a facelift in hopes that would help donations. Things hadn't exactly worked out that way. Her dad had left behind a couple of debts and after she'd paid them off, she needed what remained to keep things running month-to-month, to pay Cassidy and Xavier, her night shift guy, so she didn't have to be there 24/7.

She parked in the space next to Cassidy's SUV and cut

the engine. It looked like the sign above the door had lost another bolt. It was tilted like it was about to fall to the ground.

Luis noticed her looking at it.

"That's nothin'. I'll get on a ladder and get it all fixed up,"
he said, unbuckling his seat belt.

She climbed out of the truck, hauling along her bag of
paperwork she had to finish up. "Thanks, Luis." Seriously.
What would she do without him? Lance might be paying her
to stay with the man, but she should be doing it for free,
given how much he did to help her out.

"You deserve to be on the payroll," she told him, leading
the way inside. The bell chimed a cheerful welcome.

"Nah. I don't need the money," he insisted.

And it was obvious she *did* need some money. Jessa
looked around the reception area at the front of the building.
Buzz had unearthed the two oak desks from a trash heap in
the rubble of a dilapidated building. Sturdy as a rock, he'd
claimed, even though they both leaned slightly to the left.
And those desks weren't the only monstrosities in the room.
The stained gray carpet was pulling up around the edges. It
had been snagged from the array of paws that had walked or
pranced or scampered or cowered on its surface. Two overstuffed chairs he'd found at a garage sale provided the only
seating in the room.

She sighed deeply. It wasn't the neatest place, but it was
hard to keep things neat when you had a revolving door of
animals coming in and out.

"Hey there." Cassidy walked out from the back room,
where they kept the animal pens and supplies.

"Hi," Jessa said brightly, doing her best to cover up her
earlier irritation. "How're things going?"

"Good..." Her friend drew out the word as though she

was confused. That would be because technically Jessa wasn't supposed to come in on Sundays. Her friends were always on her about being a workaholic and making sure she took at least one day off during the week. So much so that Cassidy had volunteered to hang out on weekends for a very reasonable wage.

Before Cass could ask her why she'd come in, she got right down to business. "So how's the pig?" The day before Cam had broken up with her, someone had called to report a potbellied pig that was seen wandering around the park. Jessa had found the sweet thing down by the river, and she didn't look healthy. Too thin and very lethargic. She'd brought her in and posted signs around town, but so far no one had claimed her. Which meant she'd likely been abandoned by someone passing through town.

"The poor baby won't eat," Cass said. "I tried everything you recommended, but she just kind of nibbles, then goes back to sleep."

"I figured that might be the case." Which gave her the perfect excuse to come in on a Sunday. She'd already started the pig on antibiotics but might have to up the dosage. "That's why I thought I'd better stop and check in. I'll go take a look." She slipped past the desk and hurried to the back room. Though she'd given the pig the largest crate they had, it had curled up in the farthest corner, snout burrowed into the soft blanket Jessa had used to make a bed. When she unlatched the crate, the pig's head lifted, but it didn't move.

"Come here, sweetie." Carefully, Jessa lifted her out and held her the same way she'd hold a baby. Based on the pig's small size, she'd guess her to be less than a year old. "Why would anyone ever leave you behind?" she cooed, petting her soft head. "You're so pretty, yes you are." Downright irresistible, if you asked her, with that shiny pink snout and those black and white spots. "Such a pretty piggy."

"Think she's gonna make it?" Luis asked from behind her.

"She might have a touch of pneumonia, but we'll take care of her." Jessa scratched the pig's ears and it lifted its snout into the air. "You like that, don't you," she murmured.

The pig gave the cutest little grunt, proving that a little love can help perk up anyone.

"Would you mind if I brought her home?" Jessa turned to Luis. I'd like to keep a closer eye on her."

"Fine by me." Having brought up three boys, Luis seemed to be fazed by nothing. He'd told her plenty of tales of Lance and his brothers bringing home snakes and mice and spiders.

"Not sure Lance'll like the idea, though. He's always sayin' animals belong outside."

She couldn't fight a wicked grin. Even better.

"Got a name for her?" the man asked, scratching under the pig's chin.

Jessa held her up and carefully looked her over. "Ilsa," she said, satisfied. "Because she's fancy." And because she loved *Casablanca*.

Luis grunted out a laugh. "Never met a pig named Ilsa."

"You named her?" Cass asked, walking through the door. "Uh-oh. In my experience naming an animal means it'll be part of your family forever."

"I'd be fine with that." Jessa couldn't take in every animal that came through the shelter's doors, but Ilsa was obviously special.

"So you could've called to check on the pig, you know," her friend said as though she was hurt. "I could've handled it until tomorrow."

Guilt turned Jessa's stomach. "Oh, I know. Of course you could." That wasn't it at all! "It's just..." She paused. There was no way she'd get out of this without telling her the whole story, which she couldn't do in front of Lance's father. She turned to him. "Luis, do you mind getting started on inventory in the storage room?"

"No problem," he said, tipping his cowboy hat in Cassidy's direction as he slipped by.

Once he was gone, Cassidy plopped down at the desk with the aged computer, then rolled another office chair close and pointed at it. "Spill it. What are you doing here? You're supposed to be enjoying a day off."

Jessa sat and settled Ilsa on her lap. She *would've* been enjoying a day off if things hadn't gotten so awkward back at the ranch. In a hushed tone, she shared the whole story in what had to be record time.

Cassidy's eyes grew wider and wider. "Wow. So what're you going to do? You going to stay there?"

"I feel like I have to." She'd made a deal with Lance. Besides, she needed the money. And now she wouldn't feel bad at all taking a cut. She didn't want to give him the satisfaction of bowing out because things had gotten a little uncomfortable.

"I can't believe you kissed Lance Cortez," Cassidy blurted. Her eyes bulged and she covered her mouth. "Sorry. But that's crazy. Was it good?"

"No." *Yes it was*. Her heart sighed. *Sooooo good*.

"I can tell when you're lying, you know."

Jessa simply petted Ilsa's coarse hair and planted a kiss on the pig's head. "I wonder why someone didn't want her," she said, trying to get Cassidy to focus on something besides Lance.

Luis came back, lugging along her father's old metal tool-box. "We're almost out of dog bones," he informed her. "But from what I can tell, everything else looks fine."

Of course it was fine, because she'd done the inventory three days ago. Jessa fanned her face. "Okay," she sang. "Thanks, Luis. I'll add dog bones to the list."

He secured the toolbox under one arm and hooked the other around the ladder they kept behind the counter. "I'm gonna head out and get that sign fixed."

After he'd moseyed through the door, Cassidy looked at Jessa with shiny eyes, a grin brimming. But before the woman could ask more questions, she glanced at the call log on the desk. "Has anything else come in today?"

Cassie snorted. "No. But Hank Green called. Twice in the past half hour, even though I told him you're not in today. I offered to help him out, but it's not me he wants." She wiggled her eyebrows.

Damn it. Not exactly the kind of call she'd hoped for. Give her a fawn tangled in a fence any day over Hank Green. The retired grocery store manager had had a thing for her ever since she'd worked there the summer she'd turned eighteen. He made passes at her every time he saw her.

She sighed. "What's the problem?"

"His cat is stuck in a tree. Again." Cassidy laughed. "He probably *put* him up there so he could call you."

"Oy." Hank did have some delusions about the two of them driving off into the sunset together. Despite the fact that he was a good forty years older than her and she'd tried to tell him repeatedly he wasn't her type.

Cassidy patted her hand sympathetically. "I told him he'd have to check in with you Monday if he wanted to talk with you."

Except that would mean she had nothing to do here today. No reason to keep Luis here, which meant they would have to go back to the ranch. And she dreaded that even more than she dreaded Hank's awkward passes. "Actually, I think I'll go over there." She rose from the chair and started to collect everything she'd need for Ilsa—the crate, the antibiotics, a special bottle so she could help her put on some weight. She could easily drop the pig off at the ranch before heading over to Hank's place.

When she turned around, Cass was gaping at her. "That'll only encourage him, you know."

"The poor cat. It's not his fault his owner is nuts." She crossed to the other desk and pulled out her medical kit from the drawer, just in case Butch the wonder cat was injured during the rescue.

"I'm sure he'll get him down if you don't come," Cassidy muttered.

"I wish I had your faith." But Hank could be quite persistent. She'd been witness to that. "Anyway, this is exactly what I need today. A distraction." A reason to avoid the ranch. Okay, a reason to avoid *Lance*. "I'll bring Luis with me."

"Oh, that'll help." Her friend rolled her eyes. Hank had always had it out for the Cortez boys—called them hoodlums and troublemakers—and now the rivalry between Hank Green and Luis Cortez was legendary. "You might want to bring some rope in case there's a brawl and you have to hogtie the two of them."

"Everything'll be fine," she insisted. Even if it wasn't, it would be a hell of a lot easier than facing Lance again today.

Chapter Eleven

Though she couldn't say much for the man himself, Jessa had always loved Hank Green's house. Located only a few blocks off Main Street, it had that old, small-town curb appeal, with rounded Victorian bay windows and pointed eaves. Pale bricks set off the blue shutters and an intricate white front porch wrapped the length of the house in a charming elegance.

"Hank Green needs your help about as much as Lance needs mine," Luis mumbled as she pulled up to the curb.

"I feel bad for him," Jessa said through a sigh. "He's lonely." So he called her over to help with his animals occasionally. What was the harm in that? Though he was in his late sixties, the man had never been married, never had any family, so she could understand why he'd want some company. "Besides," she continued, withdrawing the keys and unclipping her seat belt, "I can't ignore an animal in distress." The poor cat was probably terrified.

"You sure do have a big heart, Jessa." Luis pulled himself out of her truck, and did she imagine it or was he wincing more than normal?

Before she could make a full assessment, Hank waved from the front porch.

"Jessa. Thank God you're here," he called, teetering down the steps while he clutched the rail. The rim of white hair on his head had been neatly trimmed, and the bald spot on top shone in the sun. "Butch is terrified up there. I can hear him meowing."

Luis snorted and Jessa shoved a gentle elbow into his ribs. "Be nice," she whispered. "At least you have Lance and Naomi and Gracie around."

A small smile fumbled on his lips. "And you," he said. Which made *her* smile. Though she missed her father with heart-aching sorrow, having Luis sure helped.

Hank lumbered down the walkway toward them.

Ah, geez. He'd put on his dress slacks, with a sweater vest and bow tie. If only she could convince him dressing up for her wasn't worth the effort.

"What're you doing here, Cortez?" he asked, as though perturbed that he had some competition.

"Luis is helping at the shelter today," Jessa answered for him. The less these two gentlemen talked, the better off everyone would be. Way back in a previous life, Hank had accused Levi, the youngest Cortez, of shoplifting from his store. Levi, of course, always claimed innocence, and when Luis went down there to straighten things out, it had ended in a brawl that had the town sheriff locking up both men overnight.

Hank still eyed Luis warily. "I've told you, Jessa. *I* can help you at the shelter." He shifted his body as if to block out

Luis and focus solely on her. "I have nothing but time on my hands, and as you know, I *am* an animal lover."

"Lover," Luis scoffed under his breath. Jessa did have to admit that Hank somehow made that word sound rather dirty.

Instead of indulging Hank's offer with an acknowledgment, she brushed past him and continued up the walkway toward the house. "So where is poor Butch?" she asked.

"He's out back. About halfway up that blue spruce." Hank hustled to her side, leaving Luis to walk behind them. "I don't even know how he got out…"

Once again, Luis snorted.

Jessa shot him a look over her shoulder. Hopefully it said, *Let's not make this more painful that it has to be.* Though she had a hard time choking back a laugh. "How high up?" she asked in a businesslike tone. If she could keep them on track, this wouldn't have to take long and she wouldn't risk the two of them getting into another brawl.

"Oh, I don't know…" The man led the way around the side of the house on an intricate stone path that weaved through his prize-winning rose garden. "Maybe twenty feet up."

"Twenty feet?" Was the man trying to kill her? "You could've called the fire department," she reminded him. That was the sort of thing the small-town Topaz Falls Fire and Rescue was famous for. Rescuing kitties, helping little old ladies cross the street, putting out one hell of a scorching calendar every year…

"I did call." Hank escorted her past the large white gazebo in the backyard. It was gorgeous. Flawless and lavish, adorned with hanging baskets of every kind of flower. God, maybe she should just give in and marry the man. He had the best yard in all of Topaz Falls.

"The fire department refused to come."

Yeah, and she was Dolly Parton. The thought brought on a serious cringe. Hank probably *wished* she were Dolly Parton...

This time Luis coughed behind her, but at least he was keeping his mouth shut. She gave him a surreptitious grin before glancing up into the blue spruce that towered over a white picket fence on the back perimeter of the property.

At least twenty feet above the ground, the cat crouched on a wide pluming branch, its face obscured by the pine needles.

Oh, wow. Yeah. That cat was stuck. "Have you tried calling to him? Luring him down with treats?" she asked, shading her eyes from the overpowering sun.

"Of course," Hank assured her emphatically. "I've tried *everything*. I'm so distressed by the whole thing. Butch hates heights."

Again, Jessa called his bluff. Butch did, indeed, look terrified. But there was no way he'd climbed up there by himself. Cassidy was right. Hank had probably hauled over the ladder and stowed the cat up there as a ploy to get her to come over.

"Maybe he'll come down when he sees your beautiful face," Hank murmured, leaning too close for comfort. The smell of Pepto-Bismol wafted around her, stealing the sweet scent of roses from the air.

With a quick sidestep she escaped the assault, drawing closer to Luis.

"The thing is, I can't keep climbing up your tree to get your cat down, Hank." This was the fifth time in less than two months. But this was also the highest she'd ever found Butch.

"I understand," he said through a martyred sigh. "Don't worry. I won't ask for your help anymore."

"There really is a God," Luis muttered, though not nearly soft enough.

Hank whirled. "What the hell does that mean, Cortez? Do you have a problem with me?"

"I think it was you who had a problem with me," Luis shot back.

Jessa stepped between them. "Luis, can you please go get Hank's ladder out of the garage?" she asked in her sweetest-daughter-in-the-world voice. Her father had never been able to resist it, and it appeared Luis couldn't either. He turned away, mumbling some very colorful names for Hank, and hoofed it to the path around the side of the house.

Whew. Crisis averted. Lance would kill her if he knew she'd let his father get into it with Hank Green.

Lance. Right on cue, her stomach dropped and her heart twirled and the warmth of the sun seemed to slip inside her skin.

"So what's the plan?" Hank's low and gritty tone snuffed out the sudden fire burning hot and low in her belly. Well, there it was. Her remedy for shamelessly swooning over Lance. She didn't have to worry about that when Hank was nearby. "Um." She pushed her bangs off her forehead and gazed up again.

Butch was still perched in place, frozen into a fluffy cat statue. She moved closer to the tree. "Here kitty. Come on, Butch, baby. Come down now."

The cat crouched lower and mewed. There was no way in hell he was coming down on his own. Which meant she would have to go up and get him. "We need the ladder." Luis must've found it by now, but he was probably taking his time so he could cool off.

Hank slipped in front of her, gazing down on her with an affectionate look that deepened the creases in the corners of his beady gray eyes. "Jessa... while we wait, I want to thank you. For coming. You're always there for me when I need something."

"Technically I'm always there for Butch—"

Hank didn't seem to hear. "I hope you'll let me take you out to dinner this time. Only to thank you, of course," he said quickly. "Someplace nice. Maybe the Broker?"

"The Broker?" She almost laughed. "But that's in Denver."

"Exactly. We could make it a weekend trip..." Mr. Green rubbed his hand on her shoulder.

She swatted at it like she would a pestering fly. "I'm sorry. That's not going to happen. *Ever*." And the touching her shoulder thing... that had to stop, too.

"Ever?" he repeated, as though mortally wounded.

A sigh lodged in her throat. The poor man. He wasn't so bad. Hell, at least he had good taste. And at least he didn't look at her like she was some pathetic groupie. "I'm not in a good place for anything like that right now," she said gently.

His lips pursed while his head bobbed in a brave nod. "I understand. I can wait."

Never. She'd told him never. Ain't no way he could wait that long...

"Mew." The cat's soft call commanded her attention. Jessa stood on her tiptoes and tried to see through the pine needles.

"Mew." Butch inched forward on the branch as though ready to jump down to the next one.

"That's it!" Jessa scrambled up the first couple of

branches until she was about five feet off the ground. "Come on, Butchie. Come here." She pulled herself up higher. Somewhere beneath her something cracked.

"Here. I'll give you a boost," Hank offered, raising his hands and cupping them against her ass.

"No thanks," she squawked, darting up to the next branch. The tree was thick and sturdy, shaking only slightly while she climbed higher. After pulling herself up a few more branches, she had to stop. The branches were getting thinner and there was no way they'd support her weight. Butch had climbed down a ways, but he was still a few feet above her. "Here, kitty," she crooned softly. "Come on, now. I'm right here. Jump down and I'll catch you."

The cat crept closer to the edge of the branch, head low, wide, terrified eyes focused on Jessa.

"Okay. It's okay." Hooking one arm around the trunk, she shimmied up one more branch and reached until her fingertips tingled. "There." She grabbed the skin at the back of Butch's neck. The cat hissed and squirmed but she secured him against her chest, gasping and sweating. Carefully, she picked her way back down the tree and dropped to the ground. Heaving from the effort, she handed Butch over to Hank. "Don't let the cat get out again. I can't keep doing this."

The man's chin tipped up defiantly. "If you'd agree to dinner, I wouldn't *have* to keep calling."

Shaking her head, she turned away from him and started toward the path. What could be taking Luis so long?

"Maybe you'd rather have breakfast?" Hank persisted, coming alongside of her.

Wordlessly, she shook her head.

"Coffee?" he tried.

She stopped walking and faced him. "Sorry. It's not going

to work out." This time she patted his shoulder in an effort to ease the dejected look he gave her. "What about Helen Garcia?" she asked. Helen had been the librarian since the turn of the century. "She's so smart. And ... organized." That was about where the list of her attributes stopped.

"Jessa, I know there's a slight age difference, but—"

"Slight?" she interrupted.

"I think you're the loveliest woman in the world," he finished a little desperately.

Okay, so sweet and subtle was not going to work with Hank. She had to give it to him straight. She started walking along the path so she wouldn't have to look into his eyes. "I appreciate that. Really. But it's not going to happen. I don't look at you like that, and—" When they came around the corner of the house she stopped cold.

The ladder lay in the center of the yard, crushing Hank's perfect green grass.

"My grass," he gasped, stalking toward the ladder.

Worry filled her stomach like a cold hard stone. "Where's Luis?" she choked out. The ladder looked like it had been dropped, but he wasn't there.

"I don't know, but this'll ruin my grass." Hank struggled to drag the ladder to the driveway while she scanned the empty street.

Luis wasn't there. He was gone.

Somehow, Jessa faltered to the garage, her eyes searching. It was empty. "Where could he be?" she blurted, frantically looking around.

"Knowing Cortez, he's in the house going through my things," Hank replied tightly. He marched to the garage door and threw it open. "That family is all the same. Thieves, the lot of them."

She reprimanded him with a glare. "None of them are thieves," she said sternly. "But maybe he went in for a drink. Or maybe he had to use the bathroom." Of course that was it. He had to be in the house. Jessa gulped a breath to steady her heart. He hadn't disappeared, for God's sake. She followed Hank inside, inhaling the musty scent of an old closed-in house, searching room by room, not really seeing anything but somehow finding her way. He wasn't in the kitchen or the living room or the dining room or the main floor bathroom. She bolted up the rickety staircase. "Luis?" she screeched, throwing open the upstairs bedroom doors. The house sat in a heavy silence. She broke it again with another shout, half stumbling back down the steps.

Hank met her by the front door. "He's probably gone into town for pie and coffee," he said, his nose scrunched with distaste. "You can't count on the Cortez family for anything except trouble."

"No," Jessa wheezed. Not Luis. He wouldn't leave her when she needed his help. He wouldn't have left the ladder lying in the middle of the front yard. "Oh God." Sidestepping Hank, she broke through the front door and sprinted down the driveway to the sidewalk. Trying to breathe, she looked up and down the deserted street. "Luis?" she yelled.

Nothing. No response. Hands shaking, she dug her keys out of her pocket and flew to her truck.

"Sorry, Hank!" she yelled, fumbling to unlock the doors. "Please call me right away if Luis comes back!" Before he could respond, she thrust herself into the driver's seat and gunned the engine until the truck shot away from the curb.

Chapter Twelve

One more fall like that and he'd be seein' stars. Lance hoisted himself off the ground. Not gonna lie, it was getting harder to get up. That was the third time in an hour Ball Buster had thrown him. Good thing Tucker was a regular master at corralling the mean son of a bitch so he hadn't trampled him.

Shit. He hunched, trying to even out his breathing, which was a hell of a lot harder than it sounded with the laceration and bone bruise sending flames up his rib cage.

"Hey, you okay, man?" Tucker jogged over to where Lance limped near the fence. "You're lookin' tense out there."

Tense. That was one way to put it. "I'm fine," he lied, guarding his right side. Damn bone bruise. Sure wasn't making his training any easier. Every time that pain zinged through him, he also thought back to when Jessa had touched him there. When she'd run her hands over his skin, her fingers light and gentle. That only led to another problem that pretty much made it impossible for him to ride in comfort.

"Maybe you ought to call it a day," Tucker suggested, handing him his water bottle.

Lance removed his hat and took a good long swig. He couldn't call it a day. Not until he'd gotten the better of Ball Buster. There was no way he'd be able to compete at Worlds if he couldn't even stay on that damn bull for more than three fucking seconds.

He shoved the water bottle back into Tucker's hands. "Here. I'm going again. Let's get him ready."

The man shook his head like he wasn't sure if he should pity Lance or argue. But he knew the sport. He knew what it took.

Lance climbed the fence and jumped down on the other side. He removed his gloves to check the tape on his hands. It was already frayed and torn. He'd have to rewrap—

"Lance!"

Naomi raced around the edge of the corral.

Damn. She had that look of drama about her.

"I just got a call from Ginny Eckles," she yelled as he walked to meet her. "It's your dad. She found him in front of the bakery, and something's wrong."

The pain in his ribs intensified with the hitch in his breathing. "What do you mean something's wrong?"

Naomi was wheezing like she'd sprinted all the way from her house. "She said she tried asking him some questions but he wouldn't answer. He wasn't acting like himself."

Oh for chrisssake. "Where the hell is Jessa?" he demanded, as if Naomi were her keeper.

"I don't know," she shot back with just as much attitude.

"I asked Mrs. Eckles if he was alone and she said he was. She said Luis didn't seem to remember where he was supposed to be."

"Of course he remembers," Lance grumbled, already unbuckling his chaps. His dad wouldn't forget where he was supposed to be. He was probably just being ornery. Which Jessa could've prevented had she kept an eye on him like she was supposed to.

Naomi stooped to help him get the chaps off. Always the mother. "She thinks someone should pick him up. I'd go but I have to pick up Gracie at a friend's house on the other side of town in five minutes."

"I'll get him," Lance said, kicking off the leather gear. "Tucker, go ahead and get Ball Buster settled in the stables," he called to his friend. Looked like he was done training for the day after all.

The man tipped his hat and approached the bull while Lance followed Naomi down to the driveway.

"I tried to call Jessa's cell a few times, but she didn't answer," Naomi informed him, almost like she didn't want to get her friend in trouble.

His face steamed. "Don't worry about it." Not like he could blame all of this on Jessa. Knowing his father, he'd probably lost her on purpose.

"Maybe she's really upset," Naomi said. "About your talk this morning."

"She didn't seem upset." The memory of her coy smile tugged at his gut. She seemed fine. Confident. Strong. Like a woman who could hold her own. "You're wrong about her, you know," he told Naomi. "She's stronger than you give her credit for." Strong and sexy. Enticing with that body of hers. Not that he wanted to get slapped...

"Don't you get any ideas," Naomi warned. "I don't know who that woman at breakfast was, but it wasn't Jessa. It was an act. And I don't blame her. You practically humiliated her."

"On your advice," he reminded her.

They parted ways, but before Naomi climbed into her car, she shot him a glare. "You just keep your distance. Take my word for it." Before he could answer that he was done taking her word for anything, she disappeared into her car and peeled out.

Shaking his head, Lance climbed into his truck and drove down to the highway. As far as he could tell, Jessa was a big girl and could take care of herself. He might not go out of his way to pursue her, but if something clicked between them one night, he'd let it happen. Not that he'd be dreaming about that moment. Not dreaming...fantasizing. About those slender fingers grazing his skin again, about the sexy dip in the curve of her upper lip. About the delicate weight of her body against his, all soft curves and creamy flesh...

Shit, he just about missed his turn. He jerked the wheel in a quick left and slowed as he cruised down the strip. Sure enough, a small crowd had gathered in front of Butter Buns Bakery. He slowed and pulled over to parallel park at the curb. This didn't look good.

The people who'd gathered around Luis parted as Lance jogged down the sidewalk.

"Get the hell away from me," his dad was shouting at Mrs. Eckles.

"Whoa." Lance rushed to his father's side. "Dad. What's wrong?"

"He's very agitated," Mrs. Eckles prattled in her know-it-all way. She shook her head, the bifocals strung around her neck clanking. "All I did was ask if he needed something.

He looked so confused. And when I told him I was going to call over to your place, you should've seen him. Cursing and screaming like a lunatic."

"She was badgering me," Luis put in, glaring at Mrs. Eckles like he wanted to pop her in the face.

Damn, this went way beyond ornery. "I'm sorry about this, Mrs. Eckles," Lance said, delivering the words with a polite smile. But chaos raged underneath it. What the hell was his father's problem? Making a scene like this in the middle of town? "I'll get him home." He clamped a hand onto Luis's shoulder and dragged him away before the woman decided to press charges.

His father jerked out of his grip. "I don't need you coming to pick me up. Acting like I'm the one who's crazy."

Lance growled out a sigh. Is that what happened when people got older? They stopped caring what everyone thought and did whatever they wanted? "Where's Jessa, Dad?" he asked, trying to control the venom in his tone.

"How the hell should I know?" his father shot back.

That forced him to a stop. "Because you left the house with her. To go help at the clinic."

A look of understanding dawned in his dad's blank eyes.

Tremors took over Lance's stomach. "Don't you remember?"

"Of course I remember," his father snapped. "I wanted to go for a walk, that's all. I got thirsty and I wanted to go for a walk."

Lance studied him. The man's hands were trembling. Sweat glistened on his forehead. "Are you feeling okay?" he asked.

"I'm fine," his father said, a little softer. "Just so thirsty."

Relief swept through him. He'd probably gotten dehydrated. At some point, he'd have to talk to Jessa about making sure Luis drank plenty of water. "All right, old man," he said lightly, steering his father toward the truck. "I think I've got an extra water bottle in the tr—"

"Luis!"

Lance spun. Jessa sprinted toward them, her arms flailing, long hair sailing behind her.

"Where have you been?" she rasped, pressing one hand against her heaving chest.

Damn...the way she filled out a shirt...

"I went for a walk," Luis muttered, refusing to look at Jessa.

"A walk?" she choked out. "A *walk*?" If it was possible, her face got redder. "How could you do that, Luis? Huh? How could you just walk away without telling me where you were going?"

A couple passing by on the street paused to stare at Jessa.

Yeah, she was a little fired up. "Dad needs some water. He's thirsty." Lance slipped an arm around her waist and tried coaxing her to the truck so they could move this discussion somewhere more private.

"I have the right to go for a walk if I want to," his father insisted.

Jessa halted and squirmed out of Lance's grip. "I asked you to get the ladder out of Hank Green's garage. And you never came back." She turned to Lance, her eyes wild with indignation. "And then I found the ladder lying in the middle of the front yard and Luis had simply disappeared."

What was he supposed to say? He couldn't make excuses for his father's behavior.

"I was thirsty," Luis said again. "I wanted something to drink."

"Then you should've told me that," Jessa whispered, as though she was still having a hard time breathing. "I could've gotten you a drink, Luis." She swayed a little, as if the stress of losing his father had gone to her head. Once again, Lance secured an arm around her, trying not to notice how good she smelled.

This time, she allowed him to lead her to the truck. Luis got into the passenger's seat and Lance handed him a water bottle from a cooler in the back.

Jessa had leaned against the bed of the truck, staring off into space as though trying to collect her wits.

"He didn't mean to scare you," Lance said, coming up beside her and nudging her shoulder with his. "He's always had a mind of his own. But he doesn't do stuff like that on purpose."

"He never does stuff like that to me, Lance," she said quietly. Her face turned to his, and for the first time he noticed the red rims around her eyes. She'd been crying. Some protective instinct ballooned inside him and he wanted to wipe away her tears and make sure she never had another reason to cry.

Yes, Jessa was strong. She had a lot of sass. But she was also compassionate and seemed to feel everything so deeply. Maybe he appreciated that about her even more than he appreciated her sexy legs.

"I'll talk to him. Make sure he doesn't do it again," Lance promised, and God help him, he couldn't keep his hands off her. He trailed his fingers at the base of her jaw, sweeping back the strands of hair that had escaped her ponytail.

"I think..." Her gaze strayed from his. "I think something's wrong."

"What do you mean?"

"With your father. I think something's wrong with him."

"He got thirsty and he's used to doing what he wants when he wants." That was it. The older he got, the more stubborn he got.

"Lance..." Jessa took his hand in hers and it felt so out of place but so right, her soft smooth skin covering his rough callused knuckles. "I think you need to take him to the doctor. To have him checked out."

"What?" He pulled his hands to his sides.

Jessa peered up at him, her face steeled as it had been earlier that morning when they'd had their little chat in the kitchen. "He's had short-term memory loss twice now..."

"That's not memory loss." His hands twitched and he pulled them into fists. Clearly, the man was fine. "He got turned around in the mountains. And today he just wanted a damn drink of water."

"So he left a ladder in the middle of Hank Green's yard and walked ten blocks to Main Street for a drink?" she challenged. "Why didn't he go into the house to get a drink?"

"He hates that man." Everyone knew that. Jessa knew that. Why had she even taken him there? That was probably what started this whole debacle. "He'd never set foot in Hank Green's house willingly."

Jessa stepped up to him. "I think he got disoriented. I think he didn't remember where he was or what he was supposed to be doing." Anger flashed in her eyes. "He wouldn't walk away like that when I asked him to do something. He's never done that."

Lance threw up his hands. What did she want from him? "Cut the man some slack," he said, dismissing her concerns. "He's almost seventy. He probably shouldn't be carrying ladders around anyway."

Jessa glared at him for a silent minute. Then she strode close and got in his face. "I know you don't want to hear this. But something's wrong with him."

She was right about one thing. He didn't want to hear an uneducated diagnosis. "He was at the doctor three months ago and he's healthy as a horse." Those were the doc's exact words. Trying to appease her, he laid his hand on her shoulder. "Now I'm gonna take him home. Let him rest. I'll see you later." He turned and headed for the truck before she could argue.

Chapter Thirteen

There was a reason Darla had named her establishment the Chocolate Therapist. She firmly believed that every problem could be solved with the right wine and chocolate pairing. And in Jessa's experience, she was almost always right.

In need of some serious therapy after that little exchange with Lance, Jessa marched herself down four and a half blocks and charged through the familiar stained-glass door.

A few patrons sat around the tall pub tables, leaf-peeping tourists from the looks of their designer clothing. All of them had flights of wine and an assortment of truffles to match.

Somehow just inhaling that rich, cocoa scent made Jessa feel better already.

Darla was stationed behind the counter, walking a young couple through the menu, so Jessa slunk to the far corner stool at the main bar and plopped herself down, replaying that conversation with Lance again.

He probably shouldn't be carrying ladders around anyway.

As if Luis disappearing was her fault. Her shoulders sank lower. She only wanted to help the man, and yet Lance had completely dismissed her like her opinion didn't matter at all. It wasn't just the situation with the ladder. She'd noticed the tremors, things she'd originally written off as his arthritis acting up, but now she wasn't so sure.

"Wow, who pissed in your coffee today?" Darla appeared before her with a tray of truffles and a flight of reds.

Her angel of mercy.

The woman set the trays on the counter beside Jessa and pulled over a stool. "Looked like you could use something strong, so I brought all darks and a bittersweet."

"Perfect," Jessa, said before popping one of the cocoa-dusted confections into her mouth. Then she sipped on the first glass. Closing her eyes to hold on to the taste, she swallowed. "Better already," she said with a sigh.

"You want to talk about it?" her friend asked in a tone that wouldn't take no for an answer. Who was Jessa kidding? Her face was an open comedic tragedy. She'd never been one to hide her emotions.

"This arrangement is more complicated than I thought it would be," she admitted, going for another truffle. The chocolate melted in her mouth.

"What is? Staying at a ranch with a sexy *single* cowboy while you babysit his aging father?" Sarcasm dripped from her smile. "How could that possibly be complicated?"

Yeah, yeah, yeah. She'd set herself up for this. It had all seemed so simple. Until her body and heart betrayed her and attached themselves to a man who had zero ability to commit.

"All right. This looks bad. What happened?" Darla asked, leaning her chin into her fist as though she knew they'd be there awhile.

"You have customers to take care of." And she felt more like wallowing alone.

"Beth can take care of the customers and I can take care of you." Out of all of them, Darla happened to be the most motherly. Well...if your mother liked to make off-color jokes, flirt with much younger men, and only wear shirts that showed plenty of cleavage.

"Come on," Darla prompted. "You'll feel better if you talk about it."

Not likely. But she relayed the entire story anyway, popping the truffles into her mouth and washing them down with sips of the decadent wine between sentences.

Darla said nothing. She wore the same concentrated expression she did whenever she was testing out a new recipe.

"So that's it, I guess. I think something's wrong with Luis. Lance doesn't care what I think." That about summed it up. He didn't respect her enough to value her opinion.

"Am I missing something here?" Darla leaned in, her dark eyes wide and emphatic. "Isn't *he* the one who asked for your help? For you to stay with his father and keep an eye on him?"

"Yes." Exactly. He wanted her there, but he didn't want to hear what she thought.

"Here's what you're gonna do, honey," Darla said, waiting until Jessa looked her in the eyes. "You're gonna drive back to the ranch. March that cute little ass of yours right up to Lance's front door and ask him if he still wants your help with his father."

Jessa tried to take mental notes. That sounded easy.

"Then, when he says yes—because he *will* say yes—you're going to tell him he doesn't get to ignore you. Since you are doing him a favor, he will listen and consider what you say." A grin broke through her titanium expression. "Then you tell him he's not allowed to kiss you again unless he intends to fully finish the job."

Jessa rolled her eyes. "I'll take everything else and leave out that last part."

"Come on." Darla swatted at her. "What good is taking on a second job if you can't take advantage of some of the perks?" She nibbled on a truffle. "Trust me, honey. Lance Cortez's body is one hell of a perk."

That was one way to describe it...

"Besides, maybe if you two really got it on, all this tension would go away and you'd be able to move on."

Jessa choked on a sip of wine. "I don't think so." If she was going to stick it out at the ranch until Worlds, she couldn't make things more awkward than they already were.

"Here." Darla reached into the pocket of her apron and dug out some wrapped truffles. "Take these with you. A new blend. Pop one in your mouth before you talk to him." Her eyebrows arched. "Trust me."

Jessa held out her palm and carefully examined the dark mounds of goodness. "Isn't chocolate an aphrodisiac?" Because she didn't need any help in that area. Not with Lance.

Darla simply gave her an innocent smile before she stood and waltzed away.

* * *

All the way to Lance's house, Jessa practiced. She practiced saying exactly the words Darla had given her. She practiced in a bitchy voice, an apathetic voice, then decided that was too much and tried to add a note of sympathy. All in all, she must've said the words fifty times and yet as she climbed the stairs to his front porch, her mind blanked.

But there was no turning back now. Before she could overthink it, she knocked on the door. A sudden explosion of nerves blew inside her and she quickly unwrapped the truffle that had been melting in her pocket and popped it into her mouth. Some brand of heavenly merlot leaked through the chocolate, bringing a symphony of fruity notes. *Good, fun-loving lord*, enough of these chocolates and she'd never need sex again.

The door opened and Lance stepped out. He was dressed in a faded gray T-shirt and sinfully tight worn jeans. They should be illegal in all fifty states, those jeans.

Okay. So maybe never needing sex again was a bit strong...

"Hi," he said, straightening as though he was surprised to see her. "Everything okay?"

Right. That was her cue. Everything was *not* okay. But she couldn't seem to manage the words. "Um." She cleared her throat so she didn't sound like Lauren Bacall. "We need to talk." Because she had stuff to say. Lots of important stuff...

She tried to play back Darla's badass lecture in her mind, but a steady humming drowned it out.

"Okay..." Lance stepped aside and made room for her to walk past him. On the way, she caught that alluring scent that seemed to cling to him. Something woodsy and sexy. *Keep going*, she reminded her feet. She couldn't stand too close to him.

"Can I get you something to drink?" he asked politely,

leading her through his family room and into the kitchen, where they'd had their little exchange earlier. Just like that morning, she positioned herself far away, on the opposite side of the kitchen island.

"No." No drinks. She had to get this over with. She braced her hands against the countertop and looked at him directly before she lost the nerve. "You don't get to ignore me," she announced, and wow, Darla would have been so impressed. She sounded *pissed*.

Lance blinked at her.

Courage bloomed. "I mean, I'm only trying to help, and you acted like I'm causing some big problem for your father. Instead of listening to me, you load him up in the car and get out of there like my concerns don't matter. Do you have any idea how worried I was?" She started to pace. Once she got going, it was hard to stop. "I searched everywhere. I ran up and down the block looking in everyone's yard, going up to neighbors' doors and asking if they'd seen him. In case you haven't noticed, Lance," she said glaring at him again, "I care about Luis, too." A silent round of applause broke out in her head. She'd done it! Without letting him get a word in, even.

Lance's eyes were darker, narrow. She braced herself for a defensive tirade like he'd thrown at her earlier, but instead he sighed. "You're right." His hand raked though his hair. "I'm sorry."

"You know what, Lance," she said before she'd had time to process the words. *Hold on.* He hadn't argued with her. He'd...apologized? Just like that? "Huh?"

"You're right." The man's normally broad and powerful shoulders seemed to have bent under some unseen weight. "I shouldn't have brushed you off."

She should be gloating. That was exactly what she'd

wanted him to say. But the clear dejection that pulled at his mouth halted the victory party. "Okay, then. Thank you." The words sounded hollow and awkward. There was no script for this. Darla hadn't told her what to say if Lance started apologizing...

"I should've heard you out. I'm under a lot of pressure right now." His jaw tensed as he studied her, almost like he wanted to say something more, but decided against it.

"Because of Worlds?" she asked, trying to read what he wouldn't say.

Instead of answering, he walked to the table and picked up a magazine, then tossed it on the counter in front of her. "Because of this."

She grabbed the newest copy of *Rodeo World News* and her heart sank at the article's title: "Hometown Letdown."

Her eyes scanned the editorial—written by an anonymous source—which detailed Lance's fall from the highest acclaim in the rodeo world. It outlined his entire career—the early years of his success, the World title years ago. Then it detailed his fall from glory. The disappointing times, the disqualifications, the fact that he'd barely even qualified for Worlds this year. *He has proven that he's not his father, the great Luis Cortez, who at thirty was taking the top score in every competition...*

"They've decided I'm done. Useless. According to the fans, my career should've ended years ago," he said, eyes fixed on the article.

"Unbelievable." The words were cutting. Degrading for a man who'd won so many titles, who'd once been a hero. She read the last sentence: "Lance Cortez was once the greatest rider in the world. Now he's one of the greatest examples of what happens when you don't know when to quit."

A stab of pain lodged itself at the base of her throat. "This is crap," she said, tossing it back on the counter. Her hand shook with the absurdity of it. "Utter and complete crap. You've given your life to this sport." And when he was winning, everyone loved him. They couldn't say enough about him. Hell, there was a whole display about him at the public library...

"Maybe it's not." He raised his head and looked at her but didn't seem to see her. "Do you have any idea what it's like to read that? To hear the world saying you're done before you feel ready?" Those fierce bluish eyes steeled. He snatched the magazine and tossed it into the trash can. "Everything I've given my life to for the past fifteen years is over."

Jessa watched him pace the kitchen, words and anger and passion converging. There was no script for this. No plan for the sympathy that spilled out from inside her. "I can't imagine what that would be like," she said quietly, wishing she had more to offer him.

Lance stopped and turned to face her. "I don't know who I am outside of it. Outside of being my father's son. Outside of the arena. Outside of that world."

She got that. Sometimes when things changed so fast, when all of a sudden life looked different than it had the day before, you had to be reminded of who you were. That's what had happened when her father passed away. She was no longer a daughter and everything in her life was up for grabs.

She closed the distance between them with purposeful steps. "You're a good person, Lance. A good son. You've taken care of your dad. You've worked your ass off and you've accomplished more in fifteen years than most people do in a lifetime." The words were softer than she meant for them to be, more weighted with emotion than the conviction she wanted to offer him. "You can win." She'd seen him out there—that will, the sheer determination that drove him. "I know you can win." She wasn't sure exactly how, but her hand came to rest on his forearm, fingers lightly curled around his skin.

"Don't touch me." He staggered backward. "Not right now." There was a warning in his tone that matched the agony in his eyes.

Her hand froze where his arm had been. "Okay." She studied him, trying to understand what he wasn't saying, but his eyes wouldn't meet hers. What was he thinking? Had she made him angry again? "Did I say something wrong?" she asked quietly. She didn't know what to say, how to ease that tortured expression on his face.

Lance finally looked up, eyes smoldering with a passion she'd seen in him only out in the corral. "You tempt me to forget all of it," he uttered. "You make me think it doesn't matter."

Shock thundered through her. She braced a hand against the countertop and gaped at him. "Wh...what?"

"God, Jessa." He half-laughed while his head shook slowly back and forth. "You don't even know how beautiful you are, do you?"

The words were so unexpected she almost didn't believe them. Lance Cortez was calling her beautiful?

He stepped up to her, and he seemed to be moving so slowly. But maybe it was just the shock of what he was saying...

"When you're here I have a hard time focusing on my training..."

Her lungs locked in anticipation exactly the way they had last night when he'd covered her mouth with his. "D-do you...want me to leave?" she stuttered. She was pretty sure that wasn't what he meant, but sometimes it was best to be a hundred percent certain.

"No." His hands went to her cheeks, his callused fingers stroking them softly. "It wouldn't matter. I'd still see you." He leaned in closer, so that his lips were inches away. "I'd still feel you..."

"What happened to wanting different things?" she sputtered, her throat aching with the desire to lose herself in the feel of his lips over hers, his hands on her body.

"Right now, I only want you," he growled, his shoulders rising and falling with heavy breaths. His hands anchored her face while his lips came for hers—*claimed* hers— ravaging them in a frenzy of desperation and need.

Every fragment of self-protection she'd managed to piece together shattered in the sheer extravagance of his hot mouth, his tongue gliding over hers, his strong hands sliding down her neck, then caressing their way down her chest.

He groaned into her mouth as he brought his hands lower, running his fingers over her breasts.

Greed surged through her, heating the blood in her veins until even her legs tingled. Everything in her core tightened in a hard pull of sensuous tension. Right now, she only wanted him, too. *Needed* him to satisfy this overpowering hunger he'd provoked in her. Taking his bottom lip lightly between her teeth, she bit down and pushed him against the counter, somehow tugging his shirt up and over his head on the way. Stealing a second, she stopped to admire him, the hard muscle of his chest, the sinewed flesh stretched over his abs. His jeans sat low on his carved hips. The bandage she'd dressed him in last night was still intact, purple bruising visible around the edges. She touched it carefully.

"I don't need a nurse right now." His voice ground low in his throat. A sexy grin flashed before he came at her again, this time bypassing her lips and launching a thrilling assault on her neck. It was melting her, his lips, his tongue on her skin. He edged her back against the wall and captured her hands in his, raising them up until her arms were braced above her.

God, her body was so tight, so ready, she needed him to free her, but before she could beg, he pulled off her shirt in one smooth motion. Kissing her lips, then her cheeks, then her jaw, he worked his arms around her, pulling her in tighter and unhooking her bra with one hand. His other hand tore the flimsy satin away from her body but she couldn't see where it ended up because the magic of his mouth and hands teasing at her nipples blurred her vision. He buried his face in the valley of her, sighing, uttering helplessly desperate little noises.

Ragged breaths stole her thoughts. Her hands raked his thick, luxurious hair as he kissed and sucked and nibbled until she quaked with need. *Now.* She wanted him to fill her, to take her. Right. Now. Her hands clawed at his belt buckle until it somehow came unclasped and she could rip open the button fly of his jeans.

His forehead fell to her shoulder as she slid her hands down his hips, pushing down his boxers and jeans, and wrapped both hands around the hard length of him. She started moving her fingers, tightening the pressure, but he grabbed her wrists and brought them back above her head, pinning them against the wall and kissing his way to her ear. "You first."

She kept her hands raised over her head as he kissed her mouth deeply, his fingers undoing her jeans and pushing them down her hips.

His hands cupped her ass, then one of them slid down and hiked up her leg until her knee was at his waist. The other hand snaked around her body, slicing through the swollen flesh between her legs in one long stroke.

"No need for that," she murmured breathlessly. She was so hot, so primed, she only wanted him to break her apart. Now.

The grin flickered on his lips again. He finished removing his jeans, pulling out his wallet and riffling through until he found a condom. Impatiently, he ripped open the package and had that thing on before he'd made it over to where she stood.

Her heart beat against her ribs, pounding blood all through her.

Lance slipped his hands under her and hoisted her up, bracing her back against the wall as he drove into her in one long, hard thrust.

The heated grinding pried a moan from her lips. Her fingers dug into his shoulders as he slid out painstakingly slow, watching her eyes the whole way. By the time he thrust again she was panting, bearing her hips down to meet the rhythm he was using to tease her.

"God, Jessa." He grabbed a fistful of her hair, taking it roughly back from her face, and kissing her harder, deeper. The motion of his hips came faster, all power and strength, surging into her, lifting her higher, grazing the hot wetness. Her legs tightened around his waist, heightening the sensations, until it was all she felt...him. Everywhere. Inside of her and outside of her. With a tortured grunt he thrust again and this time she couldn't hold on. With a cry of exhilaration, she let go, abandoning herself to the release of blinding sensations, floating atop wave after wave of exquisite pleasure.

Lance brought one hand to her face and tipped up her head. A spark seemed to bind their eyes together. He pushed into her faster, harder, until a long groan punched out of his mouth and his body quaked.

Winded, but somehow still holding her up, his shoulders slumped against hers. A lazy grin took over his lips and she leaned her head down to kiss them again. They were so decadent, those lips of his...so wonderfully sensual and giving.

Lance set her feet on the floor and kissed her back, wrapping her in tighter, pulling her naked body snugly against his, and they seemed to fit so perfectly together.

"You're somethin', Jessa Mae," he said, his hungry gaze lowering down her body.

"I could say the same about you." Not once in her life had sex been so spontaneous, so instinctual and free-spirited. So close to the movie sex scenes that she'd always thought were contrived and unbelievable.

One time with Lance and she was a believer.

He took her hands in his, towing her closer. "So that was unexpect—"

The doorbell chimes cut him off.

Jessa snapped her head to stare at the front door on the other side of the great room. "Who's—"

"Uncle Laaa-aance!" The door muffled Gracie's singsongy voice.

"What is she doing here?" Jessa hissed, pushing away from him, breaking their bodies apart.

His eyes squeezed shut. "I'm supposed to give her a riding lesson."

"When?" Not to be dramatic or anything, but one minute ago the girl could've walked in on them having sex in his kitchen!

He glanced at the clock. "In two minutes."

"Holy shit. Good God, Lance." She scrambled around the floor, rummaging through the discarded clothing.

"I'll tell her to go away," he said, his mesmerized eyes locked on her body.

"You can't tell her to go away! Put these on." Jessa hurled his pants and boxers at him. Then his shirt. *Oops.* That was her shirt. *Aha!* His was pooled on the island. She ran over and snatched it, shaking it out so she could pull it over his head.

A knock sounded on the door. "Hello?" It was Naomi! The heavy wood started to creak open.

Jessa hit the floor next to Lance, scooting her knees into her chest and hiding herself behind the island.

He finished buckling his belt with amazing precision, given their current dilemma.

"There you are," she heard Naomi say from across the room, thank the lord.

There was a pause.

"Why didn't you answer the door?" her friend asked, a familiar skepticism creeping in.

Lance cleared his throat. "Um. Sorry. I was…on the phone."

Wow, he was good under pressure. He almost sounded bored. And then there was her…her pulse was racing so fast and hard, it felt like her heart could tear out of her rib cage at any second.

"Oh."

Jessa held her breath. Would Naomi get suspicious and

come over to the island? She edged her back against the cabinets.

"Why is Jessa's truck out there?" the woman asked.

Damn her!

"Dunno." Lance snuck a glance down at her, flashing that grin so fast she almost didn't see it, then he walked away. "Looks like someone's ready to ride, though," he said. And he must've twirled Gracie around because she giggled and squealed.

Slowly, Jessa let out the breath she'd been holding. Footsteps traipsed away from her until they grew faint.

"I wore my pink cowgirl hat," Gracie chirped as the front door opened.

When it closed, Jessa let herself collapse on the floor. Staring up at the ceiling, she tried to grasp what had happened. One minute she was reprimanding him and the next she was practically begging him to ravage her. And it might have been fast but... wow. For some reason that had made it even better. It had never happened that fast for her. Ever.

Trying to breathe like a normal human, she sat up and started dressing herself. She never did this... a quickie in the kitchen with a man she wasn't even *dating*. What the hell had come over her?

Shaking her head at herself, she shimmied on her jeans.

It had to be that damn chocolate.

Chapter Fourteen

Uncle Lance, why aren't you listening to me?" Gracie demanded, waving a hand in his face. Her glittery pink nails caught the sunlight and practically blinded him.

"Oh. Sorry, buckaroo." He shook himself conscious. Normally, he wasn't one to dwell on the past, but he couldn't seem to bring himself back into the present. Not after that mind-blowing rendezvous in his kitchen. It had been so good he might never get himself out of the past. And it wasn't like Gracie needed a ton of supervision. Not on Esmeralda. The mare had been his mother's horse way back when. She was as old as the sun and lumbered along steady and slow no matter what a person did with the reins.

"I asked if I'm holding on right," Gracie said, her bottom lip pouting slightly. She sat up taller on Esmeralda's back. "Because someday, when I'm a beauty queen, I'll need to know how to hold on the right way."

He grinned at her. "You're perfect. Just don't grow up and become a beauty queen too fast."

"Too late for that," Naomi mumbled beside him. "I swear...I don't know where she got her diva tendencies."

He swung his head to give her a proper look of disbelief. "Really?"

"What?" she demanded, just like her daughter.

He gave her a dose of raised eyebrows and braced himself for a fist in his biceps, but she only laughed. "So I like pink. And sparkles."

"And drama," he added, making a silly face so Gracie would laugh.

"Speaking of..." Naomi tugged him back a step while they watched Gracie make another leisurely round along the fence. "You do seem a little checked out. Who were you on the phone with when we came in?" Her expressive green eyes reflected the sunlight. She was already gloating.

Aw hell. He was busted. Naomi knew good and well he avoided the phone like he avoided her drama. "It was a wrong number," he said, heading for the safety of Gracie's presence.

"Where was she hiding?" Naomi asked, following him closely. "And what the hell was she doing in your house in the middle of the afternoon?"

He stopped and faced her. "If only that was your business."

"Oh, it's my business," she fired back. "Jessa is my friend. I thought we were in agreement on this." Her eyes narrowed as though she was calibrating her intuition.

Shit. That wasn't good for him.

"You slept with her didn't you?"

"Technically no." There was no sleeping involved. No lying down, even.

"Damn it, Lance," she said, smacking a hand against her thigh.

"We don't say 'damn it,' Mommy," Gracie called over. "That's a bad word."

Lance busted out laughing.

"You're right, peaches," Naomi muttered through clenched teeth. "What I meant to say is, 'How could you let this happen?'"

He shrugged, waiting until Gracie and Esmeralda had ambled to the other side of the corral. "It just happened. Okay?" He still wasn't sure how. When Jessa had said those things to him, told him she believed in him, something else took over. He couldn't stop himself. Couldn't hold back. Part of him had thought that once it happened, he'd get it out of his system and he'd be able to stop thinking about her. To see her without wanting her so badly it made him ache.

Man, had that backfired. That little tryst had only intensified the thoughts, the physical response to her. Next time it wouldn't be fast and frantic in the kitchen. He'd take his time with her.

"So what does this mean?" Naomi half-whispered. "Is Jessa okay?"

"She sure seemed okay." Way better than okay, actually, given her sexy cries there at the end...

"I mean are you guys together? In a relationship?"

"Not that I'm aware of." Though they hadn't really made time to discuss the details. "This morning, she said that wasn't what she wanted."

"Of course she said that, you idiot."

"We don't say, 'idiot,'" Gracie admonished. "Remember, Mommy? It's not nice to put people down."

Lance laughed again. He loved that girl.

"Right," Naomi said behind a plastic smile. "Thanks for the reminder."

Esmeralda hobbled away from them for another spin around the corral, and Lance took the opportunity to argue his case.

"Why does everything have to be defined right now?" Hell, he and Jessa hadn't even defined anything. He sure wasn't stupid enough to discuss the terms of their relationship with Naomi before he'd talked to Jessa about it. Relationship? Wow...had he ever used that word before? Maybe not, but he didn't exactly mind the sound of it as much as he once had.

"Well, I'm just wondering what you plan to do now," Naomi badgered in her little sister way. "Maybe it's time for you to deal with your commitment issues so you can actually have a healthy functioning relationship with someone."

If a man said that to him, he might haul off and throw a punch. "What the hell is that supposed to mean?"

"'Hell' is a bad word!" Gracie informed him from the other side of the corral.

"Right," he muttered, wondering what would happen if she wasn't around to keep them all in line. "I meant to say heck." He turned to Naomi. "What the *heck* does that mean?"

"You know what it means."

"I've never met anyone worth committing to," he said. That was all. Good women were hard to come by. She couldn't blame that on him.

"No," Naomi argued. "You've never let yourself *trust* anyone. Not since your mom left."

He opened his mouth to object, but she went on. "I know you better than almost anyone, Lance. You have serious trust issues."

Anger rose like a shield. "You're one to talk." She hadn't even dated anyone since Mark took off.

Instead of lashing back at him like he expected her to, Naomi laid a hand on his arm. "Exactly. Which means I can recognize it."

The admission disarmed him. What could he say to that? "Maybe it'll never be possible for me." Maybe his mother's abandonment had jacked him up so bad, he'd never have a relationship. Maybe he didn't even want to try.

"So what're you gonna do?" Naomi asked again.

"I don't know." It wasn't like he'd planned to have wild passionate sex with Jessa. He'd been in a rough place when she walked in. And right when he saw her everything seemed better. The opinion of the rest of the world hadn't mattered so much. She might be the only person in the world who believed he could compete at Worlds. Who believed he could win one more title.

"Oh my God," Naomi gasped. "Did we walk in on you two?"

"Not exactly." The memory of Jessa crouched behind the island next to him baited a smile. That could be their secret, though.

"Is she still at your house?" the woman blurted. "You have to go talk to her! You have to make sure she's all right!"

"She's all right." And yes, he'd talk to her. Later. He wasn't going to stress about it. Wasn't going to force things. And he sure as hell wasn't taking Naomi's advice again. "But after we're done here, I'm gonna call Tucker and have him bring out Wild Willy." The bull should be healed up by now and he needed to get serious.

Two minutes before Jessa had shown up on his doorstep,

he'd been this close to quitting. But she'd given him the determination to train and to fight and to keep going.

And now, he'd do whatever he had to do to get back in that arena for one more dance.

* * *

She should probably leave Lance's house, seeing as how *he'd* been gone for a half hour. Jessa had managed to retrieve her clothes—which by divine intervention had been strewn around the floor *behind* the kitchen island, saving them both from a potentially awkward conversation, had Gracie happened to have caught sight of a pair of women's underwear lying out in the open.

After she'd dressed, she'd teetered around the kitchen on her still wobbly legs doing the few dishes that sat in his sink and walking around the living room like it was a museum, noting the beautiful prints hanging on the walls and the detailed woodwork and the titles of the vast array of books he kept on the shelves.

You could tell a lot from a person's book collection and Lance's was extensive. He liked local history and cowboy legends. Political thrillers and classics like Dostoyevsky and Tolstoy. She wouldn't have pegged him for an intellectual, but then again, Lance was too layered to be pegged at all.

She knew she should leave, but she liked being there. She liked learning about him. She liked seeing how he organized his space and life. And yes, she liked *him*. Not just the sex, which had been...wow. But it went deeper than that. His tenderness. His loyalty. His sensitivity. He obviously didn't want people to see those things in him, but she did.

The more time she spent with Lance, the more he revealed his true heart to her—the one that had been wounded and left him wandering, much like her own. And the more she saw of his heart, the more she realized she could love this man. If she let herself. She could. That was a dangerous prospect. Because she already knew he didn't let himself love anyone.

So she had to leave. Walk out his door and not look over her shoulder. Accept the fact that things wouldn't be the same when they saw each other again. He'd be distant like he had been earlier. And she'd be unsure.

Steeling herself, she made her way across the sitting room and peeked out one of the front windows to make sure she wouldn't be caught. If she was honest, part of her hoped Lance would come back and find her there, that they could hold on to the connection that had rooted them together when he was looking into her eyes, holding her body, kissing her. It would be like a scene from a movie. She'd swing open his front door and he'd be standing there, just about to walk in because he'd realized he couldn't live without her. Then he'd kiss her and while he was kissing her, he'd sweep her into his arms and close the front door—locking it this time—and maybe he'd take her on the soft leather couch...

But Lance didn't come. No one was outside, and while disappointment weighted her chest, that was perfect because at least she wouldn't get caught sneaking out of his house. Quickly, she opened the door and slipped outside, eyeing the horizon for any glimpse of Naomi or Gracie. Once on the front porch, she ran, stumbling down the steps before racing to her truck. She climbed inside and sped down the road to Luis's house, taking an extra few seconds behind the wheel to collect herself so she didn't seem harried and panicked.

Carefully she straightened her hair, glancing in the

rearview mirror. God, she *looked* like she'd just had passionate sex. Her face was even still flushed.

Shaking her head at herself, she climbed out of the truck. Hopefully Luis wouldn't notice...

"Hey there." The man himself greeted her from the rocker on his porch as if he'd been sitting there waiting for her. He'd even brought out little Ilsa. The pig was curled up on his lap.

"Hi," she said brightly, going to sit by him. She loved his rocking chairs. He'd made them himself from the thick aspen branches he'd found on the property.

She settled in and stared out at the view. If Luis had noticed her sitting in the truck trying to primp herself back to normal he didn't let on. And he didn't ask why she'd just driven down from Lance's place.

He probably didn't have to.

"So how's our patient?" she asked, reaching over to ruffle Ilsa's ears.

"Seems fine." He handed over the pig and Jessa nuzzled her against her cheek. Ilsa still smelled like the scented shampoo she'd used when she'd bathed her.

The rocking chairs creaked for a few minutes before Luis turned to her. "Sorry I left Green's house like that," he said gruffly.

"No." She patted his hand. "It's okay. I probably overreacted." That morning already felt so long ago. So much had happened between then and now.

"Nah. It was a fool-headed thing to do," he mumbled as though angry at himself. "There's no excuse."

That was what bothered her. Luis never did fool-headed things. He'd always been careful and deliberate. Not rash. He thought things through.

She glanced at him, trying to interpret the disheartened expression on his face. A glimmer of intuition flared inside her and she drew in a breath of courage. "Are you sure you're okay, Luis?" Because he'd left the ladder in the middle of the yard. And even if he *had* been angry at Hank or even if he'd really been thirsty, he would've propped up the ladder near the house or left it in the garage...

"There's nothin' for you to worry about," he said, clearly not answering her question. He could've simply said no, but he hadn't.

Worry weaved itself into the threads of her fears. "If there was something, you could talk to me about it, you know." Though she hadn't meant for it to, emotion laced the words. "I could help you figure it out." She would do her best. In so many ways, this man was all she had left of her father. They'd shared years together. He'd known her dad even better than she had.

Luis rocked in his chair, his old hands gripping the armrests. "It's tough getting old," he finally said. "Feeling your body give out on you."

Give out on you how? she wanted to ask. What wasn't he telling her?

"Makes you think about all the things you'd do differently." He was gazing off to the mountains in the distance as though seeing a whole lifetime of regrets play before him.

The sad pull to his lips clawed at her heart. "What would you do differently?"

"Too many things to list," he said with a humorless laugh. Then he turned to her, those eyes watery and sure. "But you know what I regret the most?"

"No," she said, her eyes locked on his.

"I regret not making things right with Lucas." He looked

away from her again, but not before she saw tears brighten his eyes. "I was hard on him when they came for him after he set that fire. Said a lot of things I can't take back."

For the life of her, she could never imagine Luis saying a mean or hateful thing to anyone. But he'd likely been different back then.

"I'm sure he knew you were just angry," she offered. The fire had tarnished the Cortez family name. It divided the town, hurt Luis's own legacy...

"I told him I never wanted to see his face again." The old man's hands trembled and his grip on the armrests seemed to tighten. "But I didn't mean it. Didn't mean one word of it."

"Of course you didn't," she whispered, hidden tears thickening her throat. This poor man. Living with that grief all these years. "Have you ever tried to contact him?"

"I've kept up on him." His gaze lowered to the ground. "Through other people. He works for the McGowen Ranch down in Pueblo. Tried to send him a letter years back, but didn't ever get a response." Another garbled laugh sputtered out. "Can't say I blame him. He's built a good life for himself. Even after all he went through. No thanks to me."

"You're the one who gave him a foundation," she pointed out.

"But I should've been there for him," he said sternly. "I should've helped him through it."

"You did your best." In her estimation, every parent screwed up in some way or another. But Luis loved his boys. That was obvious. "I mean, look at Lance. And Levi. You have a great relationship with them."

"Not with Levi. He don't ever want to come home. Stays out on the circuit, away for his training." The man looked at her with that hollow gaze again. "Truth is, Jessa, my boys deserved better than me. All of 'em."

That wasn't the truth. Not at all, but she knew nothing she could say would take away his regrets. The only peace he'd find was through rebuilding what he'd lost with Lucas.

"I sure wish I knew 'em now." She barely heard the words above the rocking chair's creaking. "The way I know Lance."

"I'm sure they wish they knew you, too." God, she'd give anything to have her father. He wasn't perfect, but he was still her dad. Surely Lucas felt the same way. "I wish they knew you the way I know you. I wouldn't have survived this past year without you, Luis."

That earned a small smile. "I could say the same," he said, patting her hand. "Buzz would be proud of you."

"Thanks," she whispered. So much of who she was had come from her father. And that had to be true for Lucas and Levi, too. No matter what had happened in the past, Luis was still part of who they were. No one knew that better than her. Her dad's death had left a gaping hole in her life, but Lucas and Levi still had their father. And what if something was wrong with him? Then they might not have him much longer. She studied the tremors in Luis's hands. What would Lucas and Levi think of the symptoms Luis was obviously battling? Would they say it was nothing like Lance had?

Apprehension built inside her. They should at least know what was going on with their father. If Lance wouldn't tell them, someone else should.

She stood abruptly, cradling Ilsa against her chest. "I should go inside. I have some work to do." For starters, she had to contact the McGowen Ranch and talk Lucas into coming home.

Chapter Fifteen

Lance slung his dirty chaps over the stable's gate and brushed the dust off his jeans. He'd had a stellar training day, no doubt thanks to Jessa's pep talk and the extracurricular activities that had taken place in his kitchen. God, had it been almost a week ago? Ever since, he'd been out in the corral at the first light of dawn until well after sunset, occasionally breaking to eat or drink something. All in all, he'd managed to bring up his time consistently to eight seconds. His ribs and back might be aching now, but it was a good ache, familiar and dull. The kind of ache that told just how hard his muscles had been working.

Every day, Jessa's words had driven him. Along with thoughts of seeing her, being with her again. He fantasized about her all the time, but instead of distracting him, those thoughts now drove him. She drove him. But between his training and her and his dad's long hours at the shelter, he hadn't seen much of her. A wave here. A quick hello there.

It was not enough for him. Anticipation had built all week, and he couldn't hold it off anymore. Soon, he'd leave for Worlds. He couldn't miss out on spending some time with her before then.

So, desperate or not, he'd decided to show up at Luis's for dinner tonight. Then maybe the two of them could get out for a walk. Or a drink back at his place.

He hauled his gear onto the shelf and stepped out of the barn into the dusky evening. The sun was already sinking behind Topaz Mountain, giving the world that surreal pinkish glow. *Perfect mood lighting*, he thought as he trekked down the driveway to his dad's place. He really should stop at home and clean himself up, but if he did, he'd risk missing dinner. Besides, maybe after dinner, he could convince Jessa to soak in the hot tub with him. Just the two of them. Under the stars...

He almost broke into a jog as he veered to the left and over the small rise to Luis's house. Jessa's truck sat out front, but there was another truck, too. One he didn't recognize. Wouldn't be right of him to barge in on dinner if they had company, but he couldn't turn around, either. Not knowing Jessa was there. Not when the thought of seeing her made him ache like this.

So he hurried up the porch steps and pushed through the door without knocking. "Hello?" he called inside the entryway, where he stopped to stomp the dirt off his boots.

"Lance?" Jessa careened around the corner and hurried down the hallway.

"Hey." He let his eyes drink her in, the soft hair that framed her face, the smooth skin that had felt so soft against his lips. She wore tight tapered jeans and a long white shirt, casual, but seductive in his eyes. She could be wearing a snowsuit right now and she'd look seductive. God, he could come apart just looking at her.

But then he noticed the thing at her feet. He blinked. A small black-and-white pig. On a harness and leash? "Uh. What's that?"

Jessa looked down as though just remembering she was taking a pig for a walk. *In* the house. "Her name's Ilsa."

"*Ilsa?*" He laughed.

"Yeah," she shot back. "What's wrong with that?"

"Just seems like there's something more suitable. Like Ham Bone. Or Pork Chop. Or Bacon," he said, eyeing the critter like he was hungry.

"Don't even think about it." Jessa scooped the thing up into her arms. "I didn't know you were coming," she said, glancing nervously over her shoulder.

"I wanted to see you." More like *had* to see her. Had to touch her again. Had to kiss her. He closed the distance between them and skimmed his hand along her lower back, nudging her—and the pig—closer.

A pink glow lit up her face just like the sunset outside.

Voices drifted from the kitchen but he tuned them out. He didn't care who was in there. He needed a minute alone with Jessa. Now if he could just figure out how to ditch the pig...

"Lance..." Jessa's breathing had quickened, and her eyes seemed as hungry as he felt. But then she glanced back over her shoulder again. So distracted. He'd have to take care of that right now. First, he gently took the pig out of her hands. The thing squealed and squirmed as he set it on the floor, then it took off down the hall. Which was fine with him. They could discuss the pig later.

"I missed you," he said, sliding his hand up her back and pressing her against him, meeting her lips in the middle. The need for more of her swelled, threatening to rip him apart. He kissed her harder and her mouth opened to his, a small moan stirring the lust he felt into a fervor.

"Wait," Jessa gasped against his lips. She pushed back. "Just hold on. We have to talk."

Right. Talk. He suppressed the urge to take her hand and tow her back to him. They probably should discuss what happened between them. He still hadn't apologized for abandoning her in the kitchen. "Sorry I had to run out on you," he said. "I didn't want to. Believe me." If she needed proof, he'd be happy to offer it. All she had to do was feel him against her to know how much he wanted her.

"It's fine," she said brushing him off with another glance toward the kitchen.

Right. The company. The voices. They'd go. In a minute. But first he had more to say. He had to tell her what her words meant to him. How they'd given him a second wind. "I wanted to thank you for—"

"You don't have to thank me," she interrupted quickly. "But I think we should talk about—"

"We can talk about it later. Right now, there's something you need to know."

"Jessa!" The call came from the kitchen and knocked the air out of Lance. That voice. He hadn't noticed when it was subdued and murmuring, but now...

No. No way. That couldn't be Lucas.

But his brother appeared in the hallway. No longer a kid, instead a man with familiar blue-gray eyes. His hair was shorter and neater than he used to keep it, and he looked clean-cut for a rancher.

Shock bolted Lance's heart to his ribs. What the fuck was he doing here?

He said nothing as his brother walked toward them. It'd been so long since he'd seen him. Since they'd agreed it would be best if he cut ties and never came home...

"This is what I was trying to tell you," Jessa whispered. Or maybe she didn't whisper. Maybe Lance just couldn't hear past the blood pounding in his ears.

"Surprise," Lucas said with a healthy apprehension weighting his eyes. They'd agreed he wouldn't come back. It was best for Luis that way. Best for Levi. For the family.

The shock of seeing him started to thaw. "What're you doing here?" he asked, carefully controlling his tone. He didn't want to startle Jessa, but what the hell? No warning or anything. He'd just decided to show up after years of being away?

Lucas and Jessa shared a look. They *shared* a look. And suddenly, he had a bad feeling.

"I called him," Jessa said firmly. "And Levi. I asked them to come home."

He didn't look at her. Couldn't. His eyes were locked on Lucas. "You should've told me." He wasn't sure if he was saying it to his brother or to the woman he'd slept with.

Lucas stepped up to him. "I didn't have time. Jessa told me she's worried about Dad and I wanted to come as soon as possible."

His head turned slowly, like someone was cranking it click by click, until he was staring at Jessa's worried expression.

"Luis and I had a talk," she said, wringing her delicate hands. "And he said how much he missed Lucas and Levi. Given the incidents he's had lately, I thought it would be nice for them to come."

Nice. She'd thought it'd be nice. Well, she didn't know a damn thing about his family. About what they'd been through. Anger prickled his neck. What the hell had she been thinking? She should've talked to him first.

He faced his brother. "Can you give us a minute?"

Lucas slipped in front of Jessa. It'd been years, but obviously his brother could still recognize when he was pissed.

"Don't blame her. She's trying to help." Lucas seemed unfazed by all of it. But then he'd always been the mellow one. The one who didn't worry, who didn't carry the weight of the damn world on his shoulders. That's why they'd decided it should be him who went away. By the time he was fourteen, Levi had already gotten caught stealing twice. He'd thrown a rock through the ice cream shop's storefront and shattered the whole damn thing. He'd been so angry at Luis, who was always out with a different woman, and he'd taken it out on the town, targeting the places where the women worked.

That's why Levi had gone to the stables that night. He'd seen Luis messing around with the commissioner's wife. So he found some gasoline and a lighter. He hadn't meant to hurt anyone, he'd said later. He was just so angry.

Lance didn't have anger issues, but he was stressed all the time. So he drank. Had two underage tickets under his belt by then. But Lucas...he was too serious for stuff like that. Serious about school. Serious about following the rules. Serious about Naomi.

So they were sure he'd get a slap on the hand. Community service. Maybe house arrest. But they hadn't counted on the judge being the commissioner's golf buddy. It seemed he wanted to punish all of them. When Lance heard they were charging him as an adult he'd tried to beg the judge to reconsider. But the man had dismissed him like he was a stray dog, threatening to have him arrested if he came back.

"It was time for me to come home, anyway," Lucas said quietly, as though he'd resigned himself to whatever consequences this little reunion would bring. "Don't you think? Dad's getting older. I want to be around."

Maybe it *was* time. But he should've had a say in it. They should've discussed this, planned out how it would go. Jessa had taken that away from him. As if she had some right to play the healer for his family. His jaw pulled tight as he stared back at Lucas. "Give. Us. A. Minute."

His brother looked at Jessa.

"It's fine," she said, glaring back at Lance and crossing her arms in a fighter's stance. She wasn't afraid of him and it was a damn good thing because they were going to have a serious chat about her butting into his family's business.

Lucas anchored a hand on Jessa's shoulder and gave it a squeeze before walking away. Seeing him touch her like they had some kind of bond didn't do much to douse the anger.

As soon as his brother disappeared Lance faced her. "You had no right to do this."

"What do you mean I had no right?" she fired back. "This isn't about you, Lance. This is about your father."

Exactly. It was about his father and Luis already carried enough guilt. How'd she think he'd feel when he learned Levi had started that fire because he'd caught him in the stables with someone else's wife?

"Do you know what Luis told me?" Jessa asked.

It must've been a rhetorical question because she hardly paused.

"He told me that his biggest regret in life is not making things right with Lucas. Did you know that? Do you know how much it tears him apart?"

He almost laughed, it was so absurd. That was nothing compared to what he'd regret if he found out the truth. "You don't understand." The anger had drained away, but he tried to hold on to it. Anger was easier than the other emotions he was going to have to deal with now that the past stared him in the face. "You have no idea what you've done."

"What *I've* done?" she repeated, her face hardened with indignation. "What I've done is brought your brothers home. And you know what? When your father saw Lucas walk through that door, he was so overjoyed he cried. He *cried*."

That revelation freed the guilt. It flowed out, overpowering everything else. He'd done what he thought was best at the time. They all had. Hell, they were only kids. The day they'd hauled Lucas away, they'd all changed, each trying to atone for it in their own way. Luis stuck around the ranch more, cooked dinner, helped with homework, all the stuff he'd been too distracted to do before. And Lance and Levi trained, taking out the anguish in the arena as if that could bring back their brother.

But it was too late.

"Lance…" Jessa moved closer, studying him carefully. "Why are you so upset? Don't you want your brothers around? Tell me how this could possibly be a bad thing."

"I can't." They'd never told anyone. They'd tried to protect their father. But there'd be no way to keep the secret now. It would come out. Everything would come out.

"What's up, bro?" Levi bounded down the hall and captured him in a bear hug, lifting him off his feet. Typical. They'd always protected him from ever having to deal with reality. He was the party boy, the fun one. Which was ironic, considering he had more to lose right now than any of them.

"Let's head out to the old watering hole and celebrate the

fam getting back together." Levi slung an arm around him. "What do ya say? Drinks are on me."

Jessa still stared at Lance, her eyes focused and intent, demanding an explanation, but he turned away and clapped his long-lost brother on the back. "As long as you're buying, I'm in."

God knew, he could use a drink right now.

Chapter Sixteen

Well, this is awkward. Jessa sat in the back seat of Lance's extended cab, wedged between Levi and Lucas. No one had said a word since they'd gotten in the truck, the jovial tone of the reunion between Luis and his two sons deadened by the eldest son's stony-faced silence.

For the life of her, Jessa couldn't figure out what she'd done wrong. Lucas and Levi had obviously simply needed an invitation to come home. When she'd called them, both of them had been concerned about their father. Both had said how much they'd missed him. *And* Lance, for that matter. Levi had gotten away from Oklahoma as soon as he could and Lucas had picked him up at the airport in Denver. Now all three Cortez boys were together with their father and no one was saying a damn word.

She drummed her fingers on her thigh. She'd had a feeling Lance would be surprised to see his brothers, but this is not how she'd pictured things going. Lucky for them, she'd always been good at breaking the ice.

Scooting forward, she peered between the seats at Lance and Luis. "So how was your training today?" she asked politely.

"Fine," he muttered.

"Training?" Levi, who was sitting behind his oldest brother, ruffled Lance's hair. "Decided not to hang up the spurs yet, eh, old man?"

"Nope." Jessa watched Lance's grip tighten on the steering wheel.

"So, Lucas," she turned to him, hoping to steer the conversation away from Lance's retirement status, which had definitely been a sore subject lately. Having Levi poke fun at him would not end well. "How are things at the McGowen Ranch?" she asked, as if she had some sort of clue as to who the McGowens were and what they did on their ranch.

"Good," he answered dutifully, but he was eyeing Lance as though watching for an impending explosion.

Another silence fell like a heavy blanket, smothering her visions of a happy reunion for a father and his sons. Yes, okay, she was a bit idealistic, but she'd imagined chatter and laughter, not a wary distance. Even Levi, who was always the life of the party, seemed subdued, staring out the window like he wanted to avoid eye contact with everyone else.

Caving under the weight of their solemnity, she remained silent, pulled out her phone, and dashed off a text to Cassidy, Naomi, and Darla.

Meet me at the Tumble Inn ASAP. In case they didn't feel the urgency, she added a *911*. Those girls had known the Cortez family longer than she had, *better* than she did, considering Naomi had seriously dated Lucas before the fire. And Levi had been like a brother to Cassidy before her brother Cash had passed away. Maybe they could help her figure out what was going on, because she was not making progress.

Good thing the Tumble Inn was only an eight-minute drive from the ranch or she might have had to start singing to break up the silence. *No one* would want to hear that.

When they arrived at the bar Lance took his sweet time parking, she couldn't help but notice.

They all piled out of the truck like they were about to head into a funeral instead of the lone country western bar in town.

She hadn't been to the Tumble Inn since the whole Cam fiasco, and now she remembered why. A huge banner hung below the sign.

Two-step Night.

Fabulous. Since she was young, Jessa had absolutely no rhythm. Her mother had attempted to put her in ballet, but after she'd knocked into another girl and caused a domino effect of toppling ballerinas during her first recital, she'd walked away from dancing and never looked back. In college, she'd tried to take a ballroom dancing class and had somehow managed to break her partner's foot during the fox-trot, so nowadays she pretty much avoided any establishment that centered around dancing.

The Cortez brothers followed their father to the entrance, but she hung back.

"I let some friends know we were coming," she called. "I'll wait for them out here."

"Sounds good." Levi was the only one who acknowledged she'd said something. "Make sure you save me a dance when you get in there," he called, working his magic charm with a wink and dimpled grin.

The man had no idea what he was asking. "Sure, I'll do that," she lied. Once she got inside, she planned to order a nice, easygoing glass of chardonnay and park it at the bar for the evening. No breaking her friends' feet tonight.

The men disappeared into the bar right as Darla and Cassidy pulled up in Darla's BMW. Naomi was a few minutes behind, probably because she had to find a sitter.

They all congregated in the middle of the parking lot.

"You told us you'd never step foot in this place again," Darla accused. Though she'd had only a few minutes' warning, the woman had somehow managed to primp and change into a low-cut shirt that displayed her cleavage.

"I didn't exactly have a choice," Jessa said, gathering them in closer. "Lucas and Levi came home and—"

"What?" Naomi interrupted, suddenly appearing pale. "What do you mean Lucas came home?"

Jessa took in the shocked—no, make that horrified— look on her friend's face. Guilt churned her stomach. She should've warned them, but she'd gotten so caught up in the plans, not to mention a crazy week at the shelter. "I called them because of the issues Luis has been having," she half-whispered, watching the doors. "He told me he missed them, so I got in touch and asked them to come home."

"I'm shocked Levi actually listened to you." Cassidy's normally sweet tone had turned bitter.

Oh boy. She really should've thought all of this through. Darla was the only one who didn't seem disturbed by the Cortez family reunion.

The woman elbowed Jessa. "Way to go, girl. About time we got a few hot men back in this town."

Naomi whirled and made a move toward her car. "I'm not going in there."

"You have to!" Jessa caught her arm before she could escape. "It's been horrible since they got home. I thought I was helping but ever since Lance saw his brothers, they're hardly speaking to each other. I don't understand."

"They went through a lot," Naomi informed her, wrenching out of her grasp. "We all went through a lot when Lucas got sent away." Emotion trembled through the words.

But that was a long time ago. It wasn't too late to work things out, even for Naomi and Lucas. Once she got over the shock of it, surely she'd be glad he was back. "I need some support in there, girls." She had no idea what to do. How to make everything better. She needed backup.

"I'm in." Cassidy sighed. "As long as there are margaritas involved." She patted Naomi's arm sympathetically. "It's not like we'll have to talk to them. In an hour this place'll be packed."

"Yeah. We can hang out on the dance floor," Darla offered with a wicked gleam in her eyes. "Or on the mechanical bull."

"I'm not going near that thing." Jessa would leave bull riding to the professionals. "Besides, we'll be too busy to dance. We have to figure out how to get these guys talking so they can get past their issues for Luis's sake." All the man wanted was for his family to be together, and thanks to Lance's rude entrance, they couldn't even give him that.

Before anyone else tried to bail, she swung one arm around Cassidy and the other around Naomi.

"I don't know how I'll face Lucas," Naomi said through a steady exhale. "I mean, I haven't seen him since he was arrested..."

"Can't blame him for not coming back." Darla followed them across the parking lot. "The whole town wanted to hang him."

Maybe back then, but things were different now. Jessa held open the door for everyone. "I never knew him that well, but he seems like a great guy." He'd been so polite to her on the phone, kind even. A little soft-spoken. Thoughtful with words.

"He was always a great guy," Naomi said, pausing before the open door as though gathering courage. "That's why I never believed he'd set the fire."

"It was years ago." Cassidy took Naomi's arm and led her inside. "And things were bad before the fire. They all fell apart after their mom left."

Was that all it was? Were they all still dealing with the resentment of their abandonment? Jessa stepped in behind her friends and let her eyes adjust to the dim lighting. Most of the tables were empty, as it was still early for the party crowd. Thankfully, no one was out on the dance floor, though music played in the background.

The Cortez men had all claimed stools at the bar, sipping their beers while seeming to avoid eye contact.

"Look at them," Jessa grumbled. "After years apart, they have nothing to say to each other?"

"Sure they do," Darla said, sashaying her way to the bar. "Men just need a little help getting the conversation going, that's all."

Cassidy followed Darla, but Jessa had to practically push Naomi. When they finally made it to the bar, her friend slipped behind her as though searching for protection and stared at the floor.

"Well, well, well," Darla said, her voice shattering the

icy silence. "It sure is good to see you boys back in town." She pulled up a stool next to Levi and plopped down. "My friends and I would like a round of margaritas, Rico," she called to the bartender.

"You got it, *mi bombon*."

Ah yes. Every male in town thought of Darla as their chocolate sweetheart. She charmed them all, just like she was doing now, chatting easily with Levi and Lance about the ale they were drinking.

Not everyone was listening, though. Lucas had turned around and was staring steadily over Jessa's shoulder.

"Naomi?" He rose slowly and bypassed Jessa.

Offering Naomi courage with a smile, she stepped aside to retrieve her margarita from the bar and to give them a minute, but stayed close enough that she overheard the nerves in her friend's tone.

"Hi, Lucas," Naomi almost whimpered.

"Hi," he murmured with this sort of awed expression on his face. It was the sweetest thing Jessa had seen since Lance had told her she was beautiful. Since he'd looked at her the way Lucas was looking at Naomi now, like he wanted to take in all the details and remember them. Like he was powerless to look away.

That lost-in-the-moment look only proved that the Cortez men might be made of steel but underneath that, they had this raw passion that ran much deeper than their brooding stares. She should know. She'd felt that passion seep into her skin and set her whole body ablaze...

Levi appeared in front of her. "How about that dance?" he asked, holding out a hand like a true Southern gentleman.

"Oh. Um." Her cheeks pulsed. "Actually, no one's even out on the dance floor."

"So?" She remembered that grin from her high school summers. The grin no girl could deny...

Jessa glanced at Lance. He'd set down his beer and was watching her, his jaw set in a hard, angry line.

And wasn't that just typical? He seemed to be pissed off at her. Again. It'd become a pattern with him. One minute he was ravaging her up against a wall and the next he was glaring at her in a pout. Well, screw that. She faced his younger brother. "You know what? I'd love to dance with you." He was fun, after all. And wearing boots, which would hopefully protect his feet from any significant damage.

"You're not gonna regret this," he promised, leading her to the dance floor.

She laughed. "Let's hope *you* don't regret it." She probably should've had him sign a waiver or something.

"Not possible," he insisted, taking her hand in his and guiding her in front of him. He wrapped one arm around her waist and drew her close, but thankfully left a respectable distance intact.

The song was slow and twangy. Surprisingly, Levi made it very easy to follow his moves.

"You're a good dancer," she said, grinning up at him as he swayed her around the floor.

"I find that dancing only helps my chance at winning a woman's heart," he replied good-naturedly.

"I find that dancing only increases *my* potential for a lawsuit," she confided.

He laughed. "Not when you're dancing with the right person." In perfect rhythm with the music, he twirled her, then reeled her back in and dipped her low. With her head upside down, she caught a view of Lance, who still sat at the bar, but he'd turned around and made it no secret that he was watching her. The dangerous look on his face dried up her mouth.

Levi pulled her back up and resumed their graceful two-step.

Not even the look on Lance's face could deter her from finishing this dance. It actually gave her the perfect opportunity to figure out what was going on between the brothers. She smiled at Levi. "Things seem a little tense between you guys."

"Do they?" he asked, spinning her again.

"Yeah. Did you all have some big fight or something?" she asked innocently. They must've had some kind of falling out. If she could figure out what happened, maybe she could help them get past it.

His charming grin dimmed. "Let's just say some of us have moved on from the past and others are stuck in it."

"You mean—"

"Mind if I cut in?" Lance had left his post at the bar and somehow sneaked up behind her.

"Course not," Levi said, opening his arms to let her go. "She's all yours."

There was never a truer statement spoken in the English language. Seeing Lance, hearing him ask to dance with her, kindled that familiar music in her heart, and yes, right now she did belong to him.

He stepped against her, resting that large skilled hand on the very small of her back, pressing her close to him, not leaving any of the respectable space intact. His other hand swallowed hers, but instead of holding it loosely the way Levi had, Lance threaded his fingers through hers and fused their palms together.

The heat from his body seemed to flow into hers as he

moved against her, sparking her lower half until she wasn't sure she could keep her feet from stumbling.

The song was something sweet and light. Lance moved with the music effortlessly, not carefree and entertaining like Levi had been but deliberate and precise.

There were a few other couples on the floor, but now they seemed so far away under the power of Lance holding her.

"I can't stand seeing you dance with my brother," he said against her hair, as though he was too afraid to look into her eyes.

Jessa could hardly find her voice. "Your brother was the only one talking to me." Somehow the words managed to hold a good amount of attitude, which was impressive, seeing as how all she wanted to do was melt into him.

"I was surprised," he said, pulling back to look at her. His eyes were serious but they held glimmers of light. "Shocked. And I wasn't the only one." He turned to gaze across the room to the table where Lucas and Naomi sat.

"I didn't think about that," she murmured. "I was only thinking about your dad. About how much he seemed to regret what happened with Lucas. I wanted to help."

He smiled, and that smile had the power to change the world. Or at least her world.

"I know," he said, sliding his hand up her back, caressing in a way that made her want to arch into him. "And things'll be fine." He said it like he might be trying to convince himself.

"Why aren't things fine now?" she asked.

His hand slipped low to her waist again, guiding her as they swayed to the music. "It's complicated."

"Families usually are." Or at least, that's how she imagined a family would be. "But even with the complications,

I'd give anything to have a family." She'd always longed for that, a place where she fit. And he might not be willing to tell her any secrets, but she'd give up all of hers if it helped him smooth things over with his family.

Lance stopped moving and gazed down at her. "Don't you have your mom?"

"She's all I have." Not that she could complain, but... "I always wanted brothers and sisters." She used to beg her mother to have another baby. Or adopt.

He pulled her close again, and now his gaze strayed. "Yeah, well, having siblings isn't always easy. Trust me."

"I do trust you." But he didn't trust her. Lance was good at kissing her, touching her, and, let's face it, giving her more pleasure than she'd experienced with any man, ever. But when it came to trusting...that wasn't exactly his strength. "No matter what it is, you guys can work through—"

"Jessa?" Cassidy tapped her on the shoulder. "Can I have a word with you real quick?"

"Oh." She hesitated. They were finally getting somewhere with a real conversation. "Right now?" she asked, hoping her friend would give her a minute.

"Yeah," Cassidy said apologetically. She leaned closer. "We have a situation."

The gravity in her tone forced Jessa to pry herself away from the luxurious warmth of Lance's body. "Be right back?"

He nodded and reluctantly let go of her hand.

Cassidy pulled her away, in the direction of the ladies' room.

She almost had to jog to keep up. "What's wrong?"

"Naomi. We need to get her out of here."

"Why—"

As they neared the ladies' room, the sound of sobbing echoed.

Jessa turned the jog into a sprint. "Good God, what happened?"

"Not exactly sure," Cassidy said as they pushed through the door.

Jessa ran to the open stall and found Naomi sitting on a vacant stool with her face buried in her hands. "I can't do this," she wailed. "I'm sorry. I wasn't prepared to see him."

Lucas. Jessa sank to her knees in front of her friend. "Oh, honey. I'm the one who's sorry. I should've told you he was coming." She knew how much Naomi still thought about him. She should've prepared her for this.

"I loved him so much," Naomi sniffled. "We never had any closure. And he's the same. Kind and thoughtful." She swiped at the tears on her face. "God, I could've married him. We would've been happy. Instead I made a mess of my life with Mark."

"You didn't make a mess of anything," Cassidy insisted, squeezing into the stall with them. "You have a beautiful daughter."

"Exactly," Jessa agreed, squeezing Naomi's hand. This had obviously been a bit too much for her. "Don't worry. We'll take you home. You don't have to stay."

They could stop by Darla's place and calm her down with some wine and chocolate. That always seemed to do the trick when one of them was upset about something.

"Okay," Naomi said, tearing off a piece of toilet paper to dry her eyes. "Just give me a minute to get myself together."

"Take your time, honey." Jessa sighed, her heart aching. Looked like a conversation with Lance would have to wait.

Chapter Seventeen

Lance moseyed over to where Lucas sat at a table. Last he saw, Naomi had been sitting with him, but she seemed to have disappeared. "Hey." He pulled out the chair across from his brother. He'd seen him only a few times since he'd left town. They'd met in Denver, just for a quick lunch or dinner if one of them was going through, but they'd always tried to avoid the subject they now had to discuss. And after they'd avoided it so long, he almost didn't know how to bring it up. "Where'd Naomi go?" he asked. Wouldn't hurt to keep avoiding it a little longer.

"Not sure." Lucas stared blankly at the full beer bottle that sat in front of him. "Didn't realize how much I'd missed her until I saw her."

"Yeah, I wondered about that." Couldn't have been easy for Naomi, either. Back in high school the two of them were pretty hot and heavy, and then one day Lucas was just gone. From all of their lives.

"She looks good," his brother said, taking a drink.

"You never ended up with anyone else." And Lucas could've found someone by now. He didn't seem to carry the baggage Lance did, even after prison. He wasn't bitter about any of it. Their mother leaving, the heavy-handed sentence he'd received...

"I've gone out with plenty of women," Lucas said, staring at his hands.

Guilt bore down on Lance once again. If they hadn't thought up that plan to protect Levi, he had no doubt Naomi and Lucas would be together right now.

"Wasn't in the cards," his brother said with a shrug.

"Because we wrote the cards." He'd never regretted it more than he did right now. When Lucas was gone, he didn't have to think about it, didn't have to face the consequences of covering for Levi. "I'm glad you're back." That surprised him. The shock had worn off and now, sitting across from him, he could see having Lucas around again. Once they waded through the shitstorm that would surely hit.

"Nice try." His brother took another sip.

"I wasn't expecting to see you. But Jessa's right. Maybe it's time." Maybe he wouldn't be able to move forward until he'd dealt with some things from his past. Something about dancing with Jessa, kissing Jessa, making love to Jessa, made him want to move forward.

"I'm not staying long."

That might be his fault. "You can stay. We'll figure out how to tell Dad everything. We'll fix it." Or at least they could try.

Lucas stared past him. "It's not worth going back. Not now."

One hour ago, Lance'd thought the same thing. But Jessa had changed his mind. "He should know the truth."

"And what would that mean for Levi?"

Lance glared over at their younger brother, who now had yet another woman out on the dance floor. What did that make? Four in the span of a half hour? Their little secret obviously didn't weigh on him. Likely because they'd always protected him. He'd never dealt with the consequences for anything.

"What would the truth mean for you?" Lance asked, looking at Lucas directly. It'd mean he'd be exonerated. At least in the eyes of the people who still despised him, who still held the fire against him. Hell, he'd noticed the whispering when people had started to trickle into the bar. The pointing. They'd all taken tables far away from Lucas—the hellion who'd burned down the stables and managed to kill the town's dreams of ever hosting another rodeo.

People in small towns like this held grudges. They wouldn't forget.

"We should keep things the way they are." Lucas had never been one to stir up trouble. "I'll stay for a while, spend some time with Dad, and lay low. Then I'll go back to work."

Except Lance couldn't get Jessa's words out of his head. She'd give anything to have a family—to have siblings— and his were right here, but he couldn't stay connected with them. "We have plenty of work around the ranch. Been leaning toward starting our own stock contracting operation." Once he retired, it would be a natural next step. "There'd be a place for you, too." Given that Lucas had gotten the McGowens' operation out of financial ruin and made it one of the most lucrative in the region, his brother could probably run things a hell of a lot better than he could.

Lucas smirked at him. "No one in this town wants me back. You know it as well as I do."

"That would change if everyone knew the truth."

"Then they'd go after Levi. That's why we protected him. And Dad." He leaned forward, his eyes never looking so much like their father's. "I knew what I was doing, Lance. And I'd do it again, too."

Of course he would. But if he had it to do over again, Lance wouldn't let him. He wouldn't let someone take the fall for something he didn't do. For something he never would've done. "I think we should tell Dad at least. Even if no one else ever knows."

"Not now. Not this trip." His brother looked over at their father, who was arguing with Gil about something. "Maybe I'll pop back in before winter for a few days." He shifted his gaze to Lance. "Jessa seems to think something's not right with him."

"He's fine." Lance brushed aside his concerns. "Just getting ornerier in his old age, that's all. He seemed happy to see you—"

"Look at you guys." Levi bounded over and grabbed a chair, turning it backward, then straddling it. "Why aren't you dancing? Plenty of women to go around."

"Not really in the mood to dance," Lance shot back. Unless it was with Jessa, but she'd been gone a while now.

"So..." Levi eyed him. "You and Jessa, huh? Should've picked up on that earlier. I wouldn't have asked her to dance if I'd known."

Nope. Not going there with Levi. He'd been gone all these years, had hardly called at all, and now he thought they could talk about Lance's personal life. They had a hell of a lot to work through before they got there. "There's nothing to know," he said with a look that would hopefully shut him down.

"Right," Levi mocked. "I saw how you were dancing with her. It was a lot different from the way I danced with her."

"Maybe you suck at dancing." He attempted to slip a warning into his tone.

"I definitely don't suck." Confidence had never been one of Levi's weaknesses.

"Are you two together?" he pressed.

"No." Technically they were not together. Not that they'd had any time to discuss their status...

"Do you want to be together?"

None of your damn business. But he went with the easier answer. "No."

"Sure seems like there's something there to me," Levi taunted. His brother had never known when to quit.

"We hooked up once. It was nothing." Classic code for *I'm not discussing this with you.* Especially when he hadn't even discussed it with her.

"So you wouldn't mind if I asked her out?" Levi clearly knew the answer to that question, judging from the smart-ass grin on his face. "'Cause she was into me once. We made out behind the barn the summer of our sophomore year, you know."

"Actually, Levi, it was behind your garage."

Shit. Lance checked over his shoulder and sure enough, Jessa stood behind them, no longer looking soft and sweet. Nice of Lucas to alert him to the fact that the woman they were talking about stood a mere four feet away. How long had she been there?

She stayed where she was, keeping her distance from the table. "I just came to tell you I have to go." The words sounded hollow. "See you later," she said to no one in particular, then spun and met Naomi, Cassidy, and Darla near the doors.

"You might want to follow her," Levi said, clapping Lance on the shoulder. "She seems pretty pissed."

Thanks to him. Instead of indulging his brother's arrogance, he leaned back into the chair. "She's fine." He hoped. Not much he could do about it after he'd told them he wasn't interested. He'd talk to her later. Right now... "We have to figure out how we're gonna tell Dad the truth about the fire."

That got Levi's attention. His back went straight as a fence post. "What do you mean?" Yeah, now he wasn't playing the funny, spoiled-boy role. He looked worried.

"We're not telling anyone anything," Lucas said, as if that was the end of the discussion.

But it wasn't. Not if Lance had anything to say about it.

* * *

She really should've seen that coming.

Jessa tuned out her friends' chatter and sipped her wine, fighting to keep her expression neutral. Difficult, considering the humiliation still burned inside. Of course Lance wasn't interested in her. She'd known that in her head. To be fair, her judgment had been severely compromised by that heated passion they'd shared in the kitchen, but still. This was Lance Cortez. Self-professed commitment-a-phobe. So it was silly that a tiny seed of hope had embedded itself so deeply in the overly fertile lands of her heart. Silly and not a mistake she would make again. Lance seemed to excel in sending mixed signals, but she wasn't up for games anymore. And she would not wait around for a man to figure out what he wanted.

"How was it seeing Levi again?" Darla asked Cassidy. They'd all gotten settled back at the Chocolate Therapist, Naomi squished between Jessa and Cassidy on the comfy couch.

"He hardly said two words to me." Cassidy laughed. "I think he's afraid of me."

"He hasn't changed at all," Naomi chimed in. "He was always the party boy. Always the center of attention. Never wanted to deal with anything real."

Though Cassidy was a few years younger than them, Jessa had always wondered about her and Levi. At one time, he'd been so close to her family. "You two never dated?" she asked. Out of everyone here, she had the least background information, seeing as how she'd been around only in the summer.

"God, no." Cassidy's nose wrinkled with disgust. "I thought Levi was hot. Like every other girl in town. But Cash wouldn't let me near him. He was over at our place all the time. Especially after his mom took off. But after the accident..." The words trailed off.

"You want my opinion, I think he took Cash's death hard." Darla leaned over and topped off all of their glasses. "It seemed like he blamed himself."

Cassidy's expression darkened. "It wasn't his fault. It's the sport. It shouldn't even be legal." Since her brother had been killed during a competition, Cassidy despised bull riding, though on a normal night—a sober night—she rarely talked about it.

"You okay, Jessa?" Naomi asked her. "You're awfully quiet." Her sweet friend happened to be doing smashingly well after a potent elixir that consisted of prosecco and lavender liqueur.

"I'm great," she fibbed. She didn't need a chorus of *I told you so*'s ringing out all around her.

"Sure looked like you and Lance were having a *wonderful* time," Darla mentioned with a probing arch of her eyebrows.

"Yeah," Cassidy agreed. "Things were looking pretty hot between you two on the dance floor."

She evaded all of their curious stares with a long, savoring sip of wine.

"Of course they were hot," Naomi said with a giggle. "Once you have sex with someone, you tend to dance a little differently." Her eyes went wide and she slapped a hand across her mouth.

"Sex?" Darla repeated.

"Sex?" Cassidy echoed.

Well. Apparently it was harder to keep secrets at the Cortez Ranch than she'd thought. Calmly, Jessa set down her wineglass. "He told you?" she asked Naomi, wishing her voice didn't sound so strange. It was one thing for her to be humiliated in private, but now his rejection was about to go public.

"No." Rounding her eyes apologetically, Naomi rested a hand on her leg. "He didn't tell me. I figured it out and he didn't deny it."

That was *so* much better.

"Oh my God!" Darla wailed. "I can't believe you've been holding out on us!" She scooted to the edge of her seat as though the suspense was killing her. "When? Where? How?"

"How?" Jessa rolled her eyes. "*You* of all people know how it works, Darla."

Her friend laughed. "Truer words."

"But we *do* need details," Cassidy urged impatiently.

"Fine." They'd never let her get out of there until she spilled her guts. Might as well get it over with. "We were in his kitchen. *Talking.* And..." The images of him holding her body flashed. She couldn't stop them. They took her over...

"And?" Darla prompted.

Jessa sighed. "And it just happened. One minute we were talking. The next kissing. Then..." She let them fill in the blank.

"In the kitchen?" Darla mock-whined. "I love kitchen sex!"

"Pretty hot," Naomi agreed. "Not that I would remember. It's been years for me, ladies," she said a bit sloppily. "I mean *years.*"

"Okay, honey. Maybe we should take a little break from this." Cassidy slipped Naomi's drink out of her hand and set it on the coffee table. "So are you two together, then?" she asked Jessa. "Because it sure looked like it."

"No." She steadied the tremble out of her voice. "We are *definitely* not together. He doesn't have feelings for me." She'd simply walked in on him at a vulnerable moment and they'd both let down their guards.

"How do you know he doesn't have feelings for you?" Naomi asked too loudly. "Because I've known him forever and I have to say...he looks different when he talks about you."

"No. Trust me." Jessa tried to laugh, but it felt more like a gag. "I overheard him tell his brothers he doesn't have feelings for me. So..."

"Are you serious?" Cassidy nearly spilled her drink.

"What an ass," Darla said, looking truly pissed on her behalf.

"I doubt he would tell his brothers if he *did* have feelings for you." Naomi reached for her glass again, her glare warning Jessa not to take it away. "It's not like they're close or anything. You saw how they were acting tonight."

"Maybe not, but we all know how Lance is." Hell, he'd told her himself how much he loathed the prospect of committed relationships. "You're the one who told me to avoid this in the first place." Then she'd thought maybe she really did simply want a one-night stand. Something easy, uncommitted. But that hadn't worked for her. Because now she knew what it could be like with Lance, how he could touch her and satisfy her and how his gaze could pierce her heart. She knew, but she couldn't have him. Lesson learned.

"Wow." Cassidy shook her head slowly back and forth. Being as busy as she was, working two jobs and going to nursing school, she didn't have a lot of her own drama. But she always confessed to loving other people's drama. "So now what're you going to do?"

"Nothing." Jessa shrugged, as though it would really be that easy to move on. "It's fine. It was fun and everything, but I'm not looking for someone like Lance, anyway." Besides, he'd gotten what he wanted. Now he'd probably leave her alone.

"Well you can't *stay* there," Darla scoffed. "For God's sake, here you are doing him a favor and he totally takes advantage of the situation."

"It's not his fault." She wasn't some naïve teenager. She'd wanted it. She'd wanted him. And the sad truth was, she still did. Even hearing those words play back in her head. That's why she had to leave the ranch. She couldn't see him every day. Not the way her soul seemed to crackle to life whenever he was near.

No. She had to walk away. Ever since she'd gone to stay

with Luis, she'd felt like she was part of a family, but it wasn't real. "You're right." She took in a breath of courage. "I need to move back home. Lucas and Levi can help out now, keep an eye on Luis."

"Exactly." Darla refilled her wineglass. "If Lance can't see what a treasure you are, he doesn't deserve you anyway. If you ask me, the best one out of that bunch is Lucas."

She had a point. While Lance seemed suspicious and closed off and Levi was capricious, Lucas was serious and quiet, but also tender, given what she'd seen when he'd been with Naomi earlier. "He really seems like a good man," she said to Naomi. "Maybe you two could reconnect..." Someone had to find a happy ending in this whole thing. And no one deserved it more than Naomi. Not after what she'd been through with her ex.

"No." Her expressive green eyes teared up again. "He's only here for a short time. Then he said he's headed back to the McGowens' place." She blotted her eyes with the sleeve of her shirt. "He seems happy. Like he's built a good life for himself down there."

A good life, but maybe not the best life. From the way he'd looked at Naomi, Jessa could swear he'd give up everything to be with her. "He wouldn't want to come back?" she asked. "Even to be with Luis?"

"He's convinced no one in town would want him back here." Naomi sighed. "Not after everything that happened."

"But that was years ago," Cassidy said. "Surely everyone's over it by now."

"Ha." Darla rolled her eyes. "Not around here. They wouldn't trust him. They'd be watching his every move. Sorry, honey. But I don't blame him for not wanting to come home."

"It's okay." Naomi finished off her drink. "It's not like we even know each other anymore."

"Except you still feel a connection to him." Jessa didn't usually resort to stating the obvious, but how could Naomi give up that easily?

A smile brought life to Naomi's eyes. "He was my first love. So I'll probably always feel connected to him."

"That's exactly why you should give it a chance," Jessa argued.

"You watch too many Hallmark movies," Darla said in her dry way.

"Maybe I do." But those stories kept her heart searching for something real and true. And not just for herself, either. "I think if you have a chance at finding true love, you should take it." No matter what. While the rest of them rolled their eyes and laughed in their *Oh, Jessa* way, she studied Naomi. She had no doubt the woman was scared. She'd been burned in the worst way possible, and now she didn't want to even consider the possibility that the man she loved might still be in love with her, too.

That was okay, though, because Jessa wasn't afraid. She had no problem launching her own secret investigation into the possibility. She had plenty of experience with these things. All she had to do was talk to Lucas.

While she might be surrounded by cynics, she still believed. No matter what happens in her own life, a true romantic never gives up on love.

Chapter Eighteen

Jessa zipped up her duffel and did a quick sweep around the room. She'd managed to shower, get dressed, and pack her things all within twenty minutes. The voices and breakfast noises from downstairs had lit quite the fire under her.

From the sound of things, all three brothers were downstairs with their father.

Levi had crashed in the other main floor bedroom of Luis's house and Lucas had stayed at Lance's place, she found out after she finally made it home around one o'clock in the morning.

Not home.

This was not her home. Luis was not her father. And Lance, while a good lover, was not boyfriend material. So, yes. It was time to go. She had to do this fast. Like ripping off a piece of medical tape that had gotten tangled in her hair while she was attempting to bandage a wounded squirrel with a major attitude problem. It'd happened to her only three times, but it hurt every time. She'd learned from experience, the faster you ripped, the faster you got through the pain.

Bravely, she stepped into her flip-flops before kneeling down to clip Ilsa into her harness. "Time to go home, lil' sweetie." She patted the pig's head affectionately. At least she wasn't going home alone. "We'll have so much fun. We can make popcorn and watch movies. You'll love it." Holding the leash in one hand, she hoisted her bag onto her shoulder. Eventually she'd have to come back for Ilsa's crate, but she wasn't about to ask for help loading her car.

Keeping her spine straight under the guise of confidence, she walked regally down the narrow staircase with her adorable little piggy and halted in the kitchen.

The men were all there together, and they were four peas in a pod. It wasn't their looks so much as their mannerisms, the way they ate, the way they sat hunched slightly, laid back and comfortable. She was glad to see they weren't silent strangers anymore, but talking easily about the ranch.

"I can help get things started," Lucas was saying. "At least from a distance. If you need me to consult on any purchases or—"

"Oh, hey, Jessa." Levi was the first one to notice her.

Lance straightened and turned around.

She looked through him. "So, the fumigator people let me know that my house is done." She gripped the suitcase strap tightly in a fist. "Which means Ilsa and I can move back home and you guys can have the place to yourselves again."

Lance's chin dipped forward slightly as he studied her from across the room. She didn't let her gaze settle in his.

"Thanks for letting me stay, Luis." She quickly led Ilsa over and planted a kiss on the man's cheek.

"Not a word about it." He reached up and pulled her into a half hug that dangerously weakened her resolve. "It's great having you here, Jessa," the man said, cutting a stern look at his firstborn. "Don't be a stranger, now."

"Why don't you stay for breakfast?" Lucas offered, rising to pull out another chair for her.

She swallowed hard. The threatening tears heated her throat. "Actually, I should get going so I can drop off my things at home before I head to the shelter." She turned before they could read any trace of sadness on her face. "But I'm sure I'll see everyone soon." Without a more formal goodbye, she stooped to pick up the pig and walked out, keeping her head low as she made her way down the porch steps. "Here we go." She opened the driver's-side door and settled a snorting, grunting Ilsa on the passenger seat. As she loaded her bag into the back, the screen door banged open behind her.

She didn't turn around. Didn't have to. She could feel Lance behind her, feel him looking at her. Unable to face him, she climbed into the truck next to Ilsa and slammed the door shut. But the damn window was open, and before she could peel out he leaned in to gaze at her with those perceptive silvery eyes. "I'm sorry," he said, slanting his head convincingly. "For what I said last night. I didn't mean...well...it wasn't what it sounded like."

Jessa kept her gaze centered on the windshield. She couldn't look at him or he'd see everything. "It's fine," she insisted, shoving the key into the ignition. "You don't owe me an apology." Technically, he didn't owe her anything. That one morning in the kitchen, she'd told him she wasn't interested in a relationship, either. She'd pretended to be just as detached as he could be.

"Come on, Jessa." His hand rested on her thigh and sent sparks shooting up her chest. "Levi was being an ass. Okay? I was just trying to shut him up."

"Sure. I get it." She moved her leg so his hand fell away, so he couldn't influence her with his touch. "The kitchen thing was…" Incredible. Impressive. Ravishingly hot. Not that she'd admit it right now. "…Fun. But you don't owe me anything. It just happened. Not like I'm expecting you to change your whole philosophy on relationships or anything." A humorless laugh slipped out. "I mean, I knew what I was signing up for. It was only a one-time thing and you—"

He pressed a finger against her lips to quiet her. "Let me take you out."

"What?"

"On a date." He paused as though the words had surprised him, too, but then he nodded. "Yeah. I want to take you on a date."

"A date?" she repeated through a laugh.

"Yes. Is that so hard to believe? Isn't that what people do when they like someone?"

"People, yes. But you?" As far as she knew, Lance had never *dated* a woman. He'd met women at bars. He'd met women out on the circuit. He'd for sure had women in his hotel rooms. But he didn't date.

"Why not me?" he demanded with that sexy half grin that had gotten her into so much trouble in his kitchen.

"Listen…" She raised a hand to stop him right there. "I know what you're trying to do here."

"Do you?"

"Yes."

He leaned in through the window, moving his face dangerously close to hers. "What am I trying to do, Jessa?"

Seduce her again. He was so damn good at it. Those eyes. They could practically undress her. "Um." She attempted to focus. "You're trying to make me feel better about things. Because let's be honest. I don't do one-night stands. Or one-afternoon stands. I've never done that. So maybe you feel bad and now you think you're obligated to take me on a date, but—"

This time he lowered his lips to hers.

A sharp breath sliced through her lungs, cutting them open. God, it was the best kind of pain...

He pulled back. "Or maybe I just want to take you on a date." His eyes held her in a daze. "Maybe I don't want you to go home. Because that means I won't see you every day. And maybe I *want* to see you. Maybe I was just trying to get my asshole brother off my back. And maybe I really do like you, Jessa. Did you ever think of that?"

One kiss and her lungs were nearly out of air. "That possibility hadn't occurred to me," she whispered, which brought back his grin.

"Please go on a date with me, Jessa. I'll beg if I have to. I'll get down on my knees right outside your truck."

He was teasing her again and damn it, she couldn't *not* smile at the man. "Um..."

He draped his arms over the open window and leaned close again. "Pretty please?" Tenderness crinkled the corners of his eyes. "You have to know I'd never tell Levi anything about how I really feel. We don't have that sort of relationship."

That was true. From what she'd seen, the eldest and youngest Cortez brothers had some competition between them.

"Let me take you out. I'll make it worth the trouble." The

promise in the words matched the one beaming suggestively in his eyes.

"Okay." She relented through a put-out sigh, hopefully covering the sudden rush that had her body humming. "Sure. Why not? I *guess* I'll go on a date with you."

His eyes brightened. "When?"

Yeah, like she had any ability to think through her schedule with her heart racing this way. Let's see... he was leaving on Friday for Vegas, so... "Thursday?" she tried.

His lips quirked with exaggerated disappointment. "That's a long time to wait."

Okay, so it didn't matter what she had going on. Based on her kitchen experience with the man, she'd cancel everything. "Wednesday?"

"Much better," he murmured, giving her lips a long, sexy glance. "I'll pick you up. Six o'clock." He glanced at Ilsa. "Leave Pork Chop at home and wear jeans."

Before she could ask him why, he walked back into the house.

* * *

He could get used to this. Having his brother home. Lance tossed his gloves onto the stable's shelf. He'd been out training this morning, and somehow with Lucas out there, things had gone smoother than they had in a long time. Not that Lance didn't appreciate Tucker, but Lucas had a way with animals. Somehow he'd calmed Wild Willy at the right moments and gotten his engine going when necessary. "Thanks for helping out today," he said, hanging the halter on a nail.

"You've still got it, you know." Lucas paced the length of the bull run, seeming to inspect it. "Same thing that made

Dad great." He ran his hand along the rotted fence railing. "Even with this shitty setup, you've got the perseverance. You can get the win this year."

"Hope so." Lance joined him near the fence, noticing for the first time how shitty it was. "Haven't had much time for keeping things up around here lately." That wasn't his thing. The equipment. The facilities. He wanted to ride. He wanted to raise bulls. "We're gonna need help getting our operation off the ground. Can't do it myself."

"I can make some notes while I'm here. Look around and give you suggestions." Lucas stuffed his hands into the pockets of his Wranglers and strode out of the stables and into the sunlight.

Lance followed. It was a hot day for the elevation. Had to be at least eighty. He slipped off his hat and swiped at the sweat that ran down his temples. "I'd sure appreciate it." He'd appreciate it even more if his brother would stay on at the ranch. He could use the expertise. But he knew when to push and now was not the time.

After latching the stable door, he followed his brother down to the driveway.

"Where's Levi anyway?" Lucas asked. "He could get his lazy ass out here and work on some of the fences for Dad."

"Think he finally went to bed." After Jessa had left the Tumble Inn last night, Lance hadn't seen much of a point in hanging out, so he'd brought Luis and Lucas home. Levi, of course, had wanted to stay. Hadn't come home until dawn, when they were getting breakfast on. Always the life of the party. Some things never changed. Lucas knew that as well as he did. When it came to the ranch, they wouldn't be able to count on Levi for much other than scoring them free booze.

"Things okay with Jessa?" Lucas asked as they neared Lance's place.

Other than the fact that he had no fucking clue what he was doing? "Think so. I'm taking her out on Wednesday." That was a real shocker, even to him. When he'd seen her loading up her bag in her truck, desperation had washed over him. He'd felt like he was losing her. Which was insane considering he'd never had her in the first place. At least not officially.

"You're taking her on a *date*?" his brother repeated with a low whistle. "Wow. So it's serious then."

The mocking tone hoisted Lance's defenses. "It's a date. Not a marriage proposal."

Lucas stopped walking and faced him. "Have you ever met a woman you *wanted* to take on a date?"

Sure. Of course he had. He scrolled through recent history. Okay. So it'd been a while. "Haven't had much time to date," he pointed out. He'd been too busy building a career.

"You don't have much time now," his brother countered. "But you're making time for this date."

Damn Lucas's insightful, philosophical nature. He never could be just another ordinary guy who stuck to safe topics like sports and rodeo gossip. He had a point, though. Lance had never bothered much with real dates. "Jessa's different." Than any other women he'd ever met. Or slept with. She didn't try too hard. Didn't fake it. She was genuine and empathetic. Honest. Real...Damn, he was whipped.

"Seems to me like she's worth a date," Lucas said, grinning as though he'd read all of Lance's thoughts. "Dad already loves her, you can tell that much. She's like the daughter he never had."

"She loves him, too." Took care of him exactly the way a daughter would...

"She worries about him," his brother said pointedly.

That knot of tension pulled in his neck. "And I keep telling her he's fine." If there was something to worry about, Luis would tell him.

Lucas rubbed at his forehead. Something he used to do when he was nervous.

"What?" Lance asked.

His brother gazed past him, out to the mountains. "He has tremors. I noticed during breakfast. His hands shake. Sometimes his head, too."

"He's gotten old." Not to be a dick, but his brother hadn't been around. He didn't know. "His arthritis flares up sometimes. That's all it is." He'd seen the tremors, too. Asked his dad about them, even. "He's almost seventy."

"You sure it's not more than that?"

Before he could answer, Naomi's car bounced up the driveway and parked in front of her house across the way.

The door opened and Gracie jumped out. "Uncle Lance! Uncle Lance!" She sprinted over and launched herself into his arms.

He swung her up into the air and twirled her around before setting her feet back on the ground. "Hey there, Gracie. Where've you been?"

"I was at my art class!" She held out a paper in her hands. "Look! I drew a picture of you riding Wild Willy."

Lance bent to study the paper, gawking at the fatheaded stick figure as though it were a work of art. "Wow." As he stood, he happened to catch a glimpse of Lucas.

His brother stared at Naomi as she walked toward them.

"Who are you?" Gracie asked, pointing a finger at Lucas.

Naomi approached looking downright spooked, so Lance answered for her. "This is my brother. Lucas."

The girl sized him up with a long glare, her lips puckered as though deep in thought. "So you're sort of like my uncle, too?"

That brought a smile to Lucas's face. He knelt in front of her. "Sure. I'd be happy to be your uncle." He stuck out his hand. "It's very nice to meet you, Gracie. Your mom is an old friend of mine."

The girl's eyes went wide. "Did you know my dad, too?"

"Oh no, honey. He didn't." Naomi lied. Mark had been Lucas's best friend in high school. Naomi's face flushed and Lance had never seen her look so flustered. "Why don't you go and get your backpack out of the car. Okay?" She sent the girl off with a light pat. "I'll be over in a minute and we can have a snack."

"Okay!" Gracie shot away from them, bounding over the ground like a happy golden retriever.

Naomi faced them, but she wouldn't look at either one of them. "Sorry about that. She's never met a stranger."

Lance stayed quiet. She definitely wasn't apologizing to him.

His brother stepped closer to her, still looking at her like she was some sort of goddess. Lance almost shook his head. And Lucas thought *he* was pathetic with Jessa.

"It's okay," Lucas said. "I'm glad I got to meet her. She's beautiful. She looks so much like you."

The compliment was met with a cold shoulder. Naomi turned. "I should get going. Gracie is always starving in the afternoon." She started to walk away, but Lance couldn't let her.

"Wait." He hooked a hand onto her shoulder and steered

her back to them. "I was thinking maybe you could sit down with Lucas and show him the books."

Her normally rosy face looked colorless. "Oh."

"He'll be consulting on our stock contracting operation," he went on before she could say no. "Might be good for him to get an idea of how our budget is allocated."

"Sure." It came out in a nervous whoosh of air. "Uh." She stared at the ground. "Yeah. Maybe this afternoon. Just...just stop by whenever." She turned and hurried away.

She hadn't even made it to her door when Lucas punched him in the arm. "Why the hell did you do that?"

Seemed Lucas didn't like people interfering in his love life, either. "It won't kill you two to spend a little time together."

Lucas glanced over at Naomi's house. "Spending time with me might kill *her*, from the looks of things."

Naomi had definitely been rattled. But not because she hated Lucas. "And why do you think that is?" Lance asked in the same mocking tone Lucas had used on him earlier.

"Same reason no one else wants me around here," his brother muttered. The moron.

Lucas turned and started for Lance's house.

Lance followed him up the porch steps. His brother had lost everything because of a decision they'd made when they were kids. He'd lived through the hell of prison time. Of being blackballed by his hometown. If anyone deserved something good, it was Lucas. "She might be worth coming back for."

His brother's back went stiff the way it used to before they'd start throwing punches. "I can't live here under a label. I'm not like you. I don't want to put myself out there for the judgment. Down at the McGowens' place, I have my freedom. I am who I am. Not the kid who screwed up." A small smile reminded Lance of Luis. "And I'm not one of the Cortez brothers. Not the son of Luis Cortez. No offense."

"None taken." Lance got that. Not wanting the labels. Hell, he'd been labeled his whole career. First as a superstar who was following in his great father's footsteps, now as a has-been.

It sounded good, having that freedom. Setting your own expectations instead of trying to live up to everyone else's. For years, the risk of failure had stalked him, driving him to become what the world needed him to be.

And now, it almost felt like it was too late to become anything else.

Chapter Nineteen

So...she was going on a date. Lance was taking her on a *date*. With Ilsa trailing behind her, Jessa pushed through the door of the shelter in a starry-eyed sort of wonder that made everything seem lovely and clean. She hardly noticed the dingy floors or the peeling drywall. The smell of dog food and animals.

She was going on a date!

"Wow, someone's chipper for a Monday morning." Xavier, her night shift guy, was hunched at the computer with his hand plastered to the mouse like he'd been in that exact position all night. Probably playing Dungeons & Dragons or something. Not that she cared. As long as someone was here to answer phones and take care of any animals that came in, he could do whatever he wanted.

Jessa floated over to the desk gracefully—probably looking like Grace Kelly in *High Society*. Well...minus the glamorous dresses, makeup, and heels. But those things weren't practical for taking care of animals and cleaning out kennels. Giving up the fantasy, she plopped down in the chair next to Xavier and pulled Ilsa into her lap. "Can I help it if it's a beautiful morning?" She swept an arm toward the streaked, grimy window. "I mean look at it. The sun is shining. The sky is so blue and perfect." That was how the world had looked ever since Lance had officially asked her out earlier this morning.

He eyed her travel mug suspiciously. "What'd you put in your coffee this morning?"

"Oh, Xavier." She sighed happily. "I don't need anything in my coffee. I'm just reveling in the beauty of the day." It wouldn't hurt him to get out and enjoy the sunshine. That long black hair of his made his skin look so pale...

"I'm headed out." He shut down the computer and shoved some books into his camo messenger bag. "No calls last night."

"Okay," she sang, scratching behind Ilsa's ears. "Enjoy the day! Maybe you should go for a hike or something. Get a little exercise."

He looked at her like she was suggesting he jump naked into a frigid mountain lake. "Why would *anyone* want to hike?" he asked in his bored monotone. "The only way I would ever hike is if the zombie apocalypse happened and I had to escape."

"That's a cheerful thought," she said, humming the sweet melody that seemed to radiate from her heart.

With a pronounced roll of the eyes, he grunted a wretched goodbye and trudged out the door, ducking his head as though anticipating the sunlight with horror.

Poor man. All he needed was a lovely goth-leaning Dungeons & Dragons princess to brighten up his world. Maybe she should start an online dating profile for him...

Instead, she logged on to the computer and checked her email, then updated the shelter's Facebook page with an adorable picture she'd snapped of Ilsa. Which gave her an idea...

Now that she'd left Luis's house, she couldn't possibly take Lance's money if he happened to win the competition. Even if she did, that wouldn't help her build a long-term donor base. It would only offer a quick, temporary fix, which was all her father could ever seem to find. *But*...if she could launch some type of brilliant social media campaign, maybe she could reach out to donors all over the country. She could have her old MBA study group help her out. Back in school, they'd worked on that kind of thing all the time together. Marketing had been her weakest area, but maybe the rest of the group would offer some pro bono work to beef up their own PR.

Her fingers tapped the keyboard excitedly as she typed out an email. Maybe they'd even know a developer who could build her an online donation page...

The door swung open, sending in a lovely autumn-scented breeze. Jessa pressed send and inhaled deeply, waving at Evie Starlington, who should have been a glamorous actress with that name, but she wasn't. She was a stained-glass artist. A recent transplant from Denver. Jessa had gone to her art show at Darla's place a couple of months ago and she'd hit it off with the woman right away. She was in her mid-sixties, but as hip as a teenager with her pink-streaked hair and bohemian clothing. Today, she wore a gauzy skirt and a peasant blouse with rainbow-colored tassels.

"Good morning," Jessa called, rising from the desk. She set Ilsa on the floor and the pig scurried quickly underneath the desk to hide. She was still working on socializing her.

"It is a good morning, isn't it?" Evie replied, snuggling a ball of fur tightly against her chest. "It got even better when I found this little charmer hanging out on my couch this morning." She held out a familiar cat. The very cat Jessa had rescued from a tree the other day.

"Oh, Butch." She took the cat out of the woman's hands.

"I have no idea how he got into my house," Evie said. "I did leave a window open last night…"

"Well, for being an inside cat, Butch here likes to go on adventures. Don't you, boy?" She held up the cat and he licked her nose as though he remembered her as his savior. "I know the owner. Hank Green. I can call him and have him pick him up." And in the process of returning the cat, shoot down every pass he made at her…

"If you wouldn't mind, that would be appreciated." The woman reached over to scratch behind the cat's ears. "Though I have to say, I did enjoy my short time with him. It was nice sharing coffee with someone. Even if it was someone else's cat."

A pang of sympathy dimmed her own happiness. Poor Evie. She seemed lonely. Her husband had passed away last year. That's why she'd moved away from Denver. She needed a new start, she'd said.

"Here." Jessa held out the cat. "Why don't you hold him while I call Hank?" And actually, the woman could stick around and meet him. He definitely wasn't Jessa's cup of tea, but he wasn't much older than Evie and they were both single.

While Evie sat in a chair gushing over Butch, Jessa hurried to the phone.

"Y-ello," Hank answered.

"Hey, it's Jessa. Butch is here at the shelter."

"What?" The word hurled through a dramatic gasp. "Why, I didn't even know he was gone!"

Uh-huh. Sure. He'd probably sent Butch out again and was getting ready to call her. Despite that, she smiled. Hank was lonely, too. And she knew how that felt. "Miss Starlington brought him in. Do you know her?"

"No. I can't say that I do."

"She's a wonderful woman. New to town." She battled the urge to start listing off all her best qualities. Shouldn't work too hard to sell her. "Somehow Butch managed to climb in her window."

Movement scratched on the other side of the line. "Well, thank her for bringing him in, will you?" he said dismissively. "I'll be right over. Then maybe we can grab a cup of coffee together..."

"Actually, you can thank Miss Starlington yourself," Jessa said before he could finish asking her out. "I'll ask her to stay until you get here."

"But—"

"See you soon!" With an extra flourish, she clicked the off button, then tossed the phone on her desk. "Hank will be over in a few minutes," she called to Evie. "Can I get you a cup of—?"

The door swung open again. *Wow*, busy morning. Jessa turned, expecting an animal situation, but instead Luis ambled in.

She popped up from her desk. "Hey, Luis. I wasn't expecting you today. Not with Lucas and Levi home."

His eyes didn't meet hers. In fact, his head stayed low enough that she could hardly get a look at his face. "I need to talk to you," he said quietly, too seriously.

The happiness that had been floating inside her all morning turned to stone. "Oh. Sure. Of course," she sputtered. She picked up Ilsa's leash and started walking toward the back room, but then noticed Evie watching them. She paused. "Have you met Evie?" she asked him. "She's new around here. An artist from Denver."

"Pleased to meet you," he said in his gentlemanly way. He crossed the room and held out his hand. The two of them shook.

Jessa tried to smile past the panic bells clanging in her heart. "Luis Cortez is..."

"I know who he is," Evie said with quite the blush. "I followed your career for a long time. It's so wonderful to meet you in person." The warm smile the woman offered him was rewarded with a humble grin.

"My career ended years ago," he said, his tone brushing away all of those famous belt buckles he'd earned.

"Maybe so, but you'll always be a legend," Evie said kindly, and suddenly Jessa regretted inviting Hank Green over.

Luis was still smiling when he shoved his hands into his pockets and strode toward the employee lounge.

Jessa followed, tugging Ilsa along behind. Whatever he wanted to say, he didn't want to wait. "Evie, Luis and I are going to have a chat in the back. Can you wait for Hank to come and pick up Butch?"

"Of course." She settled back into the chair. "I'm happy to."

They'd hardly cleared the door before Jessa turned to Luis. "Is everything okay?"

He faced her directly, steeling his hunched shoulders. "Truth is, something's not right. It hasn't been for months." His old hands folded in on themselves, fingers weaving together.

"Wh-what?" Her legs trembled, forcing her to sink to the beat-up leather couch. She swept Ilsa into her arms, holding her close for comfort. The pig nuzzled her snout into Jessa's neck.

Luis sat in the chair across from her, his expression resolute. "I get dizzy sometimes. Lose my balance. Other times I'm confused..."

The bottom dropped out of her lovely happy morning. "Oh, Luis..." *No. Please.* She couldn't do this. She couldn't face the thought of losing him, too.

He shifted, but his gaze still held hers like he was forcing himself not to look away. "When I dropped the ladder in Green's yard...I got disoriented. Couldn't remember what I was supposed to be doing. Don't even know how I ended up down on Main Street."

Don't cry. No crying. She touched a finger to the corner of each eye to catch the tears before they fell. "Have you been to the doctor?" she asked, holding her voice together with a thread of denial. Maybe he wasn't sick. Maybe he really had just been dehydrated that day...

"Yes," he said, abolishing her hope. "A couple times. The doc's done some tests. But he wants me to see a specialist in Denver. A neurologist. On Thursday."

A neurologist? This time there was no stopping the tears. They slipped down her cheeks one by one. She could be strong for him, but she couldn't promise not to show emotion. "Do you need me to come?" she half-whispered, trying to get a handle on her squeaky tone. "I can talk to Lance—"

"No." The firm denial cut her off. "I want you to come. No one else. I'm not telling Lance."

She shot to her feet, holding tightly to Ilsa, her pulse racing. "But Lance should know. He'd *want* to know."

"Not yet," Luis said stubbornly. "Not until I get a diagnosis. He's training. I can't distract him from what he needs to do."

"But…" She sank back to the couch, the gravity of what he was asking too much weight to bear. How could she not tell him? How could she go on a date with him and not tell him his father might be sick? "It's only a competition," she breathed. This was his father's life…

"It's more than that to him," Luis said sternly. "It's what he lives for. And I won't be the reason he fails."

Anger tore through the sadness. "That's ridiculous—"

"Please." The one word held enough sadness to smother her indignation. "I need to know you won't tell him. Not until I'm ready. I don't ask you for much. But I need this."

She pressed her hand against her mouth to hold in a sob and nodded. "Fine," she murmured when she could speak. "I won't tell him. But you'll have to. Eventually."

He nodded. "After the competition."

"And what about Lucas and Levi?" They'd only just reconnected with him…

"I'm not gonna saddle them with this now," he said, looking away from her as if he knew exactly what she thought about that plan.

Because she hated it. The thought of him going to a specialist—maybe hearing a grim diagnosis—without his boys there made her nauseated. "They're your family." She tried to say it gently, but conviction hurtled out.

Luis gave her a sad look as he reached across and patted her hand. "And I'll tell them when the time is right."

* * *

Lance fumbled with the buttons on his shirt. Been a damn long time since he'd worn a dress shirt. But he figured Jessa was worth the trouble, even if the collar did pinch at his neck. He tucked the shirt into his jeans and cinched his belt buckle. A fancy shirt was one thing, but he'd stick with jeans, thank you very much. Besides, what he had planned for their date tonight would require jeans. And with that thought...

He strode out into the living room. He never got nervous around women, but something in his gut churned. Which could mean only one thing. He had it bad.

"Whoa." Lucas stood in the kitchen helping himself to a beer. He whistled. "Someone must have big plans tonight."

Lance positioned himself on the other side of the counter, doing his best to appear casual. "How do you figure?"

His brother eyed him as though racking up a list of reasons. "For starters, you tucked your shirt in."

Lance looked down. *Yeah, okay.* That was a dead giveaway. "So?" he challenged, just like he used to when they were kids. That usually ended in a scuffle around the floor until one of them had the other pinned. But tonight he didn't feel like messing up his hair.

"Where are you headed?" Lucas asked, the smirk on his face making him look thirteen again.

Lance evaded his brother's amused eyes. "Gonna pick up Jessa. Take her up to the lake." A romantic evening picnic. Not that he could take credit. He'd Googled romantic dates in the mountains...

"A picnic?" His brother's jaw hung open.

Yeah, it kind of shocked him, too. But what could he say? "I like her."

"So I see." Lucas took a swig of beer and set the bottle on

the counter. "I'm happy for you. She seems close to perfect for you." The smirk reappeared. "Nice. Kind. Compassionate. Someone to balance you out."

"What the hell is that supposed to—"

The door pounded open and Levi hustled in. "Got any beer around this place? Dad's out."

Probably because Levi had downed it all. Didn't take that kid long to put back a case of beer.

"Plenty in the fridge," Lucas said, moving out of the way so Levi could open it.

He snatched a lager and popped the top like he'd been waiting for a year.

"Ahh..." He swiped his arm across his mouth and looked at Lance as though noticing him for the first time. "Why the hell are you dressed like you're doing a photo shoot for *Rodeo News*?"

"He has a date," Lucas answered for him. "With Jessa."

Damn. If only he could sucker punch him like he used to.

"Knew it." Levi's palm smacked the countertop. "It was so obvious. You were all over her at the bar."

"Noticed you avoided Cassidy," Lance said. He still knew how to put Levi in his place when the situation demanded.

Sure enough, his brother's gaze dropped to the floor.

"Did you even say a word to her?" After being her brother's best friend and practically growing up as part of the family, a hello wouldn't have killed him.

"Cassidy hates me." He took a long pull on the beer and when he set it down the spark was gone from his eyes. "She hates everyone who has anything to do with riding."

Lance doubted that. Cassidy didn't hate Levi. His brother simply felt guilty for being there when Cash died. For not being able to prevent his accident, as if he were God or something.

"Come on, you two." Lucas shook his head at the two of them. "How about we stop trying to push one another's buttons and get along? I'm only gonna be here a few more days, then I gotta head back to the McGowens'."

"A few more days?" That was it? All these years Luis had been waiting for Lucas's return, and now he was staying only a few days.

"I've got stuff to take care of down there. They rely on me."

"I gotta head back to training soon, too," Levi said, finishing off his beer. "Not everyone qualifies for Worlds with just their name." He gave Lance a pointed look. "Some of us gotta work for it."

Lance's temper flared. He *had* worked for it. His whole life. He'd given everything to it. But Levi knew that. Once again, his younger brother was just trying to poke the dragon. Besides, they had other things to discuss. If they were both leaving soon, they didn't have much time. He glanced at the clock. He had to leave in ten minutes, but they had to do this now. He walked to the counter and pulled out a stool, sitting down across from his brothers. "Since you're both here, there's something I want to say." He didn't give them a chance to respond. "I think we should tell Dad. Everything."

Lucas braced his hands against the countertop. "We've been over this."

Maybe so, but their last go-round hadn't convinced him of anything. "I think he deserves to know the truth." If he stood in the man's shoes, he'd want to know.

"There's no point," Lucas growled, more riled up than he should've been. "Not right now. What's done is done. Let's leave it be."

He couldn't. Not anymore. Not for Lucas and not for Levi. Not for their father. "No one else has to know. But he should."

Levi looked back and forth between him and Lucas, his expression unreadable. "Lance is right," he finally said.

"What?" Come again? Had those three words really just come out of his younger brother's mouth?

"You're right," Levi said again, with more conviction this time. "He should know the truth."

Wow. Lance could only stand there blinking like a fool. He'd never thought Levi would be the one to agree on this. Maybe his brother *had* grown up some out there in Oklahoma...

"You don't know what the hell you're talking about," Lucas argued. "You don't want him to know the truth."

Their youngest brother slammed his beer onto the countertop so hard Lance couldn't believe the bottle didn't shatter.

"How do you think I felt knowing you were in prison because of something I did?" he demanded. "I ruined your life."

"We didn't exactly give you a choice," Lance reminded him. He'd never thought about what it had done to Levi. It'd never seemed to bother him. He'd obviously hidden it well.

"Exactly. You didn't give me a choice." His brother's eyes had darkened. "But I could've spoken up. I could've said something. If I had it to do over, I never would let you take the fall for me."

Lucas sighed as though he was more tired than angry. "You were a kid. Hell, we were all kids. We didn't know anything."

That was the truth. For the most part they'd been on their own to make life's big decisions. And there'd been plenty of times they'd screwed up. They could always right those wrongs, though. It wasn't too late. "We can make it right now."

Lucas studied Levi. "But you have your whole career ahead of you…"

"I don't need you to protect me anymore," their younger brother said with more conviction than Lance had thought he was capable of.

Lucas still looked as surprised as he felt. "No. I guess you don't."

Levi walked over and tossed his beer bottle into the recycling bin. "They couldn't prosecute me anyway. You've already served the sentence. So yeah, it might suck if everyone else found out. They might hate me. But I won't go to prison."

Lucas still looked undecided, but Lance wasn't. "We can tell him tomorrow. At dinner," he said. "But right now I have to run." Wouldn't do to be late for Jessa. She'd already forgiven him for being an ass once. Or twice. Didn't need to add poor punctuality to the list.

"Have fun," his brothers said in unison as he trotted out the door.

Didn't need to tell him twice. It'd been only a few days since he'd spent time with her, but it felt more like months.

Outside, the early evening sun backlit the mountains with a vibrant haze. He climbed into the truck, appreciating the view as he drove toward town. Normally, he didn't consider himself an optimistic sort of fella, but it seemed things were falling into place. His brothers were back home, which meant the family was back together. After all these years, they'd put the past to rest. Worlds were coming up fast, and he'd never felt more ready for a competition in his life.

And all of it was thanks to Jessa.

Chapter Twenty

It was becoming apparent that perhaps Darla hadn't been the best choice in reinforcements to call when Jessa had started to freak out about her date with Lance. The woman had come right over and talked her into wearing her brand-new flowy, low-cut sundress that clearly said, *Make love to me in a flower-dappled meadow.*

And yes, she had to admit, it was the perfect outfit for a first date with a man who'd already convinced her he was worth the effort. But there was a slight complication. She shouldn't go on a date with him. Not when she was leaving for Denver at six thirty in the morning with his father for a secret doctor's appointment. "He told me to wear jeans," she said, glancing at herself in the mirror.

Darla only laughed. "He doesn't want you to wear jeans. When he sees this dress, he'll forget all about jeans," she promised.

"I shouldn't go. I could tell him I have the chickenpox,"

Jessa squeaked, fisting her friend's shirt desperately in her hands. "Or measles. Or a bad case of the stomach flu…" A rising panic crowded into her chest, jamming up her throat. She glanced at the clock. Lance would be there in ten minutes!

"No." Darla plucked Jessa's hands from her clothing and backed away, straightening the wrinkles out of her shirt. "You are going on this date," she said sternly. "I mean, come on! Lance never asks anyone out." Her hands flew up. "Think of what this means. This is like a record. Maybe you'll end up in the Guinness World Records or something."

Jessa deflated to the couch, suddenly exhausted from the weight of carrying such a heavy secret. "I can't go. I can't." How could she look into that man's perceptive eyes and pretend everything was all right?

Darla plopped next to her. "You *have* to go," she argued. "You look gorgeous. And you don't want to discourage his interest in you, right?"

Jessa stared at her hands, trying to even out her breathing. "Well. No. I guess not." She liked Lance. Okay. She more than liked him. But that was the problem. She'd learned enough about him to realize that keeping any sort of secret about his father would be considered an unpardonable sin in his book.

"Come on." Darla gave her shoulders a quick massage, like a coach pumping up a boxer for a big match. "Just forget about everything else and have fun tonight. Let it all go."

"I want to." She wanted to waltz out that door with him and let him sweep her off her feet like they'd been caught up in one of those wonderful Humphrey Bogart movies. Not like it would be all that hard for him to sweep her off her feet. He'd already laid a serious claim on her heart. She wanted to hold his hand and kiss him and, well, depending on where things went, maybe more than kiss him. But. "I feel like I'm lying to him." In a moment of desperation on the phone, she'd given up Luis's secret to Darla. Not that she had to worry. The woman was a vault.

"Pshaw." Darla waved away her concerns. "You're not lying. You're withholding. Totally different," she said, as though she'd suddenly become a relationship expert. "You have to respect Luis's wishes on this, Jess. This is his decision. Not yours."

And that was the sad truth of it. "I know."

"Luis is right. This would completely throw Lance off right before the biggest competition of his life. Is that what you want?"

"No." He needed this win. He needed to go out on top. Surely he'd understand. She was just trying to do what was best for him.

"Now, I'm gonna take off before he gets here and sees me giving you a pep talk." Darla pushed off the couch and walked across the room to the dog bed Jessa had brought home for Ilsa. The pig squealed when she picked her up, but Darla carefully calmed her with a smooch on the head. She'd agreed to watch Ilsa tonight. Just in case things went late.

But Jessa couldn't let things go late. She couldn't sleep with Lance! Not when she was keeping something from him…

"Call me the second you get home," Darla said for the hundredth time. "Got it? I want details. I want to know *everything*."

She followed her friend to the door and opened it for her, then leaned down to kiss Ilsa's snout. "I'm not sure there'll be anything to tell." How could she say one word to him without everything coming out? Let alone kiss the man? It would feel so wrong...

"Oh, there'll be something to tell," Darla insisted on her way down the porch. "Trust me. That dress won't let you down." With a suggestive lift of her eyebrows, she traipsed down the porch, wiggling her fingers in a wave.

Jessa didn't wave back. Her arms felt too weak to move. She tapped the door closed with her toes and paced the living room. Usually the anticipation of seeing Lance brought on the butterflies, but now it had unleashed something far more intense. What if Lance could read the secret on her face? What if she accidentally mentioned something about their trip to Denver? What if—

The doorbell chimed.

Her head whipped around. Lance's sturdy build crowded the window.

"Okay," she breathed. "Okay." Too late to cancel. Too late to make up some sort of illness. Darla was right. She wasn't lying. After it all came out, she'd simply explain to Lance how important the secret had been to Luis. He would understand. He had to understand.

Slowly, she shuffled to the door, her insides quivering the whole way. She reached for the knob and suddenly the damn thing felt like it was solid steel. Somehow she managed to get the door open, even with her failing muscles. And that image of him standing there...that burned into her brain. He was dreamy...a rugged cowboy fantasy. Dark tight jeans. Black button-down shirt tucked in so as not to hide any of his goods. His hair had been somewhat tamed but not to the point of looking like he cared all that much, and God, that made him sexy.

"Hi, there," she said as casually as she could, considering the pulse in her throat.

"Hey." His gaze lazily trailed down her body and back up to her eyes, and the desire she saw there rendered her speechless.

"I know I told you to wear jeans, but that's one hell of a dress, Jessa Love," he uttered in a rather provocative, scraping tone that tempted her to do away with the dress altogether.

Instead of disrobing, she turned away to snatch her purse off the sofa table. And to talk her cheeks out of a blush. "Thanks," she muttered as soon as she could speak.

When she turned around, he stood closer, almost right against her, and even though he hadn't touched her yet, she felt him, inhaled that dangerous scent that made her think of the powerful trees lining the mountains outside.

"I thought we'd go for a picnic." His gaze lowered to her cleavage as though he wanted her to know how much he appreciated it. "That sound okay with you?"

A picnic. It sounded perfect. In the great outdoors, maybe she could think about something besides leading him right into her bedroom. Skip the small talk. Skip the food. Who needed a date when Lance was so good at seducing her? *Ahem.* Yes. A picnic would be much safer. "I love picnics," she told him, going to the closet to pick out a sweater. Delicate and white to match the dress.

"Can't say I've ever been on a picnic," he said, holding open the front door for her. "But I figure it'll be a nice evening up at the lake."

"Mmm-hmmm," she squeaked, hightailing it down the sidewalk to his old pickup. She'd already climbed in and gotten belted before he could open the door for her.

Lance hoisted himself into the driver's seat and started the engine. As he pulled away from the curb, he glanced over at her. "You okay?" he asked, more unsure than she'd ever seen him.

"Yes." A fake laugh tumbled out. "Of course I'm okay." Oh God. She might as well have said, *No, Lance. I'm not okay. I'm taking your father to Denver in the morning.* She was terrible at pretending.

Sure enough, he gave her a skeptical look.

"Um." She scraped at a piece of nail polish on the tip of her finger. *Think. Think, damn it.* Maybe sex would've been a better idea. Then she wouldn't actually have to talk to him. "It's just...it's been a stressful week."

His eyes watched the windshield now as he navigated the town streets. "Things at the shelter okay?"

"Yes." As far as she could tell. Though she'd been a bit distracted lately, courtesy of that man sitting right there. "Just a lot to do."

The truck lurched to a stop as he waited to turn onto the highway. "My offer's still good, you know." His hand swept down her arm and brought on a rush of longing. "Even though you're not staying with Dad anymore, I'll still donate half my winnings to the shelter."

Her shoulders went stiff. "You don't have to do that," she choked out. He shouldn't do that.

"I want to." He sped onto the highway, sneaking glances at her as they headed toward the ranch. "You've done a lot for us, Jessa. Bringing my brothers home...helping out Dad."

Her hands squeezed into fists. She was still trying to help out Luis. She had to remember that. "It's nothing," she insisted, staring out the passenger window, watching the familiar mountains roll by. They'd turned off the highway and onto the ranch's vast acreage and were heading up the same switchback road she and Luis took on the ATVs. The secret seemed to sear against her chest, but she battled back an urge to tell him. "So how are things going with your brothers?" she asked in an attempt to take the focus off her.

"Things are pretty good." He kind of laughed. "Surprisingly."

That drew her gaze to him. "Why is that surprising?"

"Let's just say there've always been some things between us." He focused on the road as though he wanted to evade her eyes. "But we're dealing with them. Finally. After all these years, I think we can be like a family again." There was a gravity in his voice, half hope, half fear. But when his face turned to her she saw only strength. "Thanks to you."

Guilt spilled through her again, forcing her to look away. "I can't take credit for that." After he found out about his father's situation, he likely wouldn't be singing her praises anymore.

Silence ensued as the truck crawled up the steep incline. When the road leveled out, he glanced over at her again. "I didn't think I'd be thankful for them coming back. But I am. And Dad is." His eyes locked on hers. "I haven't seen him this happy in a long time."

She felt the color drain from her face. His father was not a safe subject right now. Not at all. "How's training coming?" she rasped, hoping to divert the conversation away from Luis. She couldn't talk about him at all or she might burst into tears. She'd nearly driven herself crazy looking up his symptoms on the Internet, fearing everything from a brain tumor to dementia to Alzheimer's.

"I feel ready," Lance said, parking the truck near the short path that led down to the lake. "I don't think I've ever felt this ready for a competition."

"I'm glad." It was the most genuine thing she'd said since he rang her doorbell. She was glad for him. After the hell everyone was giving him, he deserved to win.

Which is why she wouldn't tell him. As soon as he came back from Worlds, he'd find out everything. Right now, she had to give him space to concentrate. Comforted by the thought, she climbed out of the truck, thankful for the fresh air, the expanse of space between them. Maybe out here in the openness things wouldn't feel as intimate. Maybe she could keep her distance.

While Lance unloaded a huge basket from the bed of his truck, she wandered to the path. Evening was just starting to settle, hushing the world, making everything glow. God, it was romantic. The lighting, the soft breeze, the faraway rush of a stream. The peace of it made reality seem a little farther away, like they really had entered some dream world where happiness could never come to a screeching halt with one diagnosis, with one little lie. Her body let go of some of the tension it had been carrying as she inhaled the scent of honeysuckle and pine. So lovely, these mountains. So far away from everything else.

"Hope you like cheese. And wine," Lance said, coming up behind her.

She turned, letting herself take him in, letting her eyes linger on his. "I like both." She smiled at him. And it felt real. Not forced. "That's quite the basket. I'm so impressed," she teased, eyeing the huge woven work of art he carried.

"Borrowed it from Naomi," he admitted with a grin. "I was just gonna pack it all in a good old saddle bag. But I figured we might not want hay in our food."

She laughed, and somehow it made a surge of tingling anticipation slip through her hesitations. Lance had gone to a lot of trouble planning this date. A picnic. Something intimate and sweet. He could've taken her to a restaurant, but instead he'd brought her out here. The effort he'd put in warmed her.

They walked in an easy silence down to the lake. She'd been there a couple of times, fishing with Luis, mostly, but she'd never seen it at dusk. When the trees opened into a clearing, she stopped suddenly. It almost looked fake. The glassy surface, smooth and turquoise, fed from the glacier nestled between two cliffs above. The setting sun streaked the sky with colors, reflecting off the water. "This is incredible," she breathed.

"Yeah. Sometimes I come up here at sunset. It's probably the most peaceful spot on the entire ranch." Lance led her down to the water, where a big flat rock sat mere feet away from the shoreline.

"This is where I usually sit." He lowered the basket to the ground and took out a red-and-white-checkered tablecloth, shaking it slightly before he spread it out.

"It's perfect." She sat, letting her legs stretch out in front of her, crossing them at the ankles as her skin soaked in the gentle evening sun.

Lance sat beside her, pulling things out of the basket, one by one. A plastic-wrapped plate of some yummy-looking cheeses, a container of grapes, a platter of what looked to be prosciutto and salami. Then, two wineglasses and a bottle of merlot. He uncorked the wine and poured a glass for each of them. Then he held his out to her, a sparkle of mystery in his eyes. "To great views," he said, eyeing her dress again, and this time she let herself blush.

"To great views," she repeated, clanking her glass against his.

He pulled out two plates and served her. It was all perfectly thought out. The saltiness of the cheese with the bitterness of the wine and the sweetness of the grapes. The two of them ate leisurely while the pink hues deepened in the sky.

Jessa set down her wineglass, still mesmerized by how the lake's surface mirrored the sky. "So what do you think about when you come up here?"

Lance gazed up at the peaks above them. "Life. Competitions. Sometimes my mom." That last sentence seemed garbled with an emotion she couldn't quite peg. Anger? Resentment? Sadness?

She munched on the amazing Brie he'd selected and sipped her wine. "Did you stay in touch with her? Ever hear from her?"

Instead of answering, he shook his head. Then he popped some grapes into his mouth, chewing thoughtfully before he swallowed. "For a while I thought she'd come back. That she'd realize her mistake and make things right."

By the sound of things, he'd given up on that dream a long time ago. But she'd never been one to lose hope easily. "Maybe she still will," Jessa said, her tone treading carefully.

"Nah. She would've already. If she wanted to." He set his plate on the ground next to the rock and hunched, resting his elbows on his knees. "I've looked for her more than once. Didn't find anything. She obviously doesn't want to be found."

The pain on his face ground itself into her heart. What would that be like? To have this important piece of your life missing? Did he feel incomplete because of it? "You boys deserved better," she said, covering his hand with hers. His was warm and rough. Battered by the constant tug-of-war with leather. She loved the feel of it. Of him. His hands were so distinct, the lines and ridges and scars...

Lance scooted closer to her. "You didn't have it so easy with your family, either, huh? Always going back and forth the way you did." His arm settled around her.

"No." She let herself lean into him. "That's true. But both of my parents were always there for me." They may not have been in love, but they both loved her. She'd never had to doubt that. "I consider myself very blessed to have had that."

Lance peered down at her, his eyes searching hers. "How do you do that?"

She turned to face him. "What?"

"See the best in every situation. In everyone?"

Maybe because she'd overdosed on romance her entire life and now she thought only in terms of happily-ever-afters? That didn't sound very intelligent. "I guess I like to focus on what I have instead of what I think I need. I only see the things I'm grateful for."

His face lowered to hers. "Want to know what I'm grateful for?" he murmured, nearly against her lips.

"What?" she breathed, her heart pounding its way out of her chest.

"That dress." The grin that accompanied the words was downright naughty. And close. *So* close.

She laughed as his lips nudged hers, and he laughed, too, but only for a second before he pulled her closer, teasing her with a scrap of his extravagant mouth against hers. The heat on their lips thawed the fears and the hesitations that had chilled her heart before. Because she loved kissing him. Loved how his firm lips moved against hers, slow and sensual. Savoring. She loved the feel of his hard chest under her palms, the way his hands held her, the way his stubble scraped her skin.

"You really know how to plan a date," she whispered against his neck.

Carefully he lowered her back to the rock, then hovered over her while he traced her collarbone with his finger. "It'll only get better," he promised,

"Can't wait," she whispered, bringing her lips to his again. Losing herself in the rhythm of his kiss and the peaceful breeze and the glowing sunset, she took Darla's advice.

She let the secret between them go.

Chapter Twenty-One

This evening wasn't supposed to be about sex, but God almighty was it hard to convince his body of that. Especially with Jessa underneath him, making those hot little noises while he kissed the soft warm flesh of her neck. He wanted sex. No. He should rephrase that. He wanted sex with Jessa again. Slow this time. Deliberate. So he could touch every inch of her skin. Taste it with his tongue. So he could revel in the sensation of burying himself inside her again, taking her to that place where her control shattered and she clung to him as she rode out the pleasure he gave her...

His hands fisted and he pulled back, eased himself onto his side next to her. He wanted her more than he'd ever wanted a woman, but he wanted more than her body. Tonight was not about sex. It was about taking her on a date. When he'd picked her up, she'd been distant, and who the hell could blame her? They'd already had a quickie in the kitchen but since then, they'd hardly talked. Had hardly spent any time alone, getting to know each other the way a woman like Jessa would want to. She might say she was fine with a fling, but he knew better. She'd never given herself away to just anyone. Hell, that's what made her special. He knew she wanted more. And she deserved it, too.

"Everything okay?" she asked quietly, touching her fingers to her lips. Even in the dusky light, he could see the rosiness of her cheeks, heated and alive, the same way his body felt.

He gazed down at her, playing with the strands of hair around her face, breathing in her sweet honey scent. "Everything's more than okay." Because he had her here, alone. Because right now in this moment, she belonged to him. He couldn't say what would happen tomorrow, where tonight would lead them, but right now he had everything he wanted. "Are *you* okay?"

She smiled up at the stars that were starting to prick the sky with their twinkling light. "Yes, Lance. I am definitely okay." Her gaze met his, and he had to hold his breath and count backward from ten so he wouldn't say screw getting to know her and maul her instead. He could do this. Talk to a woman he was interested in. Talk without expecting anything else. They had a lot of things to discuss. He knew a lot about her but he didn't know *her*.

She turned on her side, so that her perfect breasts pressed against his chest. Instead of caressing them the way he'd been fantasizing about, he rested his hand on her hip. "I figured we should talk some. Get to know each other."

Jessa busted out laughing.

"What?" he demanded, though her laughter lured out a grin. She had a great laugh. Happy and buoyant. A laugh that could make even the biggest miser smile. He needed more of that laugh in his life.

"Sorry," she managed to say through a lingering giggle. "I'm sorry." She made a face as though she was struggling to put on a more serious expression. "So what do you want to know about me? Favorite color? Favorite food?" Judging from the glimmer in her eyes she was teasing him.

And he liked it. "Bra size," he shot back, though he'd had enough experience to guess she was safely within the C category.

"Why don't you take a look?" she said, temptingly.

He could. He could take the thing off with his teeth right now. But he'd already decided. Next time he made love to Jessa, it wouldn't be on an uncomfortable rock in the great outdoors. It would be in his king-size bed, where they could spend the entire night exploring each other, where he could take his time figuring out how she liked it best. Where he could send her over the edge as many times as she'd let him and then they could fall asleep with their naked bodies tangled together.

He eased out a breath. "When's your birthday?" he asked, jaw tensed with restraint.

Jessa propped herself up on her elbow and gave him that soft smile that made him want to trace her lips with his tongue. "September. The sixteenth."

He nodded as though checking her answer off the list. He tried to think of another stupid question, something insignificant, but the truth was he didn't care what her favorite color was. He didn't care what she liked to eat. That would all be learned in time. What fascinated him most about Jessa was her heart. The woman had been hurt. Engaged a couple of times, rumor had it. She'd been cast aside. Abandoned just like him.

But she had this resilience he envied. Only one person had rejected him in his whole life and yet in that one moment he'd shut himself off to the very connection he was starting to feel with Jessa. He'd ridden bulls, been bucked around, thrown. He'd broken too many bones to count. But this...this terrified him. The risk seemed so much greater than just his own life. Yet he didn't want to turn back. He didn't want to run scared this time. Jessa had managed to do what no other woman could all these years. She'd earned his trust.

He braved a look into her stunning eyes. "What do you want most in life?" he asked her, wondering if maybe he could offer it to her.

Her expression sobered. She rolled onto her back and stared up at the sky again.

Figuring it might make it easier for her to answer, he did the same.

Wind rustled the pine needles and made the water quietly lap at the shoreline. He said nothing, though Jessa's silence tempted him to let her off the hook.

Finally, she sighed, as though she'd resigned herself to honesty. "Love," she murmured as though somewhat ashamed. "That's what I want most in life. To love someone wholly and truly. And to have them love me back."

The words struck him with their simplicity. Wasn't that what most people wanted but were too afraid to admit? He leaned over, kissing her tenderly yet firmly. When he pulled back, his heart pounded. "I don't know how to do that," he admitted. To love someone. Even more than that, to let someone love *him*. "But maybe I can learn."

Jessa turned her body to his again, placing her palm at the curve of his jaw. "You're far better at it than you think you are," she whispered. "You love your father." Was it tears that made her eyes brighter? Or just the deepening darkness? He didn't know why that filled her with so much emotion, but he loved that in her. Loved how she let herself feel. He stroked her cheek, steering her lips back to his, and this time the kiss felt deeper, more meaningful. It was even harder to pull back, harder to keep his hands from wandering all of the places they wanted to go. Instead, he drew her into a tight embrace, trying to convince himself he was satisfied simply holding her. "Come with us. To Worlds." The words surprised him as much as they seemed to surprise Jessa. He hadn't planned on saying them, on inviting her. But he wanted her with him.

She pushed back and sat up. "What?"

"Come to Vegas." He sat up, too, gazing into her eyes to convince her. "We'll get you your own suite. Dad would love it."

Her head tilted to the side. "You want me to come along for your dad?"

"Yeah." He bit back a smile. She was much smarter than that, but she apparently wanted to make him say it. "And maybe I want you there for me, too." He wanted her light. Her laugh. Her smile. Her happiness. It wouldn't be easy for him to face his critics, the people who were hungrily awaiting his downfall. But something told him he could manage it better if she were with him.

Jessa's whole face lit. "Okay," she said slowly, as though it was sinking in. "Yes. I'd love to go with you."

"Okay," he repeated, already making the arrangements in his head. He'd have his agent set everything up, find her plane reservations, get her the best suite at the hotel. "You'll have a great time," he said, kissing her sweet lips again. "I promise."

She kissed him back, clinging to him, running her hands down his chest. Before they could travel any lower, he pulled back and cut off the kissing. "Right now, though, I should get you home," he growled, breaking apart their bodies before he wasn't able.

"You sure?" she whispered.

No. He was not at all sure. But the cold hardness of the rock was enough to remind him. "This isn't the most comfortable place to make out," he said.

"I noticed." She laughed. "And I really do need to get home," she agreed, scrambling off the rock and to her feet as though her balance had been compromised.

He could relate. He steadied her with a hand against her lower back. "We can go on a date in Vegas." He packed plenty of heat into the suggestive expression. "Then you can spend the night. If you want to."

The slightest hesitation flickered across her face but then she smiled. "Sure. It'll give us something to look forward to."

Hell yes, it would. He'd be counting down the minutes.

* * *

Doctor examination rooms were all the same. Bland white walls. Lights too bright. Inevitably one cheesy framed picture that someone had likely ordered as part of a special offer per dozen. From the chair where she sat next to Luis, Jessa studied the amateurish painting of an eagle perched on the sturdy branch of an evergreen tree. The creature's eyes glowered at her from all the way across the room. Not exactly the most comforting image while waiting to hear your fate.

A clock on the wall ticked off the seconds. Earlier, while she'd killed time in the waiting room, Luis had undergone some tests. Then the nurse had invited her into the exam room while they waited to hear from the doctor. And they'd been waiting ever since.

Luis sat tall and composed, much better off than she was, evidently. The anticipation of waiting for the doctor was slowly killing her. Her knee pumped with the frantic beat of her heart. What was taking so long? Had they found something terrible? Why hadn't the doctor come in yet? She watched the clock, tucking her hands under her thighs so she wouldn't fidget.

"You okay?" Luis asked, without turning his head to face her.

"No. I'm not." She couldn't lie. He'd see right through her, anyway. "This place is terrible. So depressing. I mean, would it hurt to put some color on the walls? And what's this?" she demanded, snatching a magazine off the small countertop next to them. "*Financial Times*? Are you kidding me? Who wants to sit in here and read boring old investment articles?" Indignation rolled off her face in waves, giving release to her misplaced anger. Sometimes anger was easier. Because truth be told, she was downright scared. The *what-if*s had been stirring a potion of fear that boiled in her stomach. She wanted to run from here. Far away. Before they found out the worst.

And God, she couldn't let herself think about last night. How perfect it had been. How truly wonderful Lance had treated her. Even while she'd withheld the knowledge that his father might be dying of some horrible disease . . .

"Everything will be all right, Jess," Luis said with a quiet confidence.

That only got her more riled up. "What if it's not?" Her throat was raw. How could she go through losing another father one year after her own had left her? Yes, that was selfish, but there it was. She loved Luis, and the thought of watching him suffer made her want to double over.

The old man patted her hand with warm affection. "I'm not worried, honey. Don't matter what the doc says. I've got everything I've ever wanted. My boys are all home. Together. Don't matter what's wrong with me." He spoke as though he knew something was wrong, as though he'd already accepted it.

So why couldn't she?

"Saw Lance's truck drive in awful late last night," Luis mentioned casually. "I reckon you two had a good time on your date?"

"A great time." The flashbacks of Lance touching her and kissing her with such tenderness filled her with warmth and longing. It was the best date she'd ever been on...

"You didn't tell him about the appointment?" his father asked carefully.

Her eyes fell shut. "No. I didn't."

"Sorry, Jess. I know that had to be real hard."

"It was." She tried not to glare at him. She loved the man, but she hated this. "I don't want to lie to him."

"I'll tell him when the time is right. I promise. As soon as—"

The door swung open, leaving the promise unfinished. Jessa snapped her spine to full attention as the neurologist— a short man with a neatly trimmed rim of graying hair— walked in.

"Sorry for the wait," he said briskly as he plunked himself on the rolling stool across from them. "I wanted to take a few extra minutes to go over your test results." He fumbled through a manila folder and Jessa glimpsed stacks of pictures. MRI scans, charts, diagrams. She turned to look at Luis, her mouth gaping. He must've been undergoing tests for months...

The doctor focused only on Luis, his expression a mask of polite detachment. "Based on all we've learned over the past months, and my conversations with your primary physician, I believe we have a diagnosis."

Jessa inhaled deeply, trying her hardest to be brave, trying to find strength for Luis. She snuck her hand over to his, holding on tightly, desperate to siphon some of his courage.

"I believe you're battling Parkinson's disease. And it would appear you've had it for some time," the doctor went on in a monotone.

"That's what Dr. Potter thought." Luis's voice didn't even waver. He wasn't surprised. He'd known for months. But Jessa was reeling. In anger, in sadness, in fear of how Lance would handle a blow like this...

"There's no way to know how quickly it will progress or exactly how the symptoms will manifest. Parkinson's is difficult to define. Each patient is different." The man handed Luis a large envelope. "Here are some resources. Potential treatments. Results from the latest trials. There are definitely methods we can try to slow down the progression. Medications, certain therapies."

"Is it fatal?" Jessa choked out, needing to know the prognosis.

"Not necessarily." For the first time since he'd come in, the doctor acknowledged her with direct eye contact. "But there are complications. It makes life significantly more challenging due to the mental and mobility implications."

"Okay," she whispered, nodding, trying to swallow past the emotion that snagged her throat. "Okay."

"I'd like to set up a meeting in two weeks. To give you time to digest this and read through the literature we've provided." The doctor stood, already on his way to the door. "Then we can formulate the treatment plan you feel is best for you and your situation."

He spoke like this was an everyday occurrence, like he hadn't just upturned Luis's world with one sentence. Fury climbed up to Jessa's face. She stood, too. "That's it? Shouldn't we start treatment now? Shouldn't we discuss all of the options now?" Her voice teetered on the brink of a breakdown, but seriously? They shouldn't waste any time!

The doctor looked at her patiently. "We find it's best in these situations to allow patients some time to process everything before we move forward with a treatment plan."

Her hands fisted tightly, the anger needing release. "But—"

"It's all right, Jess." Luis rested his hand on her shoulder to quiet her. "Thank you, Dr. Ellis." While Jessa wanted to wring the aloof doctor's neck, Luis reached out to shake the man's hand. "I'll see you in a couple weeks."

After the door closed, Jessa turned away from Luis so he wouldn't see her tears, but he wouldn't let her hide. The man took her arms in his hands, turning her to face him. "I'm not afraid. Not stupid enough to think it'll be easy, but I don't fear it, either." He offered her a comforting smile. "I have everything I've ever wanted," he said again. "My boys are home."

"So you'll tell Lance?" she asked, her voice watered down with tears.

"After the competition," he promised, pulling her into a reassuring hug. "After the competition, I'll tell them everything."

Chapter Twenty-Two

*H*ell yes. Lance swung himself up into the driver's seat of his pickup. He'd just finished kicking Wild Willy's ass. Clocked his best time yet. As in ever. Right after he'd hung it up for the day, he'd rushed through a quick shower and even slapped on some cologne. He may have told Jessa he'd take her out in Vegas, but he couldn't wait that long. Besides, they were supposed to leave tomorrow night for Worlds, and he wanted to bring her up to speed on the details. They'd already added her to the plane reservations and the suite had been booked. One of their suites wouldn't get much use, but it was best to keep up appearances.

Lance sped down the drive, kicking up a trail of dust behind his wheels. He could've called her first, but where was the fun in that? Since he'd dropped her off and kissed her on her doorstep last night, he'd been aching to see her, to feel that soft body of hers against his. It'd taken him ten minutes of sitting in his truck to actually pull away from her house.

He would've gone in, if she'd invited him, but she hadn't. After they shared a rather hot kiss that could've been considered a warm-up for other stuff, she'd said she had an early morning and should get inside. And he'd had to talk himself down the whole way home.

Figuring she'd still be at the shelter, he headed in that direction, tapping his hands to the rhythms playing on the country station. During his jaunt down Main Street, he waved to Kat Temple, the lone female deputy within a hundred-mile radius, and even at Hank Green, who was walking his cat on a leash. Because why the hell not?

Outside the shelter, he didn't see Jessa's car, but he parked anyway. He could wait until she got back if need be. Once he approached the windows, though, he saw that the lights were on, so he tried the door. It was open.

Cassidy sat at the front desk, working on the computer. She sat straighter as he came in.

"Hey," he said. "Didn't expect to see you here today." Far as he knew, she covered only on the weekends or when the boss was away. "Is Jessa around?"

"Oh." Her blue eyes grew round and her gaze wandered. "Um. No. Actually. She's not here." There was no evidence of her typical friendly smile. Why did she look so worried?

"What about my father?" he asked, his stomach coming unsettled. Something wasn't right. According to Levi, Jessa had picked up Luis early that morning. He'd told him they had a lot to do at the shelter today...

"Um. Your dad's not here, either."

"Where are they?"

"They're out," she said, staring hard at the computer screen. To avoid his probing gaze, if he wasn't mistaken.

"Out where?" He hadn't meant for it to sound so harsh, but this was starting to feel like a game.

"On a call."

"Oh." Why hadn't she said that in the first place? From the intensity of her worried expression, it had to be something bad. "Where are they? Maybe I can help out."

"I'm not sure," she mumbled, but Cassidy was a very bad liar. Her eyes shifted too much. And her voice carried the hoarseness of a bald-faced lie.

"What do you mean you're not sure?" He pinned her with his eyes, trying to read what she wouldn't tell him. "If she called you in to cover for her, she must've told you where she was going."

A sigh broke through her tight lips. "I think it's best if you talk to Jessa. Okay?" Without waiting for an answer, she went back to typing.

He reached over her and shut off the damn monitor. "What the hell is going on?" Something big, judging from the way she was putting him off. And he didn't like being the only one in the dark. "She wouldn't have called you in for an hour or two..." He knew that much. And Jessa rarely went out on calls outside the county limits.

"I'm not telling you anything," Cassidy said stubbornly. "It's not my place or my business. Understand?"

No. He didn't understand. Didn't understand how worry could boil up in his gut this way when he'd felt fine only five minutes ago. Was Jessa all right? Had something happened to her? "Is she with Dad?" He let his eyes beg. "Please. You at least have to tell me that." So he'd know whatever she was off dealing with she wasn't alone.

"Yes." Cassidy sighed. "She's with your father. He asked her to go to Denver with him today."

That stood him up straighter. "What?"

"That's all I'm gonna say." She walked to the door and held it open for him, gesturing for him to leave. "If you want to know more you'll have to talk to them. Okay? I'm guessing she'll have him home within the hour."

He lumbered out the door in a stunned fog. Last night, Jessa had said nothing about taking his father to Denver, but she must've been planning on it. Why would she keep something like that from him?

He wasn't sure he wanted to find out.

* * *

Jessa couldn't remember the last time she'd been silent for more than an hour. Even when she was home alone, she had a tendency to talk to herself. But most of the ride home from Denver, Luis had been quiet and introspective, as if processing what he'd learned. And she knew he had to process it alone. He wasn't like her. He didn't verbally analyze everything, so she'd let him be while she listened to the sad country songs playing on the radio.

Now that they'd almost made it back to the ranch, the urge to burst into tears intensified again. It wasn't like Luis would die in three months; she knew it could be worse. But she couldn't help wondering how long it would be before he'd have to give up the hikes he loved so much, the time wandering in the wilderness that seemed to keep him sane. *That* would slowly kill him.

"I sure appreciate you coming," he said, turning his head in her direction for the first time since they'd gotten in her truck.

"I'll do anything I can to help." She'd research until they

found the best doctors, the latest treatments. "As soon as we get home from the competition, we need to sit down with Lance and go over everything the doctor gave you." Then they could come up with a plan...

"We?" Luis asked, as though he hadn't heard right.

With all her apprehension, she'd forgotten to mention that she was tagging along to Vegas. "Lance asked me to come." Even with the sadness weighting her heart, she smiled. "I hope that's okay."

"It's more than okay," he said, smiling, too. "I couldn't be happier."

She knew he wasn't talking only about Vegas. As she veered onto the country road that led to the ranch, hope swelled inside her, seeming to stretch her ribs, to give her more room to breathe. They would get Luis through this. All of them. Together. "It won't be easy to keep it from him." Even for one more week.

"I know," he agreed. "But it's best."

She turned into Luis's driveway. "We might have to agree to disagree on—"

Her mouth froze open, the rest of the sentence disintegrating in an explosion of panic. Lance sat on Luis's front porch. As the truck rolled toward him, he looked up. Even though she couldn't see his face, she knew. He'd found out where they'd been.

"Oh God." She slowed and parked, but let the car idle. Her heart idled right along with it.

"You go on home, Jess," Luis murmured, unbuckling his seat belt. "I'll handle this."

It was tempting to take him up on that, to avoid the impending confrontation, but she couldn't. "No. I'll stay." How could she turn around and leave when Lance's expression had twisted with suspicion and anger? She had to make him understand. There'd be no way to protect him from the truth now.

Grasping at courage, she cut the engine and slowly withdrew the keys.

Luis got out first. While she struggled to find her balance, he approached the porch. "Hey, son. You've got some questions, I reckon."

Jessa hung back, bracing one hand against the truck's fender to steady herself.

Without looking in her direction, Lance walked down the steps to meet his father. "What were you doing in Denver, Dad?" he asked, and Jessa didn't recognize that voice. She'd never heard it before.

"That's my business," Luis said, not unkindly. "I'm allowed to have my own life. Don't have to answer to you."

Ignoring him, Lance turned to her. The indifference on his face sent a blow to her heart.

"Why did you go to Denver?" He repeated the question, but this time directed it at her.

Jessa eased in a steady breath, trading a look with Luis. She couldn't lie to Lance. Not right to his face. And he wasn't about to let this go. He knew something was wrong.

"I had an appointment," Luis told his son before she could speak. "And I asked Jessa to take me."

"What kind of appointment?" Lance asked impatiently.

Jessa crept closer to him. They had to tell the truth. Didn't Luis see that? The longer he stalled, the angrier Lance would be.

"I had to see a doctor. A specialist."

"A specialist." He seemed to carefully control his voice, but Jessa recognized the fury rising in his eyes, and she couldn't take it, couldn't force him to keep guessing.

"Luis saw a neurologist today," she blurted. "They diagnosed him with Parkinson's."

"What?" Lance staggered back a step, his eyes widening with a sudden wrenching pain. "Jesus, Dad." The words were breathless. "How could you keep that from me?" He shook his head as though he couldn't believe it, then set his sights on her. "And how the fuck could you pretend everything was fine? Last night. You knew. And you let me think everything was dandy." His hand raked through his hair as he paced away from them. "Jesus."

"Don't blame Jessa," Luis said, matching his son's furious tone. "It wasn't her fault. I told her to keep it quiet. I wasn't ready to tell you."

"You weren't *ready*?" Lance yelled. "Well, shit, Dad. By all means, take your time."

Jessa flinched.

"Easy, son," his father reprimanded. "Why don't we all go inside? We can tell you what the doc said. Get everything sorted out."

But Lance didn't seem to be in the place to sort anything out at the moment. He still paced in front of Jessa's truck, back and forth, staring at the ground.

She glanced at Luis. "Can you give us a minute?"

Luis hesitated, as though worried what Lance might do or say. But she could handle it. She could handle him. If they were alone, she could remind him of the connection they'd built. Just last night he'd said maybe he could learn to love, learn to let someone love him. He was still that man. He might be angry, but he was still the same Lance who'd taken her on a picnic in the mountains. "It'll be fine," she assured Luis, shooing him toward the front door. "We'll be in soon. Then we can all talk through this together."

The man nodded silently, but the look he gave his son sent a clear message. *Be careful.* Then he walked up the steps and disappeared into the house.

The hard slam of the screen door seemed to shake Lance out of his daze. He spun to face her, his face still flushed with anger, his eyes hard and distant. And who could blame him? She'd just unloaded this horrible news on him, without warning. He had to be in shock. Had to be reeling the same way she had in the doctor's office.

She approached him slowly. "I wanted to tell you," she said, reaching for his hand so she could thread their fingers together. "But I had to respect Luis's decision. He didn't want to distract you before Worlds. And it was his news to tell you. Not mine."

Lance yanked his arm away. "I didn't spend last night with him," he snapped. The ice in his tone sent her back a step. Her arms fell to her sides. She was losing him. Or... she'd already lost him. "I'm sorry. Maybe we should go inside—"

"We don't need you here for this discussion," he said, turning his back on her.

"Lance." She followed him up the steps. "Please. I was only doing what he asked me to do. I want to stay. I want to *help*." She touched his arm, tried to bring him back to her. "We can get him through this. The doctor said there are treatment options. Things that will slow the progression."

Shrugging away from her touch, he assessed her from behind a curtain of apathy. "Go home, Jessa. You're not a part of this family."

The words drove into her, sharp and cutting. And he knew. He knew exactly what kind of damage he'd just inflicted. Because she'd told him. What she wanted most in the world, what mattered to her more than anything in life. Loving and being loved. Those family connections she'd longed for to anchor her but had never managed to build.

Tears stung, but she would not give him the satisfaction of seeing them fall. "You're right. I'm not part of this family." Instead of shying away like he obviously wanted her to, she marched right to him, piercing his eyes with hers. "But I could've been." Her own anger hummed through her, building into a pressure that made her unbreakable. "And you know something, Lance? You would've been damn lucky to have me." She started to walk away, but whirled back to him. "You can think about that while you're alone in Vegas," she snapped. Then she hurried to her truck and drove away before her strength crumbled.

Chapter Twenty-Three

Instead of following Jessa like he knew he ought to, Lance hunched over and leaned his elbows on the porch railing, letting his forehead fall to his hands. All this time, he'd thought the forgetfulness, the shaking, the weakening physicality in his father was simply old age. But he'd been wrong. He'd ignored the signs, the symptoms. His own hand trembled some as he kneaded his forehead, trying to force it all to sink in. His father had Parkinson's. A label. A disease that would slowly eat away at him until there was nothing left...

Pain shot through his chest, then traveled down his arms, forcing his hands into fists. He was half-tempted to put one of those fists through the wall.

Before he could, the door banged open and Luis poked out his head.

"Where's Jessa?" he asked, glancing toward the empty spot where her truck had been parked before Lance'd gone and run her off.

He straightened, but his shoulders bore the weight of a new burden. "She went home." Because he'd been an asshole. He'd directed the brunt of his anger and shock at her. He turned to his father, trying to block out the image of her wounded eyes.

"You mean you sent her home," his father corrected.

"I was blindsided," he muttered. All afternoon, the fears and possibilities had stewed somewhere deep inside him while he'd sat on the porch waiting for Luis and Jessa to get home. Then when he saw her, without warning, it'd all boiled over, the venom spilling onto Jessa. He'd let the familiar feeling of betrayal get the best of him.

Luis stepped out onto the porch, his thumbs hooked through his belt loops. "She loves you, ya know. I've never been lucky enough to have a woman look at me the way Jess looks at you."

"I know." But he was completely unworthy of it. This little tantrum only proved he could never give her what she deserved. God, he wanted to try, though.

"I know it was a shock to hear it that way." Luis lumbered over to the old bench he'd made with his own two hands. He sat with a wince. "You don't need all this hoopla right now. I wanted to wait until after Worlds."

Lance sat beside him, letting himself notice the age spots on Luis's hands, the arthritic hunch to his shoulders. Truth is, he didn't want his father to get old. Didn't want him to get sick. He was the only one who'd stuck around, who'd stuck it out with him all these years and he couldn't imagine it. Couldn't let himself picture that day when his dad would take his last breath.

Emotion clogged his throat, but he didn't bother to clear it away. "How long have you known?"

Luis stared out at the mountains. "A while. Doc's been running tests over the past couple months."

"And you kept it to yourself." That hurt more than anything else. The fact that he hadn't trusted Lance with it. Or that he hadn't thought Lance would consider it important enough to put his training on hold. But maybe that was on him. Maybe he'd focused so much on winning that he'd made his father believe he wouldn't care. "You should've told me. I would've helped you. I would've taken you to the appointments." He would've sat by his side today while he heard the news. Instead, Luis had chosen Jessa. Maybe that was it, what had set him off. He'd chosen Jessa and Lance couldn't deny she'd been the better choice.

"I did what I thought was best." Luis turned to him, his expression donning that fatherly disappointment. "And you had no right to take it out on Jessa. She's done nothing but help this family."

"I know." Regret had already pooled in his gut, making him feel full to the gills, even though he hadn't eaten since breakfast. "But maybe it's better we end it now. Jessa deserves more than I can give her." Naomi was right. He was too screwed up to do this. He had one foot in, but kept one foot out, just in case. And when things got hard, he found an excuse to be an asshole to keep distance between them.

"That's a copout," Luis muttered. He'd always been one to call it like it was. "You're a better man than I ever was. You love someone, you gotta make it work. You gotta work hard, face up to the troubles, and get past 'em. Trust me. I wish I would've made the effort."

Before he could ask what Luis meant, Levi's truck rumbled into the driveway.

Right. He'd forgotten he'd called in his brothers. He

turned to his dad. "I should warn you. When I found out you'd gone to Denver with Jessa, I called in backup. Told them to meet me here as soon as they could."

"Swell," his father muttered, rising as though preparing to face the music.

"What's the emergency?" Lucas asked, stomping the mud off his boots as he made his way up the steps.

When Lance had finally gotten ahold of them, he'd learned the two slackers had gone fly-fishing.

"Yeah...who up and died?" Levi asked, obviously annoyed he'd been interrupted before he'd caught the big one.

Lance cringed. "No one died." *Yet.* But his brother was gonna have to grow up for this conversation. It wouldn't be easy for either of them to hear. Especially seeing as how they'd both missed out on the last ten years of their father's life.

Silence ate away at his ears, but he had no idea where to start.

"We ought to go inside, sit down," Luis said, plodding to the door. He held it open, and one by one, they headed to the same kitchen table they'd sat around every night for their meat-and-potatoes dinners growing up. Lance took a chair next to Luis while Levi and Lucas faced off on the other side of the table.

Once they'd all sat, Luis didn't waste any time getting right to it.

"Parkinson's?" Levi's voice had shrunk and he almost sounded like a little kid again.

Lucas said nothing, simply stared at Luis as though he was waiting for him to continue.

But the man was a stubborn old ox. He didn't even want to tell them what the doctor said. So Lance broke the silence.

"What's the treatment?" He steeled himself, but that was all he really wanted to know. *Needed* to know.

"Not sure, yet," Luis said, looking neither worried nor confident. "The doc gave me some information. He wants to have a meeting to discuss treatment options in a couple of weeks."

The color had finally started to come back to Levi's face. "Parkinson's isn't bad, right? It's not fatal."

"Nah." Their father dug into the wood with his fingernail. "Might make it harder for me to get around. Harder to think clear, to remember things." He shot them an ornery grin. "Hell, that's been happening for years."

Not funny. None of this was funny. There was plenty Luis wasn't saying. Lance could tell. He knew a few things about Parkinson's. One of his old high school teachers had been diagnosed a few years after Lance'd graduated. Far as he remembered, the man had suffered complication after complication until he'd passed away.

"What can we do?" Lucas finally spoke. The terrified look in his eyes reminded Lance of the day they'd sentenced him to prison.

"Nothin'. Not right now, anyway." Luis took a minute to look at each one of them. "I'm sorry I kept it from you. But I wanted to be sure. Before I went and got everyone all riled up."

"It's okay, Dad." Levi's eyes steeled with determination. "Truth is, we've been keeping something from you, too."

Tension gripped Lance's neck. This was it. The conversation he'd dreaded for years. But he nodded at his brother. It was time. Long past time. "A lot longer than a couple of months," he added.

Lucas seemed bent on fading into the background, but they had to do this. And now was as good a time as any.

Luis sat straighter, his posture apprehensive. "I don't understand."

"Lucas didn't set the fire that night. I did," Levi said directly.

Their father's head shook. He clearly didn't believe them. "But you were only fourteen. And Lucas confessed."

"Because we worked out a plan," Lance cut in. He was so ready to be done with this. To put the past behind them so they could be family for whatever time they had left. "Levi'd already been in enough trouble. We were afraid of what juvie would do to him. So Lucas said he'd take the blame instead. He had the cleanest record." It had made so much sense at the time.

"Why?" Their father was raking his hand through the tufts of white hair that were already sticking straight up on his head.

Levi's jaw tightened. "You were meeting Maureen Dobbins there. And I was so pissed off." He cut a glance to Lance. They'd all been pissed off. Levi was the one who'd caught Luis kissing Maureen in the stables, but they'd all been angry about his frequent indiscretions. They'd heard the rumors around town. And Maureen was married. To the rodeo commissioner.

Levi wouldn't look at any of them. "I thought Mom would come back. So I wanted to destroy it. The place you met up with Maureen. To make you stop."

Their father stared at the table, hands flat and motionless against the wood. "I'm sorry." His voice cracked, nearly breaking the words. "I'm so sorry, boys." An expression of stunned anguish drew Lance's hand to his father's shoulder.

"I didn't know how to be what you needed," Luis uttered.

"I didn't know how to be what she needed. I couldn't hold it all together."

"Doesn't matter now," Lucas insisted. "Things are different. You're different."

"We're all different," Lance threw in. And maybe that meant things could change now.

Luis seemed to shut everything else out as he gazed at his middle son. "All these years..." It was barely over a whisper. "I was so hard on you..."

Lucas slipped out of his chair and knelt in front of their father. "It's okay. You didn't know. I don't want you to think about it now."

The old man couldn't seem to lift his head.

"You did your best." Lance waited until Luis looked at him. "Things might not've been perfect, but we knew you wanted us. We knew you loved us. We never had to question that." Didn't matter what happened, Luis wouldn't have left them. He never would've walked out on them. And in Lance's book, that made him a saint.

"None of us care about the past." Lucas went back to his chair. "Time to move on, focus on you. Figure out how we can get you the best treatment available."

A breath lifted Lance's chest. Hope. He breathed it in. Six months ago, he would've been on his own with this. But now his brothers were home. They could navigate it together.

"I don't deserve you boys." Luis's eyes were all watery. "But I sure am glad to have you."

"I know a couple of doctors back in Oklahoma," Levi said, pushing back from the table. "I'm gonna call them and see if they have any recommendations for a good neurologist. We need the best."

"And I'm gonna call the McGowens. Let them know I'll

be delayed for a while," Lucas said, already pulling out his cell.

After they'd stepped out, Luis faced Lance. "Why'd you keep the truth from me all these years?"

That was a no brainer. "To protect you."

"Some secrets are meant to protect, son," Luis said with a resolute quietness. "Sometimes that's all you can do for the people you love. Try to protect them. Even if it backfires on you."

Ouch. Nothing like tasting the truth of your own words. He slumped against the chair back. "I had no right to get so angry at her." Jessa had the best intentions. Always. She'd already proven that more than once. "Shit." He rested his forehead on the table, trying to formulate some kind of plan for how to take those words back, how to convince her he wanted her around. To be a part of this family.

A hell of a lot of time passed, but nothing came to him.

"Got a lead," Levi said, coming back to the table.

Lucas joined them, too. "They said to take all the time I need," he said, brushing a hand over Luis's shoulder. "We'll do whatever we have to do. You're not gonna go through this alone."

A long-forgotten sting pricked Lance's eyes.

"I made a lot of mistakes," Luis said, looking around at his sons. "But you boys…you're the only thing I did right."

"Come on." Levi rose from the table. "Let's head downtown. Beer's on me."

They all stood, but Lance hung back. "Actually, I have somewhere else I've gotta be."

A knowing look bounced between the others.

"Good luck, man." Lucas whacked him on the back.

Luis only shook his head. "Trust me. He's gonna need it."

Chapter Twenty-Four

*W*e'll always have Paris.

God, was there a more tragic phrase in the English language?

Jessa blubbered into the wad of Kleenex she'd fisted in her hands. "Isn't this the best movie ever?" she asked, reaching over to pat Ilsa's head.

On the couch next to her, the pig was too busy rooting her mouth around a bowl of fresh salad to actually watch the movie. A few days on antibiotics and the pig couldn't stop eating.

Jessa turned her attention back to the television. On a normal night, *Casablanca* drew a sort of dreamy-eyed teary sadness, but tonight it *moved* her. Lance's words had embedded themselves in her heart. She heard them play over and over. Even one of her favorite movies of all time hadn't drowned them out. And maybe it wasn't so much the words as what hid behind them. He'd wounded her on purpose, and she didn't understand, couldn't fathom, ever doing that to someone.

She wrapped her father's old wool blanket tighter around her shoulders, needing to feel that connection with him. With someone. The past few weeks of her life had been so wonderfully sweet. She'd actually felt like a part of the Cortez family. But that was her fault. She'd let herself read too much into it, let herself hope for something she knew she'd likely never have.

Headlights cut across the windows outside. She paused the movie and popped to her knees on the couch, stomach quaking with that familiar hunger Lance teased out in her. All it took was one thought of seeing him and suddenly her stomach groaned as though she hadn't eaten for two weeks.

Sure enough, his truck parked along the curb in front of her house.

Damn it! She slouched down trying to hide herself from those windows. "Quiet, Ilsa, baby," she hissed. She couldn't face him right now! Her eyes had nearly swollen shut from the tears. How pathetic was that?

The dreaded knock came at the door and Jessa scrunched herself down farther into the couch.

"Jessa?" Lance called.

She didn't move. Didn't even breathe. Maybe he'd take the hint that she didn't want to talk to him. Except she did want to talk to him. She really did. Her heart thrummed and her palms grew warm. But that was why she had to ignore him. If she let things go any further with him, he'd break her. He'd hurt her and she'd never recover.

"Come on," Lance said. "I can see you sitting there. Don't make me break in again," he added.

As if he'd earned the right to be cute.

"Fine." But when he saw her ugly, makeup-smeared eyes, he'd regret the threat. She'd always known makeup was a bad idea. What was the point anyway? A girl had to be able to cry without worrying she'd scare people away.

Keeping the blanket snug around her shoulders, she stood and plodded to the door, sneaking in a fortifying breath as she unlocked the deadbolt and opened it a crack. Just a crack.

"I'm sorry," he blurted. "I shouldn't have said that. I was upset. Surely you can understand that. He's all I have…"

She shuffled out onto the porch so he couldn't step foot in her house. If that happened she wouldn't have the strength to make him leave. And she had to. She deserved more than this. The cycle of him losing his shit and apologizing to her. "I get that," she said, forcing herself to look at him. "I know you love him." Luis may be the only person in the world Lance loved. "But he doesn't have to be all you have. That's what you've chosen." He chose that an hour ago when he took the one shot at her he knew would destroy her.

A look of desperation widened his eyes. "I won't give up. I'm gonna make you forgive me."

"That's the thing, Lance," she murmured through a sigh that admitted defeat. "I've already forgiven you." She'd forgiven him the moment he'd said those words. Because she loved him. Once again she loved someone as hard as her heart knew how, but he didn't love her back. And she couldn't do that to herself. After Cam had walked out on her, she'd thought she needed to give up on men, dating, relationships…but that wasn't true. She didn't have to give up on every man. On every relationship. But she had to choose the ones that built her up. She had to be strong enough to hold out for someone who would love her the way she craved. And let's face it...Lance didn't love her. He loved that she made him feel better about himself. That she believed he could win this competition. But what would happen when there were no more competitions? When he no longer needed her to boost his confidence?

He stepped closer, gazing down into her eyes with so much emotion she had to look away. "Let me come in. Please," he begged, brushing his hand across her arm as though he knew how much weight his touch held.

It did. One light touch from him ignited her. That's why he couldn't come in. She had no self-control when it came to Lance. If she let him in, he'd have her naked and in bed within five minutes, which would only make her love him and want him more. At some point she had to stop doing this to herself. She edged toward the door, gripping it for stability. "Here's the thing," she said, scrubbing the emotion from her voice. "I can't keep loving someone more than they love me. It hurts too much." There was no other way to say it. This whole thing with Lance had been more intense, more powerful, than any relationship she'd ever had. She felt it deeper and she had to protect herself.

He held her shoulders in her hands and forced her to face him. "I *want* to love you."

"But you don't."

He sighed and let his arms fall to his sides. "I'm not sure how to yet."

The admission purged her anger and gave sympathy room to grow. "It's not something I can teach you," she told him softly. "I always thought it was. Every relationship I've ever been in. I've tried." But that wasn't the way it worked. "Turns out, it's not so easy. Turns out that it ends up only hurting me. I don't have the energy for it anymore. I'm tired." Of getting hurt, but maybe even more than that, she was tired of trying so hard.

"You don't have to be the one to teach me," he insisted. "I'll learn it on my own. I'll figure it out."

She stepped backward, underneath the open door. Half inside her house and half outside. "It's not something you figure out like some kind of puzzle." It didn't have to be so complicated. It wasn't like passing a test or forcing yourself to work hard. "Love is something you choose. Every day. In the happy moments. But in the terrible moments, too. In the moments you're so angry you want to hurt someone. You still choose love." And he hadn't.

"God." The word came out through a tortured sigh. He lifted his hand to her face and drew her lips closer to his. "I want you so much it makes me hurt." His lips brushed hers and held on, locking her in a passionate kiss.

A sigh gave her away and she wilted against him, letting him bring her arms around him and pull her close. Just once more.

"Jessa, I will make this up to you," he uttered, kissing her mouth as though desperate to prove his words.

But a kiss wasn't enough. Mind-blowing sex wasn't enough. Him running to her when he needed comfort or confidence was not enough. Not for her.

She pushed him away and held him at arm's length. "You need to go now." Before it got any harder for her. Before she wasn't able to do what she knew was best. "Good night, Lance," she whispered.

Then she turned away and escaped into the house.

* * *

It wasn't like Jessa didn't have *anyone*. Surrounded by the light of her friends, the night didn't seem so dark. Darla, Cassidy, and Naomi all sat around her in the living room, forming what had become their sacred circle. They each still wore expressions that ranged from outrage to shock to indignation based on her explanation of what had transpired with Lance.

She hadn't held anything back—nope, the whole ugly truth was out there in the safest place possible. These women would guard it with their lives. When she'd put out the SOS text, they hadn't asked why, they'd simply come over right away, toting along chocolate and wine and ice cream, even thought it was almost midnight.

Naomi hadn't even bothered to change out of her pajamas. She'd simply gone over and asked Luis to sit at the house with Gracie while she ran an errand. Jessa imagined his eyebrows had gone up, but Naomi said he hadn't asked any questions. Of course he hadn't. That was Luis. He strictly minded his own business.

So they were here. All her best girls. And her amazing little piggy was perched comfortably on her lap. And you know what? That was enough. Who needed boys anyway?

"I can't believe he said something so stupid," Naomi fumed around a mouthful of intense dark.

"Oh, I can," Darla cut in. "Lance has no clue when it comes to women. Or love."

"Seems to run in the Cortez family blood," Cassidy grumbled. Jessa didn't know all of the history between her and Levi, but the woman didn't exactly sing his praises.

"I don't know," Naomi murmured, looking down. "I always felt like Lucas understood me just fine."

Jessa reached over Ilsa's head and patted her friend's hand. Seemed she wasn't the only one hurting. Ever since Lucas had come back, Naomi had been subdued and sullen.

"I hope you told him where he could stuff his sorry-ass apology," Darla muttered, pouring Jessa another glass of the good cab.

"I stayed pretty strong." Much stronger than she'd ever imagined she could be. Of course, the confrontation had been pretty short. One more minute alone with him and she would've totally caved. "But I don't trust myself to *stay* strong."

"Of course you can," Cassidy insisted valiantly. "You kept him out of your house. That was smart."

"You got this," Darla agreed.

Jessa withheld the story about getting in the car twice to go throw herself into his arms before they'd arrived. "The thing is, I don't think I can stay away from him. So Ilsa and I are heading to Denver first thing in the morning. To spend the weekend with Mom."

"You sure that's a good idea?" Naomi asked, wide-eyed.

"Yes." She'd thought it over and she didn't have a choice. "She might say I told you so, but she'll also take me out to dinner, and we can go shopping. Maybe even for a pedi and massage." Her mother still loved to take care of her, no matter how pathetic she was. "She'll love Ilsa," she said, giving her girl a squeeze. "Besides, I don't trust myself." She had to get out of there for a while. At least until Lance left for Worlds. Then she wouldn't have to see him, or accidentally run into him at the grocery store or the bar. She glanced at Cassidy. "Can you cover for me at the shelter tomorrow?"

"Of course. I can take more shifts, too. If you want to stay longer."

"That's okay. I don't want to be gone too long." She didn't plan to put her life on hold this time.

If her many breakups had taught her anything, it was that she couldn't sit and wallow.

Chapter Twenty-Five

He sure wished talking to a woman was as uncomplicated as talking to a bull. Wild Willy didn't care what the hell you said to him as long as you fed him. Lance walked away from the corral. Last day of training before he left tonight and he didn't even feel like being out there.

As he neared the fence, he noticed Levi hanging out waiting for him. Knots of tension pulled tight in his shoulders.

"So how'd things go with Jessa last night?" his brother asked, though he had to have some clue, given the fact that Lance couldn't seem to focus.

Damn. He whipped out his bandanna and mopped his face. Levi would love this, knowing he'd struck out. "She told me to take a hike." Not like he could deny it. Levi would find out soon enough anyway.

"Seriously?" he asked through a laugh. "What the hell did you say to her?"

"I don't know." Wasn't like he'd scripted out anything eloquent. He sucked at talking. "I said sorry."

"That's it?"

Thinking back, his words did seem inadequate. He'd been so desperate, but he had no clue what to say to undo the damage. That was the worst part, that he'd hurt her. He'd caused her pain. It definitely sucked that she'd rejected him, but he could take it. What he couldn't take was the deep sadness in her eyes. "I get why she wouldn't hear me out. It's fine. I just wish I knew how to make her feel better. Even if she never wants to see my face again…"

Levi whistled low. "Good thing I came back when I did." Head shaking, he nailed Lance's shoulder with his fist. "Come on." Without an explanation, he trotted away.

"Where're we going?" he called, jogging to keep up.

"To Jessa's house, idiot. I'm gonna help you get her back."

Oh, sure. Like it'd be that easy. "She seemed pretty serious about not wanting me around." All night he'd stewed on the whole mess, trying to think up a way to fix it, and so far he had jack.

"Trust me." Levi swaggered past his front porch. "Women only need to hear the right words. She'll come around."

As they were climbing into the truck, Lucas rode up on his mountain bike. He leaned it against the garage and sauntered over. "What're you two up to?"

"We're going to win Jessa back for Lance," Levi said, turning the key in the ignition. "Wanna come?"

"Hell, yeah." Lucas ripped off his helmet and tossed it into the yard. "I could use some entertainment today."

"Great," Lance muttered, reaching around to unlock the

door for his brother. If he couldn't even beg for her back when they were alone how was he supposed to do it in front of an audience?

Lucas climbed in and belted up, just in time, as Levi gunned the engine and they were skidding down the driveway. He'd always been a shitty driver. Not surprising, given the fact that Lance was the one who'd taught him.

"So what's the plan?" Lance asked, hoping Levi could come up with something better than he had last night.

"The first thing you gotta do is admit you were wrong," his youngest brother instructed, as if he were some kind of expert.

"Did that." And it'd gotten him nowhere.

"But did you justify it?" Levi revved the truck out onto the highway. "Or did you just tell her you fucked up and you were sorry?"

He tried to think back. "I said, 'I'm sorry, but—'"

"*But?*" Levi and Lucas said in unison.

His middle brother shook his head. "Man, even I know you never say 'but' after the word 'sorry.'"

"Why didn't I know that?"

"Because the women you've tended to surround yourself with don't exactly expect apologies," Levi said. "Jessa's different."

"Yeah. I've figured out that much." As painful as it was to let his youngest brother give him advice, that's the only thing that made this worth it. The fact that Jessa was special.

"Don't worry. We'll get her back. It'll take some finesse, but I can help you out with that."

Lance shared an amused, albeit irritated look with Lucas. "And you know this how?"

"I know women," his brother bragged, in full swagger

mode. "Trust me. When you see her, you take her hand, look into her eyes, and tell her you're sorry. And that you love her."

Wait. Love? "What?"

"Tell her you love her," Levi repeated.

"But…" Did he love her? "I shouldn't say it unless it's true."

"It's true. You're definitely in love with Jessa." Levi glanced at Lucas in the rearview mirror as though searching for confirmation.

"Yep," their brother agreed. "Definitely."

He jerked his head to stare at Levi, the cocky prick. "How do you know I'm in love with her?"

"Because you care more about her than what you're missing out on," his brother pointed out. "You said you didn't care that she'd rejected you. You only care about making her happy. That clearly means you're in love."

"Okay, Dr. Phil," he mumbled.

"Lucas? Back me up?"

"I don't know what he's talking about, but I do see the way you look at Jessa." Lucas stared out the window. "I recognize that look."

Of course he would. He still got it every time he saw Naomi. "You ever sit down with Naomi? Go over any of the numbers?" Maybe have the conversation they both seemed too terrified to have?

"That's difficult when she doesn't want to be in the same room with me."

"Yeah, I guess it would be." The woman had definitely been avoiding him. "I'll talk to her."

"Not a lot of good that'll do either one of us. I don't belong in Topaz Falls anymore." He said it like it was a fact.

Lance would have to keep working on that, too.

The truck bounced down Main Street, but instead of heading to the shelter, Levi took a fast left and parked in front of the KaBloom Flower Shop and Boutique.

Despite living here his whole life, Lance had never stepped foot in that store. "What're we doing?"

Levi uttered a long-suffering sigh. "Getting flowers, dumbass. You can't expect to get her back without flowers."

"Really?" He eyed the shop windows.

"Come on." Lucas put a hand on his shoulder and dragged him to the door.

Ten minutes and one bouquet of colorful wildflowers later, they pulled up at the shelter.

Nerves lit him up the same way they did before he got into the arena. "Her car's not here." Maybe he should come back later. Alone. So his brothers didn't hear him sound like a fool.

"Let's go in and see where she is," Levi said, cutting the engine.

Since when was he the boss? Gathering up the bouquet, Lance got out of the truck and led the way inside.

Cassidy was sitting behind the reception desk. She looked up, but then turned to focus on a computer screen as though determined to ignore him.

"Hey," he said, snagging her attention back to him.

"Can I help you with something?" she asked as though she'd never met him before.

Damn. She'd obviously heard what had happened. He tried not to let her glare ruffle him. "I need to talk to Jessa. Do you know where she is?"

She refused to look at him. "Of course I know where she is."

"But you're not going to tell me." That much was obvious. Jessa must've informed her little group what he'd said to her.

"Why would I tell you?" Cassidy asked with a chilly glance.

"Because I care about her?" Love. He loved her. Why did he find it so hard to say out loud?

"Whatever." She rolled her eyes and went back to the computer screen. "Maybe you should call her," she suggested.

"Right. Okay." He retreated to the doors, ready to hightail it out of there, but Levi blocked him.

"Leave this to me," he whispered, then nudged him out of the way and strode to the counter. "Hey there, Cass. How's your mom?"

Her eyes narrowed into dangerous blue slits. "She's not so good. But you wouldn't know that, would you? You don't exactly check in anymore."

Whoa. Lance winced.

"Ouch," Lucas whispered.

"Oh. Uh. Well..." Levi sputtered. "You know how it is out on the road." The fact that Levi didn't have her swooning under the power of his signature smile seemed to throw off his confidence.

Cassidy glared at him, hands stacked on her hips. "Yeah, I know how it is. No time for the people you knew before. So you'd better get going, Levi. Rush on back to that spotlight before it gets too dim."

Lance hid a chuckle behind a hearty throat clearing. He wondered how long she'd been waiting to say that.

"Can you at least tell us when Jessa will be back?" Levi asked meekly.

"No," she shot back without missing a beat. "I can't." Without another glance in his direction, she stood and stalked into the back room.

Levi turned to them, a stunned expression flattening his normally charismatic eyes.

They stepped out the door single file.

"Smooth," Lucas said, giving their youngest brother a cheerful pat on the shoulder. "Real smooth."

Levi sulked his way to the truck while Lance and Lucas laughed behind him.

"We can swing by the Chocolate Therapist," Lucas suggested.

"Maybe Darla won't be so mean to you," Lance badgered as they all climbed into the truck. But Levi didn't grin. It seemed Cassidy had gotten to him.

After a quick stop at Darla's, where she'd flipped them off from behind the locked glass door, they stood on Naomi's porch.

Lance was almost afraid to knock. "Hell hath no fury like a scorned woman's friends."

"No shit," Levi said, shaking his head. He obviously didn't know *everything* about women. In fact, he seemed as clueless as the rest of them.

"Naomi *will* talk," Lucas said, raising his hand to knock. "She'll know how important this is."

It took a while for the door to open. Lance wondered if she'd seen them through the window and had to prepare herself. She said nothing, simply watched them all walk through her front door. Not surprisingly, her gaze lingered on Lucas, but when he came near her, she retreated to the other side of the small entryway.

Man, she wouldn't even stand next to him…

"What're you doing here, Lance?" she asked as if she already knew. Cassidy and Darla had likely warned her.

Guess that meant he had to level with her. "I need to talk to Jessa. Where is she?"

"Does it matter where she went?" Naomi's cheeks looked rosier than normal and she completely avoided Lucas's gaze. "She left. Because of what you said to her."

"It matters." More than she realized. "I'm leaving and I need to see her before I go." He needed to know she was okay. He needed to see her smile and hear her laugh and he needed to tell her he loved her.

"Jessa doesn't want to be found right now," she said, leaving them behind while she walked into the kitchen.

"Wait. Hold on." Lucas followed her.

The woman's eyes instantly went soft, like she saw some warm glow haloed around him. Man, talk about love.

"I know you're trying to protect her," Lucas said gently. "But I'd hate for her to miss out on something because she's too afraid to hear what he has to say," he murmured.

Naomi's tense shoulders collapsed under a sigh. "She's at her mom's. In Denver."

"Thank you," Lucas almost whispered. Their eyes held for a moment before Naomi turned to the counter and snatched a plate out of the dishpan, drying it with frantic motions. "You didn't hear that from me," she said, her voice shaky.

Lucas shoved his hands into his pockets, leading the way to the front door. "See you later, then." His tone was as subdued as hers.

Lance was tempted to drag Naomi over there and force her to talk to Lucas. They were obviously still hung up on each other. Before he had the chance, Lucas slipped out the front door. Guess that confrontation would have to wait. He could only manage one relationship crisis at a time.

On the porch, Levi turned to face him. "What're you gonna do?" Seemed like his younger brother was all out of good ideas.

But Lance had one more. "I guess I'm going to Denver."

* * *

If Jessa had learned one truth in her life, it was that you are never too old to bake cookies with your mom. There was something so comforting about it—being in the kitchen together, measuring out the ingredients, whipping and stirring while a sweet little pig dozed contentedly in a dog bed at her feet.

Jessa's mother had never been much of a domestic diva, but she'd always baked the best cookies, and somehow she did it in heels and a lovely fitted dress, which she'd covered with an apron, of course. Jessa, however, was still in the *I don't feel like showering* phase of wallowing, so she'd opted for sweats. Elastic waistbands always came in handy after a breakup.

She dumped an extra handful of chocolate chips into the dough and went to work folding them in with a spatula.

"Wow." Her mom peered over her shoulder. "That's some serious chocolate therapy."

"I need it." Though they'd already managed to fit in a lovely breakfast at a local café and pedicures, her heart still drooped with sadness. During the last few hours, she'd filled her mother in on the latest romantic debacle. And, surprisingly, her mom hadn't resorted to any lectures. She'd simply listened and asked her questions about Lance. It made it sort of hard to forget about him while talking about how wonderful he was.

"The oven is all preheated. Here." Carla withdrew a cookie sheet from the cupboard and set it on the counter. "Make them as big as you want."

"Don't mind if I do," Jessa said, pulling out a spoon and scooping up a huge blob of dough. These babies were going to be her lunch. Maybe her dinner, too. She was wearing sweats, after all.

"I thought we could go shopping a little later," her mother suggested. "If you—"

The doorbell twinkled a lovely tune. Good lord. Even Carla's doorbell was elegant and refined.

"I'll be right back," she said, untying her apron and pulling it over her head. God forbid anyone see her looking the least bit frumpy. If only Jessa'd inherited *that* gene. The one that cared what people thought about her appearance.

She glanced down at her attire. Nope. She hadn't. "Trust me, sweats are way more comfortable," she informed Ilsa as she continued scooping huge mounds of dough onto the cookie sheet. She'd already bought too many new clothes, but shoe shopping could be fun. At least it would momentarily distract her. And she always loved to people watch at the mall...

Her mother rushed back into the kitchen and ripped the spoon out of her had. "Lance is at the door," she whispered. "He'd like to talk to you."

"*Lance?*" She shot to the other side of the kitchen—as far away from the front door as possible. "What is he *doing* here?" How the hell did he find her?

"Maybe you should ask him," Carla said, ushering her toward the hallway.

She dug in her heels and stopped, looking down at her clothes again. They seemed to scream *You broke my heart!* and *I'm too pathetic to even get dressed!* "No." She shook her head. "I can't talk to him. I can't see him." Her heart fell to pieces just thinking about it. "Tell him to leave me alone," she said, her voice wavering.

Her mother smoothed a comforting hand down her hair. "Are you sure?"

It was so tempting. He'd driven all the way down from Topaz Falls. Topaz Falls! But this is what she did. She always gave in. She never stood her ground. "Please. I can't." Yes, she was being a coward, but they'd both already said everything there was to say. "Tell him to go."

"All right," Carla said uncertainly before she walked briskly down the hall.

Jessa held her breath, but she couldn't hear anything. After checking on Ilsa, she crept down the hallway and hid around the corner closest to the front door.

"I'm sorry," Carla was saying. "Jessa's tired and not up for company."

"I won't stay long." The sound of Lance's voice struck her. It was polite, but firm, too. "I just need two minutes."

"Well . . ." Her mother hesitated.

Come on, Mom! Jessa almost yelled. Though she understood how hard it could be to resist Lance Cortez.

"I'm sorry," Carla said again. "She seemed adamant, and—"

The pig chose that moment to come barreling down the hall, squealing like she'd been stuck with a pin, her dainty little hooves skidding on the polished wood floors.

"Ilsa!" Jessa screeched, lunging to catch her as the pig shot by. But she missed and ended up sprawled on the floor in full view of the front door.

Lance bent and somehow captured the pig while holding on to a bouquet of flowers.

Ilsa grunted and thrashed, her little legs trying to run away.

"Simmer down, Pork Chop," Lance said, subduing her in his arms. "Not gonna hurt you."

Jessa lay on the floor looking up at him, and he seemed so broad and powerful that he made the pig look like a stuffed animal.

"Hi," he said, gazing down at her.

"Hello," she managed. Not like she could avoid him now.

"I'll go ahead and take Ilsa," her mother offered, reaching out her hands. "And we'll give you two a minute."

Before Jessa could latch on to her ankle and beg her to stay, Carla hurried down the hall, calmly soothing the poor pig.

"I know you don't want to see me." Lance reached down and took hold of her hand, pulling her up effortlessly.

She glanced at her frumpy attire. "I'm not really dressed to see anyone." Especially Lance. Especially looking like this. God! Why'd she have to eavesdrop?

"You're beautiful," he said, his eyes seeming to take her—and all of her frumpiness—in. He held out the wilted and battered bouquet of wildflowers—daisies and wax flowers and snapdragons.

She took them, focusing on the vivid colors so she didn't have to look into his eyes.

"I just came to tell you I love you," he said quickly, as though afraid she might slam the door in his face. "You might not believe me, and I might not be great at show-ing it, but I do. I know I do." He handed her an envelope that had been tucked in his pocket. "This is everything you need to come to Vegas. If you decide you want to. My flight leaves soon, but if you decide to come, there's a flight and hotel voucher in there. And I put in special passes to the events."

Jessa's hand shook so hard, she could barely grip the flimsy paper. "I can't come." She wouldn't go running back to him. Not this time. She'd be like her mom and guard her-self. She'd be better than the girl who went back for another round of heartache. "Sorry. It's not going to work out." She tried to return the envelope to him, but he backed away.

"Keep it," he said quietly. Hopefully. "Just in case you change your mind." He stared at her a minute more as though storing up the vision of her face, then turned around and left.

Trying to hold it together, Jessa dragged herself back to the kitchen, the flowers and envelope weighting her hands.

Carla smiled brightly. "Is everything better?"

"No." She dumped the gifts he'd given her on the kitchen counter. "He told me he loved me. And I didn't say any-thing."

Her mother's sigh was both disapproving and sympa-thetic. Carla leaned against the counter, arms crossed, eyes so much like Jessa's honed in on her face.

"Why are you looking at me like that?" she demanded. "You of all people should be thrilled that I sent him away." She's the one who always told her she should be more care-ful about who she gave her heart to.

Instead of snapping back, Carla gestured for Jessa to sit on a stool.

"Why do I feel like I'm the one in trouble?" She slumped onto the stool. Wasn't this what Carla wanted for her? To be an independent, strong, unaffected woman?

"I guess I understand where he's coming from," her mother murmured as though the admission embarrassed her.

Where *he* was coming from? "I'm sorry?"

"I loved your father, Jessa."

"What?" She must not have heard that right.

"It took me ten years of therapy to figure it out."

"Therapy?" *Whoa.* Wait a minute. Who was this woman? "You don't do therapy." Or at least she'd never said anything.

"Actually, I do." Her mother's smile appeared almost apologetic. "You never knew your grandparents. That was on purpose. My father…he was the worst kind of bully."

Jessa had suspected as much, but Carla had never been exactly open about her own childhood. "You've never talked about him."

"There weren't many good things to say." She paused as though she had forced herself to say them now. "He wasn't abusive, but he was controlling. And he insulted my mother constantly. He treated her like a child. Wouldn't even let her get her driver's license."

"God. Really?" Well, she was glad she'd never known him, then.

"When I left home, I decided I'd never marry. Never fall in love. I thought it made you weak."

Like her grandmother. Her mom didn't have to say it. Jessa could sense the feelings of resentment.

Carla reached over and gripped her hand firmly. "But you're one of the strongest people I know, Jessa. And your father was, too." Tears glistened in her regal brown eyes, softening them. "He always told me he'd love me forever.

Even if I never loved him back. And he did. He sent me cards and letters and gifts all those years."

The mention of her father sent a wave of grief crashing over her.

"I felt so unworthy," Carla went on. "I pushed him away every chance I had. I told him to move on so many times."

"He never did." Buzz had never gone out on another date. He'd never said why, although Jessa had suspected he hadn't gotten over her mom. The two of them never dragged her into their complicated relationship, though. She'd had no clue he'd sent her mother letters.

"No. He never did move on." She laughed a little. "He was so stubborn, that man."

Jessa smiled, too. Stubborn in the best way possible.

"After you left home, I realized I wasn't healthy," Carla admitted, as though somewhat ashamed. "Emotionally. So I started therapy, and it helped me understand how afraid I'd been." Her lips pursed bravely. "The week before he passed, I wrote him a letter and told him how much I loved him. I was going to go up there to see him as soon as the summer session ended..."

But she hadn't made it in time.

Her mother's obvious pain pinched Jessa's heart. "Why didn't you tell me?"

"I don't know." Her head shook. "I guess I was embarrassed. I wasted all those years. We could've been happy. We could've been a family."

"We were a family." Definitely not conventional, but bonded by love all the same. "And at least he knew. Before. At least you told him you loved him." It changed things, knowing that. Knowing he had everything he'd wanted at the end.

Mom's eyes sought out hers. They were so solemn. "Fear does strange things to people. It makes them lash out." An unmistakable empathy echoed through the words.

"You think Lance is afraid." Yeah, well he wasn't the only one.

Carla held her hands. "I think he loves you and I think it terrifies him."

"I can't help him with that." Not again. Not this time. He'd probably just push her away like he had before.

Her mother lifted Jessa's chin like she had so many times when she was young. But this was different. She understood so much more now. Looking back at Carla, she saw a woman who had been wounded, who had spent her life running from relationships. Kind of like someone else she knew...

"How many times have you almost been attacked by an animal you were trying to rescue?" her mom asked quietly.

"Too many to count."

"Why do they try to attack?"

"Because they're in a vulnerable position. They feel threatened, and..." As she said them, the words struck her with meaning. "Oh."

"What do you usually do when an animal feels vulnerable and frightened?" She already knew, but Carla obviously wanted her to say the words.

"I move slowly," she whispered, tears weakening her throat. "And carefully. I show it I'm not there to hurt it." Sometimes it took a lot of convincing, especially when the animal had been neglected or abused.

"And you never walk away," Carla said through a sad smile.

"No." She'd never given up, even in the most hopeless

of situations. She'd always stuck it out, done whatever it took.

"What are you going to do this time?" Carla asked as though she already knew the answer.

Reaching over, she slid the envelope off the counter. "I guess I'm going to Vegas."

Chapter Twenty-Six

Lance had hardly stepped his spur inside the doorway to the swanky media reception before a curvaceous redhead cornered him. Up against a wall and way too far away from the bar for his comfort.

"Lance Cortez," she said in a flirty tone. "I'm Amber Hart."

He did his best to keep the cringe inside as he returned her dainty handshake. "Nice to meet you," he said politely, sneaking a glance at the media badge that dangled from a lanyard hanging over her fake breasts. He didn't recognize the name of the publication. Probably some small-town newspaper or one of those ad publications. They let just about anyone in here.

"So how are you feeling about the final ride?" she asked, leaning into him slightly.

Shitty. Actually, indifferent would be a better way to describe it. For the first five rounds of competition, he'd tried to maintain his focus, but each day that passed was another day he didn't hear from Jessa. Didn't know how she was doing. Didn't know *what* she was doing. He'd held out hope, and every time he went into the arena, he'd checked the seat number he'd given her. But she hadn't come.

Even with that distraction, he'd managed to maintain a spot as fourth overall in the competition, which meant he'd have to have a damn near perfect ride tomorrow to take the title.

If only he could shake the sinking feeling that maybe he'd really lost Jessa for good...

Not that Red had rights to any of that information. Avoiding eye contact, he shrugged. "Oh, you know. I feel ready."

"You sure look ready," she murmured, stripping him down with her eyes.

Five years ago that little suggestion beaming in her gaze would've invited him to take her arm and lead her to the bar, where he'd buy her drinks and charm her all the way up to his hotel room, but apparently Jessa had ruined him for any uninvolved fun because, despite the slinky dress and the impressive curves, this woman did nothing for him. "Um, will you please excuse me, Miss Hart?" He made a quick sidestep and scanned the restaurant over her shoulder. "I should go find my father." They'd come in together, but in true Luis Cortez form, he seemed to have wandered off. Smart man.

"Oh, sure, okay," she bubbled. "Here's my number." Her hand expertly slipped a card into his jean pocket, patting a little too close to his package. "Maybe we can hang out later."

"Maybe." He gave her a smile even though he had no intention of following up.

After he'd left her behind, he worked his way across the room, saying hello to some of the guys he'd competed against over the years and avoiding eye contact with every woman who seemed to be there to snag herself a stag. Finally, he saw Luis sitting at the end of the bar alone, which was exactly where he wanted to be. Head down, he elbowed his way through the lively crowd and plopped down on the stool next to Luis.

His father looked him over. "You look as miserable as a hog who's had his tail straightened," he said, taking a pull on his beer.

"I am," he admitted, signaling to the bartender to bring him whatever Luis was drinking.

"What're you doing here, son?"

He knew Luis didn't mean at the party. He meant why was he here when things weren't resolved with Jessa. Lance inhaled deeply. "Actually...I have no idea." For months he'd had this clear vision, this laser focus on Worlds. Like the closer he got to losing his career, the tighter he'd held on. Except now he couldn't for the life of him think why. It suddenly seemed a hell of a lot less important.

"This world...it doesn't give back to you." Luis looked at him square in the face, wearing the same expression he had when Lance was a teenage delinquent. "You sacrifice your body—hell, your whole life—and in the end you don't have much to show for it."

"So I guess the joke's on us, huh?" Funny. The only guarantee when you were a professional athlete was that you'd have to retire early. You had to be prepared to walk away and start something new. Walk into a whole new life. No one told you that when you were starting out, though.

"If I hadn't had you boys when I retired, I would've lost

myself." Luis turned the stool to face him. "I did for a while. Took some time to get myself straightened out. I don't want that to happen to you. You're a lot like me. The most like me out of all you boys."

"I'll take that as a compliment." Even though that wasn't how Luis meant it. And he understood. He hid behind his career. Used it as an excuse to block out everything else. He'd learned from watching his old man. He studied his father, still saw that spark of a young cowboy in his eyes, even with all of the lines the years had carved into his skin. "Why couldn't you stop Mom from leaving?" He'd never asked, but now seemed like as good a time as any, seeing as how he was going to have to deal with his issues if he ever wanted to get Jessa back.

Instead of deflecting the question with a gruff shrug of his shoulders like he usually did when Lance brought up something he didn't want to talk about, Luis set down his beer. It clanked against the bar top with the tremor in his hand. "Maybe I could've. Truth is, I didn't try." His solemn eyes lifted and found Lance's. "We got married young, and your mom...she worried an awful lot."

"I know. I remember." She was always fussing over the three of them. Though as they'd gotten older she seemed to detach herself more and more.

"It wasn't normal worry. It consumed her, made her sick." His father's cheeks hollowed. "They'd call it anxiety now. And it was constant."

"I guess I didn't realize it was so bad." But now that he thought about it, she stayed home as often as she could. Didn't have many friends. Tended to keep them home, too. She never hung around the corral, never went to any of their competitions.

"They didn't have medication for it then," Luis said. "No help. And I didn't know what to do for her."

"That's why she left?" Because of anxiety? It seemed like such a simple thing...

"She couldn't handle it. The fact that all you boys were following in my footsteps. Riding bulls. She wasn't sleeping, wasn't eating. She was so afraid something would happen to you."

Something did happen to them. All three of them. The day she left, she broke them. God, just look at them. All around thirty years old and not one healthy positive relationship among them...

"She didn't leave because she didn't love you," Luis said quietly. "I never wanted you to think that."

Remnants of the familiar anger stirred. "She could've chosen to stay." She could've tried to get help. She could've gone to counseling or something.

Luis shook his head. "Anxiety's a hard thing to understand if you've never had it. It's not just in your head. It's physical. I saw it in her. It was killing her." For the first time, Lance noticed a tremor in his father's head. It ticked, making Lance look away. He couldn't stand to see it, the evidence of a disease.

"I should've tried harder. I wish I would've done more. I wish I would've at least taken time off to try and help her before it got so bad."

For the first time, Lance let himself consider the possibility she hadn't wanted to leave. Maybe she didn't feel she had a choice. "You think it would've made a difference?"

"Maybe." Luis sighed. "If I'd fought for her. If she would've had more support." He gave Lance a long, steady glare, the same one he'd used when Lance would mouth off as an angry teen. "I know it cut you deep when she left. But it might be time to stop blaming her, son. As a parent you try to do your best with what you've got. In her way that's what she did. That fear she had...it lied to her. Told her you'd be better off without her. I know it's hard to understand, but that's the truth of it."

"Guess I don't have to understand it." All these years, he'd tried. And even knowing what he knew now, he *couldn't* understand. Luis was right. He hadn't stood where she stood. He had no idea what she struggled with. But he did know one thing. He couldn't let fear rob him of loving someone, of letting her love him. He wanted to do better than his mother had. All these years, he hadn't. When he'd lashed out at Jessa, it wasn't because he was pissed. It was because he was afraid. For his father, sure, but also for himself. "You regret it?" he asked his father. "Sticking with your career instead of walking away to be what she needed?"

A deep inhale seemed to steady Luis's tremors. "More than I can say. I was too busy collecting a whole lot of shiny shit that doesn't mean much." He looked around the party surrounding them. "Thing is, that's not my legacy. That room of buckles and trophies and news clippings. No one here gives a rat's ass who I am now."

"I do," Lance argued. His father had done his best for them. In his imperfect way. But it was enough. He'd earned their loyalty, their love, even if he didn't feel he deserved it.

Hope sparked inside of him, filling that empty coldness that'd hounded him since Jessa had sent him away. Maybe his pathetic, imperfect offering could be enough for her, too.

His father reached over and squeezed his shoulder. "You can leave your mark on this world only in the people you love. Not in the stuff you accomplish. You remember that, son."

If Luis had said that to him six months ago, he would've laughed. But now he was starting to understand.

* * *

"It's gotta be perfect, Cortez," Tucker said, pacing on the outside of the chute. "I mean, one hundred percent flawless. You gotta get your leg off him. You need the extra points."

"You think I don't know that?" Lance tightened the chinstrap on his helmet. He eyed the bull that snorted on the other side of the fence. Loco Motive made Ball Buster and Wild Willy look like kittens. The damn bull had already taken eight riders out of the competition and had sent two to the hospital.

Adrenaline boiled in his gut, shooting his body temperature up about a hundred degrees. Damn all the gear they made 'em wear these days. When he'd started out, he hadn't had to bear half his weight in body armor.

"Stay loose up there," Tucker instructed.

How was that possible when he felt this tense? He glanced around at the television cameras, all starting to swing his way. The announcers were no doubt detailing his story, his last title from six years ago to now, when he'd barely qualified to be here.

Was Jessa watching? Would she be cheering him on? God, he wanted to call her right now, tell her everything he'd wanted to say to her. But she hadn't returned any of his messages. Five days. It had been only five days since he'd seen her and yet it felt like five months.

All week, he'd held on to her words. *You can win.* They'd

kept him going. Jessa thought he could do this, so he'd ride perfect. Not for the cheering fans. Not for Luis or Tucker. Not even for himself. For her. From this moment on, he wanted everything to be about her.

The manager gave him the signal to climb up and get into position.

Here we go. He tried to clear his head the way he'd always been able to do. Took some deep breaths, inhaling that manure-tinged scent of the bull. Took about five guys to hold Loco Motive in place while Lance climbed the fence.

Tucker gave him a final pat on the arm, looking a hell of a lot more nervous than him. He couldn't blame him. Lance hadn't exactly had a stellar ride this week. Solid, but nothing that could put him on top. Not yet at least.

"You're on," the director said.

Lance swung his leg over the fence and slid onto the bull.

Instantly agitated, the son of a bitch snorted and bucked.

Lance got his right hand gripped onto the rope and kept his left hand up. Had to keep his left arm raised, no matter what happened. If it came down, if it so much as grazed the bull, he'd lose points.

The chute opened.

Loco Motive shot straight into the corral, bucking and kicking. Pissed off as all hell.

But Lance kept his form. Left arm waving, right hand fisting that rope so damn hard it felt like his knuckles would break. The arena flashed around him, fragmented glimpses of the crowd, the judges, the scoreboard.

One…

The bull's body jackknifed, but he saw it coming. His body whipped forward and he clenched his legs tight around the bull's wide girth, waving his left arm over his head.

Two...

The loud roar of the crowd muted Loco Motive's angry snorts. The bull reared up again launching them both.

Three...

Fuck! Could this get any longer? He curved his back, let his upper body jolt freely with the bull's enraged kicks.

Four...

His right hand burned like someone had stuck it in a fire. Another hard jerk sent a shot straight to his back, the muscles threatening to cave in.

Five...

Loco Motive spun in a rage, kicking up the dirt, tossing his head back like he'd had it. Lance's body thrashed, ribs separating, whiplash starting to weaken his neck.

Six...

Every muscle in Lance's body pinched, sending rivers of pain all through him. Not enough. This ride was not enough.

Seven...

He saw lights. Blurred faces. His leg. He had to get his leg up. Straining his back, he raised his left arm higher over his head and shifted his balance. His back spasmed as he lifted his right leg away from the bull, holding his posture, fighting like hell to keep his grip. The crowd's praise droned in his ears.

Eight!

His grip loosened. The right wrist was giving out. He hugged his knees into the bull's sides and flung his left arm high into the air with a whoop. Loco Motive gave one last bucking kick as though he'd taken personal offense to that, and flung Lance toward the corral fence.

A collective gasp hushed the crowd, but elation drowned out the pain in his body. That was the ride of his life. He knew it, felt it. While the bullfighter lured away Loco Motive, Lance lay flat on his back in the dirt, staring up at the scoreboard. Two medics rushed over but he waved them away. He'd be fine. As soon as he saw the score, he'd be fine. It seemed to take forever while the crowd murmured. He lay there under the lights, taking it all in, wishing he would see Jessa's face in the stands.

"Ninety-four point eight," the announcer called with an excitement that reignited the arena.

He had to blink, had to squint his eyes to make sure that was right.

Sure enough, the red numbers lit up the screen: 94.8. There were three riders left, but no one would beat that. No one *could* beat that. His eyes closed and he breathed out, now feeling every aching muscle, every sore bone.

He flattened his hands against the ground, ready to get up, but Tucker catapulted in and landed right on top of him. "Hell yeah!" his friend yelled. "Hell! Yeah!" He slapped him square in the chest. "You nailed it!"

Wincing, Lance rolled out from underneath Tucker and pushed to his feet. The crowd noise deafened him. He waved and started to limp toward the gate, trying to keep a rowdy smile intact for the cameras. But it wasn't real.

There were thousands of people here. The one person he wanted, though, the one who mattered, wasn't. He looked around, at the crowd, all watching the replay on the Jumbotron in an awed silence. And he felt no different. No better than he had twenty minutes ago. He'd just taken the world title he'd been striving for, and he didn't even feel like celebrating.

The crowd, the fanfare, the cheering...none of it even came close to giving him the same rush he got when he made Jessa smile.

Tucker launched himself into another man hug. "I can't believe it, you son of a bitch! You did it."

Lance pushed him off and backed away. He couldn't stay. All he could think about was pulling Jessa into his arms. He didn't care what she said, she belonged with him. And he belonged with her. "I have to get out of here. Now."

"You can't go!" Tucker tried to block him. "You just won the world title, jackass! They're not gonna let you cut out. You've gotta stay for the hoopla!"

He couldn't. Not without Jessa here. He never would've been able to do this if it hadn't been for her.

And she was all he needed.

Chapter Twenty-Seven

OhmyGod, ohmyGod, ohmyGod!" Jessa sprinted down some steps in the dark arena, trying to find her way out so she could get to him. That image of him flying toward the fence replayed again and again, sending her stomach into a downward spiral. When he'd hit the ground, Lance hadn't moved. And before she knew what she was doing, she'd jumped up in a panic, stepping on toes and purses and drinks until she'd made her way to the end of the row. But where was she now? And where was Lance?

Was he *dead*?

Finally, she saw a door and charged it, jogging out into the concessions area. But the place was so big—so many stairs and food stands and doors...

"How can I get down there?" she asked some poor older man pushing a trash can. "I have to find Lance Cortez! I have to get to him."

He looked down as though embarrassed for her.

"I'm not a groupie!" she shrieked. "He gave me this pass!" She tugged at the lanyard hanging around her neck. "Where's the staging area? Where do they take injured riders?"

He pointed at an escalator and got the hell out of there.

Gripping the handrail, she stumble-jogged down the escalator to the main floor and tore down a corridor, searching for a door that would get her back there.

There! Official-looking steel double doors. She bolted for them, but before she got there, they flew open.

Lance ran out. Ran! He was running!

"What're you doing?" she yelled, floating to him in a stupefied jog. "Oh my God, Lance! I thought you were hurt!"

He caught her in his arms, looking her over, touching her like he had to make sure she was really standing there. "What are *you* doing?" he asked breathlessly. "I thought you didn't come..."

Seeing him whole, strong and upright, brought a fast rush of relief that made her dizzy. "I came." She cupped her hand on his uninjured cheek. "Of course I came." A happy sigh pushed her closer to him and she felt his heartbeat against her chest. "I couldn't get a flight out until this morning. Everything was booked." And she'd had to get coverage at the shelter, and find someone to watch Ilsa, and then Naomi and Darla and Cassidy had all wanted to come, so they'd had to find flights, too...

"But you weren't in your seat," he said, smoothing his hand down her hair. "I looked for you..."

"I got here late, so I just sat in an empty seat." Who knew how long it would've taken her to find the right section?

She ran her hands down his arms, searching for damage.

"And when the bull threw you, I got up and ran." She peered up at him, all teary and pathetic. "I couldn't stand it. I thought—"

"I'm fine. Hardly felt it." He hugged her close, kissing her forehead, her cheek, her lips. "When I won, all I could think about was you. You weren't there..."

"You won?" She gasped. She'd been so panicked she hadn't even realized. She pushed him away. "If you won you have to go back in there!" What the hell was he doing standing out here talking to her?

He gazed down at her and his eyes had the power to kill her and revive her all at once.

"I had to find you so I just...ran out."

"You shouldn't have." She never would've asked him to do that. "This was your dream. You should enjoy all of it. Everything the experience will offer you."

"I guess you could say I have a new dream." He lifted his hand to her face, trailing his fingers down her cheek. "One that matters more."

Jessa pressed her hand against her chest, tears welling. His nearness stirred a craving, a tingling rush that covered her skin and while the rest of her felt weak, her heart beat strongly.

"Fact is, I'm pretty messed up," he said, pressing his hand against hers, stroking her fingers. "What I said about you not being part of the family..." His head shook. "It wasn't you I was mad at. I've blamed my mom for every-thing. Every bad thing that's happened since she left, I put it on her."

"I can understand that," Jessa whispered.

"But I'm ready to let it go. Get past it. I have to or I'll never have anything that matters." His fingertips brushed hers but he didn't hold on. "You didn't betray me. You've only been good to me. And to my family. I'm sorry I hurt you."

She peered up at him, and with that one simple apology, it seemed he'd let her see so much more of his heart. "Thank you."

"This whole week, all I could think about was how you weren't here." He inched closer, and she closed her eyes, feeling his presence up against her. "Without you, I didn't care anymore. I've won competitions. And it's never made me feel as good as I feel when I'm with you."

"Lance…" There were so many things she wanted to say, but he took her hand, stealing the words along with her breath.

"I want you," he said through an utterly helpless sigh. "I don't have much to offer. But I want to be there for you. I want to make you happy. I want to hold you in my arms and feel you against me. Nothing in my life has ever felt as good as holding you. Nothing."

The quiet conviction in his voice filled her eyes. "I want you, too."

He said nothing more, only pulled her against him and sealed her lips with his, right there in the brightly lit corridor with people walking past them, his mouth devouring hers, hungry and passionate, as if he'd been saving up his whole life to offer her this one kiss.

It carried her away, the feel of his chest heaving against hers, the strength of his hands as they held her. "Lance," she murmured, letting her purse drop to the ground. "My God, Lance."

"Let's get out of here," he groaned.

And she couldn't have said no if she tried.

* * *

"My room is closer." She wrapped her arms around his sturdy back, holding on as he urged her into the elevator.

"Floor ten," she said, against his mouth. As the elevator zoomed up, his tongue teased its way into her mouth, weakening her knees, which made her cling to him tighter. The doors rolled open and they stumbled out, moving clumsily down the hall, unable to let go of each other.

"Key's in my pocket," she breathed, already undoing the buttons on his shirt.

He groped a hand into the pocket of her jeans until he found it.

As he unlocked the door, he caught her waist and pulled her against him again, bringing his lips to hers as he somehow pushed into the hotel room.

Her feet faltered along with his and before they'd made it to the bed, she kicked off her tennis shoes while he stepped out of his boots.

"I don't know how I lived without you so long," he murmured in her ear while his hands tugged up the hem of her shirt. "I don't think I was ever really alive."

She opened her mouth to answer, to tell him that she must've never really been in love before because this all felt new. Her heart pounded her ribs so hard they threatened to fracture. And it was so good. So good it almost hurt.

He pulled her shirt over her head and slipped his fingers into her bra and *ohhhhhh*. What was she going to say again? Nothing. She couldn't speak. She slumped against him while he touched her, teasing her nipples in long strokes while she clumsily undid the rest of the buttons on his shirt until she could push it off his shoulders and run her hands over the hard muscled plane of his abs.

H-ello. Just the sight of him was foreplay...

But looking wasn't enough. She wanted to feel him, to taste him. Threading her fingers between his, she ducked her head and kissed her way down his neck to his chest, sucking and licking and breathing hotly against his skin. When she reached the waist of his pants, she let his hands go and started to work at that rather impressive belt buckle, but before she could get it undone, he hauled her back up to him. "Not yet."

Tearing back the comforter and sheets, he laid her down on the bed, hovering over her, those eyes seeming to note every detail.

"I can't get enough of you," he breathed over her. "I'll never get enough of you." With that, he lowered his lips to her neck, sneaking his hands underneath her back so he could pop the clasp of her bra. Rising, he slowly slid the straps down her shoulders as though he enjoyed the torture.

"Too slow," she breathed, pushing up to her elbows. She tore the bra away and drew his face to her breasts.

His warm tongue traced every inch of her skin, forcing her head to fall back to the pillows. Without taking his lips away from her, his hands hitched up her hips and he took down her pants and sensible cotton underwear in one fluid motion.

"Should've worn my pretty underwear," she said with a gasp.

"I like you better without any." He pulled his body over hers, kissing her lips with a sensual rhythm that charged every part of her. God, no one had ever made her ache like this...

His lips moved down her neck again, covering her chest with warm, wet kisses, then moving lower to her stomach.

Sparks flashed low in her belly, sending flares of heat between her legs. She pressed her lips together so she wouldn't moan. She shouldn't be this close this fast...

He paused and glanced up at her. "You can be as loud as you want," he teased. "No one'll walk in on us this time."

Before she could respond, he took her hips in his hands, kissing and nibbling his way down to the inside of her thigh.

Her legs fell open. She did make noise then—a long groan flowed out of her lungs, deflating them completely.

"I love turning you on," Lance said, all low and hot as his fingers parted her.

She felt his sultry breath against her most sensitive parts first, then the slick wetness of his tongue. Her hands grasped for something to hold on to, finding only fistfuls of the sheets. Cries stammered from her lips as his mouth sucked and nibbled while his fingers slid in and out. A powerful tightening in her abdomen intensified until she broke apart, and it came so fast and so forcefully she may have cried out.

Lance's face appeared in front of hers, sly grin firmly in place. "You might've disturbed the neighbors," he said, playfully kissing her forehead.

"That would be a first," she admitted, her breathing still ragged. She'd never had a reason to be so loud before. She'd never been so overtaken that she lost control that way...

"I liked it." His eyebrows danced enticingly. "Let's do it again."

"Nope." Because it wasn't nearly as fun when she was the only one being so noisy. She squirmed out from underneath him, rising to her knees, which might never stop wobbling. "This belt is coming off now, cowboy." Her hands fumbled with the brass buckle until it released. Locking her eyes on his, she gave him a small smile while she ripped open the button fly on his jeans and shoved them down, taking the boxer briefs with them. "I can turn you on, too, you know." She climbed onto him, wrapping her legs around him and grinding her hips into his.

"I'm turned on just looking at you," he uttered, pulling her so tightly against his body that nothing stood between them. His eyes locked hers in an intimate stare and he brushed some hair away from her forehead. "Seriously, Jessa. I want to give you everything. I want to be the person who loves you."

She cupped his cheeks in her hands and drew his lips to hers. "That's enough." She didn't need him to be perfect. She wasn't looking for the perfect relationship. Only someone who was willing to try every day. That was enough.

Still kissing his mouth, she straddled him and adjusted her hips until she slid onto him, pausing there, feeling him quake beneath her. He filled her so perfectly, so deeply, that her body started that delicious throb again.

His fingers dug into her shoulders, urging her chest lower until he took her breast in his mouth and swirled his tongue around the nipple. Urgency pulsed inside of her, forcing her to move. She lifted her hips and thrust down onto him hard but smooth, again and again until his head fell back to the pillow. "Hell yes, Jessa," he panted. "God, I'm so fucking lost in you."

"I have some tricks, too," she murmured, hoping she could hold on long enough. Before it was too late, she squeezed her thighs together, rocking her hips against his, cradling him as tightly into her as she could.

A cross between a growl and a groan purred against

her skin. Lance's hands went to her backside, bringing her against him faster and harder until she was completely lost in the breathless anticipation of what was coming. She tightened her legs around him even more and his body bucked beneath hers, sending a final thrust so deep into her that she came apart again, shuddering and crying out and delighting in the sound of her name on his lips as he convulsed beneath her.

A happy exhaustion took her over as she draped her body over his. He held her, nestling her head into the crook of his arm while his lips sought hers. She kissed him back somewhat lazily, given the fact that her body was sedated.

"I'll love you the best I can, Jessa Mae Love," he whispered in her ear.

And she knew it was true.

* * *

He'd never woken up with a woman in his arms. Not once in his life. And damn, it seemed he'd been missing out. Jessa lay against him, her silky back against his chest, her soft hair spilling over his arm. He didn't want to move, didn't want to disturb her and end this moment. But he also wanted to see her face.

Slowly, he eased up his head to peek over her shoulder.

Her eyes were wide open in a look of fear.

The feeling of contentment snapped and he sat up straight. "What's wrong?" How long had she been awake? Why didn't she look as calm and content as he felt?

She shifted onto her back, her captivating eyes staring at the ceiling. "I just...things moved so fast last night. We may have gotten a little carried away."

Hell yes, they'd gotten carried away and he hoped they'd do it again. As soon as possible.

"Do you regret it?" she whispered. "Walking away from the celebration? I mean, has anyone ever done that? Will you be disqualified? What'll happen?"

"Everything'll be fine." Easing out a breath of relief, he lay back down, gathering her into his arms to coax out her concerns. He didn't care what happened. "The only regret I have is that I didn't discover you sooner." The rest of his life seemed like such a waste compared to this. Compared to being connected so deeply with someone as good and bright and beautiful as Jessa.

"What about Ilsa?" she asked, suddenly looking worried again.

"The pig?" He laughed. He didn't mean to, but Pork Chop was the last thing on his mind right now.

"Yes." She searched his face. "I know you're not that crazy about her, but I love her. She's such a little sweetheart, and if we ever end up... you know... together someday..." She seemed too embarrassed to finish.

He brought her hand to his lips, kissing her fingers. "Actually, she's growing on me."

"Really?" She didn't look convinced.

"If it weren't for Pork—I mean Ilsa—you might never have talked to me again," he said, stroking her arm. "That makes her a saint in my book."

Smiling happily, Jessa propped herself up, gazing down at him, beauty spilling from her bottomless brown eyes. "I don't want the money, you know."

"You deserve the money." And she needed it for the shelter. "I always keep my word."

Her head shook. "I won't take it. You might need it. For

your dad. For his treatments." A smile plumped her lips. "Besides, some of my old grad school friends are helping me create a social media campaign to build a donor base. I guilted them into doing it for free."

He doubted she had to guilt them. Everyone who knew Jessa seemed to love her. And she would always be one of those people who gave more than she took. "We'll see," he said, not willing to argue about it now. If she refused to take the money he'd promised her, he'd simply find another way to give it to her.

"What did it feel like to win?" she asked, trailing her fingertips over his biceps.

And God she was so sexy, her blond hair trailing over her shoulder, her eyes glistening as if he could tell her anything and it would stay safely locked away in the vault of her heart.

"It felt like the end." He hadn't considered that until he said it, but the truth was, it felt like a relief.

"You're okay with that?"

"I'm ready to start the next phase." A whole new life waited for him. One he'd never thought he'd have. "I don't want to be anywhere but here right now. With you," he murmured, running his fingers over her shoulders, down her breasts. He couldn't resist the temptation of touching her. "Doing what we did last night. As many times as you'll let me."

"Mmmm-hmmm," she hummed, her eyes closing as she shimmied her hand underneath the sheets. "I can see you're up to the task." Her hand clasped the solid length of him.

Yeah, there was that. He'd woken up hard. With her in his bed, that'd most likely be the norm. He slipped his hand under the sheets, too, letting it wander down her hip...

Turning, she wrapped her legs around his waist and

brought his body against hers. "No need to bother with all the foreplay."

"I like the foreplay," he said as he sank into her. The power of it stole his breath. He had plenty of ways to draw it out as long as possible, to tease her. "It'll be worth it—"

A knock pounded on the door. "Jessa!" a woman's voice screeched from the hallway.

She froze underneath him, her eyes wide.

"Are you in there?" came from another woman.

Lance lifted his head. "Who the hell—?"

She pushed him off her and started to scramble. "It's Cassidy. And Darla!"

"What're they doing here?" he demanded, trying to pull her back to him.

"They wanted to come to Vegas." She gave him a sheepish smile. "They're staying at the Bellagio. Sorry. I forgot to mention that."

He captured her in a hug, settling her back to the mattress. "It's okay. We don't have to answer the door."

"But I was supposed to meet them for breakfast this morning..." She snatched her phone off the bedside table. "Twenty-three missed calls."

Shit. "Will we ever be able to make love without being interrupted?" he wondered aloud.

"Jessa!" Now that was Naomi. He'd heard her worked up enough times to recognize it.

"What's got them all riled?" he whispered. Maybe if they were real quiet the crazies would go away and let him finish what he'd started.

"I should've called them," she whispered back. "They get worried." Squirming out of his grip, Jessa threw on a bathrobe and unclicked the deadbolt.

"Where've you been?" The door burst open and Cassidy, Naomi, and Darla all charged in, then halted, gaping at the two of them like they'd caught them doing jumping jacks naked.

"We thought you'd been kidnapped!" Naomi squealed.

"Vegas is a huge hub for human trafficking," Cassidy added knowingly.

"Then you wouldn't return our calls!" Darla finished as if the whole thing had been scripted.

"Nope. Not kidnapped." Jessa glanced at Lance, biting her lip as though trying not to laugh. "Sorry. I kind of lost track of time."

Despite the fact that there were three high-drama women staring at him naked in bed, Lance grinned back. They'd lost track of a lot of stuff. Shoes. Clothes...

"Obviously." Darla eyed Lance like he was a big juicy cut of meat.

He pulled the covers up to his chin.

Naomi stared at him, too, but it was more of a glare. And judging from the way her hands sat rigidly on her hips, she didn't like this at all. "So you two figured things out?" she asked suspiciously.

You could say that. He still had some work to do, but he'd do whatever it took. "I realized nothing I did seemed to matter without Jessa," he said, even though there would've been a more appropriate time for this conversation. Later. After he'd had his way with Jessa and was fully clothed.

Beaming a happy, teary smile, Jessa sat on the bed next to him and took his hand.

"Awww," Darla and Cassidy said collectively.

But Naomi simply narrowed her eyes protectively. "What does that mean?"

He turned his face to Jessa's and couldn't help but pull himself up to kiss her lightly on the lips. From the sound of the sniffles in the room, that was a good move. "It means I love her. It means I'm dealing with my shit so I can be with her."

"It means that you three need to get out of my room," Jessa added. "If you couldn't tell, we were kind of in the middle of something."

"Oh! Right! Sorry!" Darla clamped her hands onto Cassidy's and Naomi's shoulders, dragging them backward to the door. "You can give us all the details later."

Lance shot Jessa a look.

"Not *all* of them," she promised.

"OhmyGod, I'm so happy for you two!" Cassidy sighed before she disappeared.

Naomi wriggled free from Darla's grasp.

Lance half-expected another angry glare, seeing as how she didn't exactly think he was worthy of Jessa. But instead, she smiled. "I'm happy for you, too. Really."

"Thanks," Jessa called, shooing her away impatiently with a hand. "Okay. Bye, now. We'll talk later."

When the door *finally* slammed, he gathered Jessa into his arms and rolled her onto his body.

She laughed. "Wow, someone's got energy."

"The pressure's on," he said, showering her shoulders with hot little kisses. "I'd better give you some incredible details to tell your friends."

Epilogue

Not once in the history of Topaz Falls had the Cortez family ever hosted a party. Until Lance started dating Jessa, that was.

Jessa stood on the front porch of Lance's home, admiring how the ranch came to life in the spring. All the aspens had their baby green leaves back. Wildflowers were starting to dot the meadows. Though they'd still likely get a few more snowstorms, the land looked like it was finally emerging from winter, so bright and fresh and new. *Every*thing at the ranch felt new and exciting and hopeful. It didn't hurt that half the town had turned out for the first shindig of the season. The laughter and murmur of gossip seemed to give the place a new life.

All winter she'd drifted in and out of this house, laughing and living and loving with this family while she and Lance got to know each other. Lucas and Levi had both stayed on for the holiday months, helping cart Luis to doctor appointments and therapy treatments. They'd all spent the evenings out by the fire pit, surrounded by drifts of crisp white snow while they roasted marshmallows and laughed as the three brothers relived their childhood antics. When the fire burned low, they'd pour the wine and listen to Lucas play his guitar. That was her favorite, snuggling with Lance and his wandering hands underneath a blanket while the soft notes of strings floated around them.

These days if anyone dared tell her she wasn't a part of this family, she wouldn't believe them. The proof was all around her. The Cortez men had actually let her plan a party at their ranch, and even though they'd grumbled about it, they sure seemed to be having a great time.

She gazed out over the white party tents they'd rented, then over to the prefab stage, where a local bluegrass band played. Okay, so it was possible that she'd gone a bit overboard. She couldn't help herself. A while back, they'd received word that Lance was being inducted into the Pro Rodeo Hall of Fame, just like his father, and right away she'd started planning the celebration of the century.

It had turned out perfectly, if she did say so herself. "Come on, Ilsa," she said, tugging gently on her not-so-little piggy's leash. They ambled down the steps and into the crowds. She almost couldn't believe how many people had turned out to honor him. She smiled at each one as she passed, saying hello, even to Hank Green, though she didn't dare get too close to him.

On the outskirts of the tent, she spotted Evie Starlington standing alone, sipping a glass of Darla's special white sangria. Still being considered a newbie in town, the poor woman wouldn't know many people, so Jessa hurried toward her.

Ilsa grunted. She didn't like hurrying. Over the winter, the pig had fully recovered and was quite a bit wider than she'd been when Jessa had found her. Wider and happier, especially when there was a party and there were plenty of scraps on the ground. "Come on, girl," she prompted. "A little exercise will do you some good." Even with Ilsa's protests, they finally made it to the tent.

"Evie! I'm so happy you could make it. Come with me." She took her hand warmly before the woman could answer, and guided her to the tables she'd happened to see Luis sitting at earlier.

Sure enough, the man was still there, chatting with Deputy Dev Jenkins about the unusually warm weather. She hated to interrupt but this was important.

"Hey there, Luis," she said, pulling out the chair next to him. Ilsa plopped down at her feet and started munching on a stray carrot that had rolled off someone's plate.

Evie took a seat across the table. "You remember Evie, right?" Jessa said, presenting the woman grandly.

"Of course." He tipped his hat to her. "Nice to see you again."

"Evie is an artist," Jessa informed him. "You should see her stained-glass work."

"That so?" The man looked at her with interest. "How'd you get into that?"

It seemed her work here was done. "Oh!" Jessa jumped out of her chair. "I completely forgot. I need to check in with Darla. Make sure she has everything she needs."

Luis squinted at her with a small smile as though he knew exactly what she was doing. But that wouldn't stop her. She waved and tugged Ilsa away to give them some time alone. To keep up appearances, she headed straight for the catering tent, even though Darla clearly had everything under control.

"This is all amazing," Jessa said to her friend as she approached what had become the food and drink control command center.

Her friend straightened her apron proudly. "Everyone seems happy and properly drunk, which means I've done my job."

"Everyone definitely seems happy." Even Cassidy was out on the dance floor letting Levi twirl her around. "She must be *really* tipsy if she's dancing with him."

"I think she lost a bet," Darla answered drily. She looked toward the corral. "Naomi's the only one who doesn't seem exactly thrilled to be here."

Jessa peeked over to where Darla was staring. Both Naomi and Lucas were mingling with a group of their old high school friends. Lucas knelt on the ground and said something that made Gracie laugh, but Naomi simply turned and wandered away alone.

"Is he still leaving tomorrow?" Darla asked, fiddling with the chocolate fountain, then dipping in a plastic spoon.

"Yes." Jessa sighed. She'd done her best to convince him to stay. "He says he has to get back to the McGowen Ranch, that they've given him long enough." He also said he'd be back and forth as much as possible, but who knew how often they'd see him.

Her friend licked the melted chocolate off her spoon and dipped in another one, handing it to Jessa. "Naomi sure avoided him the last couple of months, huh?"

"Avoided him? She pretended he didn't exist." She taste-tested the sample Darla had given her. Their friend had taken Gracie to Florida for a month to visit her parents. When she *had* been at the ranch, she'd kept herself busy with running her daughter to camps and volunteering at the school. The only time Naomi and Lucas seemed to politely chat was when they all had dinner together, but the woman always begged out early. Before they built a fire. Before Lucas played his guitar. As far as Jessa knew, they hadn't spent one second alone all winter.

A wave of panic washed over her, making her feel the heat of the evening more intensely. "I wish I could make him stay."

"Guess it's not up to us," Darla said, turning back to the chocolate fountain to refill the plates of strawberries.

"I know, it's just—"

An arm slid around her waist. "I need you," her sexy cowboy breathed into her ear. "Alone."

Those words were all it took to restart her heart. She swore it beat only for him these days.

"You can have me whenever and wherever you want me." She turned to him, and he pulled her into a scandalous hug.

Behind them, Darla made gagging noises. "Not near the food, you two!" she scolded. "And don't get any ideas about the melted chocolate."

"I already *have* ideas," Lance said, eyeing the fountain.

"He does," Jessa agreed. "He has *a lot* of good ideas."

"Okay. That's it." Her friend shooed them away. "Get out. Out of my tent."

"Fine." Jessa held out Ilsa's leash. "But would you mind holding on to her for a while? And don't give her any chocolate. I have her on a diet."

"Of course. I'd love to babysit your pig while you go off and get some." Darla rolled her eyes, but she smiled as she took the leash.

Laughing, Lance swept Jessa up the hill toward the corral. "I have a surprise for you," he murmured, drawing her close to his side.

"Ohhhh. A surprise for me? But this is supposed to be *your* special day."

Just outside the old barn, he stopped and faced her. "The surprise is for you. But I'm hoping it'll benefit me, too."

"Huh?" That didn't make any sense...

Wearing a mysterious grin, he urged her to the barn's entrance, which as far as she knew, stored their old tractor parts and animal feed.

As they stepped inside, he covered her eyes with his hand. She saw nothing but darkness, but that was okay because she'd blindly follow this man anywhere.

After a couple of steps he stopped, pulling his hand away.

Bright lights lit up the space, and this was no barn. It had been transformed into something else. Something sophisticated and clean. The walls had been dry-walled and were painted a lovely soft green. Ceramic tiles covered the once dusty floor. A long counter and desk sat at the front of the room and kennels lined the back.

Jessa gaped at him.

"Welcome to the new Helping Paws Animal Shelter," he said, spreading out his arms in grand presentation. "And don't worry. We'll get the outside fixed up as nice as the inside."

"What?" She gasped, turning herself in a slow circle, trying to take it in, but the blinding tears made it difficult. He'd thought of everything. *Everything*. From the brand-new computer sitting on the desk to the framed animal posters dressing up the walls. There were kennels and examining tables and supplies...

A happy sob squeaked out.

She turned back to him, ready to throw herself at him in a hug, but he'd taken a knee. And he was holding up a small black velvet box.

"Yes!" she blurted before he'd even said anything. Her whole body trembled with a yes. He didn't have to ask.

His exaggerated expression of shock teased her. "I haven't said anything yet."

"Oh. Right." She did her best to rein in her excitement so she didn't steal this moment from him. Knowing Lance, he'd planned out exactly what he wanted to say down to the syllable.

He took her hand in his. "You taught me how to love, Jessa," he began. "Showed me it was possible."

Tears snuck into her eyes. The man definitely knew how to write a speech...

"I know we haven't been together long," he went on. "But I've never been as sure of anything as I am of us. You brought me to life and now I want a life with you. Always. I hate it when you go home. I want the ranch to be our home now. Together. You and me and a whole bunch of kids."

The words warmed her through. Kids. A family...

"Marry me, beautiful," he uttered, tears filling his eyes, too. "Please marry me." He opened the box, revealing the most delicate ring she'd ever seen. It was a solitaire diamond, inset into a wide band, rose gold to match the necklace her father had given her. The last gift he'd given her before he passed away.

"I can answer now?" she whispered, crying softly.

He grinned and rolled his eyes up to the ceiling as though thinking about it. "Sure," he said. "I'm done."

"In that case..." She tugged him to his feet. "I can't wait to marry you. *Obviously*."

He slipped the ring onto her finger and pulled her close. "I'll make you the happiest woman in the world. I promise you." A wicked gleam lit his eyes. "And not just in bed, either."

"You already make me happy. In bed and in everything else." She embraced him as tightly as she could, holding happiness in her arms. "Oh my God, I'm getting married!" she sang, letting it soak into the deepest parts of her. She gazed up into Lance's tender eyes. Tom Hanks and Meg Ryan had nothing on them.

"I can't believe you did all of this." She looked around the room again, at all of the details, the months and months of work he'd kept secret from her. "It's perfect. The most beautiful thing I've ever seen."

"I'm gonna give you everything." He leaned down to kiss her, and she savored it, the feeling of belonging to someone again. She'd always miss her father, but for the first time since he'd passed away, her heart felt whole.

He danced her to the window and together they peered out. "Look at that. It's all ours. Yours and mine." His palms cradled her stomach. "And someday it'll belong to all of our little buckaroos, too."

She stared out at the snowcapped mountains that sheltered the houses all lined up in a row farther down the hill. "I love this place." It would be their place—a haven for their family and friends, a place where they gathered and celebrated and built a life together. All of them.

Lance drew closer behind her, wrapping her up in his arms. "Let's go out and share the news," he murmured against her neck. "Then we'll kick everyone outta here so I can try to get you pregnant."

Eyeing him seductively, she slipped out of his embrace,

backed to the main door, and clicked the lock into place. "We don't have to kick anyone out. No one'll miss us."

"In that case, come here." Her fiancé made his way to her, those breathtaking bluish eyes focused and intent. He slid his hands down her body, and she loved those big manly hands, loved how they made her feel so petite. "I love you," she whispered, kissing him again and again.

"I love you, too," he said, easing his arms around her. "And I love that you're going to be my wife."

His wife! A burst of happiness could've carried her straight to the clouds.

She'd finally found it, what her heart had so desperately craved. Love. And it was braver and bigger and deeper than she ever knew it could be.

A woman never forgets her first cowboy...

Don't miss the next installment of Sara
Richardson's Rocky Mountain Riders series

Comeback Cowboy

Available Summer 2017

Please see the next page for a preview.

Chapter One

The best thing about grand vintage houses was not the ornate crown molding or the heavy wooden five-panel doors or even the charming antique accents.

Nope. Those details were nice and all, but the best thing about old houses were the secrets protected within their walls.

Naomi Sullivan could relate to secrets. She'd carefully guarded a few whoppers of her own. While her own secrets tended to stalk her, she found other people's secrets fascinating.

Admiring the large bow window that welcomed in the early morning sunrays, Naomi breathed in the scent of old wood and dust. Truly, the place was a mess. No one had lived here since old Mrs. Porter had passed away four years ago. The original parquet floors were scuffed and dirty, the thick cherry trim discolored with grime. But somehow the Porter House still charmed her the same way it had when she was a young girl and she'd ride her bike past it every morning on her way to school.

It had always reminded her of something out of a storybook—whimsical and romantic. The structure itself was a Queen Anne Victorian with a steeply pitched roof, a dominant front-facing gable, and overhanging eaves. The siding had been well kept and was painted a lovely cloud-blue with the trim accented in an elegant cream. Classic columns held up a wraparound porch complete with intricate spindle work.

She wandered to the window and peered out at the front lawn. The gardens had gone to ruin, but the grass still grew green and thick. She supposed that was something. Turning back to Colton, her real estate agent, lawyer, and oldest childhood friend, she felt that telltale flicker of passion spark in her chest. "It's perfect. I'll take it."

Colton simply tsked at her and shuffled his four-hundred-dollar loafers over to where she stood. "No so fast. It's not even officially on the market, yet." His head tilted with a healthy dose of sass. "And how's that business loan coming, hmmm? Are the papers signed? Is the money in your account?"

"It will be," she fired back, though she wasn't nearly as gifted in the sass department as him. "It's all in process." And everything *would* go through. She *would* get that business loan. She *would* move off of the Cortez Ranch, and she *would* open her own bed and breakfast by next winter.

Damn it.

"'In process' won't cut it," Colton informed her. "If you want me to make a deal with the Porter family before they list it, I'll need the cash, honey."

"I should have it by the end of the week." At least she'd better.

She passed underneath an archway and carefully ran her hand over the solid banister that swirled up the staircase in the foyer. She'd done everything required to submit the loan application and the banker had all but told her she was a shoe in. Working at the Cortez Ranch and living there rent-free for the past ten years had allowed her to save plenty of money, so she only had to borrow enough to purchase the house, do some renovations, and buy the furniture. Besides that, she had outstanding credit and always paid her bills on time.

There was no way the bank would turn her down.

She peered over her shoulder and flashed Colton her most persuasive smile. "Tell the Porters not to bother putting the house on the market. I'll take it. As my lawyer, you can do all the paperwork and cut your rate in half."

He laughed. "You know I'm not that generous."

"Come on now," she scolded. "I've done you plenty of favors over the years. I *always* covered for you whenever you got home late." Seeing as how they'd grown up next door to each other, she'd been around to bail him out when he needed it. "And then there was that time sophomore year when I pretended to be your homecoming date so your parents wouldn't know you were really going with Thomas." Which meant she hadn't had a real date to her own homecoming. She stabbed a pointer finger into his chest. "You owe me big for that."

"True enough," he conceded heaving out a martyr's sigh. "All right. Fine. I'll have a talk with the Porters and get the ball—"

Her cellphone broke out into song and cut him off.

He eyed her with disdain. "Still haven't changed that awesome Bieber ringtone, huh?"

"I don't know how," she snapped digging it out of her purse. Her friend Darla had changed it as a joke. "If it annoys you so much, why don't you change it?" she asked, glancing at the screen.

"Who is it? Tell them you'll call them back so I can change that appalling ringtone."

Her heart sped up. "It's Lance." Her boss at the Cortez Family Ranch who'd actually become more like her big brother. The man who'd given her and Gracie a place to live after her ex walked out on them. The man who was marrying her best friend Jessa soon.

"You haven't told them you're quitting yet?" Colton asked when she clicked the phone off and stuffed it back into her purse.

"Not yet." She looked around the room again, fear swirling in with her excitement. "It doesn't seem wise to say anything until I'm sure it'll work out." There was no reason to get anyone riled up. All Jessa had talked about recently was the fun they'd have living as neighbors on the ranch.

"You have quite the connection with the Cortez family," Colton reminded her. "Once you move here things will change."

"Things need to change." Lance and Jessa deserved to have their own space. He'd just retired from bull riding and would be reorganizing things at the ranch anyway. He wouldn't need her to keep the books anymore. "Besides, this has always been my dream."

"You sure you're not just running away from Lucas?" Colton enjoyed hitting people between the eyes with the obvious truth. He knew exactly how she'd once felt about the middle Cortez brother. But she refused to flinch.

"This has nothing to do with Lucas." As the lie tumbled

from her lips, she fell back through the years, forced to relive the memories she'd tried so hard to block out.

The day Lucas Cortez, the love of her young life, had been arrested for arson. When they'd taken him away in handcuffs, she'd run after him, sobbing, begging the officer to let him go, insisting he wouldn't have done it. He wouldn't have started that fire at the rodeo grounds.

Lucas had turned to her, this seventeen-year-old man she'd known most of her life. The man she'd loved for two years. The man she'd dreamed about building a future with. His face had been cold when he'd told her to go back home. "It's over, Naomi. I'm going to prison. You need to move on."

For years, she didn't know how. Lucas had taken a chunk of her heart that day, leaving it paralyzed. That was the year she'd learned how to keep secrets. After a shocking pregnancy and a failed marriage, she'd done what she had to do to raise her daughter by herself. Then, eight months ago, Lucas had come home when his father was diagnosed with Parkinson's, and the things she'd kept hidden no longer felt safe.

"How long is he planning to stay in Topaz Falls anyway?" Colton asked innocently.

Yeah right. He knew good and well this topic was off-limits. "I don't know." Over the last months, Lucas had split time between his family's ranch and the McGowen Ranch, but eventually he'd go back to Pueblo for good. And it was just as well. She'd shut the door on the *what ifs* of her past long ago. "I haven't talked to Lucas much," she reminded Colton.

The truth was, she hadn't been able to face him. She'd made sure to keep extra busy, volunteering at school and at Jessa's animal rescue. She'd even taken Gracie to visit her parents for a month over winter break.

When she'd seen him for the first time in ten years, her heart had buckled, filling her with a pained joy. But so much time had passed. They were both different people. Now everything in her life came down to her daughter.

The moment Gracie was born, that moment she'd held her in her arms and cuddled her against her breast, every fear went away and Naomi realized she'd never be alone again. She was a mother and she would forever be connected with another soul. That bond had changed everything for her. It had made her brave.

"So this is what you want," Colton asked, dipping his chin to give her eyes a good cross-examination. "You're sure?"

"Yes." *Be brave*. It was time for her to show her daughter she could do anything she wanted.

It was time to prove she could make all of her own dreams come true.

* * *

The decision shouldn't be this hard.

Lucas brought his arm back over his head and launched the fishing line, arcing it in a perfectly timed dance, striking the fly against the water to entice the cut-throat trout he knew to be hiding in one of those deep holes on the riverbed. Ripples circled the small fuzzy hook at the end of his line, mimicking a real fly's movements on the water's glassy surface.

He did his best thinking out here—standing waist-deep in his thermal waders, still feeling the chill of the snow runoff barreling down the mountain streams and into the Topaz Falls River. It was high for this time of year—the weather had been unseasonably warm for weeks, melting the mounds of snow that had built up on the peaks.

The sun had only just started its descent to the west, hovering stubbornly over the rocky horizon, casting enough light and warmth that he didn't need a coat. In some ways, he loved it here. After being away from Topaz Falls for ten years, coming back had been nostalgic. He couldn't go anywhere in town without memories flooding him—good memories of him and his brothers riding their bikes to the general store for candy, of building forts in the woods, of riding their horses up the mountain trails.

But his best memories had taken place right on that riverbank right over there. Long evening picnics with Naomi, his high school sweetheart. The woman he'd left behind so long ago.

They'd stuff a saddlebag full of food from the pantry and ride out here. He'd spread the blanket on the ground and they'd eat in the surreal glow of a setting sun. When dusk had settled, they'd wrap themselves up in that blanket, kissing and touching each other, and eventually making love in the tall grass.

Memories of Naomi constantly seemed to churn through him, dredging up the past, giving him glimpses of their two years together. Those images were etched into his soul...her head tipped back while she laughed, that long, wavy red hair spilling down over her shoulders and catching the sun's light.

That—*she*—was what made his impending decision so hard.

With no strikes at his line, Lucas wound the fly rod's reel. He had to get back to the ranch anyhow. His youngest brother was throwing yet another shindig in honor of Lance's wedding. Or should he say Levi was throwing it for himself. No one loved a good party as much as Levi.

As he worked the reel, the fly slowly skidded across

the water's surface closer and closer, tying up his scattered thoughts along with it.

A relationship with Naomi wouldn't be practical. Hell, she didn't even seem to want him. Ever since he'd been back, she'd avoided him. And why wouldn't she? Why would any woman want to be with a convicted felon who'd done time? The rest of the town sure didn't want him to stick around. They'd made that abundantly clear.

Small towns like Topaz Falls, Colorado, had long memories and no one wanted to welcome back the guy that had supposedly burned down a stable, killed two bulls, and forever ruined the town's chances ever hosting another rodeo on the circuit.

Didn't matter that he hadn't done it. Didn't matter that he'd gotten out of prison early on good behavior. Didn't matter that he'd built a fucking empire for the McGowen Ranch outside of Pueblo in the years since.

Didn't matter who he was now.

That's why he should head back down south. Bill McGowen had called him up last week and told him he was sorry Lucas's father had been diagnosed with Parkinson's but they were gearing up for the competition season and he needed someone to run the show. Which meant he needed Lucas to make a decision. Return to manage his ranch full time, or he'd have to find someone else.

Lucas trudged to the riverbank, his legs fighting the river's current. He should've told the man then that he'd come back, but his mind had instantly conjured up this image of Naomi in his arms and, before he knew what he was saying, he'd told Bill McGowen—one of the most powerful men in the rodeo world—that he'd need to think about it and he'd let him know after Lance's wedding.

Sighing, he kicked off his rubber boots and stepped on to the soft bank where he peeled off his waders. Then he took apart the fishing pole and stored it in the cylinder carrying case.

After slipping on his leather boots and shoving the gear into his backpack, he hoisted it onto his shoulders and tramped down the narrow trail that led back to the highway where he'd parked his truck. Even before he reached it, he knew something was wrong.

All four tires were flat. Slashed, the shredded rubber lying limply on the asphalt. And then there was the glaring orange word spray-painted across the tailgate.

Felon.

That label. That damn label. It'd be slapped on him forever. He jogged down to the road to assess the damage. At least they hadn't shattered the windows. Shaking his head, he dug out his phone, but of course there was no service out here in the river valley.

And if he needed confirmation that he didn't belong in Topaz Falls, there it was.

Looking over the damage again, his hands fisted. But anger wouldn't do him much good out here. Hiking his backpack higher on his shoulders, he sucked it up and set off on foot, following the curve of the highway, boots pounding the packed gravel on the shoulder.

He'd have to walk the eight miles back to the ranch.

This was the whole reason he hadn't come back after he'd been released from prison. He'd wanted freedom—a life where no one knew about his past. McGowen didn't care that he'd served time. Hell, he thought it made him more of a badass...

The hum of an engine broke into his thoughts. He stepped

off to the side to give the car room and glanced over his shoulder.

A yellow Volkswagen Beetle blitzed toward him, picking up speed. Yep, he'd know that car anywhere. Naomi. No one else around here drove a bright yellow bug complete with flower-shaped taillights. Completely impractical for life in the mountains, but that was one thing he loved about Naomi. She didn't care much for horse sense. If something made her happy, she did it.

He watched her car draw closer and closer, and just like it always did when Naomi got near, his heart picked up. Would she stop and give him a lift to the ranch? They hadn't exactly been alone since he'd come back to Topaz Falls. She'd made sure of that.

As the yellow anomaly sped around the curve, he lifted a hand to flag her down, but the car didn't slow.

Maybe she hadn't seen him. Waving his arms, he stepped onto the shoulder...

Shit! The car was coming right for him! Adrenaline fired through him and sent him rolling into the ditch just as the car's brakes screeched. It skidded and fishtailed, likely taking out half of the tires' tread.

Breathing in the scent of burnt rubber, Lucas stared up at the sky. Well, that'd been one hell of a close shave.

The car door opened and out Naomi flew, stumbling down the embankment to where he lay on the ground.

"Oh my God! Oh my God! Lucas!" Her hands visibly shook. "What are you doing standing in the middle of the road?" she demanded, her voice about twenty octaves higher than normal.

"I wasn't in the middle of the road," he said calmly, though the swoosh of blood still roared in his ears. Couldn't tell if the adrenaline surge was from almost being mowed down, or from finally being able to stare at her the way he'd wanted to ever since he'd walked back into her life all those months ago. Whenever they bumped into each other, she always turned away from him, but now she stood over him, staring down into his eyes.

And God, she was perfection. Wavy red hair finer than silk, and those bright eyes, green as the swaying grass in a meadow. She wore a flowered dress, and her legs were made for wearing a dress. Long and toned, tensed from the way she stood in her shiny red heels.

That's why he didn't want to move. Nothing hurt, but if he moved she'd look away from him.

"Mom!" Gracie squealed from the backseat. She stuck her head out through the open window. "Is he alive?"

"I'm alive," he confirmed, waving at Naomi's daughter. "And I was standing on the *side* of the road," he said, admiring the view of the woman's tanned legs. Yeah, he could pretty much admire that view all damn day.

As usual, Naomi turned away from him. Her breaths came in gasping puffs. "God, Lucas. *God*. I was so distracted I didn't even see you." Her delicate hands covered her face. "I almost hit you. My God, I almost *hit* you." She staggered a few steps.

That got him off the ground. Didn't need her collapsing on the side of the highway.

"Hey." He hurried over to her, brushing the gravel off his ass. "I'm fine." He'd been through a hell of a lot worse than a tumble down into a ditch.

"He looks fine to me!" Gracie offered, still leaning out the window. "He's not even bleeding."

"Exactly." He ducked his head closer to Naomi's, catching her gaze. "See. No blood. I'm good."

She nodded, but seemed to be on the verge of hyperventilating. Which meant she was in no condition to get behind the wheel of that car.

"Why don't I drive you back to the ranch?" Risking her hasty retreat, he slipped an arm around her waist to support her, and he couldn't resist drawing her close to him, closer than she'd been in ten long years. She still smelled like carefree summer afternoons—a subtle hint of lemon along with the coconut oil she used to use to soften her hands. That scent, the feel of her leaning into his body roused a sudden overpowering greed. He'd never hungered as desperately for something as he hungered for her. To turn her fully to himself. To feel those breasts he used to kiss so intimately against his own chest again. He knew that body, remembered every curve and bend, every fine detail…

"I'm okay," Naomi whispered, shaking him off. "I can walk."

Of course she could. If she had a choice between keeling over and letting him touch her, she'd gladly opt for hitting the ground. But she did hand him the keys before hurrying to climb into the passenger's seat without his assistance.

Lucas folded himself into the driver's seat. Even with the seat moved all the way back, he hardly fit. But he'd take it if it meant he got to sit beside Naomi for ten minutes. Even if she wouldn't look at him. Even if she wouldn't talk to him.

He'd take it. Especially knowing he was likely going back to Pueblo in a few short weeks.

Lucas glanced in the rearview mirror. "You buckled?" he asked Gracie.

The girl nodded with a shy smile.

"All right, then. We're off." He started the engine and backed up, then turned carefully out onto the highway.

Naomi directed her gaze out the passenger's window, but Gracie eyed him dubiously from the backseat.

She looked so much like her mother with those red curls and inquisitive green eyes.

"How come you were walking on the road?" she asked.

"My truck broke down. Back where I was fishing." Not worth mentioning that it'd had some help. "So I was planning to walk back to the ranch. Until you two lovely ladies swooped in to rescue me. I'm a lucky guy."

The girl grinned, dimples poking into each cheek. "You bet you were lucky," she laughed. "Especially since Mom almost hit you!"

He stole a glance at Naomi. She stared straight ahead, her face a mask of worry.

God, he wanted to reach over and rest his hand on her thigh, tease out a smile…

"Did you catch anything?" Gracie asked, leaning between the seats.

"Nah. Not tonight. Sometimes I just go out there to think." And whenever he started to think, it inevitably led to the silent woman sitting next to him.

"I've always wanted to learn how to fish," Gracie babbled. "But I don't want to touch a worm or anything. And I wouldn't keep the fish. That would be mean."

"I never keep them either," he admitted. He'd never developed a taste for trout. "And I'd be happy to teach you how to fish sometime. If it's okay with your mom."

"Can I, Mom? Can I go fishing with Lucas?"

"We'll see," Naomi said stiffly. Parental code for *hell no*.

"What about you? What have you ladies been up to tonight?" he asked, trying to soften the woman.

"I had drama practice at school," Gracie said proudly. "I'm the fairy godmother in *Cinderella*."

"Wow." He drew out the word in a theatrical compliment. "Congratulations. That's a starring role."

Her smile was addictive. "I know! I had to memorize all these lines." The girl paused and cleared her throat dramatically. "Bibbity! Bobbity! Boo!"

Lucas widened his eyes with exaggerated awe. "You're a natural."

"Really?" Gracie gasped. "You think?"

"That was better than the movie," he insisted.

"You've seen *Cinderella*?" Naomi asked, finally acknowledging him. The skeptical curve to her sexy lips made him ache.

"Of course I've seen *Cinderella*," he said, looking at her longer than was safe. "It's a classic."

Gracie leaned forward again, straining her seat belt. "If you like *Cinderella*, you should come to my show! It's on Thursday night!"

"Oh honey..." Naomi broke in before he had the chance to answer. "I'm sure Lucas is too busy."

She likely *hoped* he was too busy, but he pretended not to notice her obvious discomfort. "Actually, I'm free Thursday night."

"Yay!" Gracie squealed.

But Naomi's worried glare returned. "You don't have to come."

"I *want* to come," he said, eyeing her. He wanted to spend time with her. To see if he had any reason to stick it out in Topaz Falls. He glanced in the rearview mirror. "One line and the Fairy Godmother has me hooked."

Gracie beamed. "Wait till you hear the rest of them!"

"I can't wait," Lucas said, directing a pleading gaze at her mother.

Naomi relented with a sigh. "It starts at seven." Her soft lips twitched as she studied him. It wasn't her full bright beautiful smile.

But it was a start.

Acknowledgments

Every time I finish a book it feels like a miracle. There's no way to describe that feeling of fear when you first create a brand-new document, when the blank page is staring back at you and you know you have to fill it, not only with characters and action and romance, but also with love and a part of yourself. After writing six books, I now know the fear doesn't go away. It's the most difficult, beautiful, heart-wrenching, exciting thing I've ever done. And I'm so grateful I don't have to do it alone.

To my fabulous readers—I hope you know how much I appreciate every review, every comment on Facebook, every note you send, everything you do to encourage and inspire me. One of the greatest blessings of being an author is sharing this journey with you.

I cannot thank my team at Forever enough for all of the work and thought they put into my books. This book took a village! Leah Hultenschmidt and Lexi Smail, thanks for stepping in and taking such good care of me through the editing process. And Megha Parekh, you have such a gift! Thank you for always pushing me to do just a little bit more. To the artists, copy editors, proofreaders, publicists, and sales and marketing gurus who never get enough credit for everything you do—I appreciate you more than I can say.

Suzie Townsend and Sara Stricker at New Leaf, thank you for taking care of the details and representing me so well. I'd be lost without you!

Thank you to my husband, Will, for continuing to be my greatest supporter. You're always the first one to comfort me or congratulate me or tell me to get my butt back in that chair. Thank you for loving me every single day, even when I'm on deadline. AJ and Kaleb, thank you for filling my life with so much joy. It's such a privilege to watch you grow and make your mark on the world.

I never have enough space to list the names of all my friends and family members who continue to love, support, and encourage me. But writing love stories is my way to honor them. They are the ones who taught me to believe in a real, raw, soul-binding love that carries so much healing power. No matter what happens in the world, we all need to believe that kind of love is possible, that we are worthy of it, and that it can change everything.

Thank you, thank you, thank you.

About the Author

Sara Richardson grew up chasing adventure in Colorado's rugged mountains. She's climbed to the top of a 14,000-foot peak at midnight, swum through Class IV rapids, completed her wilderness first-aid certification, and spent seven days at a time tromping through the wilderness with a thirty-pound backpack strapped to her shoulders.

Eventually Sara did the responsible thing and got an education in writing and journalism. After a brief stint in the corporate writing world, she stopped ignoring the voices in her head and started writing fiction. Now she uses her experience as a mountain adventure guide to write stories that incorporate adventure with romance. Still indulging her adventurous spirit, Sara lives and plays in Colorado with her saint of a husband and two young sons.

You can learn more at:

SaraRichardson.net

Twitter @SaraR_Books

Facebook.com/SaraRichardsonBooks

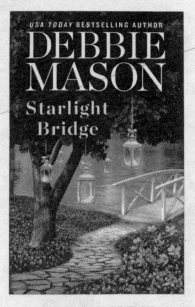

STARLIGHT BRIDGE
By Debbie Mason

Hidden in Graystone Manor is a book containing *all* the dark little secrets of Harmony Harbor...including Ava DiRossi's. No one—especially her ex-husband, Griffin Gallagher—can ever discover the truth about what tore their life apart years ago. Only now Griffin is back in town. Still handsome. Still hating her for leaving him. And still not aware that Ava never stopped loving him...

Fall in Love with Forever Romance

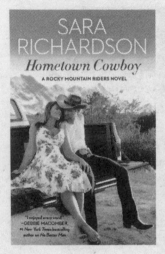

HOMETOWN COWBOY
By Sara Richardson

In the *New York Times* bestselling tradition of Jennifer Ryan and Maisey Yates comes the first book in Sara Richardson's Rocky Mountain Riders series featuring three bull-riding brothers. What would a big-time rodeo star like Lance Cortez see in Jessa Mae Love, a small-town veterinarian who wears glasses? Turns out, *plenty*.

THE BASTARD BILLIONAIRE
By Jessica Lemmon

Since returning from the war, Eli Crane has shut everybody out. That is, until Isabella Sawyer starts as his personal assistant with her sassy attitude and her curves for days. But will the secret she hides shatter the fragile trust they've built? Fans of Jill Shalvis and Jennifer Probst will love Jessica Lemmon's Billionaire Bad Boys series.

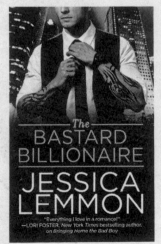

Fall in Love with Forever Romance

CHAIN REACTION
By Tara Wyatt

Alexa Fairfax is practically Hollywood royalty, but after she discovers a plot more deadly than any movie script, Alexa desperately needs a bodyguard. So she accepts the help of Zack De Luca, a true friend with a protective nature—and chiseled muscles to back it up. Zack is training to be an MMA fighter, but his biggest battle will be to resist his feelings for the woman who is way out of his league...

IF THE DUKE DEMANDS
By Anna Harrington

In the *New York Times* bestselling tradition of Elizabeth Hoyt, Grace Burrowes, and Madeline Hunter comes the first in a sexy new series from Anna Harrington. Sebastian Carlisle, the new Duke of Trent, needs a respectable wife befitting his station. But when he begins to fall for the reckless, flighty Miranda Hodgkins, he must decide between his title and his heart.